THROUGH FLOOD AND FLAME

SABINE BARING-GOULD

PRAXIS BOOKS

Praxis Books
Sheridan, Broomers Hill Lane, Pulborough, West Sussex.
RH20 2DU.

First published 1868 by Richard Bentley, London,
in three volumes

This edition 1997

ISBN 0 9528420 1 7

Printed by Intype, Wimbledon, London

British Library Cataloguing–in–Production Data.
A catalogue record for this book is available from the
British Library.

Introduction

It is difficult to give a brief preamble to this fascinating story. Such a long novel, rich and dense with the kind of sideways looks at life and thought which were so usual in Victorian fiction, yields up a host of scenes and passages for comment.

Baring–Gould is not afraid to express his own direct opinion, in the context of this romantic story. He has a profound scorn for Ranters, or Primitive Methodists, for example, and the satire with which he conveys this scorn is admirably done. The age–old debate between Justification by Faith and Justification by Works is highlighted here, in the lives of real people and the divisions in a single family. Comic Dickensian characters add froth and fun, to balance the more serious passages.

But it is the two young lovers who draw us through the story. The unwaveringly sweet and virtuous Annis, recognisably a fictional portrait of Grace Taylor, might seem a trifle too good to be true to a modern readership, but as a romantic Victorian heroine, she is classic. The familiar Victorian dichotomy, whereby a young woman is both vulnerable and strong, appears in Annis Greenwell. She hides her face and cowers away from anything loud or strange, and yet she comes through a succession of crises and dangers apparently unscathed.

Although a relatively brief period of Baring–Gould's life was spent in Horbury (the model for Sowden in this story), it was one of great influence and activity. Not only did he meet Grace there, but he wrote his renowned 'Onward Christian Soldiers' (as well as 'Now the Day is Over' and 'Through the Night of Doubt and Sorrow') there, and formed many of his lifelong opinions and interests. A fascination for local superstitions and folklore found its first real feeding ground in Horbury, with the Bogart making a personal appearance to Sabine, one dark winter night.

As with so many of Baring–Gould's novels, *Through Flood and Flame* is an extremely valuable piece of social history. Many passages are surprising in their acute relevance to our lives today. For instance, in Chapter Twenty–One, the portrait of Mr Furness (based closely on John Sharp, Vicar of Horbury) gives us an extremely relevant topic for consideration, in the Vicar's attitude to charity. Applied to the present–day debates about 'welfare' and 'aid', this section of the book has a great deal to recommend it.

The description of Christmas in Chapter Twenty-Seven; the assertion that small-town shops are too expensive in Chapter Thirty; the fact of a minor theft making a substantial newspaper report (Chapter Twenty-Eight) all add colour and realism to the time and place.

Darwin's *On the Origin of Species* was published in 1859, less than ten years before this book was written. Churchmen in particular were thrown into immense upheaval by its implications. In this novel, Baring-Gould treats us to his own humorous approach to the matter, in the shape of Richard Grover, man-monkey, and leaves us to draw what conclusions we might.

Another surprise is the severe level of pollution caused by the dyes and chemicals used at the woollen mills in the 1860s. The river Calder is stagnant and stinking in this story. A long and passionate section of Chapter Two gives us a vital insight into the attitude of the Industrial Revolution, where the advantages to humanity are seen to greatly outweigh any damage to the environment. We may not agree now, but it is salutary to read such views in a modern context. It is also worth noting that the Calder is now infinitely cleaner and healthier than it was 140 years ago.

Finally, we owe it to Baring-Gould to acknowledge his embarrassment concerning this novel. It was published in the year that he and Grace were married, making it uncomfortably pertinent to his own life. The characters in the book are almost all recognisable as real people, and he makes no bones about how he feels towards many of them. As time went by, and his family grew, the romantic idealism understandably caused him and Grace some blushes. The story of their meeting and falling in love was well known across England, with comments in *The Westminster Gazette* about them. Living up to it, in the stresses and strains of daily life, must surely have been difficult. But now, with the perspective of time, the book more than warrants a revival. It is the work of an intelligent, well-informed, enquiring man, who has inspired affection and respect in his readers ever since the appearance of this, his earliest novel.

Rebecca Smith. 1997.

Book One

Flood

Chapter One

A rainy day in autumn, of all things most intolerable, especially when that day is drawing to a close, after having rained incessantly since dawn, and gives no hope of clearing up at evenfall.

From morning till night, patter, patter on the slates of the warehouse, and drip, drip from the eaves, with a wearisome accompaniment of water guttering down the fall-pipe. It was a downright rain. It did not come with an angry plash against the window, as though a bucket of water were being soused over it, and then rush away before the wind in an eddy, but descended in parallel perpendicular lines.

The office window was dim with drops, which, after remaining stationary one moment, dribbled lower, united with other drops, and then went down the pane at a gallop. The mill-gates were open and admitted a turbid stream that was fed by driblets from every cranny, wall and causeway, and which promised to convert the mill-yard into a Black Sea. Water and dirt had penetrated everywhere. A pool was within each doorway. Mats were soaked, floors stained by wet feet, windows leaking, skylights dripping. The steam from the escape-pipe trailed along the side of the dingy red factory, powerless to rise, and obscuring the windows. The dye-house was enveloped in a rank fog. The rush of machinery was over, for the six o'clock whistle had dismissed the hands, and there only remained those who had to "side" the waste.

Away they had gone, clattering, pattering, chattering, with shawls drawn over their heads, and skirts held up; spirits rising, tongues wagging; the dull walls ringing with their merry laughter. A few blue men, their clothes reeking with oil, their arms, hands and faces, the hue which was in vogue among the ancient Britons, had charged through the slush, sending it splashing over the girls — and then all was quiet.

In the office, Hugh Arkwright was buttoning on his leggings. His books were closed, the pen laid down, and he was preparing to start.

"The river is rising fast," said his uncle, the proprietor of the factory. He was still writing: "I dare say we shall have a bit of a flood by morning."

"The Middups are under water already," said Hugh; "Jim Hirst told me that the Calder was rising three inches in the hour. That was two hours ago."

"Indeed."

"Are you leaving now, sir?"

"No, Hugh. I may be half an hour longer. Now attend, please. I want you to go to the night-watch, and tell him to rouse me should the water reach the warehouse."

"Is there any chance of that?"

"It rose ankle-deep in '34; but that was an exceptional flood and the weirs have been lowered eighteen inches since then. I do not expect a recurrence of flood, but there may be one."

"Where does the watchman live?" asked Hugh.

"You cannot miss his house, if you follow my directions. Go homeward, till you come to the fork, then, instead of taking the right-hand lane, turn left; cross the beck, and he lives in the only cottage you will see. It is in a sand quarry."

"I will go directly, sir."

"You have an umbrella?"

"I am armed against the worst weather. Look here!"

And he displayed a stout pair of boots, leggings, a water-proofed Inverness cape, and an umbrella that might have served Mrs Gamp.

"What a slop and mess everything is in," he said, taking his hat. "Now, uncle, I am off. What is the watchman's name?"

"Joe Earnshaw."

Mr Arkwright was one of the principal manufacturers in Sowden. His branch of trade was yarn-spinning. He was a practical man of business, well up in his profession, to which, indeed, he had been educated; he was diligent, cautious and thoroughly honourable. He lived quite within his means, in a small house not half a mile from the mill; and was supposed, not without good reason, to be saving money. He lived very quietly, keeping only one servant-maid and a man to attend to his horse and gig, and cultivate the garden.

He was a square-built man of middling height, with grizzled

hair which had been black, a grey beard, but no moustache. His nose was slightly aquiline, his mouth firm, his eye dark and roving. No one, judging from his features, would have supposed him to be a good-natured man; and good-natured he was not. He was fond of a joke and could make himself agreeable in society; but at his business, his natural decision and peremptoriness came out. A light humour did not sit on him as though it suited him but as though he put it upon him, because he had determined on wearing it. His dark restless eye indicated a temper which, when roused, would be violent; the lines about the mouth shewed that the same temper was under habitual control. He was agreeable in society, that is, in such society as he frequented, which consisted of the families of other manufacturers, of the doctor and of the lawyer. His wit was commonplace, not coarse, not refined, but broad. His conversational powers were chiefly exerted in what the French call *badinage*. His reading was limited to the newspapers; comsequently his style of thought was not of the highest order, nor his taste cultivated to any great pitch of refinement. He liked to quote a few Latin words in his talk, but the words had been exclusively culled from leading articles in the *Manchester Guardian* and *Leeds Mercury*.

As a master, Mr Arkwright was appreciated. His hands remained with him for years. He was perfectly just and considerate. An operative whose conduct was bad was immediately dismissed, and he never wittingly engaged one with whose character he was not acquainted. It would be difficult to decide whether Mr Arkwright was actuated in this respect by conscience or by policy. He certainly gave himself credit for acting on the purest of motives. As a general rule, men's actions are better than the moving principle; the thread is always more vauable than the bobbin round which it is wound.

Mr Arkwright was a married man, but had no child. His wife was a little German lady, the daughter of a Hamburg partner in a firm with which he had had business transactions. Quite lately, his nephew Hugh, an orphan, had come to Sowden and was living in his house, and working in his office. It was an understood thing that Hugh was to be his uncle's heir. Hugh was the son of a clergyman, the only brother of the manufacturer, who had lived on a small incumbency of £100 a year; the outs of which had devoured every spare shilling of the poor parson's income, so that when he died, Hugh was left totally unprovided for. But this mattered little to the young man, who had energy and abilities by which to make his own livelihood. His uncle had given him a home, and had found him work; and Hugh was gradually acquiring a knowledge of bookkeeping and trade, with the mysteries of which he had hitherto been profoundly unacquainted. He was very different in appearance from Mr Arkwright, being tall, strongly built, full-breasted, broad-shouldered, erect, with thick brown hair and light whiskers, and having a florid complexion, blue eyes, and, better than all, an expression of frank good humour and manly honesty of purpose which was irresistibly engaging.

He strode out into the rain, looked up at the overcast sky, which gave not the faintest sign of breaking, then at the road through the mill-gates, now a watercourse. The causeway was not totally under water, so he splashed along that.

The high road was just outside the gates; he crossed it and struck up a lane towards Mr Arkwright's house. A little stream had already furrowed up the soil and was mangling the roadway in a wanton, passionate manner; now rilling down one side of the walk, then capriciously pouring down the middle, and then betaking itself to the other side, where it swilled the causeway. The trees shivered and discharged the water wherewith their leaves were burdened, in heavy splashes on the pavement; the yellow flowers in the hedge were beaten down and draggled in the dirty water. A drain which crossed the road had burst and a succession of small fountains was boiling up, loosening the stones and cinders wherewith the way was metalled.

When Hugh had reached a sufficient elevation, he turned and looked back at the valley.

The river had overflowed its banks and the fields on either side were sheets of water. One of the mills was already surrounded, the roadway towards the Calder bridge was in one place covered and the valley appeared to contain a chain of lagoons.

Sowden was a small manufacturing town of some four thousand people; it lay up the hillsides and ran into the glens which opened into the broad vale of the Calder. The mills were all near the water and therefore liable to be flooded, but the dwelling-houses were safe, excepting only those in the "folds" or yards of the mills. Mr Arkwright's house was not in the town but outside it, conveniently enough situated, commanding the mill in the valley from the windows, and sufficiently elevated to be free of the smoke.

As Hugh walked on, he saw before him a girl returning from the factory in her white pinafore, below which showed a dark purple strip of gown. A tin can swung in her hand, her arms were bare and a red kerchief over her head was pinned beneath her chin.

The young man soon overtook her. "You will get wet through, lassie," he said. "Haven't you a shawl to wrap yourself in?"

She looked up shyly at him and answered in a low voice, "Nay, sir! One of the others has gotten it."

"Then you did not leave home without some protection this morning?"

"Nay, I'd my shawl, but one of t' lasses has ta'en it, I reckon, for I cannot find it."

"Here, come under my umbrella. You will get drenched, you poor little thing, in this heavy downpour."

"No thank you, sir."

"Oh, but I insist," said Hugh, good-humouredly. "You do not think I am such a barbarian as to pass you without offering you shelter, when I am as dry as a bone and you stand a chance of being soaked? There," he extended the umbrella over her. She seemed frightened at being spoken to, and shrank aside.

"Do not be foolish. I do not eat little girls," laughed Hugh, as he slackened his pace to hers.

It was kindly intended and she submitted, though with evident timidity. They breasted the hill without speaking.

Presently Hugh observed the little crimson kerchief turned and a pair of large soft brown eyes raised cautiously towards his face, but the moment he turned they dropped again. The young man was of a conversational disposition and he did not allow the silence to remain much longer unbroken.

"Where do you work, lassie?"

"At Arkwright's."

5

"At my uncle's!" exclaimed Hugh. "How is it you are so late in leaving? All the other girls have been gone some minutes."

"Please, sir, I have been seeking my shawl."

"What sort of work do you do in the mill?"

"Reeling."

"Do you like it?"

"It's none so dirty as some of t'other work."

"Have you worked long at my uncle's?"

'Three year, come next Whitsuntide."

"That is rather an odd manner of fixing the date," said Hugh, "considering that Whitsuntide is movable. However, you reckon by festival bonnets and ribbons."

He saw that the little body at his side was laughing, but she did not answer him.

Hugh had as yet scarcely got a peep at her face, for she held it persistently down; but when they came to the fork in the lanes she stood still and, raising her head, thanked him for the shelter. Then he saw a sweet oval face with a clear complexion, bright colour from the exertion of mounting the hill, smooth brown hair just showing beyond the red handkerchief, the largest and gentlest of hazel eyes and the smallest and freshest of lips.

The expression of the face was as pure and modest as that of one of Angelico's seraphs and the timidity which trembled in the mouth and eyes added an extra charm to the natural beauty of the quiet little face.

There is a peculiar cast of features belonging to the Yorkshire damsels of the hill-country on the eastern slope of Blackstone Edge which has in it something Flemish, something Norse. Unquestionably the dales were early colonised by Scandinavian settlers. Flemings also came over in the middle ages and established their looms in little villages amongst the hills. To the mingling of these races we must attribute the tall and sturdy frames of the men, the transparent skins, the bright pure colour, the somewhat excessive breadth of face of the women. The girls are tall, supple and graceful, not slim and angular, but with well-rounded forms. In the large towns the race is either different or has altered its characteristics, for among them, colour, height, grace, beauty — all are wanting and the women are square made, stooping, dark-haired, muddy-complexioned and plain.

The little girl who stood before Hugh was a thorough specimen of the hill lassie of Western Yorkshire, with the inexpressible beauty of a simple modest spirit beaming out of every feature with irrepressible loveliness.

"Thank you, sir," she said, lifting her eyes for one moment to Hugh's face. "My road lies yonder," pointing to the left.

"And so does mine," said Hugh; "I am not going home just now. I have a message to take to the watchman."

"Joe Earnshaw?" An expression of distress passed momentarily across her face.

"Yes; do you know him?"

"He lodges wi' us." Then, after a little hesitation, she added, "Please, sir, can I take the message?"

"No," answered Hugh. "I must give it myself and I am delighted to be able to offer you shelter all the way. Come along, my girl, and do not stand in the rain."

So they followed the lane.

"Is it far to your home?" asked the young man.

"Nay, none so very far. We have to cross t'beck."

"It is rather a lonely lane," said Hugh.

The hedges were high and thick; at intervals trees overshadowed it. In spring, unquestionably, it must have been beautiful, but on a rainy autumn day it was detestable.

On the broad roads dusk had settled down and in the lane under the trees it was almost dark. The mud was deep, the water standing in puddles. Hugh paced along and the little girl splashed at his side. Every now and then, with a dash, came the water from the trees upon the umbrella.

"What a dismal lane this is!" said Hugh again. "So you have to come along this by night alone in winter?"

"There's another road by t'river, but I mostly goes this," answered the girl; "I'm flayed i' t'dark of falling into t'Calder."

The lane descended gradually and there was a better fall for the water; consequently there was less mud.

"What time do you start of a morning?"

"A quarter past five," answered the girl.

"On a winter morning it must be dreadful," said Hugh. "How do you manage to wake?"

7

"There's a little lad lives up t'lane. He's nobut a bairn. He works down Holroyd's coal-pit and he goes past o'mornings at four o'clock. He's got wooden clogs and he clatters along t'causeway singing 'Wait for t'waggon'. Poor bairn! He's flayed o' boggarts and padfoots and he sings to gie hissen a bit o courage. But it wakens us regular."

"Poor little thing," said Hugh.

"Ay! Poor little bairn! Mother says it's a shame he should be sent all alone."

"And I think you should hardly be allowed to go alone along a dark lane like this, night and morning. Are you never afraid?"

She did not answer, but looked up at him cautiously and timidly. He caught her eye and smiled; she also smiled a little frightened smile.

"What is the padfoot?" asked Hugh.

"It's a sort of spirit, they say, like a white dog wi' goggle een."

"Have you ever seen it?"

"Nay. If I were to see it, I should dee. Them that sees t'padfoot are sure to dee — mostly, they says."

"And the boggart, what is that?"

"Nay, I cannot tell."

"I have not asked you your name yet, lassie; will you tell me what they call you?"

"They call me Annis Greenwell."

"Have you any brothers and sisters?"

She shook her head. "I've nobut a mother living. Father's dead this many a year."

"So is mine," said the young man in a sad tone. "It's a bad thing to lose a father, but it is worse to have neither father nor mother."

"Is thy mother dead?" she asked, turning her face full of sympathy towards him.

"Yes, Annis, yes."

"Oh, look there, sir!" she suddenly exclaimed.

He looked. The beck was before him; it had flooded the road, and had swept away the plank which usually served as bridge for the foot passengers. The stream which in summer was only a dribble, and in winter but a rivulet, was now a turbulent flood, rushing along discoloured with soil, and spreading over a couple of hundred yards of the roadway; the opening by which it was wont to discharge itself being far too small to allow the great descending body of water to escape. Still, water lay at their feet, a rushing, tumbling current sweeping between the stone blocks which had supported the footbridge. There was still water beyond, to a turn of the lane.

"What shall I do! What shall I do!" wailed the girl, deserting the shelter of the umbrella and running to the margin.

Hugh looked at the flood with no little dismay, measuring its breadth and speculating on its depth.

"There is no help for it," said he; "I must wade over. Have you a cart at your house which could convey you across?"

Annis shook her head.

"Very well," he said. "Take this umbrella, child, and I will go in."

"Oh, don't! Pray don't!" she entreated, catching his sleeve. But he shook her off and entered. Boots and leggings were no preservative against water now and it seemed to revel in its supremacy, entering at laceholes, buttonholes — everywhere. Hugh reached the support of the bridge and sounded the bed of the current with one foot before he ventured into the midst. The depth was not great and he crossed with ease, the water reaching no higher than his thighs.

Having satisfied himself that it was perfectly feasible to cross, he returned to Annis who stood on the brink with heaving bosom and clasped hands.

"Come," he said, "don't be alarmed, little friend; I must carry you over."

But she shrank away in terror. "I daren't, I daren't!" she gasped.

He assured her that there was not the least danger; that if she only confided herself to him, he would bear her in safety across. She was resolute for some while, and it was only when she saw that this was her only chance of reaching home that night that she yielded. She cried with fear. Hugh stooped and lifted her lightly in his arms.

"Shut your eyes," he said cheerfully; "and don't be frightened."

But to close her eyes was an impossibility. They were wide open, gazing with an agony of terror at the current in the middle of the sheet of water. Hugh, as he bore her, felt her trembling against his shoulder and he noticed the colour leave her cheek and the light desert the distended iris. Her weight on his arms and clasped fingers was great and the strain was painful. As he neared the current her alarm increased and she threw herself back.

"For heaven's sake," gasped Hugh, "Annis, sit upright or I cannot sustain you. Put your arms around me."

She clung to him in her fear, knitting her hands behind his neck, and he felt her little tin can rattle on his back. The water whirled past with tremendous velocity, rushing up his side and washing the girl's feet.

When her feet were immersed a feeble cry escaped her lips and she clung tighter to her bearer. The little red handkerchief was against his temple, the pale cheek touched his and the warm breath fanned his face.

As he emerged into stiller water she relaxed her hold and on his reaching dry land she slipped from his arms.

"You are not made of feathers," he said, laughing; "now come along to your house. I must deliver my message and be back and dried as soon as possible."

She tripped at his side, gleefully enough now, with the carmine again in her cheeks and the light once more in her eyes. She did not speak for some while, but then all at once, as though she had been revolving in her mind what to say, and had at length decided on a fitting sentence, she observed, "You are very kind."

"Not at all," answered Hugh promptly; and he added with great sincerity, "It is a pleasure."

The lane followed the brook. He could see the chimney of the cottage and the broken walls of the quarry. His walk was now nearly over. Unconsciously his pace lagged. He wished he had further to go with this poor little thing at his side under his umbrella, and he would not have objected to another beck or two. Suddenly an idea struck him.

"How are you going to get to the mill tomorrow?"

"I don't know," she answered, standing still. "I must be at my work or I'll lose my place."

"You must get Joe Earnshaw to carry you over."

She recoiled with a look of strange horror and did not answer at first, but after a while she said, "I cannot, sir. He's at t'miln when we are at home, and when we're boune home, he goes to t'miln."

"Does no one live near you who could assist you?"

"No, no one."

Hugh hesitated, looked at her, dropped his eyes and then blurted forth nervously, "I know what must be done: I must come here tomorrow morning at a quarter past five and bear you across."

"No, no," she said vehemently, her brow flushing. "No, sir; it won't do."

"Why not, little girl? The bridge can hardly be set to rights before tomorrow morning, and as far as I can see, it is your only chance of reaching the factory."

"Pray, sir —"

"It is simply a matter of common politeness," said Hugh. "I have carried you across in safety once, and I think you need not be afraid, should I venture to do so again, of my letting you fall the second time."

"Oh, no, no! But —"

"Annis, I will be on the spot at the proper time tomorrow morning. If you are not here, I shall go back; if you are here, I shall expect you to trust yourself to me."

He reached the door; the girl opened it and called her mother. A thin pale woman came to Hugh Arkwright and told him that Joe Earnshaw was out, but that he was sure to return before he went to the mill, as he had not taken with him his greatcoat and lanthorn. She thought he had gone to see the river and canal.

"You look very wet, sir," she said.

"I am wet," he answered. "Who is not wet on a day like this? And I have been drenched in fording the beck."

"Is the water out in the lane?" she asked.

"Ay, and the bridge washed away," answered Hugh. "I had to carry your little girl over or she would not have reached home tonight."

"You are very good, sir," the woman said. "Won't you step in and dry yoursen?"

"I shall have to get wet again," he answered.

"Let me make you a cup o' tea, it will warm you nicely. Now do, sir," she urged with true Yorkshire hospitality; "we're no but poor folks, but may be it will make you comfortable for going home."

Hugh hesitated. He did not wish to be late, the water might rise higher and it would be very uncomfortable to sit in wet things; moreover, his uncle's tea would be ready on his return. On the other hand, he had not seen the night-watch to deliver his message.

Undecided what to do, he poked the stones about with the ferule of his umbrella. Then he caught a glimpse of a wistful little face looking at him from behind the mother's shoulder. "Thank you," he said. "I shall be most happy," and he stepped into the cottage.

Chapter Two

It was a pleasant little room. The fire shed a ruddy glow over it, giving it an air of warmth and comfort, especially grateful after the chill and discomfort without. It was what is called in Yorkshire the house — that is, the downstairs room in general domestic use. The walls were covered with a somewhat pretentious blue paper. A large mahogany chest of drawers stood against one wall, a triangular corner–cupboard occupied an angle, and in the recess beside the fire was a cottage piano. Several coloured prints adorned the walls; two white cats on a black ground gambolled in a gilt frame over the door into the back kitchen; Garibaldi in a red shirt hung above the piano; over a black horsehair sofa was a scriptural subject in vivid colouring. On the chest of drawers was a case of stuffed seabirds — mews, gulls and a tern; and suspended above the fireplace on two crooks was a glass walking–stick, probably intended not for use, but for ornament, and only indifferently fulfilling the object for which it was made.

Mrs Greenwell had been possessed of this walking–stick for twenty–four years. It had belonged to her father. When she married she brought it to her husband as her jointure. Mr Greenwell had proved more fragile than the stick; he was gone, but the glass staff remained uninjured.

The fireplace contained a kitchen range, for this parlourlike room was the place where all the cooking was done. The washing up was carried on in the back kitchen, out of sight.

"Will you take the sofa, Mr Arkwright?" asked Mrs Greenwell; and then, turning to Annis, she said, "Now, sharp wi' t' tea things, lass."

In less than a minute a clean white cloth was cast over the round oak table and the girl — her face bright with pleasure — set on it a tray with glass plates, china cups and saucers. Then she sat down on a little stool by the fire, holding her knee, whilst her mother made tea and brought a plate of hot cakes out of the oven.

"Shall I cook you a bit o' bacon?" asked Mrs Greenwell.

"No, thank you, not on any account. I shall do very well," answered Hugh, not a little surprised at the comfort and quality of what he saw. He had been accustomed to the style of living of cotters in his father's country parish, and not to that of the artisans in a manufacturing neighbourhood. Indeed it would surprise all who know nothing of the home life of the operative in a factory, to see its comfort and refinement. His meals are good and wholesome, his house is comfortable, and his family circle pleasant and cheerful. The mill–stains washed off, the work–clothes cast aside, he composes himself to his newspaper and his tea or supper, whilst his daughter sings, accompanying herself on the piano.

Annis sat silent in the glow of the fire with her eyes meditatively fixed on the coals. She had whipped off her white pinafore and presented a pretty picture in her purple gown and crimson kerchief, with the light from the flames dancing over her bare arms and glowing face. Hugh's eyes wandered towards her continually. Annis had surrendered to her mother the part of conversing with him, so that he was obliged to talk to Mrs Greenwood, but that the girl listened and followed the thread of their conversation was evident from the changes of expression in her countenance; and Hugh marked with pleasure the smiles coming and going in her face, the dimples forming and dying on her cheek, and the light brightening and fading in her eyes, whilst he talked with her mother. What a bonny little lass she is! he thought.

And so he rattled on, talking first on one subject and then on another, for Hugh was never at a loss for matter, drawing out Mrs Greenwell's experiences of past floods; now relating his own adventures in a boat at Scarborough, which were, however, of a very ordinary type; then discussing the subject of excursions and mill–trips. Having learned that Annis and her mother had been in the summer to Blackpool and that the girl had been photographed, he of course insisted on seeing the likeness and, when satisfied with the sight of it, protested it bore not the least resemblance to the original. Then he wanted to know whether Annis had not kept the inferior copy herself and given the best to her sweetheart; wherat the little face at the fire became crimson and Mrs Greenwell promptly replied that her girl had no sweetheart and she hoped would never have one. To which the lassie said not a word.

Then Hugh was treated by the good woman to a drop of real warming cordial, made by herself from herbs, after her grandmother's receipt; this led to a digression on cordials and a vaunting by Hugh of a special elixir possessed by his aunt and brought from Germany, the secret of which he promised to obtain by fair means or foul and impart to the widow.

Still no Joe Earnshaw arrived and the evening was waxing late and dark. Hugh rose, not without considerable reluctance, and asked Mrs Greenwell to give his uncle's message to the watchman when he came in. This the widow promised to do, and Hugh thanked her for the cup of tea, which he said he had most thoroughly enjoyed, and for the cordial, which he declared would enable him to bear up against any weather without taking cold. He shook hands with her and wished her goodnight. Annis rose from her stool; Hugh did not go up to her, but with a nod bade her farewell.

When he was gone, it seemed as though the brilliancy and warmth of the room had gone too and that all had become quiet and dull. Annis reseated herself and resumed her contemplation of the glowing embers, whose light was reflected in her soft dreamy eyes.

How cheerful his conversation had been; what a palace the poor cottage had seemed whilst he was there. How kind he appeared — to carry her like a child in his arms across the beck!

Then the colour sprang into her brow, and cheek, and bosom. She had clung to him with her arms laced around his neck, and he must have thought her very forward and impudent.

But then, he had bidden her to do so; he could not have supported her unless she had thus clasped him. How strong he was; she had felt so secure in his arms. And would he really, he, a gentleman, her master's nephew, come to the stream to bear her across on the morrow? Surely not — and yet, in making the offer he had looked as though he were in earnest.

But, was it right for her to suffer him to take her up in his arms, and ought she to cling to him so tenaciously? Yet by what other means could she reach the mill? The way by the riverside was at present wholly impracticable. There was but one other girl at the factory accustomed to reeling and if she were not at her post the overlooker would assuredly be angry and "call" her, and possibly dismiss her. But perhaps the water would have subsided and the bridge be put to rights by the morrow.

So she mused, crouching by the fire with her cheek resting on her hand and the firelight caressing her face. Sitting thus she dozed off unconsciously and fell into a dream, in which she thought she stood on the brink of a raging flood, the sky dark overhead, the horizon lost in scudding vapour, and that she stretched forth her arms with a great longing towards the further bank, which she could not see, with pain and fear in her bosom, crying hot tears. And she thought she caught sight of someone plunging through the tide towards her, saying cheerily, "I am coming, do not fear!" Then her dream was broken by her mother exclaiming, "Annis, art thou boune to have any tea, lass?" And she started from her foolish reverie.

A heavy foot came to the door. "Here is Joe," said Mrs Greenwell.

Annis darted from the room and hurried upstairs.

Now, as Hugh walked home, these were his meditations: "What satisfaction is afforded by the performance of a kind act! Moralists are right when they affirm that a good deed brings its own reward. I feel at this moment a glow within me of inexpressible satisfaction at having been enabled to do a very simple yet kindly action. It would be culpable were I to neglect the opportunity afforded to me of repeating it tomorrow morning. Had I not offered the shelter of my umbrella to that nice little girl, I should have reached the brook and been across it and back without knowing that she needed to be conveyed over, and then, poor little thing! how she would have cried, what trouble she would have been in, to know how to reach home. Yes, I am thankful I was able to carry her to the other side and my conscience has been approving ever since. Virtue certainly brings its own reward."

Poor simple Hugh! You are one of the many who are ignorant of the motives about which their actions are wound. Hugh was not the least tired of congratulating himself all the way home.

"There is nothing like being brought up to feel for others, to enter into the wants and troubles of others, that is to say, to be brought up as a gentleman. My father took care to inculcate in me consideration for others, and I shall never be able to sufficiently thank him. One of these unmannerly fellows here would not have thought of offering his umbrella to a little mill-girl; would not have dreamed of carrying her over a swollen stream. If he had been going the same way, he would have plunged through himself and given no heed to the distress of a helpless child. And what a loss would have been his! I have a feeling of happiness in my bosom such as I am powerless to describe. I must set my alarum to awake me at half past four tomorrow morning."

Mr Arkwright's house was as pleasantly situated as any in the parish of Sowden. It was halfway up the hill, had a grove of beech trees behind it and in front a square garden which it was his pride to keep well stocked with flowers. This garden was well hedged on either side and railed from the road with green iron bars overhung with tea-plants. The house and garden faced south and were protected from the west winds by a row of plane trees in the hedge, under which, outside his fence, was a way leading to the stable, shared with a twine-spinner who paced up and down it all day long, whilst a little boy whirled the wheel at the end of the rope-walk. Every rose has its thorn, every sweet its bitter, every advantage its drawback. Mr Arkwright and his little German wife congratulated themselves on having such a pleasant house, but they were kept in daily irritation by the rattle of the spinner's wheel. The rope-walk was the skeleton in their cupboard. It was near their back premises and the rapidity with which the beer cask ran dry was attributed to this fact. The spinner was unwed, so was the housemaid.. Apricots were supposed to ripen on the coach-house wall, but, as a fact, they were never enjoyed by the Arkwrights; the stones, well sucked, being invariably found before they had purposed picking them, strewing the pacing-ground in the immediate proximity of the wheel. In vain did Mrs Arkwright change her servants periodically. The band-spinner, on the disappearance of one maid, promptly transferred his affections to her successor. He was provokingly good–looking, and no Abigail that the little lady could secure was proof against his bushy whiskers and dragoon–like moustache. At every change of boy at the wheel, Mrs Arkwright's anticipations of a chance being afforded the apricots to ripen was doomed to disappointment. The lads proved as sensible to the attractions of the fruit as were the servants to the charms of the spinner. The windows of the house commanded a pleasant prospect of the vale of the Calder, and the hills on the opposite side, covered with woods, rising to moor; the Black Nab, the highest point, attaining an elevation of 1700 feet above the level of the sea. To the west lay the blue ridge of Blackstone Edge. On a clear day Stoodly Pike was visible, with its obelisk erected in commemoration of the Peace of 1815, and which, singularly enough, fell the day that war with Russia was declared. The valley itself bristled with chimneys, which smoked night and day. On Sundays the air was clear, and the beauty of the hills was discernible; on other days it was seen but darkly through a veil of coal smoke. When the wind was from west or north the smoke rolled down the valley; but when from the opposite directions, it swept up the valley. It only went in two directions, up the Calder dale or down it.

How lovely the scene must have been before the manufactures disfigured the country, the smoke befouled the vegetation and the dye polluted the river, old people would relate, but it was the beauty of inanimate nature. If much of that is gone, there is a superadded charm in the influx of life and human activity. The fish no longer dart in the limpid river, basking in its shallows, lurking in its pools, for the river is no longer limpid; a reek of indigo and oil rises from it, nauseating in winter, poisoning in summer. The last trout was caught in 1845 and that tasted too strongly of dye to be edible. The wood pigeons no longer coo in the bosky nooks, for the scream of the railway engines and the discordant whistles and "buzzers" of the mills have scared them away. Yet there is something better deserving of admiration in Calder dale now than there was then. There is token of prosperity; there is work for nimble fingers, work for active brains. Intelligence which before lay dormant has been elicited, energy which before was undirected finds now a legitimate field for exercise; power which before was wasted is now gathered up into a mighty force to drive forward the social regeneration of mankind.

When the trout darted and the pigeons cooed, humanity was sparse; now it teems in dell and on hillside.

In the good old days, when the trout darted and the pigeons cooed, you might have wandered among the rocks and woods without seeing man, woman or child; now you cannot go a hundred yards without lighting on a band of little lasses clattering their cans and singing in sweet harmony as they tramp home from work; or without meeting a party of sturdy men, joyously laughing, returning to the well-spread table, to the dear "owd lass".

> "An' th' little things yammerin' reawnd."

In the good old days when the trout darted and the pigeons cooed, mankind hereabout lived a dull life of agricultural toil, with no thought above bullocks and sheep, under the despotism of an unsympathising landlord, in a bondage of body, a bondage of mind, a bondage of soul; with no consciousness of the force existing unelicited in all these poor slaves; now the shackles are broken and the captives emancipated, and men feel that they are men, can hold up their heads with legitimate pride in prosperity and in adversity are able to say —

> "Let's ha' no skulking nor sniv'ling,
> Whatever misfortunes befo';
> God bless him that fends for his living,
> An' houds up his yed through it o'!"

In the good old days, when the trout darted and the pigeons cooed, there were few to mate save the cold-blooded fish in the river and silly doves in the wood, whereas now — but on this point I can a tale unfold, if the reader has patience to follow me.

When Hugh Arkwright entered his uncle's door, he was met in the passage by the German aunt, a small woman with a brown face, lively dark eyes and hair approaching to black.

"Ach! my dear boy, you are shocking! you are *ganz*

durchnässt. What you call it in English? Oh! you go and alter your clothes immediate. I insist. Look at your boots! they are terrible–*nass*."

"Juicy, you mean, Gretchen," said her husband, looking out of the dining–room door. "Why do you not say it instead of using your stupid foreign words?"

"Why. Henry, how can you so go on! You have no nice expressions in your language. I know it is not juicy. You are poking fun at me. It is the meat is juicy and not the habiliments."

"Spell that word, Gretchen, please."

"No, *sie sind böshaft!* I will not. Go you, boy, and alter the habiliments and then you shall have your tea. *Geschwind!* Your uncle is eating of it now, and it is all warm." Then, to the maid of all work, "Sarah Ann! carry the young Herr upstairs —"

"I protest, aunt —"

"You bad fellow! you misunderstand me. You carry, for the gentleman, a jug of hot water to the top of the stairs, and *geschwind.*"

Then she darted back into the dining–room to her husband, and began to scold as she poured him out his tea.

"How can I learn the English tongue if you teach me all wrong. You teach me the bad words and people laugh over me. I have no–one to inquire of. I will *mich belehren lassen* of Sarah Anne, and you say I talk the broad Yorkshire, and the Wörterbuch gives me not always the proper expression. I will ask dear Hugh. He is a good fellow and you are very bad. You always tease me dreadful."

"I badger you, do I?"

"You what, sir! I will give you no sugar unless you tell me what that means."

"What? Badger?"

"Ach! it is naughty. I will get my Wörterbuch. Stay, you shall have no sugar till I have — How spell? Ach! see, I have it found. Der Dachs. It is a nasty beast. How you say me one nasty beast? Oh! Henry, that too bad; I shall cry."

"Nonsense, Gretchen; it means to worry, to tease, you know."

"*Ach, freilich. Zu plagen, zu quälen!* I will look out the German and see if it put badger."

"You will not find it. It is a slang term."

"That is it, you teach me more of the horrid slang than of the right English and it is too bad. Here is Hugh. I will ever ask him. *Nicht wahr!*"

And now the stream of her broken English was directed upon the young man, and to him she flew for information whenever her husband used an obscure word which she suspected of implying something very satirical at her expense. Hugh was generally able to relieve her mind, and he occasionally turned aside a joke of his uncle's which he thought might distress her. Hugh rather questioned the taste of Mr Arkwright in making the poor little woman the stalking horse of all his witticism, and was not a little wearied with the repetition of the same style of amusement at every meal; but his aunt seemed not to feel it acutely, and to bear all with perfect good nature; though occasionally when her husband had carried his fun a little too far, she would exhibit symptoms of crying. At this point Mr Arkwright became conscious that he had exceeded what was courteous and kind, and would change the topic. But the little woman was sure to revive in a moment, and not content that the talk should be monopolised by her husband, would venture on some observation so wide of the subject or so absurd as to restore the train of badinage. Probably Mr Arkwright considered this banter a lively means of exhibiting his own humour; it was therefore conducted in society every whit as much as at home. Hugh could not but feel that it exposed his uncle to be regarded as wanting in delicacy.

"Henry, mein lieber, it is so nice today."

"Then you are the first to appreciate the weather that I have met with. There is no accounting for taste. You see, Hugh, what we lose by not being foreigners."

"Oh, there now! *Sehen sie!* Not the weather, it was the band-spinner."

"Halloo! Gretchen, you following in the steps of Rachel, Jane, Susan and I suspect Sarah Anne, in declaring the moustachioed man of the rope-walk nice. I am jealous."

"This is too bad. You will not listen to what I would say. I wanted to say it was so nice this wet day, for that the band-spinner was not out here with his terrible wheel, *den ganzen tag*

21

— the total day."

"How has Sarah Anne borne up through the twenty–four hours?"

"Oh, she has been shocking cross."

"You should take the poetical view of the rope–making," said Hugh; "for there is romance in that as in everything else."

And he quoted Longfellow: —

"Human spiders spin and spin,
Backward down their threads so thin,
Dropping, each, a hempen bulk,
At the end an open door;
Squares of sunshine on the floor
Light the long and dusky lane;
And the whirling of the wheel,
Dull and drowsy makes me feel,
All its spokes are in my brain."

"It won't do, Hugh, a bit," interrupted his practical uncle; "for there is no shed with door and windows here, all goes on in the open air. And I shouldn't mind the wheel so much if it did not conduce to beer, which I have reluctantly to pay for."

"Oh, Henry, the cask is completed!" said the German wife.

"I thought as much. Wet work for the human spider. I can't see what right poets have to bring unpleasant images into their verses and try to make them go down with the public. It is bad enough to have that man perpetually supping my ale and courting my maids without having him made sentimental by becoming the subject of poetry. Come, change the subject. I cannot bear to think of that rope–walk and the eternal whirr of the hateful wheel."

"But you like the din of the mill," observed Hugh.

"That is quite another thing," answered Mr Arkwright; "I tell you, young man, I hate being *done*, I cannot endure the humiliation of being swindled. Change the topic."

"I did not see the night–watchman, sir," said Hugh.

"No great loss, either," remarked Mr Arkwright with a grim smile. "He's not an inviting object for the eyes to rest on. You left my message, I suppose."

"Yes, with the woman in whose house he lodges. I did not wait long, as there was no knowing when he would be back, and the mistress seemed perfectly trustworthy."

"That's right enough," said Arkwright; then, turning to his wife, he bade her open the shutters and see whether the rain had ceased. She obeyed. The night was dark as Erebus.

"Open the window, Gretchen."

She threw up the sash, and at once they heard the patter of drops upon the laurels.

"Confound it," said Arkwright; "there will be a flood indeed before morning. I shall go down to the mill at eleven and not wait for the watchman."

"Let me go, sir."

"Well, if you like it. Young limbs are more active than old ones; so go and bring me word of how things look. If the water does get in, we must wait in patience till it chooses to run away. None can prevent it from coming, or accelerate its departure; but I should like to know if the building is still on terra firma."

"It can hardly leave it, I suppose, uncle," said Hugh, smiling satirically.

"No, but if the water gets to the wool, there'll be the devil to pay and no pitch hot."

"I will go down at eleven."

Chapter Three

At eleven Hugh put on again his wet boots, which had been set by the kitchen fire to dry, and which were in consequence warm and steaming, buckled on his waterproof armour, grasped his shield, the Gampish umbrella, and issued forth into the night.

"Stay one bit, Hugh," called his aunt. "You must have die Laterne."

"The what, aunt?"

"The — I know not what you call it — the lighthouse, the thing that gives light, *verstehen sie*, in the blackness."

"The glow–worm, Hugh," laughed Mr Arkwright.

"No, thank you, aunt, I can find my way without the lanthorn, and there is gas at the mill."

Then the door was closed behind him and he realised the darkness and wretchedness of the night.

Carefully keeping to the causeway, he descended the hill. It is a great convenience in part of the West Riding that every road and almost every lane is provided with a broad flagged footway. The sandstone overlying the coal splits into flags and slates, and is extensively used for laying causeways and for roofing houses.

After Hugh's eyes had become accustomed to the darkness, he was able to distinguish a few objects. He saw the hedges on either side of the way, and the black trees overhead; but he strained his eyes in vain to make out the river and the mills in the hollow. Here and there a spark among the hills indicated the situation of a cottage where the inhabitants had not yet retired for the night, but in the valley reigned complete darkness.

Hugh was surprised at this, for he knew that there were gaslights over the gates of most of the factories. Presently a smile came to his lips; he was passing the spot where he had extended his umbrella to Annis Greenwell a few hours before. The image of her bright little face rose up instantly before his mind's eye, and illumined the darkness of the night to a spirit which was not altogether unaffected by the external gloom; and the return of this vision elicited from Hugh an observation which he had repeated to himself no inconsiderable number of times during the last five hours.

"What a bonny little lass she is!"

"Hugh," said a voice within him; "you are struck by a pretty face."

To which he made answer: "I! Fiddlesticks! I am too practical, too much a man of business to have any romance of that sort. I admire what is beautiful, but only as having taste. I appreciate a mountain scene, a lovely group of flowers, a graceful bird, or a sweet little face with melting brown eyes and the daintiest possible roses, and hair like spun amber — of course I do, or I should be a barbarian; but struck I am not. Who with natural sense of the beautiful does not listen with pleasure to a pure melody, to the murmur of a brook, to the fluting of a thrush, or to the warbling music of a little damsel's voice when speaking in her delightful hill–country brogue? Thank heaven, I have my natural instincts in my bosom yet, true and healthful; they are not yet mangled by the horrible machinery of a business life, and tossed into devil's dust. But even beauty," continued Hugh, "is to me nothing without soul, that soul pure and limpid as morning dew. I cannot look with complacency on a sculptured and friezed jail–frontal. I turn with disgust from its architectural perfection, for I think of the criminals behind. I should feel small charm in the beauty of the cone of Vesuvius, knowing that within was a sea of unrest and fire. However brilliant may be the red berries in the hedge, they never attract me, because I know them to be poisonous. But I love to look on a graceful Gothic minster, for I know that prayer ascends within. I delight in one of our dear limestone fells, for I am sure no volcanic forces are waiting to rend them and spurt forth desolation. I can gaze with rapture on a wood anemone or a tender speedwell, knowing that there is no deadly virus in their veins; and so I can feast my eyes on a little face that shows through its transparent linaments a simple heart ever fuming with the incense of devotion, a spirit modest and shy, a soul restful in its quiet trust. This is all practical common sense; there is no romance in this, I hope.

"Now then," to the haunting image. "Fly away you little goose! I have more important objects to which to direct my attention." Then after a minute's pause, "It is a nice little goose, though."

And so musing, he came upon the high road.

Now he could distinguish the giant mass of the factory before him, black against the dark grey sky. He could see the smoke sweeping along with the ashen clouds. But he could detect no light. Sutherland's mill, a bow-shot off, was also dark. Haigh's further up the valley showed no light, but there were sparkles about that of Kershaw. Then Kershaw's had a fold with windows facing that way. There was no fold of cottages to his uncle's mill, nor was there to Sutherland's factory, which was new, and not completed in its outbuildings. All those in Haigh's faced inwards. Hugh's eyes were sufficiently accustomed to the dark to be able to see the flooded enclosures. The water, he thought, could not as yet have reached his uncle's manufactory, but of that he could not judge with certainty without going into the yard.

He accordingly crossed the high road, passed the gates and stood in the enclosure, on one side of which was the warehouse and office, on another various sheds and outbuildings, and in the midst the huge black mass of the mill with its tall chimney.

As one watchman attended to two or more factories, Hugh was not sure whether he would find Earnshaw there or at Sutherland's. He examined the warehouse as well as possible by the dim light and was satisfied that the water had not reached it as yet. Then he passed by the factory, splashing through the mire towards the engine-house, which was on a lower level and nearer the river. Here the fold was much contracted. There was a well partially uncovered, as he remembered, somewhere near the entrance to the hoist, and to avoid it, he kept close against the outer wall. Abutting on this was a shed, in which the hand-combing was carried on before the invention of machines for accomplishing the work with greater expedition and in an inferior manner. This shed was not locked; it was used as a place for odds and ends. A couple of old combs were kept there, for orders were occasionally given for hand-combed woollen yarn for stockings.

As Hugh cautiously stole by it, running his hand along the wall, he was aware of a noise within.

He stood still and distinctly heard a peculiar voice of deep bass calibre exclaim, vibrating with passion, "Annis! Annis Greenwell! Oh, Annis! Annis!"

The blood rushed to Hugh's heart with a jerk.

"From the moment I saw you, I loved you. God! How intensely!"

The tones rose and fell with strange weird modulations and then suddenly breaking off, were interrupted by a soft mournful female voice saying: "Indeed, indeed, I love you."

Then there was a pause. And again the deep voice spoke: "You are dearer to me than life, Annis! I shall go mad!"

Then the female voice: "You know that I love you."

And this was followed by sobs.

Hugh's head swam. He waited till the sensation of giddiness was passed and then he sprang to the door, crying out, "Who is here? I will know."

A figure rushed past him and vanished into the darkness without. But he kept the doorway against the egress of the other.

"Come forward, whoever you are!" he said in a low tone. "I will not hurt you, but see you I must."

There was no answer. He waited. He did not hear a sound, save the drip through a leak in the roof upon some straw.

Again he spoke. "I must know who is here. Come to the door immediately."

He paused once more. Drip.

"Well!"

Drip.

"I have means of discovering you."

Drip, drip.

He put his hand into his pocket and drew forth his matchbox. When he tried to strike a light, he found by the trembling of his fingers how great was his agitation.

Drip.

Then the match flared up; he held it high and looked round. He could see a dangling wool–comb, an empty oil barrel, some broken iron cog–wheels.

A water–drop fell sparkling past. Then the match went out. He struck another. The yellow flare lighted on the dingy walls, illumined the straw truss on the floor, upon which the water dropped. There was a heap of something in one corner, with a black shadow behind it. Out went the match.

Drip.

He crumpled up a letter which he found in his pocket, struck another match, kindled the paper, and pushed into the corner. There he found an accumulation of sacks. Nothing more. He looked behind the oil cask — there was no one there; he went to another corner — it was piled up with hurdles. No person could possibly be secreted there.

"This is most mysterious," said Hugh, standing in the middle of the place, with the paper smouldering in his fingers. "Ah! I have not looked behind the door."

He moved towards it. Then there flashed on him from without a circle of intense light. "Halloo!" was called.

"Are you the watchman?" asked Hugh. "Here. Come and help me. There is someone secreted here. A woman."

"Who are you?"

"I am Mr Arkwright's nephew. Here, quick; give me the lanthorn."

But this the man refused to do; he turned the blaze full on the young man, dazzling him with the brilliance, then he sent the beam of light round the interior of the shed.

"Very odd," said Hugh. "I could have sworn I heard a woman speaking to a man, in here. The man dashed past me, but the woman certainly did not escape. Direct the light behind the door."

The gleam travelled in the direction indicated, but Hugh could discern no one.

"Have you seen anyone pass?" asked he, turning sharply on the watchman. The man lowered his lanthorn and shook his head. Then, putting his hand to the shade, drew it over the bull's-eye and totally eclipsed the light.

Hugh could distinguish a middle-sized man with a broad-brimmed cap, a cloak with high collars and a muffler.

"Come with me to the bottom of the yard," said the young man. "Mr Arkwright wants to know whether the water is likely to reach the warehouse."

"I will,'" answered the man.

Hugh went with him to the river end of the fold. The flood had reached the wall, but had not passed it. It must rise a couple of feet before it could wash the ground-floor of the stores of wool, raw and manufactured.

"That will do," said Hugh; then, after a few minutes of meditation, he asked: "Where were you three minutes before you came on me?"

"Coming down the fold."

"Then, Earnshaw, you must have seen if anyone had run out of the mill-yard; did anyone pass you?"

"No."

"Come, open your lanthorn. You go round that way and I will go round the other. Call me if you see anyone."

The watchman obeyed. Hugh saw the ball of fire travel slowly along the mill-wall. He followed the opposite wall, but saw no signs of living being.

"Good heaven!" he exclaimed, with a start. "He may have fallen down the well when he dashed out of the door — Earnshaw!"

"Yes, sir."

"Have you a bit of string? He may have tumbled down the well. Your lanthorn, please."

Earnshaw, however, instead of giving it him, knelt on the edge of the well, and sent the light down it. The water was not four feet from the surface. A piece of wood floated in it, nothing else.

"This is most extraordinary."

Then, as he turned to go, he said to the watchman: "By the way, how is it that there is no gas burning?"

"Water's got into the pipes," he answered.

"And mind, if the water enters the fold, come to the house and rouse us."

As he spoke, a piercing scream rang down the valley, from the steam-call on one of the mills further up the river.

"Hark!"

It was answered by a roaring vibrating buzzer from a nearer mill. "Good God!" cried Hugh. "What is the matter?"

Then there followed a rumbling, bubbling, all-pervading sound, heard through the feet, for the ears were deafened with the alarums from the mills.

A roar. A spout of water rushing up into the black air above the mill–wall illumined by the light of the watchman's lanthorn as he flashed it in that direction.

"Run for life!" burst from the man, as he fled up the hill through the mill–gates.

Hugh heard a crash, then a furious rush, felt water swirl about his feet, started forward and was in safety upon the high road.

"There's a reservoir burst," said Earnshaw.

"You run to Sutherland and I will go to my uncle!" exclaimed Hugh. "There's not a moment to be lost."

"No," said the watchman, "but nobody can do nought."

Hugh dashed up the lane, stumbling and picking himself up again, his face on fire, the discordant screams and roarings of the mill–calls reverberating through the valley, yet not obscuring the mighty growl of the descending flood. Then the church–bells clashed forth, pealed backwards and the sharp cutting note of the steel bell at Haigh's mill added to the clamour. Some half-dressed men plunged down the lane past Hugh, asking if there was fire.

"No; water. A reservoir has burst."

"By Goll! It's a bad job for them i' t' folds and by t' water side," observed one as he dashed away.

"So it is," thought Hugh, redoubling his pace. His mind flashed to the Greenwells' cottage. It stood in a peculiarly exposed position, just above where the beck flowed into the river. "Heaven help them!" he gasped. "The flood will sweep the house, to a certainty."

He found his uncle already aware that something unusual had taken place. Hugh briefly explained to him what had happened.

"Run down to the mill, uncle," he said; "I will be there presently, though I fear nothing can be done." And he rushed away from the house, turned to the left and made for the cottage in the sandpit.

He was soon brought to a standstill by the water. It was far higher than when he had traversed it before. Now the dell was half full of an eddying lake of backwater. It was perfectly impossible to pass. Hugh stood in perplexity at the margin.

The night had gradually lightened, for the moon had risen; but it was obscured by the dense vapours which crept over the sky, discharging their contents on the soaked earth. Lighter it was, however, and Hugh was thankful for it; he could see the steely reflection of the sky in the water. Then he heard a cry from where he believed the cottage to stand.

"I am coming," he answered, at the top of his voice.

He broke through the hedge, crossed a field, burst through another hedge, coursed over a meadow, then over a lately reaped cornfield, up the dell, till he reached the limits to which the backwater extended. A little higher, into a field path and cartway, which descended to the stream. Then he pulled off his Inverness cloak, threw it over his shoulders, and waded across the brook. It reached above his knees. He had expected to find it deeper, but he was above the point where it was affected by the river. He grappled with a fence of quickwood, and forced a way through; he traversed a scattered copse, came out upon the lane above the cottage, ran down it, his breath whistling through his teeth, his pulse throbbing furiously, the perspiration pouring from his face.

Once more he heard a cry for help. He had not power of voice to answer and he would not relax his pace to attempt a reply. His feet splashed into the water. He saw it occupying the whole lane, and extending through the fields, quivering, leaping, washing towards him in miniature waves, charged with straw and sticks, then retreating, as though sucked away, only to sweep forward again with greater impetuosity. It was doubtful whether he could reach the door. If he went along the top of the hill which spurred out towards the river and terminated in the sand–quarry in which was built the cottage, he would be within call of the back windows, if there were any, but he would be severed by a gulf from those who required his aid.

He would venture towards the front. He could not as yet see the house, as it was concealed from him by a turn in the lane.

He strode into the water, keeping by the hedge, to which he clung as the current rushed and spun about him. At every pace the water rose higher, and it was over his waist when he reached the wall which severed the garden from the road. To the top of this he climbed; and standing on it, had the cottage before him. The garden was wholly submerged, the lower rooms were flooded and the wavelets were plashing halfway up the doorposts. He could distinguish a figure at the bedroom window.

31

He cried:

"Mrs Greenwell!"

"Help! Help!" she screamed.

"Is Annis with you?"

"Oh yes! Do save us."

"I am coming," he shouted joyously, plunging off the wall into the turbid water.

An anxious fear had oppressed him since he had left the mill. He could not account for the strange female voice he had heard in the combing-shed. It was not like the tones of Annis, yet the male voice had uttered her name. Could little Annis have been there? he had asked; and he had replied, Impossible: how could she have been at the mill at such an hour and with the flooded beck to traverse? Yet he was not satisfied. An unrest had filled his heart, till he had heard Mrs Greenwell's answer and then it vanished instantaneously. On he went, calling cheerily to the woman at intervals, and bidding her have no fear.

Then suddenly she withdrew her head and spoke to the girl. Hugh thought he heard her say: "Annis! it is young Mr Arkwright."

And immediately a small face looked out eagerly. Hugh waved his hand and nodded. But he could not distinguish the girl's features, for the night was too dark.

The water rose to his breast and he found it difficult to keep his footing. The side of the house was towards the river and waves continually rushed against it and poured over the garden, dashing Hugh backwards and several times nearly carrying him off his feet. There was a drying-pole not far from the door. He made towards it and clung to it. As he was beaten back, an anxious cry escaped the lips of the trembling women; the moment Hugh recovered himself he called to them not to lose courage, as he would be with them very shortly.

From the pole to the cottage wall was a line on which clothes were wont to be hung. It was not strong, but it was sufficient to steady the young man as he made for the door. For a while he lost the ground and then struck out, holding with his right hand to the rope, but he found it again directly and, in a moment after, was on the doorstep. The door itself had given way before the violence of the first wave that had rushed against it, and it

32

was washing about in the room.

"Have you a light?" asked Hugh.

Mother and daughter conversed hurriedly.

"Why, Mother, of course we have. There's t' leet we went to bed wi'. And we niver thowt on't till this minute."

Then they struck a lucifer and the candle was lighted.

"It's nobut a small end, and it win't last ower long," said Annis. "I'll hold it at t'head o' stairs."

The girl descended a few steps, as far as the water would permit, and allowed the gleam of the candle to lighten the "house". Hugh made towards her, thrusting the floating door, chairs and tables aside. It was a strange scene. The brown water was above the fireplace, swirling about, rushing in and out at the open doorway and shivered window glass, the floating furniture clashing and jumbling together, the ripples dancing up the gay blue–papered walls, whilst the white cats played unconcernedly on the black ground in their gilt frame over the kitchen door, and Garibaldi stood unmoved above a piano which was dancing, and the sea–birds were perched, high and dry, on the chest of drawers; and, on the stairs, bent a fawnlike figure in purple, with pale face and large shining eyes, and a wealth of glowing straying hair about her head and white neck, holding a light which was reflected in twinkles on the dancing water.

"Ask your mother if there is anything I can bring up from this room — anything of special value," said Hugh; "but don't take the light away. I must keep off me these lumbering things that wash about."

Annis repeated Hugh's question.

"Oh, yes, sir," called the widow from the head of the stairs. "Can you, do you think, save t' glass walking–stick?"

"Well," answered Hugh, "I think it cannot hurt where it is, and I may break it bringing it to you."

"You know best, sir, but I wouldn't lose it for owt."

"Here are the birds. Annis, put out your hands."

So saying, he removed the cases of stuffed mews, guillemots and terns from the drawers and gave them to the girl, who handed them to her mother. Then he removed the perishable articles from the chimneypiece and extracted the upper drawers, which had not been submerged, from the mahogany chest. He unhooked the pictures, and seeing that the good lady would not be happy unless the walking–stick were placed in security, he brought it to her, and it was received by her rapturously and transported to the bed. At the same time Hugh ascended the stairs.

"Give me your hand, little friend, to help me," he said. Annis set the candlestick at her feet and stretched forth her arms, supposing that he really needed help. He caught the little hands in his own and held them, lifting his eyes to her large full orbs. Then the rich crimson rose to the pale cheeks once more and the bosom fluttered and the lips quivered.

"Annis!" said Mrs Greenwell, returning from having deposited the precious glass stick on the bed.

"Yes, Mother," answered the girl, nervously endeavouring to draw her hands from those which clasped them, and fly upstairs.

Then — by whom effected, I cannot tell — over went the candle and soused into the water.

"There now!" cried Mrs Greenwell.

"There!" said Hugh, giving a little squeeze to the slender fingers as they slipped away.

Chapter Four

Hugh took refuge from the water in the upper room with Annis and her mother.

The cottage was very small. It consisted of a downstairs room and back kitchen, and two bedrooms upstairs. There was a little landing at the head of the stairs, with a door opening into the chamber occupied by the two women, which chamber had a window to the front. Another door gave admission to the room let to Joe Earnshaw, the watchman. It was above the back kitchen; it did not command the backyard and the sand-rock, but had a small window to the side facing the river. It was considerably smaller than the front chamber.

Hugh went into it, to look out towards the descending flood. He could distinguish a sheet of glistening water, reflecting the pallid light from above. Far away on a distant hillside were some sparks, and he could discern a factory, like a large hulk at sea. He listened at the window, but could hear nothing. Every mill-whistle was hushed; the church bells no longer rang; no voices were to be heard calling. The only sound that met his ear was the dull monotonous wash of the flood, and the dashing of the water against the walls. Once a baulk was driven with violence against the side of the house; at another time a harsh grating attracted his attention and proved, on examination, to arise from a torn-up fragment of pasture-fence which had lodged against the house, and which rose and fell with the waves, scraping the wall as it did so. The young man heard a plantive mew behind him, and, turning to look whence it arose, noticed a white kitten on the watchman's bed, waking from sleep and stretching itself.

He shut the window and returned to the women in their room. They were seated in silence, Mrs Greenwell on the bed guarding the cherished stick of glass, Annis on a chair with her hands folded in her lap.

"I wish you had not upset the candle, lassie," said Hugh.

"Please, sir, I thought it was you," she answered.

"Oh dear, oh dear!" wailed her mother. "We shall all be

drownded! What shall we do?"

"We must wait till the water subsides a little," said the young man; "and then I shall be able to carry you to dry land. You can trust me to do that, can you not, little friend?" turning to the girl.

"Yes," Annis replied, hanging her head.

"You must assure your mother that I am very strong and that my arms are stout, and that I can carry her in perfect safety if she remains still and does not scream and fling herself about."

"Oh, I wish t'water would sipe away," moaned the widow. "I fear t'world's coming to an end. And that'll be a bad job for us. I only bought a pig last week, and I thowt to ha' fattened 'un for Christmas, but it's just so much brass thrown i' t' muck, if t'world's end is come. Tha'll niver taste none on it, lass! Thee niver will."

"Eh, Mother! I reckon t' pig is drownded."

"You may be sure of that," said Hugh. "Probably the poor thing has been carried down the river by this time."

"Eh, it's a bad job!" said Mrs Greenwell. "I wish I'd niver paid for 't, as I'll none get ony good out on't." Then, after a pause, she said, "Annis, lass, thou knows t' pig may be i' t' pighoile yet, and if she's nobut drownded, we mun boil her."

"Nay, Mother, she gone down wi' t'flood. He says so."

"Poor pig!" said the good woman, with a sigh. "It's sad to think she's gone t'road o' all flesh. Ah weel! we mun all go when t' Lord calls us." After which pious expression the widow relapsed into silence.

Hugh stood by the window, leaning against the side, looking out. The sash was up, and the cold and damp night air blew in. Now that the exertion of running and wading was over, he felt the chill of the wet clothes clinging to him, and gave an involuntary shiver. Annis looked up at him, and said in a soft, compassionating tone of voice: "You're very cold, sir! You've gotten so wet. Eh, it's a pity!"

"There's no help for it," he answered her.

"But there's no call for t'window to be open," she said; "and I'll get thee t'blanket to lap about thee, and keep out cold."

She brought him one, and he wound it round him. It was the best thing he could do, preventing the evaporation from his clothes. His hand was on the back of her chair, he caught one of the smooth straying locks and twined it round his finger. It seemed to bind the poor little thing to him and a glow passed from the slip of hair up his arm and struck warmth to his heart. She did not know that his fingers held her fast, for she was very still, with her hand doubled and her chin upon the back of it. None of the three spoke for some while. Mrs Greenwell was enduring great searchings of heart, on the score of the pig. Annis was deep in a waking dream — so was Hugh.

Without, the water moaned, in the lower room it slapped and jolted the floating furniture. The kitten mewed at the door to attract notice, and induce someone to coax it. Suddenly, there was a report like a pistol, which made all three start, and which brought the cat's entreaties to an end.

"What is it? Oh dear!" gasped the widow.

"I hope it is nothing giving way," said Hugh anxiously. "Perhaps it was only a piece of timber dashed against the wall."

"It sounded in t'house," said Annis.

"Ay, over my head and under my foot, all to once."

"There is nothing to be done, but to wait in patience," Hugh observed. "We certainly cannot escape from here till day dawns, and I hope then the water will subside."

"I think it's lightening a bit now," said Annis.

"I think so too," responded her mother; "maybe day's coming."

"Indeed, I hope so," said Hugh fervently.

"I fancy I can see yond bit o' wall," put in Mrs Greenwell; "I couldn't afore. And it's lightsomer over t' hilltop. I can mak' out trees, all sharp like."

"Yes," said Hugh, "the day is going to break. Look out, Annis!" and he let go the lock of hair. She sprang to her feet and turned to the window.

At that instant a ragged line of grey light flashed down the opposite wall, accompanied by a groaning and crackling, snapping and heaving and sinking of the floor; then a crash. Hugh caught the little girl to him, and threw the blanket over her head as a rush of slates, plaster and laths shot down.

The gash widened rapidly, and in a moment a great surface of night sky, smitten with the grey of dawn, appeared where there had been dark wall. A cloud of dust whirled around, water splashed into the room, the drops pattering over the bed and striking into the young man's face. A shrill cry of terror was uttered by the kitten, crouched in a corner, its eyes flashing green light.

Then down rushed a stone slate from the roof, and slapped the water. A quiet moment.

Then another slate fell, and struck the floor, bounced off and plashed into the flood.

Another still moment, with the rush of the water alone breaking it. Then a broad flake of plaster dropped into the middle of the room, throwing up dust and filling Hugh's nostrils with an odour of lime.

A pause once more.

And then a beam slid through the ceiling, halted at an acute angle, then swept round like a great compass–arm, smote the floor, and remained stationary, erect. Nothing further fell.

A frightened little body had been clinging frantically to Hugh, with her head against a breast which throbbed with anxiety; an arm was around her, to ward from her all danger. Now Hugh released her.

"Oh! What is it?" she asked.

"Part of the wall towards the river has fallen," he replied. "It has been undermined, and the foundations have given way."

"Will more go?"

"I think not. That angle of the house was directly opposed to the stream. You are not hurt at all are you, Annis?"

"No, no sir. Thank you so for protecting of me. But — Mother!"

Mrs Greenwell did not answer. The bed was distinctly emphasised against the horizon, as seen through the gap. The widow was not sitting up, but fallen back upon it.

"Mother —Mother, dear!" cried the girl, piteously; and in a moment she leaned over her.

The poor woman was lying with her head back and her arms stretched out; one hand clasped the glass walking–stick. A stone slate from the roof lay by her. It had struck her in falling, and she was senseless. The walking–stick was shivered to fragments.

Annis cast herself on her mother with a wail of agony,

putting her arms about her, straining her to her bosom, kissing her and pleading with her to awake and open her eyes and speak.

"Annis! My little girl," said Hugh, "loosen your hold one moment. Let me see your mother; perhaps she is only stunned. There, fill a mug with water. Quick! We may bring her round."

"Oh, Mother, Mother!" cried the girl.

"Do run for water. There is a mug on the wash-stand. Be quick, Annis!"

Then she obeyed; she took the vessel and filled it from the jug, brought it to Hugh and stood beside him sobbing whilst he splashed the water over the poor woman's face.

"She is dead," said the girl.

"I do not think it. You should not suppose the worst. I fancy she is only stunned. Hark!"

Both heard a shout; it was a loud ringing voice from the top of the sand-hill. Unfortunately no window opened that way; but Hugh, relinquishing his attention to the insensible woman, ran to the gap in the wall and called:

"Help! Help!"

Then the voice roared again: "Annis!"

"Yes!" called Hugh in reply. "Help for a sick woman and quick about it. The house is falling!"

"Annis!"

"Yes!" cried the girl. "I am here. Oh, Joe! Mother's dying."

"Who is with you?" asked the loud, vibrating voice.

"Mother. Mother's nigh dead."

"Who else? There was a man spoke."

Annis hesitated, and looked at Hugh; then her eyes fell.

"There's a man there. Who is it?" again, with a bellow like a bull.

"Only Mr Hugh Arkwright," Annis cried shrilly.

"Then," boomed the voice, "damnation! Let him save you." And they heard no more.

"Joe, Joe!" in a note of piercing agony.

No answer.

"Joe, help me! Help Mother!"

No answer.

She cried once or twice again; but no one replied, and she

returned to the bedside, on which lay the poor insensible form; and on that she now lavished all her care.

The dawn brightened. The clouds became as wool; a sickly pallor stole over the landscape. The troublous waters reflected it, showing like a sea of mercury. Trees became black patches against the horizon. The factories began to cast inky shadows over the flood and gleams to appear at their windows, the light from those to the east striking through those opposed to them. No smoke lumbered away from the tall chimneys.

A haystack drifted down the river, bobbing, lurching to one side, then to the other and then passing beyond the range of vision. Then a dead cow floated past; and after it a fleet of oil-casks. Aloft, a flight of rooks were tracing strange patterns against the grey cloud, cawing with delight, for the overflow promised them rare pickings.

Next, a strip of cloud lost its ashen hue and turned a muddy brown; presently the brown reddened and there was a bank of rust-coloured vapour towards the east. A purer, crisper air began to waft in at the chasm and to gather force. The clouds moved faster; they took outline and shape, but shape of a ragged description and an outline ever breaking up and reforming. No rain fell now. All at once the canopy of mist was criss-crossed into little fleecy packs, then a rent appeared, and a glimpse of very cold blue showed and was brushed over again, as though it had been a blot and was to be smudged out for ever. Then came a sulphur powdering and then, with a flash, a beam of sun went, as a seraph bearing a message of joy from the throne of God, flying over the hill, transmuting the flood of mercury to a sea of gold, making every bush and tree, however mean by nature, glorious by Grace; turning the drops which the breeze dashed from their leaves into showers of flame, leaping in at the gaping fissure in the cottage wall, and painting its walls yellow and carpeting its floor primrose; breaking into prismatic colours in the water-drops which trickled over the inanimate body, bringing light into the dim eyes, a flush to the pallid cheek, even crumbling into rays in the splintered glass of the walking-stick, then sinking into the bosoms of the two anxious watchers, casting out fear and doubt, and springing up in a fountain of hope, scattering its tokens from eye and lip and brow and cheek.

"A boat! A boat!" shouted Hugh, starting to the gap.

"Hoy there!" from over the water.

"Help!" called the young man, catching up Annis's crimson kerchief, which lay on a chair near at hand, and waving it.

"Right!"

Then the boat came on towards the cottage slowly, pushing past beams and rails, and fragments of broken cattle-sheds, which encumbered the backwater. The rowers thrust off the carcass of a drowned cow, but it swung round and came towards them again. They drove it off with a punting pole, and it swam a little way, and then floated to the boat from an opposite side.

There was a broken wall to be crossed. Several places had to be tried and one abandoned after another, till the gate was found and then the boat pushed through.

"How many are you there?" asked a voice from the stern.

"Three!" shouted Hugh. "But one is insensible."

"Why, good Heavens! it is Hugh!" exclaimed the man in the bows — he was Mr Arkwright. "How the deuce comes he here?"

With some difficulty the boat — it was a mere tub — was brought alongside of the cottage, floating just below where the wall had fallen. The pile of rubbish stood out of the water, and the joists of the flooring had declined, so as to make it easy to descend to the fallen stones, and then step into the boat.

Hugh carefully assisted the girl down to the heap, then lifted her into the arms of one of the men, who deposited her on a seat; then Mr Arkwight jumped out of the boat and another man followed him. With some little trouble and with great care they bore Mrs Greenwell down. The motion probably did her good, for she opened her eyes and tried to sit up. They laid her on some clothes in the boat, with her head in Annis's lap, and then pushed off.

Chapter Five

The whole of Sowden, and not Sowden only, but the entire Vale of the Calder, was in excitement early that morning. Many houses had been wrecked, much property damaged; it was feared that not a few lives had been lost. Whole families were without shelter, save such as was afforded by the charity of those whose homes has escaped; their furniture was gone seaward, their clothes were submerged in the turbid water, their little ornamental knick-knacks had vanished for ever, deep buried in an alluvial deposit, to be fossilised for the admiration of remote ages. It was ascertained that the great reservoir of Mitholmroyd had given way during the night. This reservoir supplied one of the secondary manufacturing towns of the West Riding with pure water, the drainage from the fells and scars, and was formed by drawing a strong wall as a dam across a glen, to pond back the streams. The water thus collected formed a broad picturesque sheet, a favourite visiting place for excursionists, situated among the whin-covered hills, which it reflected like a mirror, and within an easy walk of a railway station. On Saturdays this pond, or lake, as advertisements of excursion trains termed it, was a scene of great animation. Crowds of mill-people arrived by afternoon trains, in over-flowing spirits, determined on thoroughly enjoying themselves. Stalls of fruits and "spice" vendors occupied the side of the lake near the embankment, and a thriving trade in lemon-drops, kali, almond rock, sour apples and cherries was carried on. Little cock-boats were rowed over the pond by loudly laughing boys and young men, who had paid sixpence each for the privilege of paddling about the pond for an hour — a penny for ten minutes being the market value of this sport. Mauve ribbons,. magenta skirts, Humboldt parasols were scattered over the barren fells, the girls running after one another through the heather and whin, and scrambling to the top of the hill, to get a sight of the towers of York Minster, which were supposed to be visible thence on a clear day. Or, lads and lasses assembled on the turf before the boat-house, for the games of Jolly Milner and Sally Water, which were played with unflagging vigour, hour by hour, to the quaint and pretty old tunes accompanying the conventional rhymes, sung by many voices full of rich tone, such as is heard nowhere but in the West Riding.

Now this lake is no more. Yesterday afternoon a rent was observed in the wall which restrained the water, but proper attention was not paid to it. The keeper of the lock sent a little boy to look after the engineer, but the engineer was in a condition of beer, and thought there was no danger to be apprehended; so the lock-keeper, having shifted the responsibility to other shoulders, ate, drank and was merry. Before nightfall he went again to the embankment, and looked at the crack. It had not extended further; water was dribbling through it in some places; in one, a spurt shot out. Rain was falling very heavily. The pond-keeper thought it was unpleasantly moist without. He eased the lock a bit, to allow more surface water to escape, observed to himself that it was going to be a — night, the expletive not being fit to render otherwise than with a hieroglyphic blank; then he returned to his house on the edge of the embankment, and remarked to his wife that "he'd see to the wall being mended up a bit i' t' mornin', but he'd be damned if he'd do ought that night;" so he had his sup of ale, his meat and bread, whiffed his pipe, went to bed, and woke up in eternity.

The embankment gave way at once and a mighty volume of water swept down the glen, rooting up trees, brushing away homesteads, burying here, grubbing up there, building a cairn of fragments in one place, pulling down houses in another. In one great wave it burst out of the dale into the Valley of the Calder. A public-house, called the "Horse and Jockey", situated where the beck flowed into the river, vanished from the face of the earth, not one stone being left upon another. The inn-keeper's body was never found; his child's cradle, but not the child, lodged in the branches of a tree which stood its ground, whilst the flowers at its feet disappeared. The beer-casks floated ashore some miles down, were never claimed, and were tapped and drunk dry by some broken teetotallers. The sign of Horse and Jockey came to land at Goole, uninjured; it was the most worthless article the house had possessed. The sentient, soul-possessing man was destroyed; the painted jockey was

43

preserved.

There was a row of spic and span new cottages, lately erected on money borrowed from a Halifax building society, a little further down the river, of red brick, with stone heads to doors and windows; the flood carried away three out of the four.

In the first lived a respectable wool–picker, with wife and children, joined Wesleyans; he and wife and children were swept from life in a moment, to the no small satisfaction, of course mingled with acute grief, of the chapel preacher; satisfaction in that he was supplied with a subject upon which to become impressive next Sunday evening: grief, inasmuch as he had lost a pew–holder.

In the second lived a widow, who sold "spice", that is to say, sweets, together with sundry articles in the grocery line: a mighty woman very rotund, very red, with a laugh and a joke for everyone; a useful woman to wives in their confinement, and to young people with toothache and children with bowel complaint. The wives she assisted as midwife, the young folk she relieved with black bottle, the children were soothed with peppermint drops. Now she was gone down the river, her sweets dissolved, her bottles broken, her drops dispersed, her experience of confinements lost to earth. Away she had gone, floundering and spluttering in the water, till her lungs were filled with the fluid she involuntarily imbibed, and then she sank, and was caught and dragged by some sunken tree stumps.

In the third resided a musical shoemaker, a man with one love, and that love his bass–viol. A wiry, solemn man, greatly in request for all concerts, able to conduct a band, or take almost any instrument himself but loving most a viol. Of him a tale was told, how he was returning through a pasture one day in which was a furious bull, who, seeing old David with his red bag, made at him. Cobbler David did not fly; that would not comport with his dignity, and the instrument might be injured by a precipitate retreat over the hedge. The bull bellowed, and came on with lowered horn. "Steady," soliloquised the musician; "I reckon that were double B nat'ral." Again the bull bellowed.

"I fancy it were B," said David again. "But I'll mak' sewer," and opening his bag, he extracted the bass–viol, set it down, and drawing his bow across the vibrating string, produced a sound as full of volume and of the same pitch as the tone of the infuriated beast.

"I thowt I were reet," said the cobbler, with a grim smile.

At the sound from the viol the bull stood still, raised his head, glowered at the extraordinary object before him, turned tail, and fled.

Now poor David was gone, and grit and dirt had been washed into the sound–case of the cherished instrument. That was a sad night for the musicians of the neighbourhood.

In the last cottage of the row lived a drunken, good–for–nothing fellow who did odd jobs of work, sold oranges, "lead", coals, carted soil; a fellow who had driven his own poor wife, with her bairns, from the house and lived with a fat prostitute as drunken as himself. This house and those within were spared!

"They might ha' been drownded and nobody would ha' given a thowt on't," was the general verdict on this dispensation of Providence; 'it's a pity!"

After sunrise the water rapidly sank in the river, but the valley remained full of pools. Every field was overflowing, and the water could only escape slowly through the drains. It was the same with the mill–folds. The houses therein remained immersed for days. About Sowden there had been no loss of life, it was ascertained; those who had perished had lived many miles further up the valley. But though none had been drowned, many were homeless. Some poor folk had escaped from their homes as the flood first burst on them. Others had taken refuge in their bedrooms, and looked out of their windows, calling to the men who went about in boats to assist them ashore. Several had found means of saving their pigs, and had carried them upstairs. Where the water was not too deep, lads waded about collecting various articles which the flood had brought down. A number of floating oranges had lodged in a corner, and were greedily secured and sucked. One man ran about displaying a lace–up lady's boot which had been carried into his kitchen and inquiring whether anyone had seen the fellow. The rowers in a boat secured a bottle of rum, drank it off, and cast the empty bottle into the water again. There was much merriment. Yorkshire folk must laugh, whatever happens, and jokes were bandied to and fro between those who rowed or waded and those who were prisoners in the upper chambers. A very tall man, known as Flay–crow[1] Tom, whose house was submerged, strode through the water carrying his short fat wife in his arms, but just as he reached a wall, he sank into a hole and let her go. She scrambled up on the wall, laughing and chattering and not very wet, and pulled the Flay–crow out, berating him well, but good–humouredly, whilst a crowd on dry land cheered her.

"He's no better nor a great buffle–hee'ad!" she said to them in return.

In a little one–storey cot, inhabited by a lone woman, very old, a maker and seller of oatcake, the poor thing was discovered in her night–gear, seated upon a small round tea-table, with her chin on her knees, quaking with cold and fear, and the table wobbling under her. This position she had occupied for ten hours before she was rescued, and when taken off, the tea–table, relieved of her weight, rose, turned over and floated. One sturdy woman had carried her bedridden husband on her shoulders out of the house, through the water, and up the hill to a cottage, in which he and she were kindly received. That had been on the rising of the flood, now she was tramping through the water driving in at the door, examining the premises, and seeing what amount of damage had been done.

The pariahs of society were alive to their opportunities and equal to the occasion; and were descending the stream claiming everything of value that was found as having belonged to themselves. In many cases these claims were allowed; in others the finder of some article, rather than surrender it to a man whom he suspected would cast it again into the river, and bid him go further to obtain it.

A catastrophe elicits good and evil; it draws out hidden virtues and it manifests unsuspected vice. Fraud, theft, lying, selfishness were exhibited on this occasion. Deserted houses were entered and robbed; assistance was refused unless paid for exorbitantly; goods known to belong to neighbours were taken possession of, and sworn to as having been the property of the finder for weeks or months. But, on the other hand, an amount

[1]scarecrow

of kindliness, unselfishness and sympathy was manifested for the sufferers which went no little way towards consoling them for their losses. The homeless were received into the houses of those who had homes unvisited by misfortune. People vied with one another in showing attention to those who were deprived of all. They were clothed and fed and sheltered and warmed, and men spent their time in helping the helpless, and in protecting their goods, without looking for repayment.

Mr Arkwright was a man of feeling, and he insisted on having the poor widow moved to his own house. Mrs Greenwell had revived sufficiently to look about her and inquire after the pig and bewail the broken staff, a fragment of which remained in her hand. The slate had cut and bruised her scalp. Annis and one of the boatmen bound a handkerchief round her head, and a shutter having been found, the widow was laid on it, and borne up the hill by the men, whilst her daughter walked at her side.

Mrs Arkwright was at the garden gate. She had been desiring to assist some one of the sufferers, and now her delight at having the opportunity of lavishing her sympathy and care on one who was not only outcast, but badly hurt, was excessive. Few of the houses round were without some inmates thrust on them by the catastrophe of the night, and now the little German lady was gratified in her most sanguine wishes in being afforded scope for the display of attentions like her neighbours.

"What the deuce took you to that cottage?" asked Mr Arkwright of Hugh.

"Humanity," was the prompt reply of his nephew.

"Where did you go, after giving me warning of the flood, boy? I thought you told me you would be with me directly. I expected you all night. There was not much to be done at the mill, except to get the books safe from the reach of the water, but you should have been there."

"So I would have been, dear uncle, but my assistance was needed for the preservation of life, and I could not well refuse it."

"What took you to that cottage?" again inquired Mr Arkwright.

"I believe it was presence of mind. You know that you sent me there at half-past six."

47

"Yes, I know I did. What of that?"

"Well, fortunately — I will rather say providentially — I observed the position of the house, with its angle to the river; and directly I knew that a reservoir had burst, I felt sure that the cottage in question would stand very little chance of escaping destruction. My father, I am thankful to say, always taught me to observe and to think, and I am fortunate in having profited by his instruction."

"There were other houses in equal peril," said his uncle.

"Yes, there were," Hugh answered. "Those, for instance, in the mill-fold; but I knew on them would be directed all care and attention, whereas this house was out of the way, and there were no men near to give help. It really was most fortunate that I went there."

"Humph!"

His uncle seemed partially satisfied with the explanation. Mr Arkwright had been out all night himself.

"You see, when once I got there, there was no getting away," added Hugh. "I had not the inhumanity to leave a dying woman, and I very much question whether it would have been possible for me to have left. It was bad enough reaching the cottage."

"Change the topic," said Mr Arkwright. "You are wet through; go and alter your habiliments, as Gretchen would say, or you will be laid up with rheumatic fever."

"Rheumatic fever is a dreadful complaint," observed Hugh.

"Ay," said the mill-owner, "I believe you, my boy. And the worst is, that it leaves after-effects. It often affects the heart."

"I feel a sort of queer sensation there now," said Hugh.

"Stuff!" laughed his uncle. "It follows, does not precede, the disorder. Go and slip on your dry things and we'll have some hot toddy to set us right. Be sharp!"

Mrs Arkwright had in the meanwhile seen her patient into bed, had bustled about the house first after one thing and then another, in the exuberance of her sympathy. The doctor was sent for, cordials were applied, and there was no fear of Mrs Greenwell suffering for want of attention. If there is one thing a woman revels in, it is having a sick person in the house; if there is one thing, however, that she prefers, it is having a corpse. Mrs Arkwright was likely to be gratified in both respects, for the poor widow was doomed not to recover; but of this the lady was not certain now, though flutterings in her bosom had told her that it was not impossible. Had her husband given her the choice of a sick woman or a silk dress, she would have accepted the former; had he offered her a set of diamonds or a decease, she would have enthusiastically elected the latter.

Let no–one deem the little German lady unfeeling. She was the impersonification of tender compassion and sympathy. Her own comfort, her health, her leisure she would sacrifice without a moment's regret to her solicitude for another; but there is a certain satisfaction in being enabled to exert the human instincts, in having an object on whom to lavish the sensibilities, in having something to harrow the feelings, which is to most women positive, though unacknowledged, pleasure. A man loves to be placed in a position which shall draw out his resources of mind and body, however exhausting to the mind and wearying to the body. It is precisely the same with the woman, and sick and death beds are the fields upon which she can best display her powers of sympathy and endurance. What forethought has to be exerted! what protracted watchings! what perpetual cookings! what interminable fidfaddling, wearing to the frame and to the spirit! yet gone through with an enthusiasm unabated, because it springs from a consciousness that she is fulfilling her vocation, and moving in the sphere for which she was designed before the creation of all things.

"*Ach, die arme liebe Frau, es thut mich herzlich weh!*" said Mrs Arkwright, arranging the sheets round Mrs Greenwell. "Now there! I do forget, and speak my own tongue. You are shocking bad. You are — *freilich*. Ah! My ivers!" — Mr Arkwright had taught her that expression — "You will eat nothing, but you must and you shall. Ver–well, you may stay till the doctor comes, and he shall say. Then we see; you will have to gobble, gobble! Will you taste *eine Brühe*, a — what you call it? — a broth of beef? No! Ver–well, we shall wait a bit."

Annis stood by her mother's side, very anxious. Mrs Arkwright directed her attention next to her.

"You poor little lassie! have you had to eat some breakfast? You must," then she summoned Sarah Ann. "You, Sarah! shall see to the Mädchen, and give her something. She is hungry, she is thirsty, I know ver–well; and you shall give her a brush and comb, and made her nice and all right."

The servant–girl entered on the employment with delight; took Annis to her room, and let her wash her face and hands and smooth her hair; then brought her down to the kitchen, and gave her coffee and buttered toast. Annis was not long at her breakfast, for her heart was with her mother, and she felt restless when away from her room. Sarah Ann talked incessantly, asking more questions than it was possible for the little girl to answer, being anxious to know who she was, what was her age, where she worked, how she liked her work, had she ever thought of going out into service, how her mother had been injured, did she think she was badly hurt where she lived, was she very frightened when the water came into the house, did it waken her by its noise, or was she awake already, what did she think it was when she heard the noise, did she scream and cry, had she lost much in the flood, were her Sunday clothes spoiled, how many gowns had she, did she like hats and bonnets, flowers or feathers, how was she rescued, was she not very glad, would she like to have the same thing to happen over again? and similar questions, some of which Annis replied to, whilst others she left unanswered.

"You are not going yet," remonstrated Sarah Ann, when the girl rose to return upstairs; "you've not told me nowt yet. Stay a bit longer. Your mother's all safe, there's Mrs Arkwright with her, and she'll let ya know if there's owt amiss. Stay, lass, till t' doctor comes — I reckon he'll be here directly." Then she recommenced her string of questions. Sarah Ann knew nothing of the part Hugh had taken in the rescue, and Annis did not think it necessary to inform her.

In a very short while the servant had acquired the following facts, which, as they may be of some interest to the reader, are recorded here.

Annis was seventeen at her last birthday in March; she was the only child of her mother, and had lost her father five years before. She had no kindred of close relationship to her in Sowden, but her mother's brother had a farm in the hills near Keighley. She had been there one Whitsuntide feast, but had only remained there a few days. She had a cousin in Sowden, "they called him Rhodes," that is to say, in plain English, his surname was Rhodes, whose daughter Martha worked at Arkwright's mill, and was her great friend.

"I know her," said Sarah. "She's a Church Sunday-school teacher; I see her wi' t' bairns every Sunday. She's got a black hat wi' a blue ribbon, and a black silk mantilla. Her folks is all Ranters, but she's all for t' church." How this came about Sarah Ann professed not to know, and she declared she was "fair down capped wi' it."

The information obtained by her touching Annis's wardrobe is calculated to interest lady readers, and as this book will probably have a preponderance of such, it is here inserted by us, professing to be perfectly ignorant of the subject ourselves.

Annis had three gowns. The purple dress she then wore had once been a best, but that was very long ago, and now it was worn for work. She had a second best, a blue Coburg at one shilling and threepence a yard, which she usually wore of an evening at home, and on Saturday afternoons, and on rainy Sundays. Her best gown was of purple French merino, at four shillings a yard; she had had it new last Whitsuntide. On Sarah's inquiring how many breadths there were in her skirts, Annis replied, four; the dressmaker she employed was Miss Hamshaw. She had a white bonnet with a rose in it, and a hat edged with blue velvet, and with a blue feather in it — this had been worn new with the blue dress, but Annis was thinking of altering the trimmings to suit the purple French merino. She had a brown cloak, and a black silk jacket, which latter had been a mantilla, but had been altered. None of her clothes were likely to have been injured by the wet, as they were in her box upstairs.

Sarah Ann then inquired whether Annis had taken any precaution against the house being robbed. It would be a pity to have the French merino lost for want of proper care. Would it not be as well to speak to Mr Arkwright about it, or to Mr Hugh?

Suddenly Annis looked down. They might send and see that nothing was taken, or, if the house was in a state of ruin, might have the things transported to a place of security. There was Mr Hugh coming downstairs; she would tell him about it — she professed to be a little afraid of the master.

51

So Sarah Ann went into the passage, and begged Hugh to let her speak with him for a moment; as the little girl had told her that her property was exposed to the risk of being stolen. When the young man heard this, he stepped into the kitchen and asked Annis what it was she wanted. The girl explained to him that she should like to have all her own and her mother's things placed in safety, and that she thought her cousin Rhodes in Kirkgate would take them in, if they could be transported thither. "But," she added, "I don't like to trouble you any more, sir, you have been so kind to Mother and me. If John Rhodes could be told about it, I think he'd have us things flitted, but I do na' like to leave Mother, to tell him."

"I will see to it, so have no fear," answered Hugh; "put that trouble off your mind. I will either tell Rhodes, or see myself to the transporting of all your goods and chattels."

"You're so very kind," said Annis mournfully.

"Not a bit," answered Hugh. "I am only acting in accordance with the dictates of Christian humanity, just as scores of others in Sowden are acting this morning towards those who, like you and your mother, are for a while homeless. So do not fret about troubling me, for trouble there is none; it is our duty to assist one another in misfortune. Why, little girl, if anything were to befall me, I should expect you to exert yourself to help me."

"I would; eh, I would!" she looked up full of intense eagerness.

Hugh smiled.

"Sarah Ann," said he, "I hear the front door bell. I think the doctor is come; show him upstairs at once."

The maid ran out; Annis rose to go, too, but Hugh stopped her. "Wait a moment, little friend; tell me if there is anything that wants to be taken care of. You had better let me know where any money is, that I may secure it for you."

"Oh, sir," she replied, "i' t' box upstairs, you'll find there's a little brass i' t' left–hand side down at t' bottom, under my clothes. Mother put away a few pounds there. There's none anywhere else."

"Then I will have the box moved, and, indeed, anything that is not injured, as soon as the water is low enough, and someone shall watch the house till then."

"Thank you, sir." Then she hesitated.

"What is it, Annis?"

"Please, sir," she hesitated again.

"Well, speak out, what do you want?"

She lifted her shy brown eyes to him timidly, and said in a low voice: "Please, Mr Arkwright, I think you've my red handkerchief; I think I seed you put it by mistake into your pocket, when we were boune to leave t'old house."

Hugh coloured, then laughed. "Now, Annis," he said, "I think you might let me keep that, as I took care of you and your mother."

"Eh! Do you want it, sir? It's nobut a poor cotton handkerchief."

"I should like to have it so much, as a little remembrance of the adventures of last night."

"Oh, you're heartily welcome," she said, looking puzzled. "But it's nowt but t' handkerchief I wear on my head at miln; and I thought I'd maybe wear it now. I've no hat here."

Hugh drew it very sheepishly from his pocket, held it between both his hands, and extended it to her.

"Stop! not in such a hurry," he said, as she was about to take it. She at once dropped her arm.

"Now, Annis," he said, "I will let you have the red kerchief back on one condition, and that is, that as soon as I have got you another, you will give me this one back. I value it as a memorial of a very adventurous night. I am fond of keeping memorials. I have got a thread from the chair in which George the Third sat when he was mad; and a bit of the fringe of Mary Queen of Scots' robe; and some leaves off the willow in St Helena above the grave of Napoleon; and so, you see, I should like also to have this, if I may. Promise?"

"Yes," she said, "you shall have it when you want it; but it's just nought."

"Never mind that, I shall treasure it. There, put it round your head, you little Red Cap."

"It's not a cap," she said, smiling.

"Pin it under your chin. That's it. No, I know it is not a cap, but you remind me of the little girl in a picture-book I had when I was a boy; she had a bit of crimson round her head, just like you, and she was in a wood, with a great wolf looking at her, ready to eat her up. There! now, with your gold-brown hair peeping out, your pink cheeks and saucy eyes, you are just like the little Red Cap of my boyish dreams. I used to think how I wished I was in the wood, too, with a big stick, that I might protect the poor little thing against the monster; then I warrant you, no wolf would have come nigh to devour her. Now, you will remember your promise, Red Cap?"

"Yes, sir. May I go now to Mother?"

"Go; and pray God your mother may get better."

"I'm very sorry t'glass stick were broken," said Annis, sighing.

Then she tripped upstairs and Hugh went to his uncle.

"You have been a long time changing your clothes," said Mr Arkwright; "or you have been delayed. I thought I heard you descend the stairs some minutes ago."

"I have been in the kitchen."

"In the kitchen! what doing there?"

"Why, sir, I have been considering about having the poor woman's traps moved from her house. You see, they are now exposed to the chance of being stolen by any passerby. She has here, I have ascertained by enquiry, a cousin named John Rhodes; he works at the mill, I think, and the poor creature would feel ease of mind if her goods were placed in his care. Had I not better see to it, Uncle?"

"All in good time," replied Mr Arkwright. "You shall not go till you have had breakfast and some hot toddy, or we shall be charged with you sick on our hands. After that, go. You take a great interest in those people, Hugh?"

"Of course I do, sir," said the young man, slightly colouring. "I should be an inhuman monster were I not to feel for the sufferings of that poor woman, with her head smashed and her house fallen, and her little trifles of comfort destroyed. It really is distressing to any man of sensibility. I noticed that you, uncle, behaved most kindly to her, as you lifted her into and out of the boat, and you have certainly evinced considerable kindness in bringing her to your house to be nursed."

"For the matter of that, Hugh, I could do no otherwise; I could not leave them where they were. As everyone about here is affording shelter to those who have been driven out of their homes, one must do as others do, or one gets regarded as destitute of feeling."

"Exactly so, sir," responded Hugh, with great cordiality. "You and I feel precisely alike on this point."

"Humph! Well, change the topic."

"By the way, uncle," said Hugh, after having sipped his cordial, "did anyone tell you that I was at the cottage exerting myself to rescue those poor creatures?"

"No, Hugh."

"Nor anyone tell you that they were in danger and needed help?"

"No, no–one."

"Not Joe Earnshaw?"

"Certainly not."

"Very odd," mused Hugh. "Someone, I suppose it was the watchman, came to the top of the quarry and shouted; we called in reply, telling him that assistance was needed, but he went away."

"It cannot have been Joe," said Mr Arkwright; "he was with me nearly all the night. He was not half an hour away; and he would of course have told me. Probably it was someone else, who went off for assistance, only we came before he could obtain it."

Hugh thought again. He did not tell his uncle of the last words of the mysterious voice, but he said to himself, meditatively, "Heaven help me! There may be a wolf after my little Red Cap; but I will protect her with my strong arm."

Chapter Six

Hugh was as good as his word to Annis. He communicated with John Rhodes, who readily agreed to find room for his cousin's articles of furniture, clothing, etc, till Mrs Greenwell had moved into a new house. A cart was obtained, and Rhodes and Hugh drove down the lane, through the water, which had subsided in the glen almost as rapidly as it had risen, and crossing the beck, reached the widow's house. The two men had to wade to the door, but the water reached no higher than their knees, and in the downstairs room was only ankle–deep.

The first object that attracted Hugh's attention was the fallen candlestick, still half immersed. They removed to the cart the mahogany chest of drawers, the sofa, the piano and then the chairs and tables.

"I think that is as much as can be carried," said Hugh.

"I guess so," answered Rhodes. "I'll drive t' load home now, and return, sir, if you'll be good enough to bide here till I comes back."

"Yes, I will remain; but shall you not want me to help you to unload? I can go with you, and assist in doing that, if you like."

"Nay; there'll be scores o' willin' hands i' t' town," replied Rhodes; "and you can do better here, samming[1] up bits o' odds and ends."

"Very well then, I am willing."

So Mrs Greenwell's cousin drove off.

Rhodes was a wool–sorter in Mr Arkwright's mill, a respectable, well–conducted man, of middle age. His peculiar branch of work demanded a sharp eye, great practice, and considerable patience. He was well paid, and John managed to live very comfortably on his wages and on the profits of a little draper's shop kept by his wife. They had several children, but the elder were married and had left their parents. Rachel, Martha and Susan remained. The eldest of the three assisted her mother

[1]picking

56

in the shop and house and professed to be a milliner. Martha and Susan worked in the mills — Martha in that of Mr Arkwright, Susan in a cloth-mill.

John's wages amounted to twenty-one shillings a week; Martha had a regular wage of ten shillings; whilst that of Susan, who was paid by the piece, varied from seven to ten or even twelve. How much clear profit was derived from the shop and from Rachel's sewing, it would be difficult to estimate, but it was not inconsiderable.

Mrs Rhodes was not a general favourite among the people of Sowden. She was gifted with an unfortunate facility of tongue, and a devotion to the feminine science of slander, which made her a dangerous acquaintance. No one trusted her as a friend, everyone feared her as an enemy. Her eyes were everywhere, so also were her ears. What was whispered in the closet at one end of the village was proclaimed by Sarah Rhodes on the housetops at the other end.

She knew who passed up and down Kirkgate in the day, and their reasons for passing — these were generally of a criminal character. She was acquainted with the opinion formed by everyone of everyone else; this was invariably unjust and spiteful. The motives actuating every person in Sowden in whatever they did, were bare to the eye of Mrs Rhodes and she had the satisfaction of discovering to the world their viciousness. Sarah Rhodes was an excitable person and in her spiritual affairs excitement supplied the place of religion. She was a Ranter, or Primitive Methodist, a denomination which supplies sensationalism and excitement to those who have a natural or acquired taste for them. The programme of the devotional dissipations for the season consisted of: a revival in early spring, in summer a camp meeting or two, beginning with invocation of Divine aid, and ending with sweethearting in dark corners. In the autumn a miracle play — Joseph, a sacred drama composed by the Rev. Joseph Hibbert, performed in the chapel; the pulpit serving as a well into which a blooming youth, impersonating the son of Rachel, was lowered by pocket-handkerchiefs. The pulpit also was made use of for a prison, and into it a class-leader acting the part of a jailer, violently thrust the youthful Joseph with glances of fury and a speech in rhymed heroics.

At Christmas approached, missionary sermons, with exhibitions of reclaimed savages, formed an attractive feature in the Sunday evening entertainments. At the time of which I am writing a converted man–monkey, of whom more anon, was drawing a crowd to the chapel. This man in his days of darkness had acted as gorilla in a caravan, had found his way into Armley gaol and had emerged a preacher at two guineas a week, and the privilege of selling a history of his life at the chapel doors, at sixpence each copy. These cheerful diversions in the religious line revolted Martha, the best of the Rhodes family, and she had broken with the Ranters, and had become a Sunday–school teacher in the Church. Susan was giddy and had no convictions. She went to church when there was a school festival or a missionary sermon, and to chapel when there was a man–monkey, navvy, prize–fighter or dwarf, to hold forth.

John Rhodes himself was not a cordial dissenter, he went to chapel because his wife took him; but he would far rather have spent his Sunday evenings at home with his pipe and newspaper. He thought there was a deal of humbug in religion. He knew that the preachers were not sincere, that revivals made some worse than before, and others spiritually proud, that camp meetings resulted in "misfortunes"; but he shrugged his shoulders, saying that there was little but humbug everywhere, and that there was no avoiding it. He was alive to the fact that a saving faith meant doing the works of the flesh, and that election signified an obliteration of all scruples of conscience. He listened with profound attention to the converted dwarf, standing three feet in his boots, declaiming in a squeak on the terrors of hell flames, and in his own mind he suspected the said flames had as great a probability of existence as the Bogart, and when he was expected to sing about Meeting being a little Heaven here below, he devoutly hoped there was no such thing as a future life. John Rhodes was rapidly approaching a condition of disbelief in revealed religion, brought on by the humbug and hypocrisy of the phases of Christianity with which he was brought in contact, but he conformed to Primitive Methodism, to insure domestic peace. Of all his children Martha was the dearest to him, perhaps because she was the least appreciated by her mother, perhaps also because she had clung to him with greater love than the others. When his children were little, he had forbidden their going to camp meetings and revivals, lest they should contract a contempt for religion, but when they grew up they had followed their own wills. Martha had always obeyed his wishes on that point as on any other; and when she had taken up with Church, he had resisted the coercion which her mother had advised, and had suffered her to follow her own religious predilections.

But we must return to Hugh in the ruined cottage.

Having cleared the downstairs front room, he examined the kitchen and collected all the utensils he could find into a heap on the table. He opened the cellar door and looked down, but as he had expected, he found the cellar full of water.

Then he ascended the stairs and entered the women's bedroom. He found the box, raised the lid and, feeling under the articles there, in the left-hand corner, touched and then extracted a clasp purse containing the widow's money. He opened it, and counted four pounds, twelve shillings; he slipped into it a sovereign from his own pocket, then made a memorandum of the money on a piece of paper, closed the purse and placed it in his waistcoat pocket so as to be able to deliver it over, without chance of its being lightened of its contents, to the owner. He next proceeded to roll up the bedding, so as to be ready for transport, and in so doing, under the pillow, he lit upon Annis's hymnal and prayer-book. He opened them, and saw on the flyleaf of each,

ANNIS GREENWELL
From her dear friend
MARTHA RHODES.

"Steal not this book for fear of shame,
For in it is the owner's name."

He raised the books reverently to his lips and then placed them in his breast pocket. Then it struck him that very probably the little girl would like to have her hat or bonnet, so he looked for it and found both in a blue bandbox, which he brought downstairs, intending to take it to her at his uncle's house, instead of sending it on with John Rhodes.

Having finished his examination of the front room, he went to the door of the other, and was surprised to find it locked. He pressed against it, and would probably have forced it open, had not a heavy tread sounded within, and someone come to the door and said in a deep ringing voice: "Leave my door alone. This is my lodging."

"Are you Joe Earnshaw?" asked Hugh, with surprise.

"Yes."

"Will you help me and John Rhodes to move the things to the cart? We are taking everything away."

"No."

"Will you open the door?"

"No."

"Why not?"

"Because I won't."

"Are we to leave the furniture in your room?"

"It's all mine. You touch it if you dare."

Just then Hugh heard the rumble of the cart, and John's voice; so he ran downstairs, walked through the water to him, and said: "Do you know the night-watch is there?"

"Joe Earnshaw?"

"Yes, he lodges there."

"I know he does."

"Well, he is locked in his room and will not come out."

Rhodes shrugged his shoulders, and with a peculiar expression of face, said: "Tha'd better let 'im alone. I doubt he's none so varry right here," and he pointed to his head. "Let 'un gang his own road. 'Twon't do to mell[2] wi' him. He's a right to stay if he wills. Tak' no notice of 'un, lad. We've plenty to do without, we shall be thronged shiftin' traps."

The kitchen utensils, the box of clothes, the bedding, and everything of any value that the two men could lay hands on, were moved to the cart. Then Hugh mounted, holding the stuffed birds, Garibaldi, the white kittens and the scriptural picture in his hands, lest the glasses should be broken by the

[2]meddle

jolting of the wheels. He seated himself on the bedding and John drove. After that he had seen the birds and pictures conveyed in safety into the house in Kirkgate, Hugh departed amidst the thanks of the family and hurried home, carrying the bandbox with Annis's hat in it. Her aunt had removed the bonnet, which she thought there was no occasion for him to take. Mrs Rhodes begged him to tell Mrs Arkwright that as soon as ever the widow could be moved, they would be glad to receive her into their house.

On reaching his uncle's house, the first thing Hugh did was to inquire after Mrs Greenwell. His aunt told him that the doctor had been there, and had given no hopes of the poor woman's recovery, and that there was, of course, no possibility of removing her. Hugh delivered the bandbox to her, and asked her to give it to the daughter, and tell her that the money and everything else was safe. Then he went in search of his uncle and found him at the mill.

The flood had sufficiently abated to give employment to all hands, and Hugh found plenty of occupation for the rest of the day. The water had been in the warehouses and much damage had been done. Wool was soaked and therefore liable to catch fire by spontaneous combustion, unless carefully watched. As much as could be accommodated was conveyed to the drying-house, where it was spread on the iron floor and the fires relighted. The packages of yarn were brought out and laid to dry in the sun and wind. Girls were employed all day in washing the floors after the men had scraped the silt away and cast it forth in shovelfuls. The dye-vats were emptied, as the water had got into them and spoiled their contents — a loss to Mr Arkwright of some fifty pounds. Bales of wool were broken and spread on every available dry spot. The machinery which had been in contact with the water was carefully cleaned and oiled.

By evening the mill began to recover its usual appearance. The yard was, however, still full of pools; one wall had been laid flat by the force of the current, and the fold was full of ruts and heaps of gravel, ash and slime.

"We shall not get started this week," said Mr Arkwright; "and we may consider ourselves lucky if we can bring the place into working order again during the early part of next. Now, Hugh, it is drawing on to evening and I am as hungry as a hunter. I have had no dinner, have you?"

"No, I could not get away."

"Well, come along. Gretchen shall give us a high tea. There's nothing more to be done this evening. I shall keep three men watching the mill at night till the wool is dry. It will be a wonder if there are not fires after this."

So, leaving the factory, uncle and nephew trudged up the hill to the meal, which their exertions had prepared them to appreciate with unusual zest.

Chapter Seven

During the day Mr Furness, the vicar, called to see the sick woman, and on the following morning administered the Sacrament to her; after which Mrs Greenwell awaited her end.

The widow was neither excited nor depressed at the prospect of leaving this world. She was of a naturally phlegmatic temperament and readily acquiesced in the inevitable, especially if that inevitable were invested with religious solemnity. She had a natural vein of heavy piety in her composition, as she had also a natural vein of commonplace. Some people are heavily religious, others are frolicksomely religious. Mrs Greenwell could not tolerate the latter form of piety. She was addicted to funerals, and failed to appreciate christenings and weddings. She was opposed to exciting sermons, but highly valued moral exhortations. She was diligent in the discharge of all her duties, and she was resigned to the dispensations of Providence. If a hole were burnt in the bottom of her kettle, she did not murmer, because she knew it was "ordered"; if the fowls made havoc of her seedlings, she was satisfied it was "for her good". When cholera broke out in the land, it was to teach folk a lesson to be humble; when the potatoes were diseased, it was to give them a warning to labour for other meat than that which perishes. She was strongly impressed with a belief in judgments. The Crimean war was a judgment on the land for its impiety; the scarlatina, in her immediate neighbourhood, was a judgment on it for its neglect of the Sabbath.

The opportunity afforded her by the consciousness that she was to die was greedily seized upon by Mrs Greenwell for the purpose of pointing morals; a pastime for which she evinced a marked partiality. It may be questioned whether, in her case, the curtailment of life was not counterbalanced by the exceeding gratification afforded her during the rest of her sojourn in the tabernacle of the flesh, of expressing her religious convictions in the ears of Annis, Sarah Anne and Mrs Arkwright.

It is not worth while recording these reflections, as they were, though very true, deficient in originality.

Hers was not a poetic deathbed. She did not extend her arms to the vision of the departed husband, the lamented Mr Greenwell, nor did she hear angels singing, nor did she ask what the wild waves of the Calder were saying; neither, again, did she bid the vital spark of heavenly flame — meaning her soul — "Quit, O quit this mortal frame!" but she turned to Annis and said with gravity:

"My dear, I'm sorry I murmured against Providence, agaite of that pig. I know it were for t' best. It were ta'en to prepare me for another world, that I should na set my affections on things here. Thou knows, lass! And may it be a lesson to thee, or ever thou grows up."

"A pigue!" exclaimed Mrs Arkwright; "ah dear, drive the pigues out of your head."

"Annis," continued the dying woman, "one thing after another is ta'en from us, and all for our good. First thy father, then t' pig, then t'walking–stick, and now I'm boune home. Never mind! we'll all meet again i' another and better world."

Then she paused for some quarter of an hour and seemed to be dozing.

Mrs Arkwright and Annis hoped she would have a little sleep; she had been talking incessantly for a quarter of an hour on religious topics.

At last the poor woman opened her eyes, looked towards the good lady, who bent over her and said: "I think I could fancy a pickled onion."

Mrs Arkwright rushed off in search of one, but the poor creature never ate it in this world, after having expressed this wish. She fell at once into a state of coma and remained in that condition for three hours and forty–eight minutes, at the end of which time she expired, going off in a state of sleep.

There is a little Methodist work on the dying speeches of true believers, full of very edifying moral discourses. There is also a little Roman collection of the last words of saints. Mrs Greenwell was neither a Methodist nor a Roman, so there is no chance of her dying words being inserted in a future edition of either of these little books, but if a collection similar to these above mentioned be made of the last speeches of Church of England folk, it is to be hoped that the final utterances of as pious and humble and devout a soul as lived under the Christian dispensation will find admission therein: — "I think I could fancy a pickled onion."

Story writers seem to regard a death as inevitably the most romantic event in life, scarcely second to a proposal. They suppose the poetic instincts to be at that time most highly developed, and the accidents to be all of the most suitable and picturesque description. The departing are thought to retain their faculties to the last moment, to do much talking and indulge in a profusion of sentiment. Such deaths are extremely rare. Usually the mental powers fail along with those of the body, and the interest completely evaporates. Deaths generally arrive imperceptibly, when the patient is in a condition of insensibility through weakness or pain. Dying speeches usually precede death by a long interval, and are not often of much greater value than that of Mrs Greenwell: — "I think I could fancy a pickled onion."

It need hardly be said that for a few days Mrs Arkwright was so thoroughly engrossed in the Corpse that Hugh and her husband were left to their own resources.

Mr Arkwright was very much annoyed at having the woman die on the premises; and he vented his ill-humour occasionally upon his nephew. But fortunately the work which had to be done at the mill to get it into proper order again, to remedy the damage effected by the flood, and the attention which had to be devoted to the damp wool, lest it should ignite, were sufficient diversions to prevent the misfortune of the death becoming a serious grievance. He laid all the blame upon Hugh, and declared again and again that he should never forgive him for having brought him into this predicament, and that he would rather have given twenty pounds than have had the event take place in his house.

Since the day that Annis had entered with her mother, Hugh had seen nothing of her. He spent the greater part of his time at the mill; and on Mrs Greenwell's decease the little girl had gone to her cousins, the Rhodes. The funeral took place three days after the widow's death; consequently, for four days Hugh had not met his "Little Red Cap" as he delighted to designate the girl to himself. During these four days her image had constantly been before him, and he had longed for an opportunity of speaking to her. There was much that he wanted to ask her about. He was anxious to know something of Joe Earnshaw, of the strange voices he had heard on the evening of the flood in the combing-shed; of that call to her from the top of the quarry, and the cruel desertion of her when in peril of her life. He wanted to know what were her future plans; whether she purposed remaining in Sowden, and working, as before, at his uncle's mill. But he could not speak to her of these things in her present distress; he must wait for a more convenient time. Still, he wished to have a few words with her; he knew that the poor little heart was now very sore and tender, and he hoped that an expression of sympathy might go some way towards healing it.

"It is only natural," said Hugh to himself, "that I should take some interest in her welfare, considering the part I played the night of the flood. It would be unfeeling in me not to exhibit commiseration at her loss, and I have been taught that the comforting of the sorrowful is one of the spiritual works of mercy incumbent on all Christians. A reasonable interest I certainly take in her welfare — of course nothing more."

That reasonable interest, we will suppose, made him go daily round by Kirkgate to reach his home — which was a circuitous route. This way obviated the ascent up the steep part of the hill, Hugh explained to himself.

The same reasonable interest, probably, induced him to walk on eagerly till he came opposite Mrs Rhodes' shop, then to look at the windows, to slacken his pace, and, seeing no one, to go along the rest of his way with depressed spirits and drooping eye.

Was it from the same reasonable interest, or was it the effect of the damp and exposure of the eventful night, that he has now a dull, craving, aching sensation across his breast, which deprived him of his spirits and consequently of his conversational powers?

One day he walked to a neighbouring town, three miles off, the market town of Sowden, which was only a large manufacturing village, and bought a black silk handkerchief, and a little jet brooch, very neat and quiet, with a Cornish crystal in it.

"One must keep one's promise," said Hugh; "and I told her I

66

would give her another handkerchief for that dear little red one she used to wear. Poor Red Cap! I wonder whether she is crying now; and the drops, brighter than this diamond, are falling from those bonny, large, sad eyes. Oh me! I must have a word with her again!"

Having possessed himself of these articles, he carried them about with him all day long, in the hopes of having an opportunity of presenting them. Annis was sure to keep her word of letting him have the handkerchief: she did not look like one who would break a promise. No. Hugh felt certain that the coveted handkerchief would be his one day; and till he received it, he kept hostages — which were the hymnal and prayerbook he had found under her pillow. The purse she had, for he had given it to his aunt to convey to her; rightly judging that it would be needed at her mother's death. With the purse he had sent the memorandum of the amount in the purse, and beneath that he had written in pencil: — "I keep your books. When you let me have what you promised, I will return them. — H.A."

Possibly it was a reasonable interest only which induced Hugh every night before he went to bed, in the quiet of his own room, to draw these books from his breast-pocket and study them, wondering which were Annis's favourite hymns and collects, and then to lay them under his own pillow; but interest, when reasonable, does not generally manifest itself in this form; neither, most certainly, would it lead a sleeper to thrust his hand beneath his pillow and rest with it upon the books.

That Hugh exhibited an interest in the girl, we allow, but to its being reasonable, we demur.

On the fifth day they met; but only for a moment. Annis had come to the house to thank Mrs Arkwright for her kindness, and to take away her bandbox and one or two other trifles which had been left in the room when her mother had died. Hugh had been upstairs to wash his hands for tea, when he observed a little figure in black on the landing, just emerged from the room of death. He guessed in a moment who it was. Something in his breast gave a great flutter and nearly choked him. He darted forward, and catching Annis by both her hands, drew her to a window.

The dull evening light struggling in showed him the little girl who had been haunting him day and night, but she looked so different now. No red kerchief, no purple dress, no white pinafore, nor bare arms and neck, but a plain mourning bonnet, and a black dress and a white collar round the slender throat. But it was the same peaceful pure face, full of innocence; the same clear complexion, looking now very transparent; the same soft eyes, glowing with tender light, but now brimming over; the same delicate mouth, but now tremulous with suppressed emotion.

Hugh looked into her deep eyes, raised full of confidence and entreaty for pity. The hands he held tight in his own. His heart was swelling, and speech was difficult.

"Annis," he said in a low tone, "my little friend, I am so glad to see you again. I have been longing — " he stopped. "I wanted to — to tell you how deeply I felt for you in your trouble. Annis! I can't express myself. But I am full of sympathy for you."

He could not let her go. There was rest and peace and relief in holding her, and in looking at her sweet simple face. That gnawing weariness in his breast was gone now; that wasting anxiety in his heart had vanished. That longing expectation was satisfied at last — as he held her and gazed on her.

"Your promise, Annis," he said, slowly, at last.

She drew her hands out of his; and he produced his little present and her books, as she offered him a very small parcel in brown paper. A long sparkling drop ran over from her eyes, as Hugh looked at her. Her lips were quivering with the scarcely restrainable sob.

The door of the dining-room opened.

"I must see you again, Annis," he said, earnestly; "I must." Then he rushed from her downstairs.

That evening, Hugh was cheerful; he chatted with his uncle and aunt in the usual way, and made himself very agreeable.

"I have got a bit of news for you, my boy," said his uncle. "We shall have the mill running again tomorrow. I have been talking it over with the foreman and engineer, and we see no reason why the work should not go on as usual tomorrow; so I have told the stoker to get the fires up, and have sent to the hands to announce it."

68

"I am very glad to hear that," said Hugh. "And I hope we shall have no more floods."

"And no fires," added Mr Arkwright.

"Why, how now," put in Gretchen; "you said you had commanded the man to get ready the fire and *nun! Sie wünschen. Ach*, you are a funny fellow. Now you hope there will not fire be."

"My dear, there's a place for everything. I like to have the water in the boiler and not sousing the machinery. I like to have the fire under it, and not consuming the warehouses. Do you take?"

"Take what, Henry?"

"Look out in the dictionary."

"Look out what? Take — I know ver–well what that mean, it means, *zu nehmen, zu bekommen. Nicht wahr?*"

"It means to understand, you little stupid."

"I don't believe it one bit, one atom. I will get my *Wörterbuch*. Stay. I have it. To take — there now! *zu nehmen, zu mitführen, annehmen, bekommen, führen*. There, *mein lieber Herr!* not one meaning to understand, *zu verstehen*. You see. You use the word all wrong. I know the language much better as you. You are be–conquered, mister. I triumph."

Later in the evening Mrs Arkwright broke forth in praises of Annis, relating to her husband how the girl had been to thank her for what had been done for her mother.

"She is extraordinarily *zärtlich*, so, you have no nice word in English; so *besicheiden*, so modest and sweet, and she is so *reizend hübsch*. Do you not think the same, dear Henry?"

"I am no judge; ask Hugh."

The young man coloured deeply, and became confused. His aunt did not notice this, but insisted on having his opinion.

"I am so very glad she is nice. I should not have liked one very nasty girl in the house, smelling of oil. Don't you think she is very pretty now, Hugh? You answer not."

"She certainly is not offensively ugly," said the young man, putting on an air of indifference. "My uncle will agree with me in my verdict."

"She is so nice, so *sittsam* — where you have one word in your English, we have *tausend*. She is in your mill, Henry? *Ach, es ist Schade.* Then she will learn bad and be noisy."

"Now, come Gretchen," said Mr Arkwright. "I won't have you maligning my little lasses. I believe you will not find a better conducted set of girls anywhere. They are merry, poor things, but there is no harm in that; they have their fun and jokes, but so have you. And I'll answer for it that you may compare them with the same number of girls in any other rank of life, high or low, and for modesty, self-respect, and delicacy of feeling they will not be easily surpassed."

"Hear, hear!" said Hugh.

"Yes," continued Mr Arkwright, "in these large villages or small towns they are not demoralised. Of course there are bad ones and frail ones and foolish ones; but so there are in every class of life. Those poor children are exposed to temptations from which those above them are carefully screened. But they learn self-control and self-respect and there is a truth about them which is wanting in their betters in social position. Now Gretchen, not another word against my lasses."

"Ach, weh! I have poked up the lion."

"I am sensitive upon the subject. I like those I employ to have the credit due to them for those virtues they possess. Now, Gretchen, you know what shoddy cloth is?"

"*Jahwohl!* It is cloth made of the dust of the nasty black fellow."

"Of devil's dust. You are right. It is cloth made of very little staple and very much trash. It looks exactly like good old stuff which would stand a tug one way and a strain the other, and which, however long worn, would never wear to holes and rags; but it resembles it only in appearance. Give it a wrench and it is at once in tatters. The provoking thing is that when you buy the cloth you cannot tell that it is made of shoddy, it looks so good. Experience alone convinces of its worthlessness. Gretchen! I very much fear that ladies in the upper classes are made for the market, like shoddy cloth. They have an air of refinement, of candour, of modesty and of amiability, which is very engaging. Some unfortunate man invests his honour, happiness and welfare in one of those precious articles, and when he takes it home to his bosom he finds it is all devil's dust. But I will say this for the poor girls of whom I am

70

speaking. When there is bad, it shows it is such; and when there is loose texture, it lets you see that it is such; and when it looks to be stout material, as, God be thanked, there is in plenty, then never fear, it will wear old, but never wear out. Do you understand me, Gretchen?"

"*Nun! für was halten Sie mich denn?* To be sure."

"My dear, I hate shoddy. Wherever I go now, I find shoddy. There is shoddy in trade, in literature, in politics, in morals and in society. Every advertisement in a paper is shoddy. I have not read many good books lately, because before I have got through half a dozen pages, I see the devil's dust fly out. Poetry is full of it; so are the leading articles in newspapers. Look at morals. My good friend and neighbour, whoever he may be, has his vesture of morality most sound and substantial in appearance to his own eyes, and to those of his fellows. Alas! it is shoddy too. However excellent we may think his moral character to be, till the wrench comes, he cannot be sure whether it is made of the staple or the dust of virtue. How surprised he is when, with the first pluck, it flies to tatters! But if you want to see devil's dust bona fide, without an atom of good wool in it, look at political speeches. Here is one by the member for B——, my dear. You know I am tolerably radical in my views, but I should like my politics better if they were not so confoundedly mixed up with shoddy. Have you ever seen the manufacture of felt? No! well, it is not woven at all, the hairs are rubbed and rubbed together until they become entangled into a web, but there is not an atom of fibre running directly through the fabric, not one straightforward thread, longitudinally, latitudinally or diagonally, in the whole texture. There you have a figure for this speech. It looks very tough and very substantial, very homogeneous. Gretchen, every fibre of thought, every thread of principle in it, is twisted and contorted; not a thought, not a principle there is other than devil's dust. Gretchen, in society there is an intolerable amount of shoddy passing as real staple; we call it the civilities of life. They are not real. Do you know, I find a positive pleasure in conversing with my operatives, because they are manly, and straightforward and real. One hears a great deal of shoddy talked about the skilled artisan and his intelligence. I will tell you what I think of the West Riding specimen, who is the cream of English operatives. I believe him to be a soft-hearted, hard-headed being, who can be turned round the little finger by one man, but who is impracticable to another. He has his good points, and he has his bad points. He is shrewd, he is suspicious, he is perfectly truthful, very self-reliant and outrageously conceited. When his suspicion is overcome, he is cordial. His respect and affection gained, he is ready to exhibit the greatest self-sacrifice and docility, but if his self-love be wounded, he shows an implacability and ferocity worthy only of a heathen. He is a lover of order and of method. In short, he is by nature adapted to be the most dangerous and desperate of ruffians or the noblest specimen that can be found, the world through, of God-made man. Now, Gretchen, let us have some supper."

"In the winking of an eye!"

Chapter Eight

Marriage is an interesting relic of a barbarous age.

In times of ignorance, when the sun was believed to revolve round the earth, it was fondly held that wives were conducive to the happiness of men. Education has dispelled this absurd theory, and civilisation is rapidly abolishing the institution of matrimony based on the fallacious axiom..

Aristotle, in his "History of Animals", tells us that the scolopendra having swallowed a hook, turns itself inside out to rid itself of the barb. Modern naturalists deny that the scolopendra acts thus. Most of the facts established by the ancients have been demonstrated to be false by the moderns.

The ancients believed that woman was a warm–blooded domestic animal of gentle disposition, living on love, whose ornament was a meek and quiet spirit. But the moderns assure us that she is cold–blooded, restless in disposition, a devourer of gold and stirrer–up of strife, whose ornament is varnish and tinsel. Society having once swallowed the matrimonial hook is now, like the scolopendra, turning itself inside out and evacuating the fretting and burdensome encumbrance. The scolopendra accepted the hook, supposing it to be meat; finding it to be barbed iron, it discharged it. Society gulped down matrimony as a blessing; finding it a curse, it is getting rid of it with expedition.

A wise rabbi married a very little wife, and excused himself to his scholars by observing, "Of evils, I choose the least." Young men of the present day go beyond his teaching, and of evils choose none. Why so? Not because they do not fall in love as men fell in love in days of yore, but because, though they may lose their hearts, they do not at the same time lose their heads. Their hearts urge them to marriage, their heads restrain them from indulging in a luxury beyond their means.

Girls of the period are like the lilies of the field; "they toil not, neither do they spin and yet Solomon in all his glory was not arrayed like one of them." What may be laudable in the lily is objectionable in the woman. And few men can afford to unite

73

themselves to one who sins by omission as well as by commission, by omitting to share the labour of her husband, and by committing the offence of squandering the results of his toil. If she does work at all, she reverses the task of the Danaids. They strove to fill a bottomless well, but she buckets indefatigably out of a well which is shallow, but which she persists in regarding as unfathomable, — her husband's purse.

Young men know this well, and are exceedingly cautious and shy of marriage. A man of fortune may possess a wife, just as he may keep a hunter or a shooting-box, but to a man of limited means such extravagance is impossible.

Human nature, however, remains the same, and young men still fall in love, but reason restrains all but the foolish from giving rein to the tender passion. In these times, the affection of love is something that is born to be killed, like a flea; and no man of sense and a small income is easy, if he feels the irritation, till he has crushed the sentiment out of his soul.

The first sensation produced by a consciousness of being in love is abject terror, — terror lest the heart should win the day, and the intellectual powers be unable to assert their proper pre-eminence.

Poor Hugh! with a feeling of terror, when he retired to rest that night, did he realise the fact that he was in love, not a little, but with his whole being.

Poor Annis! her timid, tender spirit leaned towards him, unconscious that it loved him, but conscious that, in his presence, it tasted unwonted happiness.

Hugh remained awake the greater part of that night immersed in anxious thought. He felt that his peace of mind was bound up with that little girl. How this had come about was more than he could tell. What it was which had influenced him he could not discover. He had been much in society, he had mingled with a great number of the other sex, — yet had never felt drawn to any one of them in the way in which he was conscious of being attracted towards Annis. He had talked by the hour to the Misses Jones, the belles of Sowden, without feeling the slightest interest in either of them; he had played croquet every evening in the week with Miss Barden, the fascinating daughter of the squire of his father's parish, and had never felt his pulse throb quicker when he met her than when he parted from her. He had danced five times in an evening with the gorgeous Miss Pinkney, who was regarded as one of the finest women and most eligible matches in the county, and the thought of her had not deprived him of an hour's sleep. He had picnicked at Bolton with Miss Fearne and lost his way with her in the woods, and she was a quiet, modest and natural little maiden, daughter of a neighbouring vicar; but he had felt very glad when they found the high road again. And now, his heart was full of strange cravings, his soul yearning with indescribable earnestness for one whom he had seen very little of, knew less of, who was not his equal in station and education. How was this? All day his thoughts were full of her; he could not sleep for trouble connected with her; her happiness was to him the dearest object of life; one glimpse of her was like a sunbeam entering a gloomy apartment and lightening it up. The sound of her foot made his pulse leap, the touch of her hand kindled a fire in his bosom, the tone of her voice was music to his soul. Why was this? He tried to argue with himself that it was not so. He laboured to convince himself that he was influenced by humanity, not by passion. But his arguments broke down one after another.

"Yes!" he said, starting from the bed on which he had been sitting in the dark, and clasping his hands to his brow. "I love her, I love her. And it is a bad job, too!"

Then he reviewed his position. Was it right for him to give way to this feeling? Ought he to persevere in the course he had unconsciously taken? What was Annis? A poor girl, working in a factory, without social position and education and money. What was he? A gentleman by birth and by bringing up, with no means of his own, but with the prospect of becoming partner in his uncle's business and of finally inheriting his savings.

It would not be politic for him to anger his uncle, nor wise to run counter to the decision of society against unequal matches. There was everything to be said against his giving rein to the passion which consumed him; there was little to be said in its favour.

That little may be summed up in a few words; but they were dilated on by Hugh to himself, and repeated with unnecessary frequency. The girl was good, gentle and modest. There was a certainty that she was not made for the market, but was of true strong material, following his uncle's illustration. This attraction he felt had come unsought and unexpectedly, and natural instincts were more likely to guide aright in the choice of a mate than social advantages. But Hugh felt that the balance of reason was against his giving way to his passion. "It cannot be," he said; "no, it cannot be! Heaven help me! I must take my firstborn love and destroy it. I have not betrayed myself to the little girl, and she can have no idea of what is raging within my breast. I must not speak to her any more, I must not see her any more. I must forget the past, and bury my secret in my own bosom. She can never be mine. One thing I have which shall be sacred to me" — he unfolded the red handkerchief and spread it before him in the moonlight, and leaned over it; his face working with pain, his hand upon it, his eyes directed towards it, but only dimly seeing it. Then his breast shook, something rose in his throat, a great sob burst forth — two jewels spangled the little kerchief. He caught it up and kissed it, and bound it round him over his heart, and cast himself on his bed. "This is all I have of her, and I shall never part with it."

The week passed and he kept his determination; but the struggle was greater than he had anticipated; and only by the acuteness with which he suffered did he realise how intense was the love which he felt, how far the rootlets of that plant had spread; how that they had bound themselves round his heart, and had struck into every nerve, and penetrated his whole system. Night and day there was a gnawing pain in his breast, a pressure on his heart. His spirits failed, he became grave and abstracted. His eye lost its brilliancy, his cheek its colour, his step its elasticity. Mrs Arkwright noticed the alteration and bewailed it; her husband attributed it to over-exertion during the flood and prophesied his speedy recovery. Hugh felt a continual restlessness, impelling him to break off whatever he was engaged upon to commence some other pursuit, in hopes of obtaining relief, but invariably without success. When in the office he was constantly making mistakes in his books. Towards twelve o'clock, when the mill would "loose", his pulse quickened and a feverish heat manifested itself in his cheek and

76

eye. He knew that a little foot would pass the office door, but he would not turn his head towards the window. As he walked with his uncle to dinner he felt a longing which he vainly strove to suppress, to see a figure in purple moving up the high road; in the dusk of evening he would wander down the lane to the left, so well remembered, and linger by the beck, then retrace his steps, and arrive in time for his uncle's supper. During meal-time he spoke little, and longed for it to be over, that he might seek the quiet of his own room, where he could stand at his window, leaning his cheek on his hand, and look out over the valley at the black moors, absorbed in thought, with no eye but that of God to mark the workings of his countenance; or he would lie on his bed, with his face in his hands, hour by hour, without moving. And night and day there was a red kerchief knotted round his breast, rising and falling with his breath, and throbbing with the beatings of his heart. His long night reveries always ended in one way — by his kneeling down by his bedside, and putting his hands together, and bending his brow to the counterpane, and praying for her whom he could not forget, that she might ever be good and pure and simple in mind and soul and body, and love God and be happy. That gave him some peace. There was One to whom he could speak of her and speak without offence, for he was asking blessings upon her head. But for that relief he could not have borne his pain.

When a man loves, the whole force of his nature impels him towards the object of his passion, and, in proportion to the energy and power of his character, is the intensity of the feeling. A woman's love burns slowly, with great warmth and light, but steadily. A man's love rages hot and furious, and consumes fuel and furnace.

One day, at six o'clock, Hugh was in the office door, waiting for his uncle, and Annis passed. He knew she was coming up the mill-yard, though he would not look in that direction. He felt her approaching, though he saw her not. He determinedly kept his eyes depressed. He caught the strip of deep purple below the white cover, and two small feet moving nimbly towards him — past him. Then — though he tried his best — look up he must. And he saw a sad little face turned towards him, with two large melting eyes resting on him. A delicate glow of pleasure stole into the girl's cheeks as their eyes met: a scarlet spot burned on those of Hugh. He turned hastily round, and darted into the office, calling his uncle.

On Saturday he saw her again, when Mr Arkwright paid the hands, but he would not look at her: he kept his eyes on the book, but he saw her through every fibre of his body. On Sunday, at church, whilst singing one of the hymns, quite unexpectedly his eyes fell on a demure little figure in black, behind one of the pillars in the aisle, with a black silk handkerchief round her neck, and a jet brooch on her bosom, on which sparkled a Cornish diamond.

Martha Rhodes had not seen her cousin dressed for church that morning, as she had gone early to school, but on their return from service, Martha said: "Annis, where ever did'st thou get yon bonny brooch? I thought we'd gotten all thy black things, lass, and I never saw yon brooch afore."

Annis hesitated and coloured. After a little while she said, in a low voice, with her eyes down: "It war given me, lass."

"Given thee!" exclaimed Martha: "why, whoever gave it thee, I should varry much like to know."

But her cousin did not seem as anxious to tell. Martha, however, was not to be put off. She was a girl who would have her questions answered, and she stuck to her point till that point was gained.

"It war Mr Arkwright," answered Annis, at length, on compulsion.

"Which of 'em, dearie?" asked Martha.

This was coming to close quarters, and Annis endeavoured to evade a reply. But her cousin was not disposed to allow her questions to be evaded, so she repeated it in a resolute manner.

"It was Mr Hugh," said the poor little thing, in a faltering tone, becoming very red; "that is, — he gave me t' parcel wi' kerchief and brooch, but, thou knows, it maybe war Mrs Arkwright as sent 'em me. It's none so likely he'd give them, lass."

Martha looked gravely and steadily in her cousin's face. "What art thou blushing so very red for, lass?"

"Nay, Martha, am I? I reckon I'm varry hot. Thou sees it's over warm today."

78

"I don't think 't were Mrs Arkwright gave thee t' brooch," said Martha Rhodes. "Did she say aught to thee about it?"

"Nay, lass, she said nowt."

"Then it war Mr Hugh as gave it thee."

Annis made no reply, but hung her head.

"I don't think thee ought to ha' ta'en it," continued Martha; "it's none right for thee to wear it."

"Eh! Why not?"

"It's none right," repeated Martha; "and I'm sorry about it. What made him give it thee?"

"I cannot tell. Thou knows he saved Mother and me i' t' flood, and I reckon it war for a bit o' remembrance o' that, thee sees. I'm varry sure there's nowt wrong i' it. I'm varry sure, Martha, deary!"

"Maybe there's none. Hast thou had much speech wi' him?"

"Nay, not over much."

"Thou mun have none at all," said Martha.

Martha Rhodes was a noble-looking girl, with abundance of dark-brown hair, a well-formed face, bright colour, a somewhat heavy brow and fine dark eyes. Her features were not regular and she was not handsome, but her countenance was very pleasing and full of dignity, and when she smiled or was interested, its expression rendered it lovely. In manner she was blunt; she was frank and candid, truthful and upright. Few but those who knew her could judge of the depth of heart and tenderness of feeling which existed in her, and which were concealed beneath a brusque manner. She was a very thoughtful and a very determined girl. She seldom acted on impulse, generally she long considered before she took any step of moment; but, when once taken, she held on her course with resolution which could not be overcome. There was not the slightest pretension in her, no affectation, no vanity. She held her own in her family and in the mill, by the quiet strength of her character, not by outward demonstration. At home, her mother respected and disliked her: respected her for her reliability, disliked her because she had broken away from the religious traditions of the family. In the mill she was the central figure in the group of those who were quiet, modest and womanly, without arrogating to herself that position, or exhibiting consciousness that she occupied it: but it was a position she had won for herself by her consistency, and her right to fill it was generally acknowledged. Human nature is the same all the world over, and in every rank of life. Among all peoples, under every clime, are the same phases and varieties of character, that meet us among our own immediate acquaintance. We are very much mistaken if we suppose that in classes socially removed from our own there is not the same difference of temperament, the same shadings of character as in that in which we move. To those who look down on the men and women below them, they seem of a level, but they differ among themselves as much as do those who contemplate them from above.

Said the sun to the eagle: "The earth is without form and void. It is all quite flat."

To which the bird replied: "Not so, O sun! from thy exalted height thou canst not discern the valleys, the ravines, the hills, the mountains, teeming with life in varied forms of beauty. Descend, O sun, for a little while, and thou wilt find glens deep and gloomy, valleys profound and umbrageous, hills swelling, and lofty mountains ever white with unsullied snow. The earth is certainly not flat, neither is it without form, neither is it void."

We hear people speak of the vice and immorality of the classes below them. I would have those people pluck out the beam from their own eyes before they cast out the mote from their brother's eyes. I would have them know that there are special vices and hidden immoralities in their own class, and that some men's sins are open beforehand, going back to judgment, and some men they follow after. I would ask them, whether vice loses its viciousness because it is hidden in their class and becomes exceeding vicious in that below them, because it is visible? Granted that there is much sin, much degradation, much moral corruption, much that is foul, loathsome, sickening in the social depths; yet, let it be known, that it is with its roots in slime that God grows his lilies. Supposing — for I am far from granting — that there anarchy, lawlessness, rebellion, seethe, that there moral corruption festers, that there fraud and dishonesty are rife; supposing that thence goes up the malarious reek which poisons and blights; well, granted that there is the haunt of the paddock, the newt and the worm; yet it is there that God grows his lilies, white-petalled, gold-stamened, sunward-spreading, unmarred by one foul stain.

Cover your face, hold your nose, restrain your breath, and hurry past this nasty pool — and miss God's lilies.

Search where you will on earth, you will find that the Creator has made some form of beauty to live and thrive. There is not a turbid pool, nor decaying refuse heap, not a mouthful of the most unwholesome air, not a drop of the most stagnant water, that does not teem with life, perfect in its loveliness. Only, you will not see it unless you seek with reverence and with love.

And can it be that souls and human natures, so far excelling diatoms, desmids and animalcules of every sort, full of beauty, perfect in loveliness, shall not be found adorning and glorifying every stratum of society, however low, however degraded, however despised? But the operative class in the manufacturing counties is not low, neither is it degraded; whether despised or not, it little cares; and through it you have not far to look before you find souls so lovely in their whiteness, so refined in their delicacy, so beautiful in their simplicity, so noble in their truthfulness, so glorious in their courage, that you will be convinced it is not in the conservatories of the rich alone that God delights to grow his lilies.

Chapter Nine

At this time Richard Grover, the man–monkey, was conducting a series of exercises at the Primitive Methodist, or, as it was commonly termed, the Ranter Chapel. He received two guineas a week for his services, and was entertained in turn by the leading dissenters of the Primitive Methodist persuasion.

On Friday evening he became the guest of Mrs Rhodes to tea and supper. John absented himself. He had particular business — a game of dominoes at the Mechanics' Institute — which called him away and deprived him of the gratification of doing the honours of his own table to the itinerant preacher.

Richard Grover was a middle–sized bony rather than muscular man, with all his joints sharp, very long–backed and short–legged. The upper part of his person hardly accorded with the lower; the latter belonged to a small man, the upper to one of large proportions. His arms were long, his hands enormous. His hair was curly and black, cut over the ears in half–moons, running back at the temples and descending to a point in the middle of his forehead. His eyes were grey and glittering; his lower jaw huge and his mouth big.

Probably the horrible simian proportions of this man and his hardly human countenance, had made an exhibitor of wild beasts hire him a few years ago to impersonate the African gorilla. He was by no means ashamed of this episode in his past history; it was one he delighted to speak of in private and in public, and when he went about to preach, he was invariably advertised as

RICHARD GROVER OF MANCHESTER

The Celebrated and Converted

MAN–MONKEY!

The parlour of the Rhodes' establishment was very comfortable. It had its piano, its sofa and its pictures; one of the latter an oil–painting by a local artist, representing John Rhodes, senior, by trade a slubber, father of the present John Rhodes, not in slubbing costume, which would have become him, but in his Sunday best, which did not become him.

If there be any truth in the Darwinian theory, then *that* man — judging from his portrait — was derived by a process of natural selection from a turnip. There was no contemplating the picture without having the conviction forced on one, that the ancestral turnip nature inhered still. Turnip was in all the features; there was turnip on the brain, turnip lodged in the stomach, and the soul of a turnip looked out of the eye. Unpleasant as the painting was, no one who looked on it could doubt its fidelity as a portrait.

A picture is about to be presented to the reader, which is exceedingly disagreeable; but, odious as the representation may be, it is a faithful portrait of one of a class terribly numerous in the northern manufacturing counties, where they are doing an incalculable and irreparable amount of injury to religion and morality.

Richard Grover was seated at the tea–table discussing some buttered cakes studded with currants. Mrs Rhodes made tea. Rachel ate by snatches, being occupied with the kettle, the muffins, the cakes and the bacon which was being fried.

Martha remained as much as possible in the back kitchen, only coming when necessary into the room where the man–monkey was being regaled.

Annis and Susan took their tea at a side–table; and Annis, having finished hers speedily, settled on a low seat by the fire, and relapsed into her usual meditative position, with her cheek on her hand; but now, instead of contemplating the coals, observing the preacher with wide, astonished eyes.

"You'll have a snack o' bacon, Mr Grover?" asked Mrs Rhodes.

"Thank'y, I won't say nay. I like it fat and cut thick. That's the ticket. Just so. Now I'll trouble thoo to teem[1] th' gravy over 't; I'm partial to th' drippings. Come, now! though I be a Manchester man, I'll say this, mam, I never i' all my born days

[1]pour

saw a better rasher nor this. Glory be!"

"It's our own fattening, Mr Grover."

"I'd be sworn to 't. I can smell thy handiwork i' th' reek — I can taste it i' th' drippings. Hey, lass! pass me over th' spoon. It's a long way handier for swallowing th' drippings. Thae may teem out another cup o' tea, and put in more shuggar."

"Nay, help thysen, lad."

He did not need twice telling. "I mak' mysel at whoam, thou sees," he said; "it's a glorious thing that wherever one goes, there's servants o' th' Lord to give a chap his vittles. Hallelujah!"

"Them as is i' th' right road is always provided for," said Mrs Rhodes.

"Eh! that's sure enew," added Rachel.

"Thou's making a poor tea," observed the hostess; "let me do thee another rasher."

"I could pallate it," answered Richard Grover. "And mind, lass, thae cuts i' th' fat, and never fear about it being over thick for me."

"Thou'st done a glorious work here, Mr Grover!" said Mrs Rhodes.

"I have that," said Richard, approvingly. "Wherever I go, it's all th' same. The folks was stirred up grand at Hanging Heaton, where I was Sunday three weeks back. They was converted as thick as blags[2]. I'm in mighty request, I can tell thee, owd lass! Go where I will, they want me i' th' next parish. It's grand, thae knows, for an earthen vessel to be a hinstrument o' glory."

"Have you been long converted, Mr Grover?"

"Only a twelvemonth, mam. Did you never hear th' tale?" He finished his rasher, and thrust back his chair. "You mun be siding th' table," he added, "and when you've gotten all sided, and will clap you down and be quiet, I'll tell you. And I'm thinking," he added, fixing his glittering eye on the corner cupboard, "that you've sommut i' yond place as would be nice wi' a drop o' warm water and a lump o' white shuggar."

"Ay, I have," answered Mrs Rhodes, gleefully. "I think I know that you like something comforting. You're not a

[2]blackberries

84

teetotaller, I reckon?"

"Nay, I'm no teetotaller. But don't think I'm ought again them total chaps. They're a good sort, mind you."

He looked complacently round the room. Mrs Rhodes was seated on the other side of the fire, Rachel near her; Susan was perched on the sofa-arm. Martha came in and sat in a corner, where she might not be observed. It was dull in the back kitchen among the slops and saucepans, with the cat for company. On the table was a bottle of gin, a tumbler, hot water and sugar. The man-monkey mixed a stiff glass for himself.

"I'm weak i' my insides," he explained. "And preaching takes a deal out o' me. The sweat fair siles[3] off me; you might wring a bucketful out o' my shirt. Now I'll show you sommut, lasses. Look here!"

Suddenly he threw his foot up, and placed it on the table. "Dost thae see my boot, and th' big nails i' it, mam? It were wi' this same boot I killed my missis, wi' poising[4] her when I was druffen[5]. Eh, lasses! I were a bad un i' my unconverted, unregenerated state. I swore awful. I cussed, and it's mercy o' heaven I warn't struck dead wi' leetning for th' foul words I spake. I'd a tidy sort o' a missis and two small bairns, but I used 'em shameful when I were i' liquor. I never gave 'em enew to eat, I drunk up all as I ever addled[6], I may say, like he i' Scripture. I've been extortioner, unjust, adulterer. Eh! I could tell you some rummy tales as would make these lasses blush and throw their aprons over their faces to hide their giggling. I could tell you some rummy things I ha' done," with a significant wink and nod at Mrs Rhodes. "But mebbe you're fain to hear th' worst I did. Well!"

He looked proudly about the room with straightened back and

[3]runs

[4]kicking

[5]drunk

[6]earned

85

erect head; "I'm a murderer! Ay! Th' Lord be praised. I may say, I'm a murderer. I killed my missis wi' this here boot thae sees. I only wear these boots when I'm preaching or visiting special friends. I wouldn't wear 'em out for nowt, for I can show th' very article as did th' job, and it's a great attraction. Glory be!"

"I've a'ways heard," said Martha from the distant corner, "that the biggest rogues are them as is unhung."

"Right, lass!" replied the man–monkey, wheeling round. "The Lord be praised! And I believe there never was a more hawful offender agen th' laws o' God and o' man as mysel. Weel! you sniggering kitlings" — to Susan, Rachel and the other girls — "you want to hear all about it; but I'd as lief not tell."

And here we may remark that not one of the girls was "sniggering". Martha looked disgusted; Annis's face was white and frightened; Susan also gave signs of being alarmed.

"And so you're all on tenterhooks to hear how I killed th' owd brid. Why, thae sees, I did it this road: — Poor lass, she were a'ways a looking out, wi' her pale hungry face, after me o' nights, and I didn't fancy it. She'd come hanging aboot th' beershop, and axing after me, and fretting and trying to persuade me to come away along wi' her. And folks laughed and said I was looked after shameful by my missis. So I tou'd her, next time I caught her coming after me that road, I'd gi' her summut as she'd never forget. Weel, lasses, would you believe it, next Saturday neet she cam' fratching and fretting as afore. I sent her home wi' a flea i' her lug, and when I cam' whoame I fund her there, sitting up biding till I cam'. So I up wi' my foot and I poised her i' th' breast, and she never said owt, but fell as if she were dead. Then I were a bit flayed; I thowt I'd done the job over fast. I took her up, and I laid her i' th' bed, and doused her wl' cawd water; and bym–by she cam' round. Well! she took bad after; she never got over that, it had brussen summut i' th' inside, I reckon, so she deed i' th' back end o' th' year. But I never got owt done to me, for, thae sees, nobody could say 'twere I killed her, or trouble. Mebbe a little of both. She suffered awful bad, I've heard say, but I didn't heed her much mysel. I went off wi' another woman, and left her and th' bairns to fend for theirsels; and I reckon that had summat to do wi' settling of her. So if 't war'nt kick only, 't were t'other thing; and

86

as I did both, I don't see as onybody else can lay claim to being th' death o' her but myself. What do you say, mam?"

"Eh! but t'Lord's been gracious to you."

Martha, unable to control her disgust any longer, said: "I'm very sure, if you had your merits, you'd ha' swung."

"I'm very sure," replied the man-monkey, turning towards her, "if I'd ha' had my merits, I'd ha' been boiling and frizzling i' hell fire. But glory be! it's none by merits, lass, but by faith, we're saved."

The strange man spoke with vehemence, whirling his long arms like the wooden soldiers who spin their flappers in the wind to scare birds. Ever and anon he drank from his tumbler, replenished it and drank again. His wild grey eyes flashed, his monstrous jaw worked as he spoke, and his black hair bristled with excitement.

"Merits, lass!" he cried; "dost thae think we shall be axed one word o' that score? Never a word! Dost thae think thy morality and respectability will save thoo? Never a bit! What's thy morality and respectability but filthy rags and dust and ashes? Dost thae think th' Almighty cares one farthing whether thou'st moral or not? Never a farthing? Thae'll be axed about thy faith, and not about thy works, lass. Shall I tell thoo where thy moral lass will be? Hoo'll be i' th' outer darkness, and hoo'll hear nowt thro' eternity, but th' tick-tack, tick-tack o' th' great clock o' time that'll never be wound up, because it'll never run down. I can tell thoo, there's not a bad deed I've not done, there's not a commandment I've not broken; and now I'm justified, I'm sanctified, I'm regenerate. Th' owd things is passed away; I'm no more i' th' flesh, but i' th' spirit."

Martha laughed.

"Ay, I am. I've th' witness i' myself. I'm one o' th' elect. I cannot commit sin, whatever I does now, because I'm born anew. Thae may read that i' Scriptures, lass, if thae doubts me. See one, John, three, nine."

In his excitement he rose to his feet and sudenly throwing back his head, burst forth into a hymn, sung with loud but rich voice. It began:

"Just as I am, all over muck,
Without a grace, or plea
Who've wallowed in the mire of guilt
With th' devil basting me."

Then, flashing his eye round, and whirling his hands, he roared
forth, "Chorus, lads! Out wi' th' chorus, lasses!

I am coming, I am coming,
I am coming, I am coming,
Unto Sion, unto Sion,
Unto Sion, unto Sion,
Faster, faster, faster, faster.
I am coming o'er the sea."

This was joined in vociferously by Mrs Rhodes, Rachel and
Susan.

"I have been sunk in awful sins
That shameful was and foul,
I never gave a single thought
Unto my precious soul."

"Out wi' th' chorus!"
"I am coming, I am coming,
I am coming, I am coming,
Unto Sion, unto Sion,
Unto Sion, unto Sion,
Faster, faster, faster, faster.
I am coming o'er the sea."

The rollicking air, the excitement of the leader, his vehemence
in singing and the wildness of his appearance, produced a
mesmeric effect on all in the room. The mother and Rachel
sprang up and threw their arms about. Susan moved excitedly,
at one moment off the sofa, at another on it again. Annis
clasped her hands to her face and recoiled against the wall;
Martha, even, was not unmoved.

"Heigh!" yelled the man-monkey, suddenly becoming rigid

and fixing his eyes on Martha, whilst his arms and hands were levelled at her. "Heigh!"

Martha started back and caught the arms of the sofa, her eyes fixed involuntarily on the wild eyes that glowered at her.

"What do you want?"

"Thee knowest not of the truth! Thou art i' th' gall o' bitterness and bond of iniquity."

"Eh!" cried Mrs Rhodes; "she's not found th' Lord yet, she's none tasted that he is gracious."

"I knows it," growled Richard Grover. "But the Lord is wrestling wi' her soul."

Martha recovered herself, sprang from her seat and dashed out of the room.

"Divil's gotten how'd of her," said the preacher, composedly. Then his eye ranged the room, and in so doing lit upon the upturned blanched face of Annis, who, having never before witnessed a similar scene, was nearly frightened out of her wits by it.

"That's a gradely bit o' lass," said Richard, turning to Mrs Rhodes. "Is she i' th' state o' grace?"

"Oh! nay," replied the woman; "she knows nowt about saving faith."

Immediately Grover fixed her with his eyes, and waved his hands over her. Annis trembled with alarm, and her lips became pale.

"Jump up!" he thundered. She was too frightened to obey, so he caught her under her arms and heaved her to her feet.

Then he began to pray over her in a loud wailing voice, pausing at intervals for the women to groan and cry for mercy. "Down on your knees," he roared, forcing the girl down. "Pray! pray out! Cry out for forgiveness! Call out, lass!" Then he burst into spasmodic cries of "Mercy, mercy, mercy!" swinging himself up and down and waving his monstrous hands about, and over the poor trembling girl. He plucked her up again, and, holding her at arm's length, bent his head and glared into her face, calling, "Do you feel it? Say you feel it! Aren't you saved yet? Can't you cry?" Then turning to those around, he bellowed forth, "Ax the Lord for her. Call it down. It's coming. It's coming. I knew it. Heigh! she's off!"

Annis had suddenly shaken herself free and had fled across the room with a shriek.

"After her! After her! Don't let t'owd chap have her. Th' grace o' God's coming. I' another minute! Eh! stop her, catch her!"

Mrs Rhodes rushed one way, Rachel another and Richard Grover bounded across the room and grabbed Annis by the waist, raised her from her feet, and shook her, crying, "Heigh! heigh! Praise th' Lord! It's coming! Heigh! sing out. Desn't thae feel it? Dost thae know whither thae'st boune, unless thae'st converted? to th' lake o' brimstone and fire, where there's reek of sulphur iver i' thy nose, and fire iver i' thy bones, and the worm iver i' thy flesh, and blackness o' outer darkness iver i' thy eyes, and the shrieking o' divils and damned souls iver i' thy ears. Heigh! dost thae not read thy title clear, to mansions i' th' skies yet? Call out, lass! Call out!" and he shook her again.

A piercing cry of agony escaped Annis's lips. Mrs Rhodes and Rachel pleaded for grace on their cousin; Susan, in a state of the wildest excitement, clung to her, crying and pulling at her, and imploring her to speak out. But the poor child battled frantically with the man who shook and lifted and cast her down, and roared at her.

"Let go!" said a firm voice, in Grover's ear. He paid no attention. The room was ringing with cries and groans and exclamations. "Let her go, I say!" again very decidedly, and the preacher caught Martha's eyes flashing defiance at him, and felt her hands on his arm, endeavouring to wrench them off Annis.

"Not for thee!" he shouted. "Thou shan't mar th' Lord's work!" Then to Annis again, "Pray! pray! Call to th' Lord; say, I'm coming, I'm coming, I'm coming! unto Sion. Faster, faster, faster, faster! I am coming over the sea! ween't thee, but thae shall! I'm none going to let thee escape! I've a call to —"

Martha sent the contents of his tumbler of scalding gin and water full in his face.

"Thou shalt let her go this minnit, thou druffen vagabone!"

Richard fell back, blinded and tortured with the sting of the hot fluid. Mrs Rhodes, Rachel and Susan ceased their exclamations, their voices failing them in their astonishment.

For a minute only was there silence in the room; and then with a howl, like that of a wild beast, the man–monkey leaped on Martha, all his old fierce, brutal rage excited by the pain and by the liquor he had already imbibed. He caught her by the throat and flung her back against the sofa, his eyes glaring like metal at white heat, his face crimson with its scalding, his hair erect as though electrified, his huge jaw snapping; oaths, curses and words of horrible obscenity pouring in a filthy torrent from his lips. In vain did the girl attempt resistance, her strength was as nothing compared with his, now strung to its fullest power by fury, madness and drink. The women shrunk away alarmed; Annis had not sufficiently recovered her own fright to be able to assist her cousin.

"Gie me th' poker! gie me a knife!" roared the infuriated man.

John Rhodes had done his game of dominoes, had read the *Leeds Mercury* and looked twice through the *Illustrated London News*, had gossiped with a friend, and at last, thinking to himself that all would be quiet at home, the preacher gone and his wife waiting to lock up, was returning to his house, pipe in mouth.

"There's grand goings on," said a man to him, grinning, as he approached his house.

"Eh!" said a woman, with enthusiasm, "Richard Grover be a working of 'em off i' grand style, I reckon."

Then John noticed a number of people assembed in the street outside his door, and was aware of a considerable noise issuing from his own premises.

"It's like a second day o' Pentecost," said another woman. "He'll ha' made that lass o' thine, John, gie ower goin' to chu'ch."

Rhodes set his teeth, his brow grew dark; he forced his way through the people without answering some sportive sallies from men of his acquaintance, opened his door, and shut it again upon himself as he went in. He strode through the shop, and entered the sitting–room, the windows of which looked out, as did that of the shop, on Kirkgate.

He saw the man–monkey holding Martha down, and heard his yells for a weapon. In an instant John caught him, pinioned his arms behind his back without speaking a word, and began to thrust him before him from the room.

91

"Look out!" howled the infuriated man. "I'm punishing that
bad 'un, that her spirit may be saved. Let me aloan, man! What
art tha' doing? Let my hands go!"

John did not answer a word, but drove him forward.

"Thou'll burn for this i' flames o' hell!" raged Grover; "th'
divil'll ha' the roasting o' thee, I swear. Let me aloan."

John held him with one arm as he opened the street door,
then he thrust him out on the doorstep, and with a blow between
his shoulder–blades, sent him flying into the middle of the
street. Then he shut and locked the door, and returned to the
parlour and the discomfited women.

"Eh, who iver?" said Mrs Rhodes, drawing a long breath.

"Oh, father, how could'st tha?" gasped Rachel.

John made ne reply, but sat him down in the chair vacated by
the preacher, and mixed for himself a glass of spirits and water.
As he drank it he heard in the street a loud voice singing —

> "Just as I am, all over muck,
> Without a grace, or plea,
> Who've wallowed in the mire of guilt
> With th' devil basting me."

which was followed by a chorus, joined in by the rabble
without:

> I am coming, I am coming,
> I am coming, I am coming,
> Unto Sion, unto Sion,
> Unto Sion, unto Sion,
> Faster, faster, faster, faster.
> I am coming o'er the sea."

"Wife," said Rhodes gravely, "nobody in my house, if I can
help it, shall iver go to a place o' worship agin."

It was well he said, "If I can help it," for next Sunday his
wife and elder daughter went as usual to chapel.

Martha passed him, dressed for church.

"Where art tha' boune to, lass?" he said.

"Church, father. And I'm sorry to ha' to go again' thee i' this, but I mun go, and Annis wi' me."

"If tha' mun, tha' mun. But I'm capped thou should go onywheer after what was agait Friday neet. There shall be no more religion for me but that o' nature, which mebbe is t' best a chap can have."

So the women followed their course as before, but John was no more to be seen in his place at meeting.

Chapter Ten

Another week slid by and Hugh believed that he had successfully mastered the passion which had taken possession of his heart. It had been hard work, very hard work indeed, but by desperate struggling with himself and by resolutely staring in the face the difficulties which stood in the way of his persevering with it, he had obtained the supremacy. The tender flower of love which had sprung up and fascinated him with its beauty and filled the chambers of his inner being with its fragrance, and had bidden fair to expand into such spotless glory of blossom, had been ruthlessly smitten down. He had trodden on the wounded plant and beat its buds into the soil. Again had a feeble shoot appeared, looking sunward, and spread its little leaves as hands praying to be spared, but again had he struck it down, and now the soil was black and trampled, and strewn with the bruised and mouldering remains.

At times, Hugh had been inclined to yield, feeling himself unequal to the effort. This sensation generally came on of an evening. Then he would rush into the little conservatory adjoining the house, and pace up and down it. The poor fellow had never felt love before, and now the master passion had seized him and was grappling with him, exerting all its force, and convincing him of his own powerlessness to resist effectually. In such times he felt inclined to rush off in quest of Annis and to pour out his heart to her and ask her to comfort him by the promise of her love. Then he pictured to himself the rapture of seeing those dear brown eyes filled with light, and beaming on him, and feeling all his griefs and pangs disperse and fly away, as clouds before the morning sun. Then he thought how the waves within would sink and fall to a calm, how the deep waters of feeling, now convulsed and tempest-tossed, would repose, and bask in the glory of that love, desiring never to be stirred again.

Then Hope drew for him a fair prospect — the familiar deceptive picture it delights to present to lovers, with cottage and trellised roses, and, of course, jessamine and sheep, and cows, and doves, etc; but prominent in the foreground was Hugh himself, with his arm round a little wife, in purple, whose cheek was on his shoulder and one hand in his. Considering how impracticable was such an image, it is surprising that Hugh should have allowed his eyes to rest on it lingeringly and with frequency. One night he dreamt of this cottage. He thought he was standing with Annis, in the above-mentioned attitude, looking at the setting sun, which glimmered over a distant sea. From the door, led a straight path between rows of hollyhocks, yellow, crimson, white and maroon. Coming up the path, he beheld his mother, dead long ago, advancing towards him, with grave, peaceful countenance. He thought she took Annis by the hand, and, leading her away, said, "I wish to see whether I like her."

Then Hugh thought he watched the two pace up and down the hollyhock walk for nearly an hour, speaking to each other in tones which he could not catch. But he thought he saw his mother addressing questions with great earnestness to the girl, which Annis answered with equal seriousness. At length, a beautiful light fell over the faces of the two, as they came smiling, hand in hand, towards him; and his mother put the hand of Annis in his, saying: "Take her, I love her well. You will be happy together; she is good and true."

Hugh was more impressed with this dream than he chose to acknowledge to himself. The different points in it rose before him throughout the day, and he had difficulty in repelling them. It was the first time he had dreamt of his mother since her death, and her face and her tone of voice had presented themselves before him with a vividness not a little startling.

If she were alive, reasoned Hugh, she would be more distressed than anyone else at my having lost my heart in the way I have; she would be the last person to say to me, "Take her, you will be happy together." I can fancy I hear her now pouring forth arguments why I should not yield. But then, he mused further, who knows whether after death the soul does not see things very differently from the way in which she beholds them in life, and judge not by the accidents of station and birth, and education, but by the intrinsic worth of the heart? Who knows whether those things which, with eyes of sense, are judged to be of the utmost importance, fade altogether from the vision of spirit and the disembodied soul, failing to perceive at all these colours wherewith social life invests every individual, realises only the chiaro-oscuro of the character, its strong shadows and vivid lights.

But, after all, continued Hugh, what should there be in a dream to influence one this way or that? What caused me to dream? — a heavy supper, of course. Away with these vanities! I will think no longer on them.

At last Hugh was, as he believed, victorious; and he even dared to look at Annis as she passed the millgates. Indeed, he sought the opportunity of so doing, for it afforded him an occasion of glorying in his triumph. When he stood in the office door, as Annis went by, she seldom looked towards him, except she felt very sure that he was not observing her, when she would furtively glance up and lower her eyes again.

It would be difficult to analyse the girl's feelings. She did not dare admit to herself that she loved him, and yet she really did love him with her whole soft warm heart. There was no one for her to cling to, now that her mother was gone, but her cousin Martha, and Martha did not engage her whole affections, for they stretched forth, feeling after another object, the nature of which she had not realised. She did not ask herself the question whether Hugh cared for her, for she did not think it possible that he should. There was no future to her love, very little present, it was nearly all past, and that past confined to the evening and night of the flood, and the moment of meeting at the head of the stairs in Mr Arkwright's house. All that Hugh had said and done she attributed to his kindness, never imagining the possibility of any other motive lurking behind. She felt nothing of the struggle that went on in the young man's bosom, because there was no possible future open before her, in which he figured. She was glad to see him. Her spirits failed when the day passed without her having rested her eyes upon him, and yet, when she was in his presence, she seldom had the courage to look at him. If Hugh had died or gone away, she would have spent her days in the same patient, unrepining manner, working diligently for her bread, loving to dream about him who had borne her so bravely over the beck, and had stood by her in the falling house, and had held her by the hands and asked for the red handkerchief, as a memento of the past, and such reminiscences would have satisfied her.

One day Mr Arkwright stopped Hugh, as he was starting from his seat, when the whistle had sounded for the operatives to break off work.

"Hugh," said his uncle dryly, "I observe that you run to the door whenever the mill 'looses'. I hope it is not to look at the girls."

"Girls, sir!" exclaimed Hugh, colouring very red; "what on earth can they be to me?"

"Oh, nothing at all, I hope," said Mr Arkwright grimly; "only you must excuse the remark, when I see you rush to the door the moment the shawls begin to pass the window."

"My dear uncle, I am only looking at the weather."

"I should prefer your taking your observations at a quarter to twelve and a quarter to six, than punctually at the hour."

"Why, you see, uncle, I am so busy with my books, that the time slips by, and, till the whistle sounds, I do not know what the time is."

"I will trouble you to resume your seat," said Mr Arkwright, "and to change the topic."

How brutally suspicious uncle is, thought Hugh.

Annis had for some time been longing to revisit the old cottage in the sand–quarry. She had not seen it since the flood, and, after the first excitement of moving into her new home was passed, and the first grief over the loss of her mother had abated, the desire to visit the house, where she had spent many happy years, became daily stronger.

One evening there was no cloud in the sky, and there seemed to be more light than usual. So she said to Martha, "I think I'll just tak' a look at t' own place once again, afore I go home. Wilt tha' come wi' me, lass?"

"Nay, Annis, I cannot; I've a deal to do. But if tha's a mind to go, go thysen; but be sharp, and come home afore dark."

"Ay, I'll not be long. Tha's none occasions to be flayed for me, lass, I know t' lane so weel now, I'd as lieve go there neet–time as day."

"But it's none likely to be dark yet, tha' can come back afore neetfall, if thou mak's speed."

"I'll be back, never fear. But I must see t' place again."

Hugh passed at that moment and caught her words. As he went up the hill, he knew that she was not far behind him. Once he turned, to observe the beauty of the valley, with the evening light upon it, and the last glow lingering on the moors opposite. The view was much improved by a little figure in purple and white ascending the path in the foreground, a point of life in the still prospect. Then he resumed his ascent. Presently, he observed a green caterpillar with a pink stripe down its back and a horn on its head, traversing the causeway. Having been impressed in youth with a love of animals, Hugh stooped to remove the insect from the stone it was crossing, lest it should be injured by the foot of the heedless passerby, and one was approaching already, and was not far off. The caterpillar was not satisfied with the pacific intentions of Hugh, and resenting the interference with its liberty of action, rolled off the leaf upon which Hugh was conveying it to a place of safety. This occasioned a further delay, and obliged the young man to lift the insect again. At that moment Annis came up.

"Look here," said Hugh, suddenly rising, and exhibiting the creature.

"Eh! it's bonny!" And the little face glowed and the eyes brightened.

Then Hugh cast it away, and, suiting his pace to that of the girl, said: "Do you remember our coming up here together, nearly a month ago, one very rainy evening?"

Annis looked up in his face and made no reply. Could she forget that walk? Never, as long as life lasted! That was the answer of her eyes, but her lips did not move.

"Annis, whither are you going now?" asked Hugh.

"Please, sir, I wanted to see t'owd house again, and I'm boune there."

"Do you think the bridge is put to rights, little friend?" he asked, with a smile, looking slyly at her.

"Yes, sir," she answered faintly, without looking up.

"You'll not need help over the beck, then?"

She blushed and gave no answer.

"You are very sure that the bridge is set up again? Perhaps it is not."

"Ay, sir, it is. I'm very sure."

"And you are not afraid of going alone down the lane?"

"No, sir."

"Nor of remaining alone?"

"No, sir."

"Annis, I have not seen you since — since you gave me the —"

Oh, Hugh! Hugh! where is that red kerchief now? Is it not fluttering at the present moment over your heart, which is agitated with reasonable interest, not love, for that has been conquered and completely trampled out.

"My little friend," he added, leaving the other sentence unfinished, "I feel a very strong interest in your welfare as, of course, is only natural. So I am anxious to know if you are happy where you are? Are the Rhodes family kind to you?"

"Oh, yes, very."

"I hear Martha Rhodes is a great friend of yours. She is a very good respectable girl."

"She is that!" said Annis, brightening, and looking up; "she's a very dear girl."

"I am glad you like her, for I hear a good account of her from everyone. Have you any other great friends?"

"No, sir, none at all but Martha"; then, after a pause — "Please, sir, I must go down the lane. Martha'll be angry with me if I'm late, and I said I'll be back soon." For they were at the fork of the roads, and Hugh seemed inclined for a little more conversation.

But Annis, with a quiet, "Good evening, sir!" slipped away, and was lost behind the first turn in the lane.

Hugh did not hurry home. He stood where he was and mused. Was the bridge put to rights? Yes, he knew by the testimony of his own eyes, that it had been replaced three weeks ago. Was Annis safe alone? Certainly, she had been along that lane night and day for years. Then — all at once — there darted into Hugh's memory the conversation he had heard in the combing-shed. So many events had taken place since then, and he had been so busily engaged in conquering his passion, that he had not thought much of the incident, but now it recurred to him in all distinctness.

"I told Annis last time I saw her that I *must* see her again; it was about this matter. I really must ascertain who the speakers were; I am in duty bound to mention the circumstance to her. I consider I should be morally culpable were I to conceal it from her. How odd! I thought when she tripped off that I had something very particular to speak to her about, but I could not at the moment recall it. However, there is time now. I will follow her."

And he hurried down the left-hand lane.

He expected to catch Annis immediately, but he was mistaken. She was anxious to see over the old home before dark, and to return to her cousin as speedily as possible, and she had hastened down the lane at a good pace. Consequently, Hugh did not overtake her. He crossed the little stream on the footbridge and, on reaching the cottage, found the garden-gate open. It was apparent that Annis had gone into the house.

He passed through the gate, and went in at the front door. She was in the house, at the cellar stairs, seeing whether the water had subsided there. When Hugh entered, she started, and uttered a little cry, not perceiving in the dusk within who it was.

"You need not be frightened, little friend; it is I."

"Oh, sir!"

"Annis, I forgot something very particular I wanted to speak to you about. Come here! — what are you doing there?"

"There are some bunches of herbs, some marjoram and thyme, hung up at t' cellar head, I'm getting down. I think Mrs Rhodes may like them."

"Bother the herbs," said Hugh, impatiently; "I want to talk to you. Will you come to me, Annis? Don't you know, I told you when you gave me the red handkerchief — you remember — well, I told you then that I *must* see you again. Did I not, Annis?"

"Yes, sir," she answered faintly, coming towards him.

"I am afraid of your running away," said Hugh.

"I won't run away."

"But you'll be after that pot-marjoram and thyme."

"No, sir! I won't."

"I cannot be sure of that, unless I hold you as a prisoner." He caught her gently by the shoulders. "I really want to speak to you very seriously," he said, drawing her gently from the back part of the room towards the broken window, which, facing west, admitted a feeble light from the evening sky. "Annis!" he continued, "will you hold up your poor little face and let me look at it? I don't think it looks well; it is sad, and looks paler than it was once. You must not let your troubles weigh on your spirit too much, my dear little girl."

Then he paused and contemplated her by the soft twilight dying out behind the western hills. She made one little trembling attempt to slip from his hands, but he would not let her go.

"You will be after the marjoram," he said; "I must hold my bird fast, or it will fly away." Again he paused.

"Annis, I must tell you what I have on my mind, and what I want to speak to you about. On the night of the flood, I was at the mill, just as the reservoir burst, or, at all events, as its waters came on us. You know the combing–shed?"

"Yes," in a very low voice.

"Well, I was going past it in the dark, and I heard two people talking — at least, I think it was two, but I only found one. There was a man's voice, and a voice like that of a woman. I went into the shed, and a man rushed past me, but I could see no signs of the other, and yet I searched all through the place. I heard what the man said. He used your name. He mentioned you — Annis Greenwell; and I thought the other voice answered. You were not there, then?"

"No, sir! How could I have been there?"

"Of course not; why should I doubt? Is there another Annis Greenwell in the neighbourhood?"

"I'm very sure there's none," answered the girl.

"Is there an Annis?"

"I do not think it. But, please sir, who was t' man?"

"That I do not know."

"What did he say of me?"

"He said that he loved you more than his life; that he was mad with love of you."

"Then it was not of me he spoke," said Annis. "I do not think there's anybody would have said that of me."

Hugh did not speak. His heart beat very fast; he had

101

misjudged his strength. All the bulwarks he had erected gave way, as do the pebble and sand walls which children set up on sea-beaches against the advancing tide. Impregnable they had seemed, but the wave rushed on, and they dissolved and vanished at once.

"Are you very sure, dear Annis," he said with agitated voice, "that no one loves you?"

"Ay! there's Martha, and there's Rachel and Susan."

"But no man?"

"Nay," she answered, shaking her head.

"Annis," said Hugh, earnestly, letting go her shoulders and putting his hands to her temples and holding back her brown hair: "Annis, dear Annis! and do you love no one?" She shook her head, as he held it, and looked full in her eyes.

Neither spoke, except with those mute tell-tales, and it was now so dark that they only dimly saw one another's faces. He pressed back her brow, that the faint light might rest upon it, and let him read the language of the great mysterious eyes.

"Annis! there is one who loves you, and loves you with his whole heart." He spoke low and softly, holding the little head, which he felt trembling, between his palms: "one who has fought very hard against his love for you — has battled with it, as though it were a mortal foe — has thought to conquer it, but who cannot." The little girl did not speak; her bosom heaved, and the tears of joy and wonder rolled out of her eyes and over her cheeks. "He has struggled desperately against his love, and been miserable. Dear, dear Annis, tell me you do not dislike me; tell me you may get to like — to love me. I cannot live without your love."

Suddenly a dazzling gleam of yellow light shot across the deserted room and struck the girl's face, then lit that of Hugh. Then they heard a click, and the blaze disappeared. Hugh had seen a ball of flame, nothing more. Now he heard a deep sonorous voice: "You cannot live without her love! You must!"

And a black figure stood at the foot of the stairs.

"Who are you?" asked Hugh angrily. "What are you doing here?"

"Annis!" said the voice, in low vibrating tones: "Poor child! go home — it is late."

"Oh, Joe," said the girl, feebly.

"Go home at once."

"That is the voice I heard in the shed," Hugh exclaimed. "I am sure of it."

"Mr Arkwright, if you will meet me in that shed tonight at ten, I will tell you all. Let the girl go home."

It was impossible to resist. Hugh could not prolong his interview with Annis in the presence of this mysterious third; so he said: "Yes, return home, Annis. I will accompany you," and he drew her with him from the house.

They walked hastily along the lane, knowing that they were followed by the man.

"Annis," said Hugh, in a low tone; "who is he? You seem to know him."

"It is Joe Earnshaw."

"The night-watch!" exclaimed Hugh.

It was now dark: the wind had risen and was rushing through the trees and hissing in the tangled hedge. Hugh was irritated at the interruption whilst telling the girl the secret of his heart, and especially at that secret having been heard by another. The wind made sufficient noise to allow him to speak to her in a low voice without having been overheard.

"How came he to be in the house?"

"I fancy he must be living in his lodging room still. Maybe he had not flitted," answered Annis.

"I had so much to say to you, dear little girl," whispered Hugh. "May I see you again sometime? We must have our talk out. I had not said half that I had to say when that confounded fellow came blundering in on us."

They reached the end of the lane. Where the roads diverged stood a girl, with a shawl round her head, fluttering in the wind.

"Annis!" she called.

"Yes, Martha."

"Oh, lass! what a time thou hast been!" She eyed Hugh. "Is that Mr Hugh Arkwright?"

"Yes, it is," answered the young man, in a tone of vexation.

"Oh, Annis, dear lass," said Martha Rhodes wailingly; "come along wi' me. Why hast thou been —" Her voice broke and she burst into tears.

"Martha, what's agait?" asked Annis, rushing to her.

"Come along, come along, dear lass," said the elder girl, dragging her away towards the town.

Hugh stood still and looked after them. He was annoyed beyond measure. He had been heard telling Annis his love, and he had been seen walking with her in a lonely lane at night; next day this would be all over the place, would reach his uncle's ears, and —

"At ten o'clock, in the combing-shed," said the ringing bass voice in his ear, as the watchman strode past him in the dark, and took the way towards the mill.

"I'll be there," shouted Hugh after him.

Chapter Eleven

Martha said nothing to her cousin on their way to Kirkgate, but she held her by the hand as though afraid of losing her again. Martha had a great deal more knowledge of the world than Annis, and she was full of apprehension for her friend.

She knew that her heart was true and right, and that she would not wilfully go wrong, but she feared lest her simplicity should be taken advantage of by the unscrupulous.

Martha, with a practical knowledge of the world and its ways, was not injured by that knowledge. She had been brought into contact with it from childhood, and had been moulded by it into a self-reliant, courageous and high-principled girl. The world does not always destroy, it often builds up; it does not always ruin, it often perfects. It may fairly be questioned whether the system of education for girls pursued in the upper classes is that best calculated for the development of the character, and whether the gain in ignorance of evil is counter-balanced by the loss of vigour of the moral constitution. Conventionalism is too often elevated to the rank of a first principle, and becomes a motive power in the place of self-respect. Mothers entrust the formation of the characters of their daughters to governesses, whose system is to break up and to destroy the strong, yet delicate mechanism of the child's moral nature, and to replace it by clumsy imitations devoid of the living principle. Simplicity is banished and affectation occupies its room. Shamefacedness is cast out to make way for mock-modesty. Truth is obliterated, that insincerity may reign supreme.

And when the work is complete, these dolls of society are thrust upon men in the hopes of charming them, and convincing them that they will prove agreeable companions to them on life's journey. But men are not always in a doll-loving babyhood, nor are wax faces, and an interior of wirework and brass and rolling blue eyes, and squeaking mouths a source of perennial delight. Woman, as made by God, is the fairest of his creatures; as recreated by the governess she is beneath contempt.

When Martha and Annis went to the little room they occupied

together, the elder girl made her cousin sit beside her on the bed, and then, for the first time, she spoke.

"Annis, deary!" she said. "I were fair downcapped to see thee wi' Hugh Arkwright. I can assure thee I were."

Annis remained silent.

"Lass! why dist tha' tell me tha' wanted to see t' house i' t' sand–pit, when all along tha' was boune to meet Hugh Arkwright?"

"Nay, Martha," said Annis piteously; "nay, I did not go to meet him."

"Tha' hast been oft wi' him," Martha said.

"It's not true," answered Annis; "I never was wi' him afore t' flood, and I've never been down that road wi' him since."

"But tha'st met him elsewhere."

"I have not, Martha, barring when he gave me t' brooch."

"Thou must go wi' him no more. It's not right for thee to be seen walking i' t' neet wi' thy master's nephew. How did he fall in wi' thee?"

"Oh,Martha, he came to t' house."

"And what kept thee so long?"

"We was just talking."

"What about?"

"Eh, lass! A deal of things."

"Annis," said Martha, in a tone of pain, "this munna go on. Tha' knows not the foul things folk'll be saying o' thee; an' gossiping tales there'll be about."

The little girl crept up to her cousin and put her arms round her neck. "Don't fret, Martha dear; I would not grieve thee for aught."

"It's not grieving me that matters," said Martha mournfully; "it's just nowt else but t' right and wrong o' th' case. I'm feered for thee, dear lass."

"I think there's none occasion for that."

"Thou poor little innocent lamb, thou knows nowt o' t' wickedness o' t' world, and thou'll fall i' t' snare o' t' devil afore thou knows."

"Nay, Martha, I will not."

"But thou wilt if thou goes trustin' grand folks like that Hugh Arkwright, and walking o' neets wi' t' lads."

"I'll never do it any more."

"I hope thou wi'nt. Annis, wilt thou tell me t' truth if I axes thee?"

"Ay, a sure."

"Annis, did he say owt to thee?"

"He said a very deal."

"Nay, I know that. Did he speak soft like to thee?"

"Ay, he did."

"Did he say owt about love, dear lass?"

Annis hid her face in her cousin's bosom, and made no reply.

"I thowt so! I thowt so!" wailed Martha, clasping the girl to her, and drawing her shawl about her, as though she were a mother–bird sheltering her young from the hawk. "And dost thou like him?" she said, in a low, tender, pitiful voice.

Annis clung tighter to her, with her arms knit about her, and the little hands working convulsively at her back. Martha kissed her brown glossy hair and laid her cheek on the little agitated head which lay in her bosom, swaying herself from side to side as a mother nursing her babe. "My own little lass," she said, with a broken voice; "thou mun break thy heart rayther nor go wi' him again; he'll do thee a terrible harm if thou trusts him."

"Nay, nay, Martha!" exclaimed Annis, with energy, raising her face and looking full in that of her cousin. "That he never will."

"Do not be over sure. Keep off t' danger and thou'll no fall. I think I'd niver hold up my head again if thou did get to shame. I'm a'most heartbroken now."

"Nay, Martha," pleaded the little girl. "Don't fret. I've done nought to occasion that, and I hope I shall never do that as'll make thee cry. Give ower, lass."

"Wilt thou promise me thou'lt never walk wi' him more?"

"Nay, I cannot promise; but I don't think I shall."

"Did he ax thee to meet him again?"

"Ay, he did," murmured Annis.

"Look up, lass!" said Martha, firmly. "This'll niver do. Thou'rt going same road as many as has led to shame and sin, and thou gives no heed to what I warns thee of, and thou cracks ower thy power to resist temptation, and thou'rt running fair into 't. However, canst thou say t' Lord's prayer, and ax not to be led into temptation, when thou'rt going head for'ard as wilful as owt into t' midst of it? Eh, lass, if thou goes on this road thou'll come to t' same end as Nancy Eastwood, lass."

The scarlet colour rushed over Annis's face and neck and bosom and she put her hand on Martha's mouth.

"For shame, Martha! for shame! Dost thou think so bad of me as that?"

"Annis," said her cousin, drawing the hand away; "that poor girl was a tidy, decent lass as ever thou seed at miln and Bob Atkinson's lad took after her, and she wor stuck up wi' having such a grand follower, and wor lifted up wi' pride, and she thowt mebbe he'd marry her, and thou knows what that came to."

Annis made no answer. The case was somewhat parallel; the son of the village lawyer had kept company with one of the girls from Sutherland's mill, and they had met clandestinely, for Mr Atkinson had threatened his son, if he did not conduct himself respectably, that he would turn him adrift. And it had ended in the shame of the girl and the young man leaving the place. It had caused considerable scandal in the village, and the conduct of both had been severely commented on. The young man met with harsh judgment for having led the girl astray, and the young woman was not compassionated, because as the folk said, she ought to have known better than to have encouraged her lover.

"Thou knows very weel," pursued Martha, "that as soon as ever it's known that Hugh Arkwright is courtin' thee, folk'll be saying o' thee just the same as they said o' Nancy Eastwood."

"Thou'll never tell that thou seed him and me!" entreated Annis.

"Nay, I'll not tell," replied Martha, "but if thou'rt wi' him again, mebbe others'll see thee too. Did none see thee this time?"

"Ay," said Annis despairingly. "There was Joe Earnshaw."

Martha Rhodes mused for a little while; at last she said, "I don't know what to make o' Joe, he knows nobody, mebbe it'll go no farther." Then suddenly turning on her cousin, she asked, "Lass, did Hugh ax thee to marry him?"

"Oh, nay!" replied the poor little girl; "I never thought of that nor he neither. He just looked i' my face and said, 'Dear Annis, I have loved thee a very long time, and I have striven hard to conquer my love, and now I feel that I cannot live any longer without thine.' He said no more and then Joe came up and bid me go home, and Hugh went wi' me, and he said nought further, but that he'd a deal more to say, and he mun see me again."

"Annis," said Martha, "go to bed, my poor little lamb. I'll go see Hugh Arkwright mysen."

"Not now!" said Annis, startled.

"Nay, not now, some day when miln looses."

Chapter Twelve

At ten o' clock that night Hugh went to the mill. He was glad to have some distraction to thoughts which were none of the pleasantest.

He knew that, in a day or two, he would become the butt upon whom all the scandalmongers in Sowden would exercise their wit, in inventing or embellishing tales detrimental to his character. He knew that these pests of society are ever buzzing round their more respectable neighbours, like wasps about apricots, probing them with their probosces, searching eagerly for the slightest fracture in the skin of their propriety, that they may work it to a large rent, and mangle and devour, and pollute what is within. He knew that a sound skin was to them a constant cause of annoyance, and that the minutest defect therein, giving them an opportunity for sucking the fresh sweet juices, and rendering it a tasteless, shrivelled husk, was greedily seized upon by them; so greedily, that at the first symptom of a rent, in a moment they would be in legions on the spot.

Several of these hateful beings might be found in Sowden, sitting in their nests, whirring with their wings, thrusting forth their antennae groping for food, turning their eyes from side to side, ever watchful for a chance of rushing on their prey.

There was Mrs Jumbold, the doctor's wife, a thin scarecrow of a woman, with wiry black ringlets and a pointed nose, who thrived on the most virulent acids in her husband's laboratory. She was sure to be down, one of the first, on poor Hugh. In a minute after having heard the gossiping tale, she would have on her black poke bonnet and her grey mantilla, and come shuffling along the causeway to call on Mrs Arkwright and express to her the distress occasioned to her own feelings by the scandal she had heard of the lady's nephew.

There was Mrs Cordale, the relict of the deceased postmaster — would to heaven he had taken her with him, or stamped and posted her for the remotest region in infinity, ere he left this world of care! Wise postmaster! he insured his peace by leaving her behind!

110

There was Mr Metcalf, an elderly party with dropsical legs; a godless old man, who hoped to win heaven by making out everyone to be worse than himself, and to be saved, as best out of a bad bunch, lest heaven should be empty — a man who, too infirm to work, spent his days in hobbling on sticks from door to door, getting drinks of beer, and retailing in return slanderous stories.

There was Priscilla Walker, the milliner, unmarried and misanthropic, who loved to hear and speak evil of the other sex, the cause of all the mischief in the world.

There was that gossiping, restless Mrs Rhodes, with Annis under her immediate eye.

Hugh was of a sensitive nature, and peculiarly fearful of spiteful comment. Physically courageous, he was morally timid. He would have faced a lion's claws and teeth, but he could not stand against a woman's tongue. Had he been a soldier he would not have shrunk before a storm of bullets interspersed with occasional cannonballs, but the slightest breath of slander made him succumb.

He was certain that every possible variation would be played on the theme of his evening walk with Annis. His motives would be misconstrued; designs of a base and dishonourable nature would be attributed to him. Persons he met would pass with a smirk, infinitely more galling than a spoken insult; he would overhear a group speaking of him, and at the sight of him they would laugh, and quote a familiar and offensive proverb. Respectable people would shake their heads at him, and exhibit coldness; the worthless would triumph over his supposed fall.

Feeling poignantly for himself, he felt equally keenly for Annis. He knew that she too would be the subject of rude jest and ugly insinuations; that bold and prying eyes would watch her; that her every act and word would be distorted and made occasion of scandal; that, at home and in the mill, she would have no peace; and that, in her isolation, she would suffer acutely the slur which would be cast on her character.

How could he prevent all this dreadful misery falling upon their heads? He looked round, vainly searching for means. Slander was hydra-headed; if he met and exposed one malignant lie, from its stump would spring seven worse falsehoods. Was there any possibility of checking the story before it spread, of strangling it at its birth? He questioned the possibility. Of Joe Earnshaw he knew little, and could form no opinion as to the likelihood of his repeating what he had heard. Of Martha Rhodes he knew also but little, and he had no opportunity offered him of securing her silence. Probably, as soon as she and Annis reached home, the girl would tell her mother what she had seen, and when once a secret was in Mrs Rhodes' possession, it became the property of the parish.

It was sickening to the sensibility of Hugh to know that the outpouring of his heart had been overheard by the watchman. He recoiled from the prospect of his words to Annis being retained at public-houses over pipes and beer, amidst the roars of laughter of the drunken sots who there congregated. He thought of Hezekiah exhibiting his treasures to the messengers and thereby insuring their seizure and his own captivity. "And I," said Hugh, "have I not opened the treasure-house of my soul, and shown all its richest feelings and most precious desires to one who will carry them and me to Babylon!"

He asked himself whether he could defeat the anticipations of the scandalmongers by taking a further step. Should he ask Annis to be his wife? Impossible! he had no home of his own, and he knew not whether his uncle would tolerate such a move on his part. Annis was too young and inexperienced and ignorant to become his partner, at all events, at present.

Then why had he spoken to her? Why did he declare to her his love, when he had no future open to him, and the way before him was dark? — Because he had been mastered by that passion which he had deemed destroyed. He had followed her to the cottage, relying on his ability to control himself, and his resolution had broken down, his victory had proved vain, his strength had given way.

Should he for the future hold aloof from Annis? His whole sense of honour and right revolted from such a thought; he had told her that he loved her, and bidden her encourage a love for him in return; he had brought her into great trial and difficulty, and had launched the wave over her head, and he could not — he ought not — to suffer her to struggle alone.

Through all his darkness and perplexity one strong clear light

112

beamed unwaveringly — his faith in Annis. That, nothing could disturb. He believed her to be true, and good, and noble, and worthy of his love, worthy of the pain he should have to bear for her sake.

It may be years before I can claim her as my wife — years before I have the means to support a wife — years before she can be moulded and adapted to what society will demand of my wife; but if we live, and she can learn to trust and love me, Annis, and no one else, shall be mine.

Do I desire for my wife one in whom I can repose perfect trust and confidence, knowing that such trust and confidence will never be betrayed?

Such is Annis!

Do I desire one who is true as steel — whom affection will never swerve for one moment — whose thought even will never be false — whose heart will wear green, and will stand sunshine and storm, frost and fire, and like the ivy, will clasp its support in life and death; which, though you may slice through its trunk, will die as it lived, clingingly, without a muscle relaxing, a tendril unloosening, a fibre yielding?

Such is my poor little Annis!

And do I seek a white unstained soul, as unblemished as when breathed forth from God; as fragrant in its childlike simplicity as mountain thyme; as transparent as the moor spring running over a gravelly bottom?

Such, I know, is the soul of Annis!

And do I ask for a brave little spirit, full of confidence in its rectitude and courage the steadfastness of its faith?

Such again is that of Annis!

What more do I ask? Fortune, position, talent, education? Can I insure the most precious jewels of all — truth, trust, simplicity and courage, with these other gifts, which are, after all, not gems but settings? These are well enough if one can have them, but without the others they are nothing — worse than nothing, for they make more conspicuous the paste which they enshrine and endeavour to pass off as crystal.

Hugh was young. Self-control grows with years, and is only acquired by experience. Hugh felt with sufficient acuteness that he was in a hobble, that he had committed himself without

113

having calculated the cost beforehand. If the reader supposes, from our having made Hugh the hero of this tale, that he is a model of intelligence, of judgment, of prudence, he is vastly mistaken. The young man was simply worthy, true-hearted and frank; his youth made him impulsive; his education had not fitted him for self-discipline, such as a man has acquired at forty by battling with the world. Had Arkwright been selfish and dishonourable he would have shrunk from the consequences he had incurred by his rash, unpremeditated act. But selfish and dishonourable he was not, though impulsive and wanting in judgment he might be.

And moreover, in his inmost soul, Hugh was not sorry that he had spoken to Annis. It had been a relief to his feelings, but he was intensely mortified at having been overheard.

He realised now that, sooner or later, he must have spoken, and that it was simply a question of time when he made the avowal; what he did deplore was the fact that this avowal had been made in the presence of a third party.

He asked himself again and again why he had been such a fool as not to see that the house was empty before he began to speak on private matters to the girl. He remembered now that Earnshaw had retained his furniture and room when all the rest of the articles in the cottage had been removed, and that therefore he had probably resolved on continuing to inhabit it. He ought to have remembered that at the proper time and occasion, and have ascertained whether Earnshaw had left the house before he rushed upon a declaration.

How much had been overheard by the watchman Hugh did not know, but he was aware that the man had heard quite sufficient to have a very precise notion of Hugh's meaning when he spoke, for he had repeated the last words Hugh had made use of.

These thoughts had revolved incessantly in his mind since he had parted with Annis. They recurred in the same order, unbidden, unvaried, with distressing iteration. In vain did the young man attempt to banish them, it was as though they were affixed to a Buddhist praying machine, which rotates in the wind, reproducing the same images, the same prayers, the same ejaculations, at regular intervals, morning and evening, noon and night, whether observed or not, in man's absence equally with in his presence.

Which slip of thought was uppermost when Hugh reached the mill we cannot say; it does not matter; one was as absorbing as another.

The night was dark and blustering. The wind growled about the deserted factory in the gloom, tossing little wisps of straw, and noisily flapping some wool bags which hung on lines. Sunderland's mill was just distinguishable as a dark stain against the sky, its chimney looking of a ponderous height, lighted by the gas lamp which flickered over the doorway and was reflected by the opposite wall of the stable.

Hugh passed under the light above the gate to his uncle's mill-fold, and went towards the combing-shed, looking around him for the watchman, but not perceiving him.

On reaching the shed door he looked in. Within it was as black as pitch, and he could see nothing.

"I suppose I am early," he thought, and leaned against the side-post, waiting the arrival of Earnshaw. It had struck ten when he left the house, and it must have been half-past when he reached the fold.

"Well," said a bass voice from within. "I am ready."

Hugh started; the sound was unexpected. "Yes, I am ready too," he answered; "what have you to say to me?"

"Come inside."

Hugh stepped through the door. The watchman must have been seated, for the young man heard the sound of displaced fragments of iron and wood as he rose.

"Come nigher."

"I will come further if you will let me see my way by your lanthorn, but I am afraid of falling over something."

"Afraid!" with a deep booming laugh.

"Afraid of stumbling," said Hugh. "Show a light."

"No."

"Then I will stand where I am."

"Do so."

Hugh heard the man stride towards him. "What do you want with me?" asked the young man.

"What do you want with Annis Greenwell?" inquired the

115

other.

"Nothing but what is honourable," said Hugh, in a tone of decision. "Why did you act the listener to me when I was speaking to her?"

"Why did you act the listener to me?" asked the other.

"When?"

"The flood-night, in this shed."

Neither said anything for a moment. Hugh kicked the straw about with his foot, doubting what to say.

"I will not have thee following Annis Greenwell," Earnshaw said, breaking the silence abruptly and with a loud voice.

"I shall pursue my own course," Hugh replied, composedly. "You overheard me tell her that I loved her, which is the truth. You have no right to exercise authority over her, or over me."

"You shall not follow her."

"I tell you, I shall take my course independently of you."

"You daren't!"

"I dare not. indeed!"

"No, you daren't. Do you know what nice tales which will be spread abroad of you? Are you ready to be the object of every jest and lie in all Sowden?"

"I tell you, Joe, that with a clear conscience, I will face all that Sowden and the world may choose to say. I would not do that girl an injury for any consideration; and if you fear that, set your mind at rest; she is safe with me."

"And you'll give her pain and misery. That's love!"

"I will cause her none that I can help. If our interview gets to be known, it will be through you or Martha Rhodes."

"You need not fear that I will tell, and you need not doubt Martha."

"Then I am obliged to you. It was distressing to me that you should have overheard me — "

"And to me, that you should have overheard me."

"I will repeat to no one what I heard."

"You told Annis."

"Because you mentioned her name, and said you loved her."

"And so I do. I love her — ah! madly." The rich voice thrilled with emotion, rising in volume till suddenly it changed to a soft musical note of feminine sweetness and tone. "Dearly, and for a long while have I loved her; and she knows it."

"No, no!" said Hugh. "She told me no one loved her."

"She must know it," again in the rich bass. "I have watched her and lived near her, and do you think she would not read my heart? Is she so blind as that, imagine you?"

"You never spoke to her?" Hugh said, with intense interest.

"No, I never spoke. I am not one to speak. What would it avail me to speak? — to bid a girl look in my eyes and love me, and cling to me, and put her hand in mine, her lips to mine. — See!"

Suddenly the lanthorn–shade clicked, a gleam shot across the shed, and Hugh saw the watchman slowly raise the ball of fire. He noticed the coat–buttons lit up one after another, then the dangling ends of the comforter; and then the light fell over the FACE!

Hugh recoiled with a shudder of horror, and turned his eyes away. He saw a countenance the like of which he had never beheld before: blood–red, welted and mangled, and scarred horribly, as though it had been torn with the iron teeth which rend the cloth in the shoddy mills, and then had been suffered to heal up as it would in lumps and ridges and rents and cavities. Two dark, deepset eyes watched him from under fragments of bushy brows.

Then the light vanished.

Hugh felt sick. The horrible appearance of the face, suddenly flaring out of the deep darkness of the shed in the night, upon him away from the presence of other men, startled and almost unmanned him. The slit lip, with the glittering teeth showing beneath, the torn nose, the riven cheek, the streaked brow, were visible to the eye of his mind still, though hidden from that of his body. He had, in one second, beheld a countenance which had indelibly impressed its hideousness on his memory to haunt him through life.

"Well," said the voice, in sweet musical tones, "you have seen me now. Am I one to ask a girl to love me? Can I hope to win the heart of woman, think you?" Then the bell–note of his strange, changeable voice sounded again. "But I can love. Ay! I can love; and I do love; and with a madness of passion, because it is hopeless — a madness that makes my brain burn,

117

and impels me to strange deeds. Do you wonder now that I hide myself from the sight of men; that I act as watch at night-time, when there is darkness to veil my face, and that I keep close by day? What sort of life do you call that? I dare not meet men, or I should have all eyes following me, all heads turned to look at me, all faces expressing that feeling which I observed in yours — horror and disgust."

Then Hugh heard the gulping, gurgling sound of restrained sobs.

"If I show myself in the street, the men stare, the women shrink away, the children scream and then rush after me; the gentle turn their faces aside and I know that aversion is their feeling; the coarse titter and remark on my appearance. I feel this keenly, and I fly to my chamber, where I may hide my revolting features. I do not look like a man, but a man I am, and a man's feelings I have. I suffer in my solitude — I suffer tortures — I think I shall go mad. For two years I have lodged at the little cottage in the sand-pit and have been watchman to the mills at night, when I can walk about and breathe the fresh air under the canopy of heaven, without the prospect of being stared at with horror, disgust and pity. During those two years I have seen much of Annis Greenwell, and seeing her I have loved her; how intensely, none but myself know, how despairingly, how hopelessly, you may judge. Every hair of her head is precious to me; every look at her fair face is a transport of heaven. But she cannot love me. I know it. It is impossible! I see that she shrinks from me, and that there is abhorrence which she strives to conceal, whenever her eyes rest on me."

He spoke in broken sentences, pausing between each, and his voice ran through wide variations of tone, now thrilling low like a deep organ note, now tremulous and sweet and high-pitched like that of a female. So great were the differences in the tone of the sentences, that Hugh could hardly convince himself that they all proceeded from the same speaker.

"I was not always thus," the watchman continued; "there was a time when I was young and good-looking as any other man might be."

"Then how —" broke in Hugh.

"I am coming to that," said Earnshaw, interrupting the

question. "I was in the tool–setting trade at Manchester. And I did well and was thriving. But there was a strike of the operatives. There were two or three of us wouldn't strike, and I was one. I thought we didn't ought to strike; we were in the wrong; and what was more, I couldn't afford to strike. I was earning good wages, and I thought them fair. So I stuck to my work. Then one day, as I was sitting at my table, the door opened suddenly, and something was cast in, almost at my feet; it was a tin box, or very like one, but I don't remember very well; I know I bent down from my seat to look at it, and pick it up, and see what it was, and all at once it burst, and I do not know more. That was a trade–union outrage; and it was one of their infernal machines, full of broken iron and glass and vitriol and nails, that exploded. You see what it has done to me. Would you see again?"

"No, thank you!" quickly and involuntarily.

"No, I dare say you would not like to see. But the face you saw is the result of that damned wicked, cowardly malice of the idle fellows who wouldn't let me work when they wouldn't work themselves."

"Were the authors of the outrage discovered and punished?"

"No. They were not."

"Are you sure it was done by the trade–union?"

"I know the man who did it."

"Then why was he not punished?"

"There was no evidence."

"Nothing, then, was done to him."

"Mark me," said Earnshaw in a low whispered tone, "if ever I meet him, something shall be done to him; that I swear."

"Do you know where he is?"

"Yes."

"Where?"

"I will not tell."

"What is his name?"

"I will not say."

Neither spoke for about five minutes. The one to break the silence was Earnshaw, who said in his deep notes: "I have bidden you meet me here, and I have told you this for a purpose. You know now who I am, what my feelings are, and how I suffer."

"You have my most cordial commiseration," said Hugh.

"I don't ask for it; I don't want it," answered Earnshaw fiercely. "Wait and offer it when it is sought. No! I do not desire it. But I desire this, that you should fear to enrage me. A man thrown on his own thoughts, with all his feelings torn, his sense of pride mutilated, his hopes in life blighted, is not a man to be trifled with; he is desperate as a tiger deprived of her whelps, or as a boar at bay. I am maddening over my love, which can never meet with a return; a very little, and I become raging as those of old possessed of devils. I feel it in my blood, I feel it in my heart, I feel it in my brain. Young man, beware of me; beware of how you exasperate me! I tell you this: Annis shall never be yours! If I cannot have her myself, no one else shall possess her. I shall watch about her, and defend her with fury from the touch of another. You said you could not live without her. *I* cannot live without her. You approach her at your peril! I warn you off."

"I am not to be moved by these threats," said Hugh.

"Be wise in time! Your making love to Annis can come to no good. She cannot be your wife, she is not your equal in station and in education. What would your uncle say to such a match? He would cast you off. You do not intend to marry her."

"I do," answered Hugh. "I will have no other wife."

"I do not believe it! You deceive yourself and you deceive her. You are trifling with her feelings and a young girl's feelings are sacred and precious things, not to be stirred with wanton finger."

"You misjudge me, I assure you."

"I think this," said the watchman; "you are not wilfully proposing her ruin. No! I do not think so vilely of you as that. No! or if I did —," he paused and drew a long breath, which sounded through his teeth — "you would not leave this shed alive! I believe you mean honourably; but I will not suffer this to continue. You must give her up."

"I cannot, I will not! True, I cannot hope to take her to be my wife now, dependent as I am, but I shall work for the time when I may claim her."

"That shall never be. I shall see to that. Young man, I have

120

some regard for you, and therefore I give you this warning. You slight it at your peril!"

And he went past Hugh, swept him aside, and vanished into the night.

Hugh remained no longer at the mill. It was becoming late and his uncle would miss him. He ascended the hill meditatively, entered the garden, swinging to behind him the iron gate, walked to the front door, and opened it.

Mr Arkwright came out of the dining-room into the passage, with his pipe in his hand and his collar and cravat off.

"Where the deuce have you been all this while?" he asked.

"At the mill, uncle."

"At the mill! and pray what have you been doing there?"

"Only having a talk."

"Humph! talk!" Mr Arkwright frowned, took a long whiff at his pipe, then looked grimly at Hugh, and said, interrogatively, "Petticoats?"

"No, sir," answered Hugh, in a tone of irritation; "why are you always suspecting me? I was having a chat with your watchman, whose acquaintance I have been making."

Mr Arkwright eyed him steadily. "Not a pretty face?"

"No, a fearful one," answered Hugh, shuddering.

"You don't take," said Mr Arkwright bluntly. "I mean you have not been chatting with a pretty face?"

"Uncle, I beg you not to worry me with these sort of hints."

"Humph! I see. Change the topic — have some spirits."

Chapter Thirteen

Next day at the dinner hour, as he was returning from the mill to the house, he found Martha Rhodes leaning against the lane gate, as though awaiting him.

The girl had resolved on speaking to him about Annis, but it cost her such an effort, that nothing saving her anxiety for her cousin, and sense of responsibility for her welfare, would have induced her to undertake the task. She felt that much depended on the way in which she managed her part, and she was fearful of being unequal to it. It was with no little agitation that she waited at the gate for Hugh; her heart beat very fast, and her breath came short.

Hugh was glad of the opportunity of speaking to her, and securing her silence respecting what she had seen the evening before.

"Martha," he said, coming up to her, "how do you do today?"

"Very nicely, thank you, sir."

"Are you not going home to your dinner?"

"Presently."

"Are you waiting for anyone?"

"Please, sir, I was waiting for you."

"For me! well, do you know, I wanted to have a word with you myself. I dare say you were rather surprised to see me walking with your cousin Annis, so late last night."

"I was very much surprised."

"Of course you were." Hugh began to fidget a little. Martha turned her dark expressive eyes on him; they seemed to him full of reproach. "Well, you see, I had something particular to say to her. You know I — I had to do with bringing her and her mother into safety during the flood. Well, I had something respecting that about which to speak to her. Now I want to ask you not to gossip about having met us together, for if you do, you may do Annis a great deal of harm, and cause her a great deal of annoyance and pain."

"You may be very sure I'll say nowt about it."

"Thank you. Of course it was an accident our being together, but it was one which, if maliciously taken advantage of, might occasion much distress. You understand me?"

"Ay."

"Thank you, Martha; and now, good day!"

She held out her arm to bar the way. "Nay, nay!" she said, hastily, "don't go."

"Have you something to say to me?"

"Ay; a deal. Wait a bit."

She was gathering up her courage. Her noble face was full of passing lights and shadows, kindling and darkling in her eyes. She did not look at him, but turned towards the valley, resting her chin on her hand, and her elbow on the gate. The other arm she kept extended.

Hugh waited a little while, and still she did not speak, so he said: "Martha, what is it?"

She turned to him with an effort, and said, hurriedly: "You must leave Annis alone. She is a poor simple bit o' thing as onybody could twist round t' little finger. She's a'most too simple, and she thinks there's no harm and danger where there's most."

"I will do her no injury, Martha."

"Ah! thou thinks not; but don't thou know o' Nancy Eastwood and Bob Atkinson, lad? I would na' have things go t' same road wi' our Annis for a'most onything."

"You must not think that, Martha. You have no right to suspect evil, merely because you saw me walking with Annis."

"But it's not that alone," she said, speaking fast; "thou knows thee's told her that tha loves her, and — "

"Martha! what makes you say this?"

"I know it; never heed how. I cannot have thee do owt wrong to my poor little Annis. She's a dear good lass, and thou'lt none find a better, choose how."

"I am sure of that; but you really must not think evil of me."

"I think this," answered Martha, "that thou dostn't know thy own sen where thou'rt leading her to. Thou loves her, maybe, and loves her dearly. But what then? Dost thou think thou can make her thy wife? Nay, lad, she wi'nt frame for that, and thou dost not think it. Thou'rt ta'en wi' her face and her pretty ways, thou'rt goin' forward 'bout[1] thinking whither 't 'll lead thee. If thou see her and speak wi' her, and gain her love, that leads to nowt but broken hearts and sad actions. Nay, nay! leave her alone, it's better for the both o' you."

She paused, out of breath.

"Martha," said Hugh, earnestly, "I admire and respect you for speaking out. You have shown yourself a true friend to Annis, and a brave, right-minded girl."

"I want none o' your fine speeches," said Martha sharply. "It's them fine speeches as has done t' job wi' our Annis. Nay! keep off me and keep off wi' fine words and civilities; we can do very well wi'out, and mebbe be more heart-whole i' t' end. Eh! it's a shame to go and steal t' affections o' a poor little lass as knows no better, and mak' her fret as though she had t' wark[2] i' t' heart."

"You must really listen to me," Hugh said. "I tell you, you need not entertain the least fear that I will conduct myself otherwise than honourably towards your cousin. Her character, her reputation, are sacred and dear, and neither shall suffer at my hand."

"Why! thee'st axed her to love thee!"

"What if I have?"

"Didst thou say owt to her about making her thy wife?"

"No, I did not."

"And why not, if thou meant honourably?"

"Because I was interrupted. Martha, it is very odd that you should know all about what I said. Are you imagining it, or were you told it?"

"I got it all out, somehow," answered the girl; "I wasn't boune to rest till I knew all. I was too feared for Annis, I can tell thee."

"And you have constituted yourself her guardian?"

"I s'pose I have."

"And now, as her guardian, you have come to ask me my

[1]without

[2]pain

124

intentions?"

"Yes," answered the girl, brightening. "It's just so."

"Now, suppose I do not answer, nor acknowledge your right to assume this office; what then?"

She looked intently and sorrowfully at him; then she said, clasping her hands: "Why, then — Nay! I cannot tell. I'll ax t' Lord to take t' lassie into his own protection. I'll do all I can to save her from you, and when I can do nowt, t' Lord'll do t' rest."

She spoke confidently, with her face lighting up with earnestness and faith, and becoming beautiful through the strength of zeal which shone through her countenance, spiritualizing her features.

"Eh!" she continued; "it's not much I can do, my poor sen, but I'll not suffer her to fall into thy power wi'out a great fight for it — not wi' weapons of flesh, but wi' those o' prayer. And I reckon, if tha' does owt again that lassie, t' Lord'll avenge his own on thee terribly."

Hugh caught her hand and shook it. "My dear Martha," he said, "I desire no better guardian for Annis than you. I trust you. You are worthy of the office, and I acknowledge your right to demand an explanation of me. I do, indeed, love Annis: I told her the truth when I said I loved her; and, Martha, I promise you, no other woman shall be my wife. How to make her mine, I cannot tell now; the way before me is dark. I am poor and must wait till I have means of my own before I can ask her to share my lot with me; but as soon as I am in a position to marry I will entreat Annis to be mine. Are you satisfied now?"

"I think so," said Martha, examining his face, and endeavouring to read what was written there. She saw nothing save frankness and truth there. "But, sir! you must see it's none weel for her to be seen wi' thee. Folk will not believe that thou means right, and her character'll suffer; and, if thou hopes to mak' her thy wife, thou mun tak' care that nobody has owt to fling i' thy face o' that score. Folks is over fond of casting muck."

"They are, indeed. Now, Martha, one word. I should like to see Annis again, and tell her all my hopes and desires."

"I'll say nowt about that till I've thowt it over. Maybe I'll do thee that turn, but I'd better not promise. I think I may trust

125

thee; thou looks honest, and thou speaks honest." Then, with a shake of her head: "But I fear thy civil speeches. Them as talks most grand does the worst. I've heard say; and David says, 'Their words are smoother than oil, and yet be they very swords.' I hope thou'rt none deceiving me."

"No, Martha, I am not. I think you may trust me. Have I not trusted you, and frankly told you all — told you enough to make me the laughing-stock and sport of the place, if you were to betray the confidence I have reposed in you? Can you not in return place confidence in me?"

"It is true," said the girl, musingly; "you've told me a deal. Ay! I see what thou'rt driving at. It's right. I see, thou'st been free and open wi' me. Well, choose how, I'll trust thee. There, lad! I ha' said it. Please God, I shanna ha' to rue it."

"That you never shall."

A moment after Hugh exclaimed, with a look of vexation: "Bother! Here comes my uncle. I wouldn't have had him see me talking with you for something. Good-bye, Martha!" And he hurried off.

Mr Arkwright walked leisurely up the hill to his house, hung up his hat, wiped his brow, sat down at the dinner-table, with an ominous frown on his face, and said, "I thought so — Petticoats!"

He made no further remark during the rest of the early dinner, till a dessert of unripe apricots — in number five — was produced, home-grown, the only fruit which had escaped the marauding band-spinner's boy. Mrs Arkwright looked at him and shrugged her shoulders. "My dear Henry! This is all — it is shocking!"

Whereat Mr Arkwright sternly said: "If the apricots were the only shocking things, I should not mind so much; but when Hugh — " He turned full upon him and looked at him gloomily.

"Well, sir!"

"I'll tell you what, young sir. I give you timely notice, I'll not have you dangling after my girls."

"My ivers!" exclaimed Gretchen; "What is dat?"

"Never mind," said Mr Arkwright; "it is no concern of yours,

Gretchen. I am speaking to you, Hugh. Do you understand me? I'll not have you sawneying and slobbering about my lasses!" The manufacturer was rather vigorous than refined in his expressions. "They are good enough little bodies, and I'll not have you or anyone else turning their heads, and making them pert and giddy."

"You need have no fear of me."

"Herr Je! what is de matter?" asked the little German woman.

"Nothing that concerns you," answered her husband, shortly. "Hugh, what did you mean by talking to Martha Rhodes, one of the best and most well-conducted girls in the place, and turning her into a flirt?"

"I was doing nothing of the kind, sir," said Hugh, with some exhibition of temper. "It is really very hard if I may not open my mouth to a young woman, without becoming a victim of your odious insinuations."

"I make no insinuations. I simply tell you that I'll have no more of this. You understand me — no spoonying, no slobbering — "

"Sir, your expressions are exceedingly offensive."

"Oh, Heinrich, what is dat?" from Gretchen.

"Never mind."

"But I will look in my Wörterbuch." *Sotto voce.*

"Well, you know my opinion, Hugh; I beg you will act upon it. And now, take an apricot and change the subject."

Chapter Fourteen

It not unfrequently happened that visitors at Sowden came to Mr Arkwright's mill to see the processes of yarn and worsted-spinning. Those visitors were sometimes taken round by the overlooker; but if they were acquaintances of the owner, or persons of distinction, by Mr Arkwright himself, or his nephew.

Hugh had undergone the regular round several times, and was sufficiently posted up in the intricacies of the machinery and the processes gone through by the wool, to be a fair guide to the uninitiated. He could explain the mysteries of "willying", "slubbing", "doubling", and reeling, hanking, pressing and making up, with tolerable accuracy and lucidity.

A day or two after the event recorded in the last chapter Hugh was commissioned by his uncle to take some ladies over the mill. Mr Arkwright had business of importance, or pretended that he had, that he might escape the infliction of an hour with folk who had only come to while away idle time, and who would derive no possible benefit from the visit, taking no interest in what they saw. Mr Arkwright would not have grudged half a day to a man of an inquiring mind, who exhibited intelligent enquiry, but he had no patience with sightseers, who came and went with no advantage to their minds. On the present occasion, he could not well commit this party to the overlooker, as it consisted of relations of the principal doctor in the place, his own immediate friend. So he entrusted them to Hugh, observing to his nephew: "You are more a lady's man than I am; and, as this party consists exclusively of ladies, I think you will be in your element. I would not rob you of the pleasure on any consideration."

"I think, when they have seen the mill, I will bring them here for you to run them through the books."

"I will not have them here," said Mr Arkwright, sharply; "I can't be pestered with a lot of tittle-tattling, empty-headed women. I am not of the age to appreciate it, but you are. I am satisfied you will immensely enjoy your morning."

"Really, uncle, I think you understand the machinery so much better than I do, and are able to give so much more lucid explanations of its operation, that I feel I am taking an office on me which becomes you better."

"By the way, Hugh, I want you to keep your eyes open. There is an heiress in the party, a Miss Doldrums, a nice enough girl, with lots of the summum bonum. Her father made a fortune out of a patent smoke–jack, and when he died, left it all to her. Now's your time to do the gallant and insinuating."

"She may keep her smoke–jack money to herself. I do not want it."

"Yes, you do, my boy; a little money is a glorious thing, and a great deal is glory itself. By Jove! I'd take you into partnership directly, if you could put a few thousands into the business."

"But I have no inclination to take the lady into partnership," answered Hugh, laughing. "What is she like? Has she red hair and a squint? Does she limp and is she freckled?"

"No such thing: she is a handsome dashing girl. You might do worse, Hugh; indeed you might."

"Shall I take them through everything?" asked Hugh.

"Oh, that is just as they fancy. Probably the usual round will suffice — drying, dyeing, willying, spinning, reeling, packing. Take care that you keep their crinolines off the machinery, and don't let them get fast in any of the bands."

"I'll do my best. But I must say, sir, you show more interest in these ladies than you do in me."

"How so?"

"Why, you are so preciously eager to get me entangled in the worst bands of all, from which I could never break free — the matrimonial bands."

Mr Arkwright enjoyed a joke, especially if of a simple and punning description: refined wit was quite beyond him. Hugh's sally was highly appreciated by him.

"Get along, you rascal," he said; "I see a flutter of parasols outside the window, awaiting you. Look out for Miss Doldrums, and lose your heart, if you can possibly manage it, and take her fortune and her strapping self in exchange."

"Thank you for nothing."

Hugh went out with the ladies. He found Mrs Jumbold, in her black bonnet and grey shawl, with the end of her nose very red and her curls very wiry, in charge of four ladies: Mrs Doldrums, the relict of the smoke–jack patentee, who had issue, Laura, there present, in a blue gown and hat trimmed with yellow, a green parasol, and magenta gloves. The other ladies were Miss Thomson and Miss Mergatroyd, the former a relative of Mrs Doldrums, the latter a schoolfriend of Laura's.

"I think," said Mrs Jumbold, in her harsh voice, pushing towards Hugh, "I think you have not had the pleasure of making the acquaintance of these ladies; let me introduce you."

That ceremony having been gone through, Hugh proceeded down the yard in their company. Mrs Jumbold fastened herself on him, and began confidentially to poke him under the fifth rib with the ferule of her parasol.

"Doldrums," she said, in a half whisper, looking out of the corners of her eyes and shaking her ringlets. "You know the name?"

"I have that pleasure, now that you have favoured me with an introduction."

"Good name," said she. "Very."

She spoke abruptly, with little snapping sentences.

"Silver medal at 'International', you know."

"Indeed," Hugh observed, slyly, "I was unaware that medals had been awarded for names."

"Smoke–jacks!" She discharged the word as a pea from a boy's shooter.

"I am glad to learn it. Miss Mergatroyd, allow me to caution you against letting your shawl trail on the ground; the pavement is very dirty."

The young lady smiled and took the necessary precautions to avoid the soiling of this article of vesture.

"It is not a shawl, Mr Arkwright," she said, with a wriggle and jerk of the chin, intended to be childish and fascinating. "It is a pelisse."

"This way, Miss Doldrums; you are going towards the dye–house."

"I particularly wish to see the dye–house," said Miss Doldrums. "Do let me run in, I'll be out in a moment."

"We shall come to it in turn."

"Oh, but I hate going in regular order, let me pop in and out

130

where I like; I shall see so much more."

"You may get into mischief."

"I always am in mischief," she said. "Let me get into some frightful scrape. Do then! Let me tap one of the dye-vats, and waste ever such a lot; or let me burst a boiler or pull down a chimney or something."

"Nonsense, Laura," said Miss Thomson. "Keep with us, or you will get upset into some cauldron of boiling water or chopped to bits among the wheels, and that would be dreadful."

"But I must see everything. Promise me, Mr Arkwright."

"Yes, you shall see all that is to be seen."

"I should so like —." She paused and looked up to the mill chimney.

"Well, my dear," put in Mrs Jumbold, "what would you like? I am sure, with your means, no wish need remain ungratified."

"I should so like —" Then she turned sharp round at Hugh, and said: "Here, tell me, is it possible?"

"What, Miss Doldrums?"

"Could I possibly get to the top of that chimney?"

"Good gracious!" exclaimed the doctor's wife. "Why, what an idea!"

"I should love it," said the vehement young lady. "It is so tall, there would be such a view from the top, and it would seem so funny looking down. Mr Arkwright, take me up it, and all the others shall remain below, and we will pelt them with oranges and nuts."

"I am afraid you must do without the ascent. There is no means of climbing it," Hugh observed.

"But isn't there a ladder inside?"

"No, none."

"But there is in church-steeples, and I have often been up, taking jackdaws' nests."

"This is not a church-steeple, you see."

"No; but there is a ladder in deep wells."

"Neither is this a well, exactly."

"Well, no; but it would appear like one, if you were at the top and looked down the inside. I don't see why they should have ladders in wells and not in mill chimneys. Mr Arkwright, don't you think you could tie two or three ladders together and put them up outside?"

"I am sure there are none long enough."

"Well," said the young lady, "come along, show us something else. I am disappointed, or you are cross."

"I am certain, my dear," put in Mrs Jumbold, in her croaky voice, "that Mr Hugh would not be cross with anyone, least of all with *you*." Then aside to the young man, "I have it on good authority, she has about fifteen hundred a year. The smoke-jack did it. They were nothing before. Only in a small way, you understand. But Mr D. made a hit. The hit was unusually successful. She will have more when her mother dies." This was loud enough to be heard by Mrs Doldrums.

"Yes," said that personage, a very stout, wheezy woman, with grey hair, who walked slowly and like a compass, supposing a compass could walk; her joints being stiff, each step necessitated a semi-revolution of her enormous body. "Yes, when I'm dead," said she, "Laura will have three hundred more. Three hundred a year is settled on me for life, after which it passes to Laura; and as I am sixty-five, the chances are that she will have many years' enjoyment of it. I have got such a sweet corner of Sourby churchyard set apart for me, next to Mr Doldrums. I had a very nice stone put up to him, or rather, over him. It was a walled grave, and there is a large slab on top. I bought enough room for myself and for Laura, and for her husband, always supposing she will have one, and there are some odd corners for her children, should any die young. I haven't provided for them as grows up, you know. I didn't see that there was any call for that. I was not going to be stint in anything, Mrs Jumbold, you understand. I'm a large woman, and I shall take up a deal of room, so I've had an extra width of grave, and I paid for it. But, perhaps, 't won't be needed, for I may fall away a great deal in my last illness, especially if it be a long and painful one. I hope I've left margin. What do you think, Laura, is there margin enough?"

"What, Mother?"

"Is there margin enough, think you? You see, it won't do to be too tight; it's a pity for an inch or two to be thrussen for room." Mrs Doldrums gave way to Yorkshireisms occasionally, not being a highly educated personage. She was an exceedingly matter–of–fact person, and had her hobby, which was forced on all her acquaintance. This hobby she was unfortunately given an opportunity of mounting on the present occasion, by the remark of Mrs Jumbold on her daughter's prospects in the event of her decease.

Mrs Doldrums had been provided for years with a shroud and a coffin, or rather with several coffins, for as her body increased in size, she being "in her fattenings", as she termed it, the coffins, one after another, became too narrow for her to lie easy in them, and a fresh one was ordered of the undertaker and she was remeasured for it. The old ones she kept. "They may come in useful some day," she said, and indeed, one of them had served Mr Doldrums for his last bed. When very intimate friends had a death in the family, the old lady was wont to send a polite message to say that if she could oblige them with one of her old coffins she should be happy, only they must send the measure of the corpse and she would let them know if it would fit.

There was a story told of this good lady, that a year or two ago she had a nephew in a decline. The poor fellow was very reluctant to believe it, and when the Whitsuntide school feast took place in the parsonage garden, adjoining the cemetery, he was blithe as any of the children. Mrs Doldrums, seeing him in a jubilant mood, caught him by the arm and drew him into the churchyard, and pointing to the tomb of her husband, said, "Charlie, I've bought room enough to accommodate you very comfortably in there; you shall lie next to Mr Doldrums, on the opposite side to where my coffin is to be, and so you'll have the side next the wall."

"Oh, dear!" exclaimed Miss Mergatroyd. "What a horrid smell!"

"It is the oil," said Hugh. "All the wool — indeed everything here — is saturated with oil. One soon gets accustomed to the smell. I do not mind it in the least, whereas the odour of indigo dye is to me sickening and I shall never get used to it."

"My! What a din!" from Miss Doldrums, as they entered the long room, full of rattling wheels, whirling bobbins, flying bands, rotating cylinders and little figures with smudged pinafores darting about under the control of an elderly man in a white linen coat, very much discoloured with oil.

The ladies stood at the door, bewildered by the motion which pervaded every object on which their eyes rested, by the thrumming of the boards under their feet and the discordant metallic clatter in their ears. When they spoke, they spoke loud, to be heard.

The man in white jacket shouted.

At once a shoal of little girls scampered from some lurking-place behind a line of whirling bobbins, and rushed across the passage, down the centre and dived out of sight behind some other piece of mechanism. As the ladies went down one side of the room and up the other, Hugh explained the processes which were going on to Mrs Doldrums, Miss Mergatroyd and Miss Thomson.

"I have been over the place so often," said Mrs Jumbold, "that I know every inch, and all the ins and outs are quite familiar to me."

Presently Hugh felt a poke in his ribs, and turning sharply round to find the cause, discovered the surgeon's lady attempting to attract his attention to Miss Doldrums by lunging at him with her parasol.

"Look at her," she said; "so rich and so playful."

The young lady to whom Mrs Jumbold alluded was conversing with the overlooker in a familiar manner.

"Are you called Tom?"

"No, miss. My name's William Fanshaw."

"Oh, Will! Will, may I put my finger there? I wonder how it would feel? How fast it goes round. Do you think I might touch it?"

"Why, miss, if you want to have your finger taken off, you may. Look here. Hey! Emma Varley!" He called and a girl of twelve trotted up. "Look here, miss! She put her finger where you want to put yours, and it's gone." He caught the girl's hand and showed it to the young lady.

"Oh, you poor little darling!" exclaimed Laura. "When did that happen? How dreadful. I wish I were Queen and I'd stop children working in these mills, that I would."

"I don't fancy they'd thank'y over much for that," said the overlooker, smiling. "But you see, miss, everyone as has to work for their living has to run some risks. There's sailors have to chance being drownded, and there's soldiers to being shot, and them as works in factories to be lamed. But you wouldn't put down all sailing and soldiering and manufacture, would you?"

"Come along, Emma," said the volatile girl; "I want to see what you are working at. Do tell me all about it. I can't listen to Mr Hugh's long story. I'd rather hear you; and then you can show me." And she ran after the little lassie to the row of bobbins where she was piecing.

"Look here!" said Laura, casting her eye round; "break one of those threads, do! I want to see what will happen."

"Please, miss!"

"Now, do, there's a dear child. I'll say I did it, if anyone begins to scold."

Little Varley snapped a thread, and then stopped the bobbin.

"What are you doing there?" asked Hugh, coming up.

"Mischief," answered the young lady, with twinkling eyes. "Now get along, I'm not going to have you to explain things; I have a little friend here who knows all about the wheels and crinkum crankums better than anyone else. Emma, come along and tell me what that great joggling contrivance is for. Oh! look, there's a great squirrel's cage. I must see it!" and off she darted, holding Emma Varley by the arm, across the great room, towards the reeling place.

"Why! I thought there would be a squirrel inside," said Laura in a tone of disappointment, when she came to the wooden circular frame on which the worsted is wound previous to being made into hanks.

"Emma! What is this for? Tell me."

The girl explained to the best of her ability.

"Did it hurt you much having your finger off?" asked Laura, suddenly adverting to another subject.

"Nay, miss, not over much. I didn't feel a'most no pain at all."

"And what did Mr Arkwright do?"

"Eh! he were kind. He paid t'doctor's bill, and cam' to see me, and gave' me a present o' five pound. He put it i' t' saving bank for me. He's a grand master is Arkwright. Art thou onyways akin to him?"

"No; what made you ask?"

"Nay! I cannot tell. Please, miss, I mun go back to my piecening."

"Well, go." Then suddenly coming upon Annis, she said, "Is your name Mary or Susan or Maggie, or what?"

"Annis."

"It's a funny name, but I like it. Annis! I think it's very pretty. Oh! here comes Mr Hugh; I want to know whether you don't think Annis a very pretty name, sir?" asked Miss Doldrums, turning sharply upon him. Hugh became scarlet and looked askance at Annis.

"You must not ask me," he replied; "I am not a judge of names."

"Annis," said Laura, "let me tie up one of those clues. How fast you move your fingers. Give me one of those bits of yellow worsted. Stay! steady the squirrel cage. There! I've done it as well as any of yours. Do you not get tired of spinning that thing round all day long?"

"Oh, no, miss! I'm used to it."

"I never could get accustomed to such monotonous work, I'm sure. Goodbye, I am off. I want to see something else."

"Don't get entangled in the machinery!" called Hugh to her, but she did not hear him; the rush of the wheels, the clack of the bands, and the shivering of the windows, drowned his voice.

The reeling did not detain the other ladies long; they walked towards the door, as this was the last of the processes gone through in the great room. The packing was done elsewhere.

Before leaving, Hugh stepped back to Annis, and whispered to her: "Dear little girl, I must have a word with you. I have not said all I want. When can I speak to you?"

She looked at him timidly and said nothing.

"Shall you be at liberty at twelve?"

She nodded slightly.

"I am not going home to dinner today," she said falteringly. "Mrs Rhodes has sent us dinner here."

"Well. Will you come to Whinbury Wood at noon? I must finish what I have to say to you."

"May Martha come too?"

Hugh hesitated and looked provoked.

"Very well — yes — bring her. But you I must see."

Then he ran after the ladies and caught Miss Doldrums' hand away from a strap which was revolving rapidly, and which she wanted to try her strength upon. Mrs Jumbold suddenly came up. Hugh started; she had been behind him and not with the other ladies.

The overlooker gazed after Laura as she left the long room, and said, grimly smiling: "I never seed owt like her, she's as wick as a scoprill," by which he meant that she was as lively as a teetotum.

At twelve o'clock Hugh made his way to Whinbury Wood. It was a little broken patch of ground covered with rocks and trees, hardly deserving the name of a wood, not extending over more than some ten acres, the trees wide apart, the ground ferny and straggled over by blackberry brambles. It was a favourite resort of the girls in summer, when they did not go home to dinner; they were fond of taking their tins and sitting on the rocks under the shadow of the oaks and beeches, to eat their frugal meal. A little footpath led to it from the back of the mill, above the drying-ground for the dyed wool; the distance was nothing considerable — perhaps ten minutes' walk. There was another way to the place, through a gate opening out of the high road, some distance up the hill. Hugh went this way, so as not to attract observation. It was considerably longer; and, by the time he reached the wood, Martha and Annis were already there.

Martha had been rather startled when her cousin told her that Hugh had appointed them to meet him in the wood, and at first felt disposed to object, but afterwards she yielded, for she considered that it was best that Hugh and Annis should meet again, and come to an understanding together, and she was glad that it should take place in broad daylight and in her presence.

Hugh came towards them, his face glowing with pleasure.

"Annis, I am thankful that you have come; Martha it is very good of you. You will let me have a few words with your cousin, will you not, staid guardian that you are?"

"Ay, sir, you may speak to her; I came for that purpose. But don't be long about it, for I wouldn't have onybody see you together for owt."

"Martha, I shall not be long, but I cannot say what I have to say in the presence of a third — this time."

The girl smiled, and walked away; seated herself on a rock at a little distance, with her face towards the mill, and opening her tin, began her dinner.

"Annis," said Hugh; "I began to tell you how I loved you, but was interrupted, once before. Now I tell you the same tale again. I tell you that I love you deeply, intensely, truly, with my whole heart; and now I want to know if there is some little nook in your bosom in which the thought of me may be cherished with love."

The girl looked down and trembled; she could not answer.

"Dearest Annis," Hugh continued, "let me tell you what I offer you. I have no means and no home of my own; I am poor myself, and I only ask you to be a poor man's wife. I cannot, however, demand you to be mine now. I see no way open as yet, all is uncertain before me, and I know not how I may get on in that world in which I have now only begun to struggle. But, believe me, if you will promise to be true to me and will try to love me, I will fight my way on bravely and with good heart, and trust God to make the path clear, and open a road where now I see no way."

The little girl shook with agitation and her lips were quite unable to form words.

"Annis," said Hugh, "put your hand in mine. You shall say nothing. Here, if you are willing to look forward with me and wait in hopes, press my hand; if you refuse me, let go."

He held the slender fingers in his. They were not withdrawn. Presently, very timidly, they were contracted on his and at the same moment her full moist eyes looked him in the face.

He stooped and kissed her white brow.

"My own little love," he said softly; "so be it. We shall be one in heart. We may not meet often, but we shall trust one another, and cherish the love of one another as a precious jewel in our breasts. God knows how things may turn out! I doubt not that if we are loyal to one another all will come right in the end. Give me one kiss."

She put up her bare arms and wound them round his neck, and he folded her to his heart.

"Annis!" cried Martha, suddenly; "come along, lass."

She dropped her arms, the tears were streaming down her

glowing cheeks, tears of joy which welled up in her soul, like one of the fountains of living water of Paradise.

"Annis," called Martha, anxiously; and turning hastily round, she made a sign to Hugh to be off.

Hugh's sharp eyes all at once fell on a black poke bonnet, a grey shawl, a pointed nose, wiry ringlets and a pair of sharp eyes.

"I *am* astonished!" said a shrill voice. "Well, indeed!"

Chapter Fifteen

Mrs Rhodes having sent their dinners down to her husband and daughter at the mill, had the coast clear for regaling Richard Grover. She knew that her husband would not consent to the man entering his door again, and therefore she took care to invite him when John Rhodes would not be at home. It was some way to the factory, and there was a long hill to ascend, wherefore it was Mrs Rhodes' wont often to send the dinner to her family, unless it were of such a nature as to render it advisable that they should return to Kirkgate to partake of it.

Richard had been a fortnight or three weeks in Sowden, where his ministrations had proved exceedingly acceptable, but the society being financially incapable of accepting a prolongation of his favour, had passed him on to the adjoining parish, where he was conducting a similar round of religious exercises to that he had carried on in Sowden.

He did not forget his old friends in the latter place, but looked up one or two of those whom he held in highest favour, and among these was Mrs Rhodes.

The little awkwardness of the cursing and swearing, foul language and assault on Martha, was put aside and forgotten by him and the elect lady.

"You see th' owd chap war agait of bringing me agin into bondage. He thowt he'd gotten me then. We're all tried mortal bad. Paul stood Peter to th' face, and I warn't going to stand your lass's imperence."

So he explained away the affair, and Mrs Rhodes was quite disposed to accept the explanation, such as it was, in a friendly spirit.

"Thou knows," said the preacher, "what we *do* ain't nothing. Glory be! We're justified by faith alone."

Richard Grover was a scoundrel and a hypocrite.

For many years of his life he had been a thorough-paced scoundrel, and he was a hypocrite in addition. Shortly after his release from jail he had attended a Revival in a dissenting chapel. He had been awakened to a consciousness of his state, and had felt sincere, but transient, compunction; sufficient, however, to make him cry out, in the midst of the assembly, for mercy.

To those who have never attended a Revival, and are therefore unaware of its character, a brief sketch of the proceedings may be of interest. It is preceded by a sermon, interspersed with hymns and extempore prayers, often of an unexpected character, and the sermon itself of singular vigour and considerable eloquence, delivered with tremendous energy and action. At the conclusion of the discourse, those who would leave the chapel are prevented. If a person, especially a female, is seen to open a pew-door, the preacher, or one of his satellites, rushes up and thrusts, or drags, the person up the chapel. The whole place rings with shrieks and groans. The noise becomes deafening; everyone who considers himself or herself in a converted state, cries out to the Almighty vociferously; in the meantime the patient is forced onto a cushion, about which men stand crying and exhorting and calling on the Spirit to descend. Pray, pray, pray! is roared into the frightened person's ears, whilst the waving hands, the passes, and the fixed eyes of the operators, produce a mesmeric condition in which consciousness is suspended, and the individual performed on does what he is bidden without feeling power to resist, or retaining afterwards a reminiscence of what has taken place. If those who have been converted at a Revival are questioned, in many cases it will be found that what transpired has been completely forgotten, and that the whole has seemed like a frightful dream. Others become hysterical and scream convulsively. Their state is secure, the agonised shrieks are tokens of the operation of Divine grace. Sometimes the patient attempts to run away, and is pursued by the elect; the doors are shut, and he is hunted down with demoniacal howls. At a camp-meeting he is raced round the field, whilst the preacher calls to the pursuers to have him fast and not let the devil run away with him.

It happens often that the excited condition of the whole congregation, the noise, the lights, the heat, the magnetic influence, affect a witness who is not of the elect, and he lifts his voice in the chorus of yells. He is instantly pounced upon, dragged forward, thrown on his knees before those assembled, and made to pray aloud; any words, however few and incoherent, are accepted as tokens of a regenerate heart, and the congregation bursts forth in shouts of Glory! Glory! Hallelujah! The Lord be praised!

It was in this manner that Richard Grover was converted; and having once been regenerated, he was forced on to narrating his experiences, conducting prayer and preaching.

He was undoubtedly in earnest at first. Of the fundamental truths of Christianity he knew nothing, except that there was a flaming hell, a glorious heaven, and that by faith only the first was escaped and the second secured. Richard found that his rant proved attractive; the owners of the chapel discovered that he drew; he continued to declaim, and to his delight found, not only that it was gratifying to his vanity, but filling to his pocket. The sermons he preached were not sermons, but narrations of his own diabolical past history, the horrors of which, the wickedness of which, was immensely interesting. The revolting tale was interspersed with exclamations of praise to God for having saved and justified him, and laudation of the effects of conversion. After a while Richard found that one congregation became tired of hearing the same narrative over and over again, and so he took to wandering from place to place, repeating the story, occasionally enlarging beyond the truth on the loathsome particulars, and conducting revival meetings. The first glow of enthusiasm soon wore off, the first sincerity died away, but the preacher was still required to exhibit the appearance of sincerity and enthusiasm; consequently he was forced to simulate what ceased to exist. This became habitual, and he was hardened into an hypocrite. The old vile propensities of his brutal nature regained their ascendancy, but had to be concealed. It is a terrible fact, but the veil beneath which he hid them was religion.

Such is the history of one, but it is also that of the many.

The result of the proceedings of these men is that the connection existing between religion and morality is being steadily broken down among the lower orders, and that the less gullible and less excitable, are filled with a disgust against religion in any form.

In the West Riding the principal religious communities are the Church, the Weslyan body, the Baptists, and the Ranters or Primitive Methodists. The Weslyan Society, once so powerful, is losing its ground. It fails to make proselytes, it numbers the old and middle-aged, respectable, well conducted and solemnly pious artisans and shopkeepers, and principally is supported by mill-owners, who like its respectability, and who, having been brought up dissenters, choose a solemn form there of which will flatter them, and not exact of them much scrupulosity as to their trade conscience. But Weslyanism presents no attractions to the young, and children who have been marched twice a day, morning and afternoon, to the Methodist chapel, will be found in the evening at Church or Ranter meeting-house, and at either place they acquire a taste for something very different from the dull and ponderous services of their chapel.

The Baptists are patched about; certain districts are entirely free from them, and there Independents are to be found. In some places they are very powerful, and are an energetic and an influential body. But the Primitive Methodists carry with them most of the lower class. The manner in which they keep up a succession of excitements has already been sketched. The Ranters are more in earnest and more real than the Weslyans. They have no fixed principles; anything that has go in it is adopted by them; the last roystering popular song is parodied, and its tune adopted as a hymn melody. For instance, before service on Sunday, a band of men will be seen marching in procession down the street singing at the top of their voices such a song as Richard Grover's "We are coming" or the following arrangement of Russell's favourite song:

Cheer, saints, cheer! we're bound for peaceful Zion;
Cheer, saints, cheer! for that free and happy land!
Cheer, saints, cheer! we'll Israel's God rely on,
We'll be led by the power of his right hand.

Cheer, saints, cheer, etc..

But there is a lower depth of Yorkshire religionism still, and that is the Glory Band — a band of maniacs performing the

143

most frenzied antics, seizing in the street on any casual passerby, and forcing him to cry out that he is saved, waking the sleepers at night by their discordant howls.

The great mass of the intelligent men in our manufacturing districts are thoroughly dissatisfied with dissent. They have seen through its hollowness, and they are becoming daily more impressed with the hypocrisy of its professors, and the majority are falling into a coalition of disbelief and contempt for all forms of worship and professions of faith.

If the Church did not present such a lamentable picture of a house divided against itself; if it were better manned than it unfortunately is, in the centres of mental and bodily activity; if it displayed its energy and above all if it kept clear of *Humbug*, it is scarcely possible to doubt that the great body of noble, clear-headed, truthful, vigorous-minded men which form the muscle of England in the North, are ready at once to submit as children to a mother, thankful to escape from the cant and profanation of all that is holy which abounds in other quarters.

Religion is a powerful force everywhere, especially among the lower classes. This sketch would be incomplete without a picture of what meets one at every turn among those whose manners and habits we are describing. The drawing of Richard Grover may have startled, but it is by no means overdrawn; and if revolting, it is yet hatefully real.

"I think I could sup a drop more ale, lass," said the man-monkey, extending his empty mug. "Eating mak's a chap dry, thae knows."

"You shall have it and welcome, Richard," answered Mrs Rhodes.

"I say, owd lass! I want a word wi' thee. Th' Lord's work were agait grandly t' other neet, if that blasted wench hadn't come and sassed th' gin and water i' my face."

"She's a bad 'un!" remarked Martha's mother. "Bad she ever were, and no mistake."

"Whoo'll come to no good end, I reckon," said the man-monkey. "Whoo'l be cast i' th' lake o' burning brimstone an' vitriol, wi' t' devils pokin' her about wi' red-hot irons. I'm very sewer o' that, if she gangs th' same road all her life through."

"I s'pose she will."

144

"And yond other gradely lass. Eh! but she wor a glorious vessel for grace, an' she knowed it."

"Who dost thae mean, our Rachel?"

"Nay, t'other little lass o' thine wi' great shining' een."

"Eh! thou means Annis. She's none o' ours."

"I'd ha' been th' makin' of her, an' thy dowter Martha hadn't hindered me, wi' her cuss'd interference."

"I reckon thou would. She's a tidy lass, but she's none converted, thou knows. She's i' th' flesh still; she's not gotten set at liberty yet."

"Eh! but whoo mun be."

"I'd be fair glad she wor, but I don't see how I can fashion it. Thou sees, she's set on Church wi' our Martha, an' I reckon there'll be no breaking 'em off. Them's ever together, and thou can not get one apart from t'other; and Martha'll set her again t' truth strongly, and they'll be as stiff as owt."

"I very near did th' job t'other neet," said Richard. "An I'd had another fi' minutes I could ha' settled th' whole bag o' tricks. It wor a pity, it wor."

"Thou'rt right there, Richard."

"Ay, I know varry weel I could ha' done it, an I had time; I felt th' inspiration comin' fast; I felt it i' my finger ends, and flashin' frae my een, an' whoo wor goin' fair dazed, and that's a'most ever th' sign that th' works begone. I were tewing hard, an' then thy dowter set all to nowt. Eh! but it's sad to ha' th' Lord's work marred and brought to nowt by a ower forrard lass as thy Martha. I seemen inclined for to ha' another try."

"I wish thou could, Richard, I do upon my soul."

"Dost thae think thae could get it i' tew this road?" asked the man-monkey. "Dost thae fancy thae could get thy John away sometime, and thy Martha too, and let me ha' a try again? I should like to convert her, that I should."

Mrs Rhodes thought a while, and after having poked the fire, and looked in the oven, and shaken her head, she answered:

"Nay, I don't think that's possible; an' my John were to find thee here, he'd use me shaeful. Eh! deary! the names he'd call me, and he'd take the strap to me, mebbe."

"Now, dost thae fancy thae could send yon little lass some evening after th' miln looses to a fair lonesome spot, an' thy

John and Martha know nowt about it? Then I could meet her there, thae sees."

Mrs Rhodes took a brass candlestick and began to rub it bright, whilst revolving in her mind the feasibility of the suggestion.

"Happen I might," she replied at last.

"Eh! that's right. Glory be! And wheer wilt thae send her?"

"Dost thae know t' lane doun to t' sandpit? They call it Sandy-pit Lane."

"Out by Askroyd?"

"Ay."

"I knows it middlin' weel."

"I'll send her there an errand toneet."

"Nay, lass, not toneet; I've a sermon at Askroyd Chapel."

"Then tomorrow, that's Wednesday."

"Nay, I've a lect'r on the unmasking o' th' Confessional at Gordown."

"When shall I say?"

"Put it at back eend; say Friday. I'll be i' th' lane o' Friday next — about what time?"

"I cannot say to the minute. Happen I say eight o' clock."

"Thae'll be very sewer not to forget."

"Nay! I'll none forget; thae mun reckon on me, Richard."

"Now gie me another sup o' ale, and I'll be makin' tracks."

She at once poured him out the beer and he finished his meal. After a little further talk, he rose and took his hat.

"I thank thee kindly for coming," said Mrs Rhodes.

"Now," said the man-monkey, "thae'll not forget Friday neet at eight o'clock!"

Chapter Sixteen

Alas for Hugh! Mrs Jumbold had overheard him appoint Annis to meet him in the Whinbury Copse, and had taken care to be present. She has seen her guests home and had then sallied forth full of eagerness to find out what was meant by the assignation.

In the long room of the mill the noise had been too great for her to hear much, but she had distinctly caught Hugh's words — "Will you come to Whinbury Wood at noon? I must finish what I had to say to you." It was enough to excite the lady's curiosity to fever pitch, and she had been on thorns till twelve o'clock struck, and she was able to escape from her visitors and make her way to the trsyting wood. There she appeared suddenly and unexpectedly, to see Mr Arkwright, junior, with a little factory girl clinging to him, and he bending over her and kissing her.

"Upon my word!" said the lady, "who would have thought it? Ha! Good morning again, Mr Hugh. I have surprised you, I see. Dear me! You have taken my breath away. I didn't think it of you. Well, we live in a sad world — a world of wickedness! Of course, Mr Hugh, your uncle knows of this, and of course you have informed your aunt."

"Mrs Jumbold," said Hugh, angrily, "your conduct is monstrous. What right have you to follow me, and pry into my conduct, in this outrageous manner?"

"I have a right to take a little walk in the woods, I suppose," said the lady, tossing her nose and sending her ringlets flying about her face: "I am fond of privacy, and I find this a retired place, Mr Hugh."

"Annis," the young man said sorrowfully, to the little girl, "go away, my pet; I have nothing more to say to you now."

"Annis," said Mrs Jumbold, "the daughter of the woman who died after the flood! I know. Jumbold attended Mrs Greenwell. How long have you been carrying on your intrigue, I should wish to know?"

"Then you may wish," answered Hugh, sharply. "I shall answer none of your questions, for I do not acknowledge your right to put them. I see popular report is not wrong in the character it assigns to you."

"Pray what character does it assign to me?"

"Ask others." Hugh was boiling with indignation at the mean inquisitiveness of this social wasp, and his passion overcame his natural politeness. "It is no very savoury character, I can tell you."

"You are exceedingly rude," said Mrs Jumbold.

"I am exceedingly incensed," retorted Hugh.

"Of course, you know that I shall feel it my duty to report to your relatives the scandalous scene I have had the misfortune to witness. I should be lacking in my obligations to those who have always been objects of my liveliest respect were I to fail in so doing."

"You are perfectly at liberty to blacken my character to the uttermost," answered Hugh fiercely. "Go along with you to the town, and spend the rest of the day in rushing from house to house retailing slander, and rejoicing in your hateful business. I cannot hinder you; no mortal can. A poisonous tongue will spit its venom everywhere."

And he strode away from her.

"Dear, dear!" gasped the lady; "this is awful. What a vicious young man!"

Hugh was silent and abstracted at dinner. He knew that Mrs Jumbold would make the worst of what she had seen, and that it would not be long before the story reached his uncle's ears.

He determined that he would speak to Mr Arkwright first; but when he came to be face to face with him, his courage failed. The manufacturer rattled away with some story, and then chaffed his wife, and sent her to her dictionary in a state of bewilderment, so that Hugh found, or thought he found, no opportunity for broaching the subject. He then resolved to defer his announcement till they walked together to the mill; but when the time for returning to his books arrived, he ascertained that Mr Arkwright would not be at the factory, but was going to drive to a neighbouring town on business.

"Well," thought Hugh, "I will tell him about it in the evening; he cannot well hear the gossip till tomorrow, unless that detestable woman comes here this afternoon, and poisons my aunt's mind."

Mrs Jumbold did call on Mrs Arkwright that afternoon. There was a radiance in her face as she came in and sat down, an *empressement* in her greeting of the little German lady, and a cheerfulness of manner which made Mrs Arkwright exclaim: "Ah, now, this is lovely! You are so well and spirited this after-midday. Are you not, *meine liebe*? I am quite sure you are splendid."

"I am very well, thank you," answered Mrs Jumbold, with a peculiar and expressive smirk on her face. "I think I never enjoyed better health, but generally, you know, I am a poor sufferer."

"So! I am sorry. You have paid dreadful; where then?"

"In my liver. It is to liver I am a martyr. I have had to take a deal of calomel to keep my liver in control. I have been salivated frequently. But you know, Mrs Arkwright, we can't always order things as we best like them, can we?"

"Oh, no," answered the little woman, vainly endeavouring to attach an idea to the words "calomel" and "salivate", and only dimly guessing what was signified by "liver".

"Wait — I have a capital thing for sick in all bones; it is nice to rub in with a *stück flanell*. Shall I fetch it?"

"No!" entreated the doctor's wife. "I implore you not. I said I was very well now, but that I am often ill. Not now, you understand."

"*Richtig!* I understand."

"And are you pretty middling, my dear?" asked Mrs Jumbold.

"What you say?"

"Are you well?"

"Oh, very well, thank you. How are the young ladies?"

"We have been all over the mill this morning; your nephew Hugh was so civil; he took care to explain everything to us so nicely, and, I am sure, my companions were most gratified. I have been through the place so often, you know, that I understand all about it; but Miss Doldrums and Miss Mergatroyd were quite new to anything of the kind. The smoke-jack trade, you know, is very different — more lucrative, you see."

"Yes, I see."

"The late Mr Doldrums rose from a mere nothing. He chanced on an invention which took with the public, so he made a great

149

fortune. But" — and she lowered her voice — "I have heard say that the invention was not his, but that of a workman in his employ, and that Mr Doldrums took advantage of it and got a patent, and so secured the credit and the profit; but, you know, I can't say it was so, only people talk, you understand."

"Oh, yes, they do, ver–much."

"However, he is dead; and, whilst on that subject, I cannot help alluding to the extraordinary way in which Mrs Doldrums thrusts her contrivance for her own funeral upon one at all times. It is an absorbing idea with her: and, you will allow, it is an exceedingly displeasing one. She is fond of introducing it at mealtime, especially when there is cold meat on the table. I think she might have better taste."

"Ach! but I think the meat cold is so nice, with sour kraut, and I just chop up a little egg, and put it about of it; and, indeed, *es ist mir sehr ang–enehm.*"

"There's no wonder she's fat," pursued Mrs Jumbold, "considering the amount of bottled stout she takes. But, then, she can pay for it, or, if she can't, her daughter can. You'd hardly believe, my dear, the quantity she drank at lunch today. Jumbold helped her twice to porter, and she had some shandigaff too, and then she took claret and sherry like a fish, and after all asked for some spirits."

"And was she tossicated?"

"No, not that; cheerful — very cheerful. I observed her colour deepen, and her eye glisten, and she talked rather boisterously about how she had buried Mr Doldrums handsomely, with plenty of mutes, and a nice hearse and plumes, and got him a roomy walled vault, and so on."

"Where, now — in her house?"

"No," answered Mrs Jumbold, "in the churchyard."

Mrs Arkwright looked somewhat perplexed; at last she enquired: "Is he not dead then?"

"Yes; he died some time ago."

"Then, why wrong to have him put in the grave?"

The doctor's wife gave up the subject in despair; the little German woman could not follow her. So she led off on another topic: "I dare say you wonder to see me today?"

"But, no."

"I called only on Saturday, and here I am again."

"The more the merrier, as Henry says. I am heartily glad to see you ever."

"Thank you; you are exceedingly kind. But I would not have inflicted myself on you today, but that I felt it right to tender my best thanks for your nephew's civility to us, in showing us round the mill; and, I am sure, we must have taken up a great deal of his valuable time."

"Oh, no; he is delighted."

"And, then, I wished —ahem! I wished to say — you must excuse me, my dear friend; I am in hopes you will."

"You are not going yet; no — stay!"

"No; I have something I feel it incumbent on me to mention, though, I am sure, it will cause you an infinity of pain."

"Oh, but I like Mr Furness ver–much."

Mrs Jumbold did not trace the connection between the remark of Mrs Arkwright and her own preliminary observation. The link was the word "incumbent", which the German lady did understand, having looked it out in her dictionary the day before, and, hearing it used now, she guessed the relation borne by the rest of the sentence to it.

"It is about Hugh I want to speak," said the doctor's wife, very loud and harshly, as though she were talking to a deaf person, and hoped to make her comprehend by increasing the volume of tone in her voice.

Mrs Arkwright nodded, and said: "He is a nice fellow."

Then Mrs Jumbold sighed, and looked commiseratingly at her hostess. "I am afraid I shall distress you," — leaning forward.

"Oh, no, indeed," said Gretchen promptly.

"Do you know, I overheard Mr Hugh speaking to one of the millgirls."

"To be sure; he does that very often."

"And he made an appointment with her." Then Mrs Jumbold fell back, and stared glassily at the lady of the house.

"*Freilich!*" exclaimed Gretchen, complacently, not understanding in the least what "an appointment" signified.

"In Whinbury Copse."

Mrs Arkwright nodded.

"Do you understand?" asked the visitor. "Mr Hugh told one

of the factory girls to be with him in the Wood." She spoke distinctly and slowly.

"You say true!" Mrs Arkwright looked a little surprised.

"And," continued the doctor's wife, in her harsh tones, "I saw them meet."

"That was well," said the little woman.

"I actually saw your nephew" — here Mrs Jumbold assumed an air of solemnity and mystery. She thrust forth her parasol and poked Mrs Arkwright in the chest, nodded, winked, coughed, looked round the room, sighed — then shot her lead and lips forward, close to the other's ear, and said, in a loud, hoarse whisper: "Kissed her!"

"In my country everyone do kiss," said Mrs Arkwright, with composure.

"Smacked!"

Mrs Arkwright smiled.

"I must get my *Wörterbuch*; excuse me!" and she ran in search of her book. On her return she found Mrs Jumbold, stern, upright and presenting an exceedingly forbidding appearance.

"Now," said Mrs Arkwright, opening the dictionary on her knees, "I am ready. Go on, *Geschwind!*"

"I saw them kissing — yes, kissing," continued the visitor. "Horrible. And it was that Annis Greenwell, whose mother was nursed and died here. The base ingratitude of the thing disgusted me, apart from her shamelessness."

"Ah! Annis, the dear little lassie! She is so nice, so *zärtlich*, so *bescheiden*! — so very gentle and modest."

"What! modest — meeting your nephew and kissing him!"

"Ach!" said Mrs Arkwright, shrugging her shoulders, "I do not understand English ways, but I think her very nice."

"I think both she and Mr Hugh exceedingly wicked."

"No, no," exclaimed the little woman. "Hugh is a good fellow. Annis is a ver-good girl."

"Do you call it good, meeting in a dark wood and kissing?" The wood, by the way, was not dark, for the trees were scattered.

"It is all right. I know Hugh is a good fellow. I will not hear bad of him."

Mrs Jumbold stared at her, elevated her eyebrows and

compressed her lips. "Am I to understand, mam," she said, in a freezing tone, "that hugging and kissing are, in your eyes, morally right?"

"How you spell it?"

"Spell what?"

"H — hugging."

"Really, Mrs Arkwright, I cannot stay to inform you. I am amazed. Positively, I am flabbergasted —"

"Oh, stay!" and the little lady plunged into her dictionary.

"I am aghast at your insensibility to the outrageous immorality of your nephew. Do you think, mam, that one who thus flies in the face of all propriety is to be received into our society as fit to mingle with those who have at least some respect for the decencies of life! — is one who chooses to associate with the very rag–tag and bobtail of — "

"Oh, stay!" pleaded Mrs Arkwright piteously. "I have not got that other word yet."

"Do you think that one who lowers himself to base amours is to be suffered to approach our daughters?" By the way, Mrs Jumbold had none, and there was no immediate prospect of an arrival; the idea of daughters was, therefore, figurative and poetical. "No! certainly not. And, I must say, that I am shocked and pained to find that you, mam, whom I had regarded as a friend, should suffer yourself to so lose all sense of your position as to connive at the moral degradeation of your nephew."

"It is not in the *Wörterbuch*," said Mrs Arkwright, suddenly looking up, with an air of triumph.

"What is not?" asked Mrs Jumbold.

"Flabbergast. Now, that other word."

The doctor's wife made a formal bow, and retreated towards the door.

"Do stay!" exclaimed the German lady; "I will give you some nice grapes. They are in the *Gewächshaus*."

"Certainly not," answered Mrs Jumbold, sailing out of the room.

"It began with one R," murmured Mrs Arkwright.

Before evening, the story of Hugh's meeting with Annis in Whinbury Copse was public property.

153

Mrs Jumbold spent the rest of the afternoon, as Hugh had anticipated, in circulating the tale, with additions of her own, not the least considerable of which was this:" And, strange to say, Mrs Arkwright is at the bottom of it all!" Everyone to whom this was told by the doctor's wife became a fresh centre from which the scandal could spread, and, as a story never loses in the telling, it became vastly transformed before it had passed through many hands.

Poor Hugh, as he sat over his books, knew what was going on in Sowden. When the whistle sounded for work to cease, he found by the significant glances of those he encountered, that the story had already reached the mill.

He heart almost failed at the prospect before him. He knew there would ensue weeks and perhaps months of misery — for it is miserable to an honourable man to have mean and cowardly actions attributed to him, and it is miserable to a modest man to know that he is in the mouths of everyone, to be commented on and criticised.

He had brought it all upon himself by giving way to an attachment which must only become subject of gossip. He said to himself: "I ought not to have spoken, I might have kept my secret in my breast till time had passed, and I had an opportunity of seeing my way clearly. I was too precipitate; I would that I had been more patient, and had had more self-control!"

But then he made answer to himself: "I could not but speak, I should have gone mad without; my declaration has relieved my soul inexpressibly. Now I must bear the storm for Annis's sake."

But for her he would have been tempted — against his own convictions — to hide his head somewhere. This was a temptation and he knew it to be such. No! he would stand to his post, and face all that Sowden had to say, with frank assurance that what he had begun, he would go through with, and show to all that he was not ashamed of what he had done.

Hugh had never before been brought face to face with the world. He had fallen into the eddies of a mäelstrom; and he had nothing to clasp, to stay him up. To descend a mäelstrom; and come up alive, we must judiciously select the object to which we cling. A boat goes down into the abyss keel upwards, and comes up battered and crushed, without him who held to it; a beam of wood fares no better. Drowning men catch at straws, but straws are obviously incapable of sustaining their weight on a placid sea, much less are they of avail in the vortex of the mäelstrom. A hencoop has been recommended by some parties; Edgar Allen Poe prefers an empty cask. As a general rule, the more light, hollow and valueless the article, the safer it is to hold to. Anything solid and sound is sure to be sucked down, and crushed, but straws, feather, hencoops, float. Hugh did grasp something — his faith in Annis, true, and strong, and firm and good; that was certain to be engulfed by the mäelstrom.

Eminent geographers assure me that the mäelstrom does not exist except in the imagination of romancers. Don't tell me that! I know it whirls with increasing fury every day, sucking into its hideous throat men, and women, and children. I hear its mutterings, I am in it myself, my head is spinning, my feet have no footing, my arms are extended to cling to whatever at the moment promises to stay me up.

I see the carcases of the dead disgorged; and fair vessels, which went down with flags flying and sails spread, I see come up, mast and keel all shattered and crushed, out of the depths of that deadly grave of hopes, and lives, and fortunes, whilst the hencoops and empty casks swim uninjured.

Don't tell me that because now all is smooth and calm on the surface, there are no currents below. I hear their mumbling, deep and suppressed, swelling till they burst into voices like those of the daughters of the horse-leech, crying, "Give, give, give! Give lives, give reputations, give hopes, that we may mangle and destroy them!"

There is a smooth surface to tempt yon lighthearted boy to bathe in the treacherous waters — to allure yon tender maid to loose her skiff from the shore and slide over it — to induce yon calculating fisher to cast his net in it. But the current is working as a churn beneath, and the swimmer feels himself caught and sucked downwards, and the maiden finds her skiff drawn further from the shore, and the fisher is conscious of a strain upon his net, like a strong hand in the deep dragging it below, and he clinging to the net will go down with it. Alas! poor lad! we shall see thy shattered frame cast up with all life beaten out of it. We shall see thee, poor girl! broken on the rocks below, and flung ashore, mangled out of all semblance of thy former self. We shall see thee too, hapless fisher! strangled in the coils of thine own net. Don't tell me there is no mäelstrom!

Es wallet und siedet und brausst und zischt,
Wie wenn Wasser und Feuer sich mengt,
Bis zum Himmel spritzt der dampfende Gischt,
Und Fluth auf Fluth sich ohn' Ende drängt.
Und will sich nimmer erschöpfen und leeren,
Als wolle das Meer noch ein Meer gebären.

The hermit on his rock views this, and rings his warning bell, and the novelist points out the dangers, too, and then plunges into the gulf himself.

Don't tell me there is no mäelstrom, when I see kings casting into it their crowns, and men their fortunes, and women their honour; when I see fathers hurl down it their sons, and mothers their daughters, and husbands their wives. Good God! No mäelstrom! Mäelstrom is the supreme Moloch of the universe, to whom all nations and kindreds worship, and do sacrifice of their best and dearest, of themselves, and their all.

No mäelstrom! when the diver comes up from the deep, with haggard eyes and sunken cheeks, to say that there *is* a mäelstrom, and that he has been down it, and has seen the ghastly sights below, which are hidden beneath a glittering surface — the dragon, the shark, the snake, the sepia stretching its horrible arms, the shapeless hammer, the loathsome dogfish.

They who say there is no mäelstrom dream. I have tasted of its brine, I have battled with its waves, I have had a glimpse of the horrors of its womb, and I know, in verity, that there is a mäelstrom.

Chapter Seventeen

When the wave broke above the head of Annis, she extended her hand to Martha, and Martha sustained her.

As they left the mill, a party of girls attacked Annis with exclamations of —

"Eh, lass! thou'rt deep!"

"Whoever would ha' thowt it o' thee!"

"How could thou fashion to go trailin' after thy betters!"

"Eh! I thowt, wi' all thy still ways, thou wor ower deep."

"I'se sorry thou'rt a bad un."

Annis shrank from them in a blanched, quivering state, with her great eyes distended with terror, unable to say a word to protect herself.

"Ya mun kep off, everyone o' you," said Martha Rhodes, looking round on the group. "I tell thee, Hannah, she's no more a bad un than thee. She's as good and modest as any one o' ye all, and you've none occasion to be casting stones at her afore she's down."

"She'll come to no good, lass," said the girl Hannah. "Thou knows Nancy Eastwood; weel, it's a bad road to be taking after her."

"She's not taking after her," answered Martha; "if Hugh Arkwright chooses to ax our Annis to be his wife, it's just nowt to thee. He mun please hissen and happen he might do wor."

"Eh! dost thou think they'll be wed?" said Hannah derisively. "That'll never be. He talks about it, but he doesn't mean it."

"That thou'st no call to think," said Martha. "Mak' room."

She led Annis through them and away up the hill home.

"Mebbe it's true," said one of the girls, after they had gone. "Martha wouldn't be so stiff about it, an' there were owt wrong."

"Happen she's mistaken."

"We shall see." And so they dispersed.

The storm broke on Hugh next day — not more fiercely, not more crushingly.

Mrs Arkwright said nothing to him. The little woman was not in the least disturbed by Mrs Jumbold's story; she believed Hugh to be an honourable and right-minded fellow, and she did not trouble herself to inquire into the charge brought against him by the spiteful scandalmonger.

"It is sure to be right somehow," was her internal conviction, expressed mentally in her native tongue. "There is no occasion for me to ask questions about it; I should only get laughed at for my pains."

Neither did she speak of it to her husband till he mentioned it to her.

Hugh noticed all breakfast time that something unpleasant was brewing. He was anxious to have it over, so he broached the subject himself.

"I suppose, sir, you have heard the reports circulating about me?"

"Yes."

Mr Arkwright looked thundery; with his brows contracted and his eyes glittering. His way of eating indicated that he was angry, for he broke his victuals, and put it into his mouth jerkily, and between each mouthful scowled at his newspaper, without speaking.

"You have been told that I made an appointment with one of your mill girls to meet me in Whinbury Copse, and that I kept it."

Mr Arkwright put down his paper, put his elbows on the table, and resting his head between his palms, looked straight in his nephew's face, and said, "Go on."

"I do not know, sir, what you have heard. Most probably a tissue of lies, for the originator of the whole story is unscrupulous."

His uncle looked gloomily at him still, and did not speak. Hugh found a difficulty in forming his sentences, on account of his agitation, he therefore paused after each to recover himself, and take breath. Mr Arkwright offered no interruptions.

"Mrs Jumbold overheard me tell Annis Greenwell that I wanted to speak to her in Whinbury. She followed me thither, and found me conversing with the girl, not alone, but in the presence of Martha Rhodes.

"I tell you the reason why I desired to see Annis. I love her. I have loved her ever since the flood. I have tried hard to conquer my feeling. I believed I had mastered it, but it conquered me. I may have acted rashly. I have asked her to be my wife."

Mr Arkwright snorted.

"I dare say you think me exceedingly foolish, and exceedingly headstrong —"

"I do." Like the stroke of a sledgehammer came the words from the manufacturer.

"But I do not regret having taken this course. I have acted with honour, and have not said one word of which I am ashamed, or which I wish recalled. I love Annis dearly — how dearly I cannot express. I also reverence her as one in every way deserving my regard."

"Except in station," put in Mr Arkwright, abruptly.

"You are right, except in station and education. I recognise in her every noble quality of Christian womanhood. Station matters little to me, poor and isolated as I am; education may be acquired."

Hugh, beginning to warm with his subject, overcame his nervousness.

"Yes, sir, I wish for, and I will have, no other girl for my wife but Annis. My love for her came unsought, it was struggled with desperately, it would not be overcome, and I firmly believe that where Providence draws two hearts together, it intends to unite them. It may be years before I am able to ask Annis to join her lot with mine, but I shall steadily look forward to that and work for it."

"Let me tell you," said Mr Arkwright, raising his head, "that you are a confounded jackass."

"Sir!"

"A confounded jackass."

"Uncle, I cannot hear such expressions used, and I will not."

"You must bear what you have called down on your own head. Are you prepared for the consequences?"

"What consequences?"

"The consequences of being regarded henceforth in the light of a *jackass*."

"I will endure whatever I shall be called on to endure. I have taken my line. It is not a usual one, and will therefore arouse attention and elicit comment. It will be distressing, I know, to have to run the gauntlet of all the gossips in the place, but I will do it. I have done nothing wrong."

"Hugh," said Mr Arkwright, "I am glad of that. That is a relief to me to hear. If you had, I would have turned you out of my doors, and you should never have set foot within them again; for the man who takes advantage of woman's weakness to bring shame upon her, is, in my opinion, the most detestable and contemptible scoundrel unhung. I will say this to you, I never suspected you of that. I never thought you a scoundrel, but I do think you a jackass."

"Oh, my dear!" exclaimed Gretchen. "What is it all about? Mrs Jumbold told me one tale — *ganz märchenhaft* — yesterday."

"Hold your tongue now," said Mr Arkwright, turning sharply on her; "do not interrupt. Go on, Hugh."

"Well, sir, I have spoken to Annis, and told her that I see no prospect of making her my wife now, but that I will take her to me one day."

"Go on."

"I have nothing more to say."

"You are a fool," said Mr Arkwright. "I did think you would have been wiser. This comes of being brought up out of the world; had you been reared in a town and not in the country, among men of business and not parsons, this would never have happened. You must think no more of it. It can never be."

"It shall be, some day, if we live."

"Nonsense. Don't make matters worse by obstinacy. You have done an idiotic act, don't stick to it."

"I shall stick to it."

"We shall see. In a few months the fancy will have worn off, and you will hear reason."

"It is no mere fancy, uncle."

"That time alone will prove. We must quiet the girl with a present of a few pounds, and marry her to some young fellow or other, and so settle the matter."

"That shall never be."

"Now, Hugh, listen to reason. You cannot possibly marry a girl so beneath you in position; if you were to do so, she would not be received into society by those who rank with you, and it would be a constant source of humiliation to you, to find your wife looked down upon. Her way of thinking will be entirely distinct from yours. At first, the charm of a pretty face, and a simple, unsophisticated nature would delight you, but after these attractions were worn off, you would feel the want of education, and refinement of manner; in society you would be liable to meet with a thousand rebuffs, and to have your sensibilities hurt by casual remarks, which will strike home to you as barbed arrows. You do not know what effect a change of station would produce on a girl of this sort; from being a quiet and modest lass, she might develop into a vulgar and coarse woman. If you had children, they would take after the mother and your home would be miserable, your temper would sour, and you would seek in dissipation the happiness which your own house ceased to afford. Ill-assorted marriages rarely turn out well. There, Hugh, I have told you what is before you if you persevere in your madness. Now look to the other prospect open to you. Without intending to flatter you, I may say that you have qualities and looks which will put you in a good way to make a fortune. A little attention and application, and you will be qualified to become partner in my business; you may look about you for a young lady with money — such as Miss Doldrums, whose means would be invaluable, and you could buy a country house, and set up as a country gentleman, become a magistrate, and make a family."

Hugh did not speak immediately; when he did, he said, quietly and firmly: "I have made my choice."

"Well, well!" said Mr Arkwright; "the event will not always follow our wish and planning. We shall see! Only, would to heaven you had not made a fool of yourself. You will have all Sowden gossiping about you for some weeks. Now, if you please, let us change the topic. I shall want you to go to Bradford for me today, on business."

Hugh was surprised at Mr Arkwright having kept his coolness; he had expected him to have burst into a fit of anger and to have threatened to turn him from his door and disinherit him.

But Mr Arkwright was a man of the world. He knew that young men fall in love, generally very foolishly; that, when they are in this condition, they are not amenable to reason. He took Hugh's affair to heart, chiefly because it was likely to cause scandal; that it would end as Hugh anticipated, he never for a moment supposed. His course was to pooh-pooh the whole concern, throw a blaze of commonsense over it, and leave time to cool the ardour of youth. He expected to find his nephew full of sentiment, romance and obstinacy at first, and he had no doubt that after a few weeks or months, his resolution would waver, the sentiment would dissolve before matter-of-fact, the romance would leak away, and the obstinacy break down, and then some arrangement could be come to, agreeable to both parties, to break off the silly engagement and laugh it away as a folly of the past.

Mr Arkwright knew that if he were to go into a passion and threaten Hugh, it would make the young man ten times more resolute, but that if he passed this act over, his nephew would feel the kindness, and consider himself under an obligation. He was a kindhearted man also in his rough way, and he could not help compassionating the young man in his awkward position, as the object of all eyes, ears and tongues in the place. He considered Hugh a fool, but he was deserving of commiseration rather than chastisement.

Chapter Eighteen

Mr Furness, Vicar of Sowden, was walking to the parsonage with short, rapid steps, his head a little on one side, and his shoulder very close to the wall. He was an old man now. He had been moulded by Oxford in its ancient days, when Newman and Keble were presiding spirits, and from the former he had inherited the trick of wearing his hat on the back of his head, and from the latter he had imbibed a devotion to swallow–tailed coats.

He was a Yorkshireman by birth and parentage, but no Yorkshireman in appearance. From the county to which he belonged, he had derived a strength of purpose and determination of character which no opposition could break. To his parentage and education he owed a refinement and courtesy of manner belonging to an old school of politeness, that has, alas! almost disappeared.

He was a short, dapper man, without colour, closely–shaven and with short–cut grey, or nearly white, hair, frail in constitution, and with little bodily strength. He belonged to an ecclesiastical type rarely met with. We are accustomed to the self–asserting, self–centred Evangelical; the blustering and secular Broad Churchman, and to the dilettante Honeyman of Ritualism; but Mr Furness was detached from any one of these classes. He was an indefatigable parish priest of the old Tractarian school, who clung to the traditions of his youth, and reverenced the names of Pusey, Newman, Froude, Williams and Keble, as those of redoubtable leaders, in whose traces he was proud to walk.

The Weslyans of his parish shook their heads over him, and declared that he preached nothing but morality; but when the vicar was roused night after night by the noise of drunken riots in the street, when he found that trade was fast degenerating under competition into fraud, and when he saw that the number of bastards was rapidly on the increase in the parish register, he convinced himself that morality was, on the whole, not a doctrine so unnecessary to be taught in the pulpit as the advocates of justification by faith and free grace supposed. Indeed, it is a pity that the worthlessness of virtue is so eagerly insisted on by dissenting and evangelical preachers, for their hearers have taken them at their word, and combine immorality in every form with the most fervent professions of faith, and confidence in their election. Suddenly Mr Furness was brought to an abrupt standstill by means of an umbrella handle which caught him over the shoulder.

"You can stop a minute," said Mrs Jumbold. "I've got something to say to you, vicar."

Mr Furness turned round and, smiling, extended his hand. "A beautiful day, Mrs Jumbold."

"So, so. I say, have you heard?"

"Heard what?"

"Oh! the news."

"Really, I have no time to look in at the Institute now. I get up all my news of the week from the *Guardian* on Saturday, and today is Friday, you know. Tomorrow I shall be well posted up. Today, I am ignorant of all that has taken place the world through during the last six days."

"Oh! I don't mean news of that sort. But, vicar, first of all, I want to know why that curate of yours left out the General Thanksgiving on Sunday, eh?"

"Did he? I did not observe it. It was omitted by accident, I suppose?"

"No, no. There was some meaning in it, some object. Now, none of your popish ways with me. I won't have any of your ritualism, I can tell you; so you speak to him, will you? Now, the news; of course you have heard it, about Mr Hugh Arkwright?"

"I have heard nothing more than that you have been talking about him all round the parish," said the clergyman, giving her a quiet stab.

Mrs Jumbold coloured; her nose became purple. She had received similar thrusts on other occasions, and she did not like the vicar for that reason. To her friends, she explained that she did not approve of his opinions.

As a general rule, people hold those religious views which best suit their convenience, sometimes they form their opinions

164

in a spirit of opposition. Not one in a thousand in High Church, Low Church, Catholic or Protestant on conviction.

"I saw what took place," said Mrs Jumbold.

"Did you indeed?" The tone of the vicar's voice deprecated persevering in the subject, but the doctor's wife was not disposed to be silent, or to turn from that topic.

"Yes, I saw it all. Very immoral conduct."

"What do you mean by immoral?" asked the vicar; "words should be well weighed before they are uttered, especially when they touch the character of another."

"Immoral! Of course I know what I mean by immoral — licentious. There, sir!"

The vicar looked up at the church clock. "I think you must excuse me, Mrs Jumbold, it is near my dinner hour, and though that is not an excuse to be ordinarily made to a lady, yet you know me, and that I depend on my meals entirely, and utterly collapse if I do not have them at the moment that nature cries out."

"But you haven't heard me," said Mrs Jumbold, throwing up her umbrella again, with the crook towards her pastor, as though she were about to catch him by it, and retain him till he had heard what she had to relate.

The vicar dreaded this umbrella handle. Once it had caught in his coat–pocket, and had torn the cloth. On another occasion it had nearly prostrated him, by catching his knee.

"I say," pursued Mrs Jumbold, "one of your Sunday–school teachers, too. I always said you did wrong in getting young men and women to take classes. They bring discredit on the church. Of course you will dismiss him from the school?"

"Certainly not."

"What! allow a profligate, licentious, dissolute —"

"Mrs Jumbold, I want my dinner. Nature cries out, I shall collapse."

The handle of the umbrella clasped him at once.

"You will turn that libertine out, will you not?"

"My good lady, I have already hinted to you how distasteful this subject is to me."

"Of course it is!" exclaimed the doctor's wife, in a tone of triumph. "What else could it be, when Hugh Arkwright is one

165

of your teachers, and the young woman was one of your confirmation candidates last March."

"I daresay you will detain me no longer. An engine will not work without coal, and my system must have its carbon supplied at the right moment — "

"You will dismiss him, won't you?"

"I shall not, Mrs Jumbold. Hugh Arkwright is an honourable man. He may have been foolish, but he has not done anything which is wrong. Have you never acted in a precipitate and injudicious manner, may I ask?"

"Never, Mr Furness," replied the doctor's wife, bridling up.

"Not when — " He was on the point of alluding to an exceedingly silly act of Mrs Jumbold in forcing her husband to leave a good practice for that of Sowden, to please a whim of her own; but he restrained himself.

"You must allow me to speak one word to you, as your friend and pastor," said the vicar, laying his small and delicate hand on the lady's wrist: "I think I have read somewhere about a good man who passed everything he wished to say of another person through three sieves. The first was, 'Is it true?' The second, 'Is it kind?' The third, 'Is it necessary?' Might I commend that example to your consideration? Now, good morning."

Turning sharply round, he saw a lady in a pearl–grey silk dress, with a black belt and a rose in it, step towards him across the road.

"Bessie!" he exclaimed with joy. "My dear sister! How unexpected this is. Did you drop from the clouds, or rise through a trapdoor in the earth?"

Then, turning to Mrs Jumbold, he introduced his sister to the doctor's wife.

"How did you leave my mother?" he asked, looking radiant with delight and pride on Miss Furness.

"She is very much the same as usual, William."

"We're likely to have nasty trying weather for old people," said Mrs Jumbold. "This month generally uses them badly, the wind is so keen."

"We shall do our best to keep her out of the wind," said Miss Furness, smiling. "Our house is draughtproof, I assure you."

"Ah, you can't keep out east wind. There's a nature in it

166

which penetrates everywhere, a life–destroying nature I call it. It comes in with the air. You don't hermetically seal Mrs Furness up, I suppose?"

"Bessie, you must be quite hungry," said the vicar.

"I am indeed. The journey from York is tedious, on account of the stoppage and change of trains at Normanton and the delay at Wakefield."

"You are famished, are you?" asked Mr Furness.

"Well, I can't quite say that; but I shall be ready for your dinner. You dine at one, do you not?"

"At one, punctually," replied the vicar. "And now," looking up at the clock, "it is ten minutes past."

"Ah!" put in Mrs Jumbold, "servants ain't punctual. It's no use expecting it. I've given over looking for times to be kept. Domestics are not what they once were. I can't keep cook or housemaid; they give themselves such airs and demand such wages, and do so little that it puts me out of patience. This comes of your education. I never liked the scheme of education — you went too high."

"Did you find your servants highly cultivated in intellect and refined in taste?" asked Miss Furness.

"No, that they are not. I fancy sometimes we shall have to scrub our own floors, we are come to such a pass."

"I think it would be well," said the vicar slyly, "if all people would scrub and clean their own houses, and then they would be less disposed to observe, or imagine they observe, dirt on their neighbours' walls and floors. I wish you good morning." And he dexterously slipped beyond reach of the umbrella-handle.

When Mr Furness entered the parsonage with his sister, he gave a sigh of relief.

"What is that sigh for?" asked Bessie.

"Never mind, dear, or you will make me say something which will stick in one or two of the sieves, though it would pass only too readily through the first. What have you popped in on me in this unexpected manner for?"

"Oh, William! let us have dinner first, and then I will tell you. I knew what you were driving at, when you asked me whether I was hungry. Men are egotistical things — even the best of

167

them, and their thoughts are centred on self. When you pretended such sympathy with me, you were thinking of yourself all the while."

"I protest, Bessie, I did think of you."

"Yes, but only because you were yourself in want of dinner."

"What have you come about, tell me?"

"Not till you have had something to eat."

"Is it anything touching my mother?"

"Yes."

"Nothing serious?"

"No; don't be frightened. She is as usual."

After the roast leg of mutton had been removed, and the tapioca pudding was brought on, the vicar, unable to repress his curiosity any longer, said, "Bessie, what have you come about?"

"I will tell you now. I want someone to help me in looking after Mother. I must have a little relief. The dear old lady is somewhat exacting, and I can scarcely get out of doors for fresh air, or to buy what is necessary for the house. Do you know of anyone who would do?"

"There is Susan Glover," said one of the curates.

"I think Elizabeth Jessop would do better," observed the second curate.

"Elizabeth Jessop wouldn't do at all," remarked the first, sententiously.

"Why not?"

"There are reasons" — mysteriously.

"Excuse me," said the vicar, "but I doubt whether Susan Glover is *quite* the person who would do."

"She is a very respectable person."

"I readily allow that, but she is too old for the peculiar sort of work, and has not tenderness sufficient for a nurse."

"Then Elizabeth Jessop," suggested the second curate again.

"I tell you she won't do," said the first, impatiently.

"I do not see why not."

The first curate bent over towards the younger and whispered, "Erysipelas."

As he was an authority on parochial infirmities, from whom there was no appeal, not even to Mr Jumbold, the second curate relapsed into silence, with a shudder, and gave up his opinion instantly.

"I will think it over," said the vicar. "If you hear from me in a week or fortnight, it will do, I daresay."

"Yes, William, very well."

"Do you go back to York tonight?" asked one of the curates.

"I return this afternoon," replied Miss Furness. "I have come to take a peep at my brother, but I am not able to spare much time, as Mrs Furness is so poorly."

The vicar rose and said grace, and then retired with his sister to his room, and was closeted with her, till it was time for her to return.

Chapter Nineteen

At twelve o'clock, Mr Arkwright put his head out of the office door, summoned John Rhodes, who was passing and said, "John! send me that girl, Annis Greenwell. I want to speak to her while Mr Hugh is out of the way."

"All right, sir," answered the wool-sorter, with a grin. "I reckon these young things is like barrels o' gunpowder."

"A little cold water is wanted, John. Nothing like a souse."

"I'm afeared t' cold water did t' job," said John.

"How so?"

"Why, 'twor flood set it all agait, if what folks say be true.You see, sir, many waters will set love ablaze, and won't quench it, nother."

"But they may slake it," said Mr Arkwright.

"Happen t' may. But when t' prophet Elijah built his altar a'top o' Carmel, they teemed a deal o' water over 't. However, when t' fire fell fra' heaven, it just made t' water o' no account, but it licked up meat and wood and stones and water, and all t' bag o' tricks."

"Well," said Mr Arkwright observed, "I believe women are like those torpedoes or infernal machines which blow up under water as readily as on ground. I remember to have read somewhere that old Romans, when they were burning their dead, used to put one female corpse to three males, because it was supposed to contain so much more oil than the others that it facilitated their incremation. For my part, I think there is combustible material in one woman to set any number of men in a blaze."

John shook his head and chuckled. Then, composing his face, he said: "I think Annis would ha' been right enew if Mr Hugh ha' let her alone, poor lass! I doubt she'd ever ha' given him a thowt if he hadn't trailed after her. So tha munna lay 't all to t' lass's account. She's as good and modest a bairn as tha can find, choose how; but ye canna expect that a flock o' wool wi'nt burn if ya put it i' t' middle o' a blaze."

"Well, John; send her to me."

A few minutes after the poor little thing came quaking into the office as frightened as a mouse under the paw of a cat. Mr Arkwright sat at his desk making entries in his ledger, and pasting letters into the correspondence book without appearing to notice her. He had observed her alarm, and he considerately gave her a little while in which to compose herself. But much time could not be wasted; he wanted his dinner and after the lapse of a few minutes he looked up sharply at her and said: "Now, then, what's all this nonsense about?"

Annis made no answer. She stood in the door fumbling with her pinafore, and with her head bent down. She had a new crimson kerchief on her head. Girls do not wear mourning when they are at their work and Martha had given her this one. There came in a sunbeam at the office window, and fell over her head and breast, bringing out the colours in all their intensity against the grey shadows of the outer passage into which the door opened. If Mr Arkwright had possessed the slightest artistic feeling, he would have been charmed with the subject before him. A patch of crimson, a bent face, with half–lit, delicately–hued cheek of the softest rose bloom, a white pinafore, with the shadow of the bowed head striking across it, a graceful pair of nervously–moving hands plucking the white smock into knots with deeply–marked folds, and then changing them, and over the brow two little sweeps of the brightest amber gathered back beneath the handkerchief, but sufficient to arrest the sun; and below, out of the full light, the purple of a skirt, and a couple of little feet in black shoes, which could not keep quiet.

But Mr Arkwright had not a trace of art–appreciation in his whole being, and he saw nothing before him but a little girl who received seven shillings a week, on an average, for reeling, and who had brought his nephew into a hobble.

"Shut the door behind you."

The girl obeyed. It was a glass door. The passage without was a roomy entrance to the woolsorting and packing departments.

"Now then, tell me how you have got into this pickle."

She could not answer. Her employer saw it; so he spoke again: "Annis Greenwell, you and Hugh have made great fools of yourselves. I believe the fault lies with that great blundering booby, my nephew, and that you have been only soft and not

171

designing. I do not believe that you made any attempt to entrap him."

The girl looked up earnestly and attempted to speak, but the words died on her lips.

"I understand you," said Mr Arkwright. "I quite believe what you wish to say, that you had not thought of Hugh till Hugh thought of you. Is it not so?"

She nodded.

"You must think no more of him, and he must think no more of you."

She glanced at him with an imploring expression; spots of carnation starting to her cheek, and as suddenly dying from it.

"You absurd little creature," said Mr Arkwright, "do you think it possible that your silly romance should be suffered to go any further? Of course not. You must see very well that it is folly. Does not everyone around you say so? What advice do John and Mrs Rhodes give you? What do the girls you work with cast in your teeth? Has it brought you happiness? Tell me now, are you not very wretched?"

She put her hands over her face and her bosom tossed convulsively.

"Sit down on that chair whilst I talk to you rationally. I will not speak to you violently, but reasonably and temperately. Do you think that you are a suitable companion for my nephew? Now answer that; I really must have your reply."

She clasped her hands on her lap as she sank on the chair. After a brief struggle she said, in a faint whisper, "No."

"No, you are not. Hugh is a man of education and accustomed to society perfectly distinct from that in which you move. His speech is quite different from yours, and still greater is the divergence in your ways of thinking. If I were suddenly to transport you to my drawing-room and bid you spend your day there receiving visitors and entertaining guests, you would be at a loss how to act: you would feel that you were in a sphere with which you were wholly unacquainted, among people before whom you would shrink with humiliation, conscious of your inferiority in breeding, in manners and in expression. You would want to run away to the kitchen. Hugh's wife must not be a cook, but a lady. A life in a forced and unnatural position would

172

be a daily misery to you, and you would sigh for the freedom of your old associations and habits. Ladies in the upper classes have their minds, their words, their bodies put into stays at early infancy. Their thoughts, their conversation, their bodies grow in stays and live in stays, and can never get out of stays. They do not feel the restraint because they have never known what it is to be without stays; but you, who live in a natural condition, would feel it intolerable to be all at once seized upon, and surrounded, body, soul and spirit, with whalebone and irons, from which you were never to escape. How would you like me to take a great strap and fling it round your chest, and gird it tighter, tighter, tighter, till all power of respiration and circulation was at an end? Now, if you became a lady, my poor child, we should have to lace up your thoughts tighter, tighter, tighter, till they could not flow, and your words till they were stiffened into the most rigid platitudes. Why! when you felt the great iron bones beginning to encircle you, and the laces to be drawn tight, you would give a scream, and away you would fly to your freedom and nature again; and then what would become of Hugh?"

He paused and looked at her. She was listening intently, with her right elbow on the desk — Hugh's own desk — and her head resting in her palm, whilst the other arm hung on her lap, listlessly. There was a gloss on her cheek, such as we see on a leaf after rain, for the tears trickled silently over her face.

"Poor child!" said Mr Arkwright, "I am sorry you are in trouble, but it is the consequence of your own folly, or rather of that of Hugh, for he is to blame in the matter, not you. Tell me now, should you like to be a grand lady seeing plenty of company?"

"No, no, no, sir!" she said, sobbing out.

"Come, wipe your eyes and be quiet. I must put the case very plainly before you, because you young folk see nothing but the glitter of the outside, and never get below the surface, unless an older and wiser hand obliges you. Do you not find, Annis, that your way of talking is very different from ours? and do you think that you could learn to give up the old brogue for proper grammatical English? Would not you fear whenever you opened your mouth that you were saying something wrong which would

173

make others stare and laugh and fill you and Hugh with shame?"

She answered with a long–drawn, deep sigh, and a clear drop sparkling in the noonday sunbeam, which fell on the desk.

"Now, what has your love–folly brought you to? And not you only, remember, but Hugh as well. You are both wretched."

She looked up suddenly, with her great lustrous eyes dulled with tears and asked in a plaintive tone: "Please, is he very wretched, Mr Arkwright?"

"Yes, Annis, very. He must be so, with all Sowden gossiping about him, and saying very bad, very wicked things of him."

She put her face down on the desk and threw out her bare arms over it, with her hands spread out, as though repelling something, and hiding her eyes from some object and stopping her ears to some voice.

Mr Arkwright left his seat and went over to her, and putting his hand gently on her shoulder, said in a kindly tone: "My poor, silly little thing! I will not distress you more than I can help, but you must hear to what a pass you have brought matters. Will you sit up and listen to me?"

She half raised her head and then let it fall again.

"Well, never mind, hide your face like that, but keep your ears open."

He resumed his seat, and continued: "This romantic passion will soon evaporate and Hugh will be exceedingly sorry for what he has done. Mind you, Annis, he is honourable, and he will not forsake you; he will not surrender you, without your frankly accorded permission. I speak to you now in a way I would not speak to any other. You have it in your power to ruin my nephew's happiness and prospects if you choose. You may hold him to his engagement if you like. His welfare is entirely in your hands; you may think me unwise to tell you this, but I do so because I believe you to be as honourable and as willing to do what is right as — as — as Hugh, I will say. Now, it is for you to make your choice. If you keep Hugh to his word, I wash my hands of him; I shall send him about his business, he can no longer remain here, and I cannot allow myself to be brought into relationship with half the working people in the place. He shall go from Sowden and shift for himself elsewhere. I intended to teach him the trade, and then to admit him to

174

partnership with myself, and finally to surrender the business into his hands; but that will be frustrated by his taking you to wife. I cannot, and I will not allow that. You may saddle yourself upon him if you will. Then, in future years, he will have to thank you if he loses my property and if he comes to poverty. Perhaps elsewhere he may obtain a clerkship and struggle on, but he will not be able to educate his children, and bring them up as he was brought up; and he will look repiningly to the past and wish he had not been such a fool as to cast his eyes below his station in life, and lose thereby the friendship of the only relative who could have advanced him. Now, Annis, I ask you a question. Do you really love my nephew, Hugh?"

She looked up and turned her head, without lifting her arms from the desk on which they were extended. With a wailing reality in her words, she answered: "I do. Oh! indeed; wi' my whole heart."

"The question is, whether you love him so selfishly as to desire to ruin his prospects rather than lose him?"

"I wouldn't do him a harm for owt."

"Will you give him up, Annis? It comes to this, he or you must leave Sowden. If you refuse to surrender him, I walk him out of my house and wash my hands of all concern in him: but if you have the courage and right feeling to take the course I suggest, you may both be happy some day, but — not together. What's that noise?"

The noise was the rattling of the desk against the wall, occasioned by the agonising struggle in the girl's bosom.

"I love him. I love him over weel!" she said between her sobs.

"If you really love him well, you will consider his advantage rather than your own."

"I'll go," she said, without looking up; "I'll go, and I'll never see my own poor lad more."

"You have relations to go to, I suppose."

She made a motion with her head, which might be taken either way; Mr Arkwright took it for assent. She was too agitated to be able to bear much further exhortation, and the manufacturer considerately turned upon his seat and continued his work at the correspondence–book.

It took him ten minutes or a quarter of an hour to finish what he was about, and when it was done, he shut the book noisily, took his hat, left his seat and looked at Annis.

She lay still at the desk, with her bare arms stretched towards the window and her crimson coif resting between them, and one foot turned round the leg of the stool.

"Come, Annis," he said, "you must go now. I am going to lock up."

She rose mechanically from her place, her face tear-stained and pale, and she moved towards the door without showing symptoms of an inclination to speak.

"Little girl," said Mr Arkwright, holding her back with one hand, and looking gravely, almost sternly, into her twilight eyes, "may I trust you to hold your determination?"

"You may."

"You will give up all hopes of being Hugh's wife?"

"Yes."

"You will leave Sowden as soon as you possibly can?"

"I will."

"You will cease to love Hugh?"

"That can never be," she answered, with vehemence, the faded light shooting once more into her eyes and the colour leaping into her cheek.

"Well, well, you will try to forget him."

"I cannot promise that," she said, sadly. "And please sir," she asked, piteously, "may I see him once more to say goodbye?"

Mr Arkwright hesitated. "Only once," he answered, making a virtue of necessity, feeling sure that whether he gave leave or not, the two would not part without a farewell; "only once, and that on condition you do not tell Hugh where you are going to, or give him any clue to discovering your whereabouts."

"Varry weel," she said. "I shall see him once more."

"Stay, Annis," Mr Arkwright called after her, as she stepped through the doorway, "here, take this to help you on your way. Mind, I trust you." He held out to her a five-pound note.

"Nay," she said. "I do not want it."

"Annis, I insist. It is but just; I am sending you from your work, where you earn your livelihood, to where you may be long before you find employment. It is a matter of conscience

176

with me. Take this. And now go home, never mind about coming back to the mill this afternoon. Your heart is sore and you will be better out of the way of the chattering prying girls, who are sure to fly at you the moment they have an opportunity."

The poor child left the office and walked slowly up the yard. At the gate was Martha. She had waited there patiently, with her eye on the door into the entrance passage, from the moment that the whistle dismissed the hands, till her cousin came out. Her father and Susan had gone home to dinner without her.

"Oh, Martha!" said Annis, sadly, "hast thou not been home?"

"Nay, lass; I wouldn't go bout thee. It's over–late now and we mun do wi' no dinner today."

"I'm boun home," said Annis; "I'm not coming to t'miln no more."

"Eh!" then, after a little thought, "but it's best so."

Then putting her arm round her, Martha accompanied her the greater part of the way home.

"Tha looks rueful," said Martha, parting with her.

"Gie me a kiss, lass!" pleaded Annis, despairingly. "I'm ower sick at heart."

When she reached home, she hurried upstairs and cast herself upon her bed, to weep unrestrainedly.

The afternoon glided by, and still she sobbed, and at intervals her feeble voice was lifted with the cry: "I cannot bear it! Oh, Lord! thy will, not mine, be done! but I do love him, and I ever shall!" And she took a little brooch of jet, with a crystal in it, and buckled it on the bosom of her smock, and drew the coverlet over her, for she was cold, crossed her hands on the ornament, pressing it to her, and cried, and fell asleep.

That same afternoon Hugh returned from Bradford; the mill was near the station, so he went straight to it, and entered the office, where he found his uncle busy, with his back to him, writing.

"Here are letters to write; be sharp!" said Mr Arkwright, without looking up, thrusting some memoranda towards him.

Hugh brushed them up and went towards his desk.

"Uncle," he said suddenly, "who has been here? The desk is wet; it looks as if tears had dribbled over it."

"Annis Greenwell has been there," answered Mr Arkwright, still bending over his correspondence.

Hugh glanced at his uncle, and seeing that he was not observing, put his hand into his bosom, and drew forth a crimson handkerchief, wherewith he tenderly wiped up the drops, tenderly as if he had wiped them from the glistening cheek of his poor little girl. Then he replaced the kerchief near his heart and leaning over the stained board, he said to himself: "She has consecrated this place and it is holy ground henceforth."

Chapter Twenty

Mrs Rhodes had observed Annis enter and run upstaurs. Supposing her to be unwell with headache or some trifling malady, and being very busy herself, she did not trouble herself about her till it drew near to six o' clock, when, her work being over, she went in search of the girl and found her asleep on the bed.

Mrs Rhodes proceeded to arouse her, and bid her come and have her tea. Annis opened her dim eyes as consciousness returned, and with her hand on the brooch, answered that she would be ready directly. Then she washed her face, feeling refreshed by her nap, put off her working–clothes and descended the stairs.

"You look badly," said Mrs Rhodes. "Take a sup o' tea; maybe it'll bring you round a bit, it does me mostly when I'm out o' sorts."

"I don't think it'll mend me," answered Annis.

"Eh, lass," the woman said, with a sly look, "there's somebody wants to see thee this neet; he's bid me tell thee to meet him i' t' Sandy–pit Lane, at half–past eight o'clock."

Annis's face kindled, she looked up at Mrs Rhodes and saw a twinkle in her eye.

"Is't truth? Tha'rt none boune to deceive me?"

"Nay, what should I be deceiving thee for? It's truth what I said."

She spoke sharply, knowing that though her words were true, they conveyed a wrong impression to the girl; who supposed Mrs Rhodes referred to a person very different from the man–monkey.

For the next two hours the colour shone brightly in the girl's cheeks. She thought that Hugh had been to the house and left the message for her, and now she was to see him for the last time and bid him farewell. It would break her heart to part with him, but there was pleasure in the prospect of seeing him once again, and hearing him tell her how precious she was to him, and how dearly he loved her. The little heart was warm within.

179

A while before it had been as a stone. She put from her the thought that she was to be separated from him forever, and yielded, for the little while that remained, to the pleasing prospect of being once more by his side.

When Martha came in, her mother, suspecting that Annis would want to take her friend with her, sent Martha off on an errand which would prevent her accompanying Annis.

At ten minutes past eight the girl fastened her silk kerchief round her neck with the brooch Hugh had given her, put on her black gown and a black bonnet, took an umbrella, as the night was cloudy and there might be rain, and started for the lane.

The moon was up, but it cast a dim watery glimmer over the country, making the black outline of the hills and moor-tops distinct against the white curdy vapours. Occasionally a silver pencil of light pierced the veil, and traced a line of glaring white along the slopes of the fells, catching Stoodley Pike, diving into one of the cross vales, then climbing a spur of Blackstone Edge, illuming the gaunt ridge of Tom Tittermans, turning the dingy stream of the Calder into a flood of liquid silver, as it leaped upon it, then running away over Black Nab and vanishing. The furze, or whin, as Yorkshire people call it, was alight on the Nab. It had been fired during the day, and the hillside was starred with winking sparks, whilst near the top the dry, prickly growth was flaming and dusky figures were visible moving about the fires, running here and there, urging the conflagration onward, leading it from one whin-clump to another and rejoicing when the flame roared up from a dense mass of dry shrubs.

The rush of the water over the weir was audible, swelling into distinctness on the wind, and fading into a murmur as it died away. Over Halifax the clouds reflected the illuminated streets, ruddy on their under surfaces, pallid towards the moon above. To the north-east, where there were ironworks, over the hill, the clouds glared in throbs, pulsating into fire and falling back into gloom.

Annis, as she stole along the lane leading to the fork whence branched off the way to the sandpit and the other by Mr Arkwright's house to the village of Askroyd, passed some solitary pairs of lovers talking, and heard one girl say to her sweetheart: "Si' there, lad, yond's that lass as Hugh Arkwright's followin'. I reckon she's boune to meet him now."

"Eh!" said another, addressing Annis with a laugh, "tha'rt i' grand fettle toneet!"

A little out of the town, however, there was no-one. Annis reached the point where the two lanes diverged, and with beating heart turned down that leading to her old home, a lane which was called after the sandpit in which her mother's cottage had stood. Here the hedges were high and shut out the prospect towards the valley, and trees hung overhead, so that the way was exceedingly dark. It had lately been stoned for some distance, and it was very unpleasant walking over the slag which had been used for the purpose. Large cakes of vitrified material, the refuse of the iron furnaces, are employed through the neighbourhood for the mending of highways and parish roads, to the great detriment of boots and shoes, till the glassy fragments are resolved into dust, which becomes very disagreeable in windy weather, for then eyes, nostrils, ears and mouth are filled with tiny vitreous particles, causing acute pain.

In walking over the fresh-metalled way, Annis's footsteps were audible as she dislodged some stones, and stumbled on others. She was glad when she had reached the unstoned path, a hundred yards from the entrance of the lane.

It was there that she saw someone awaiting her. When she caught sight of the figure her feet moved more nimbly and in a moment she was by him.

"Oh, Hugh!"

"That ain't my name," said the voice of the man-monkey. "So you little roguish kitling, you're come to me!"

She started back in terror. He put his hand out to her, but she drew away.

"Didn't you expect to see me here, eh?" he asked. "Didn't yer mother — nay, but whoo ain't your mother nither — didn't whoo tell thee I were here awaitin' for thee?"

"Oh, no, no! I thowt 't were someone else," moaned Annis.

"Eh! you did, did you? I wi'nt do as well as another, happen. You don't fancy me, eh? Now, lass, bide still. I've a deal I want to say to thee. Bide still, I say, or I'll ma' thee!"

She stepped backward, but remained paralysed with terror as

he waved his long arm over her, and the black hand smote across the moon, casting a shadow on her face.

"Let me go — oh, Mr Grover, please let me go!" she pleaded.

"I reckon I'll do nowt o' th' sort," answered the man-monkey, with a loud gulping laugh. "Come along th' lane wi' me."

"No, no!" she said, agonised with fear. "Oh, Mr Grover, please say what you have to say and let me go home."

"So you cam' out to meet another, eh? And who may he be?" She would not answer.

"You've yer sweetheart, I reckon. Lasses a'most a'ways has if they can get 'em. Times they has three or four if they be good-lookin' as thou art. Hast thou got more nor one, eh?"

Annis stood quailing before him, fascinated by his glaring eyes and wild gestures. In the moonlight, which for a while broke over the lane, his horrible malformation became doubly frightful. The short bowed legs, the long body and lengthy arms ever in violent motion, cast a shadow on the ground that fearfully caricatured what was actually monstrous. Every now and then the man's face, with the flat nose, huge jowl, protruding eyebrows and retreating forehead, became vividly distinct in the moonlight.

"Look you here, lass," continued the man-monkey, "I'm just goin' to ax you to put your horses along wi' mine. What d'yer say to that, yer minx?" and he chucked her under the chin. She recoiled from him with curdling blood; he did not, or would not, notice the repugnance expressed by her moon-illumined countenance, but went on: "Yer gigglin' kitling! I think we'd do grand togither. Ya sees I'm doin' nicely i' my trade o' th' Gospel. Th' Lord blesses me and I'm middlin' off for brass. Si' there, lass!" He drew a handful of silver from his pocket, and poured it from one palm to the other, letting it glitter and tinkle before her. "I get on famous. Ya can ha' bonnets and feathers and crinolines, and owt tha' likes, if tha'lt come wi' me. Happen tha might turn out a rare good preacher, too, byme-by, an' that 'ud be a new sensation. Eh! lass, but it's a grand life going about frae place to place an' getting a bellyfu' whereiver one goes, and given th' best o' all. I've tried a many trades, but I fancies preachin' best. It brings in a vast o' brass, and there's a deal o' pleasure in it. For thou sees it don't matter a damn what one does when a chap is justified by faith. Come, lass, tha'lt be mine, I know tha wilt. Glory be! I said so"; and he stooped over her to kiss her.

With a feeble cry she beat him off with her umbrella. "Keep back!" she said. "Don't touch me!"

"Nay!" laughed he, "tha'lt know better nor say that to me. Do'st thae know who I am? I a'most known ower Yarkshire and all th' world. Eh! I'm a famous man; I'm a man mony a lass 'ud gie her lugs to be able to call her aine, or mebbe to ha' a smack o' th' lips frae. Lass! iverybody's heard o' Richard Grover, th' converted man–monkey, as went i' th' caravans, and wor showed off as a live gorilla frae th' wilds o' Africa. I used to eat rats afore th' folk — rats as wor wick[1]. I napped off their heads and I rived th' skin off, and I ate 'em rair[2]. I'm varry sure tha'll none say tha wi'nt come along wi' me and be glorified and justified."

Annis suddenly turned and fled.

"Heigh!" roared the man–monkey, leaping baboonlike after her, and catching her by the shoulders with his great hands. "That wi'nt do, nohow. What do'st mean, eh?"

A wild bitter cry of "Hugh!" escaped the poor girl's lips. It rang out in the still night with piercing distinctness, and was caught and flung back in a lower tone by the wood up the glen.

"I'll stop that," growled Richard, whose blood began to rise. "Run if thou durst."

He let her go cautiously and put his hand in his pocket. In a moment she started forward again. At once a handkerchief flapped in the wind, was whisked round her throat and twisted by a huge hand with violence at the back of her neck.

At the next instant the arms of the man–monkey were wrenched away, a huge black shade fell over the road.

"Run, run!" bellowed a thrilling bass voice.

Annis was free; without turning to look who had liberated her, she ran, tripping and falling and picking herself up again, and running further till she had cleared the lane, and was in the

[1]alive

[2]raw

183

road, flying home.

Grover was in the hands of one mightier than himself, who held him pinioned, with his arms behind his back till the sound of the girl's feet had died away in the distance. Then the man-monkey felt himself swung round, and grasped on the shoulders, and shaken furiously, and then steadied. He looked up terrified in the face of him who held him.

"Earnshaw!"

"Dick!"

The man-monkey cowered before the black glowing eyes which were fixed on him — cowered, bending and quaking as though palsied, with livid face, and lifted deprecating hands, and knees that failed to sustain him.

"Dick," said the bass voice in its deepest tones, "I have you now. You d----d sneaking villain that you are, skulking hypocrite that you are! I have you at last!"

"Joe! oh, Joe! do nowt to me!" gasped the writhing, quivering wretch. "It warn't me. I swear it warn't."

"It was you, you villain. I know it was you. Look at your work!" The watchman turned himself about that the moon might glare over his maimed features. "Look at your work!" he roared, dragging Grover up from the ground on which he had sunk in a great bony straggling heap. "Up with you! Look, look, look!" and then cast him on his feet and shook him again, and flung him to the ground and picked him up again, and laughed and jabbered and growled.

All at once a dense cloud, heavy with rain, swept across the disc of the moon and a blackness of great darkness fell upon the lane.

"Joe," moaned the horrified preacher, "let me alone. You are mad!"

"Mad!" answered the other. "And who was it drove me mad, eh? Answer me that. Who ruined the happiness of a quiet diligent man and shattered for ever his hopes in this world, and maybe in another? Who would not let another work steadily when himself was idle? Who half-murdered another better than himself and is unpunished, eh? I will tell you this, Grover: I have waited and prayed for the chance of meeting you, as I meet you now. I have waited and prayed, knowing that the time would come when you and I should stand face to face and I should be able to pay you for the wrongs I have received of you."

A groan from Richard.

"Ay! groan if you like, it's many thousand groans you've cost me."

"Joe, spare me for mercy's sake!"

"Did you spare me? Do you remember that case, the broken glass, the rusty nails, the powder, the vitriol? Do you think there was mercy in that? And now this night, were you ready to spare one poor little girl a moment since? I tell you, if I'd been inclined to show mercy and to spare, a while ago, I've no thought of doing either now that I have caught you at your villainies again. Look there!" he thrust the man-monkey towards a heap of large prongs and blocks of vitreous slag at the side of the road, waiting to be broken up and strewn.

"Can you make out that? That is to be your bed. A nice bed that. How do you like the thought of sleeping there? I might have done something less, but you've put the sum and crown to your wickedness by touching *her*." Again, and furiously, he shook the wretch.

"Remember the case! Remember the vitriol — and the nails!" Suddenly he heaved Grover above his head, and held him there, writhing like a hideous spider, then he cast him with all his force on the snags of dross.

Martha was returning from the errand on which she had been sent, when she happened to meet a girl with whom she was acquainted.

"Eh, Martha, where art t' boune to?"

"I'm boune home, lass, as fast as I can."

"Thou'st not been there wi' Annis."

"Nay, I've been after some yeast for Mother, down to Bessy Fawcett."

"I met thy Annis, none so varry long sin. I reckon she were after her young man, thou knows."

"You're mista'en, Polly."

"Nay, I'm not; she were i' grand fettle, wi' all her Sunday

185

clothes on. She were going along t' road to Askroyd."

"Art thou sure?"

"I'm very sure, there was Ellen Smith saw her too."

"It's strange, is that," mused Martha. Then, turning to the girl, she said: "Good neet, lass!"

"Good neet to thee."

Then Martha went on. She was vexed to think that Annis had gone off without telling her, and that by letting herself be seen on the way to Hugh's house, she should give additional cause of scandal.

"I'll go after her," said Martha, striking up by a ginnel[3], into the Askroyd road. She found it deserted as far as the diverging roads. She went up the road to the Arkwrights' cottage, but saw no signs of her cousin. Then she returned to the fork, supposing that she should find her with Hugh walking in the old familiar Sandy-pit Lane.

She picked her way, by the moonlight, as well as possible over the stones, stumbling where the trees cast their pitch-black shadows, looking anxiously before her for her friend. She stood still and listened, without hearing any sound.

"I'll go no further," she said; "she cannot be here." Then, however, she changed her mind. "Nay, I'll just go to t' turning."

And at the turning she saw something straggling across the road. Her heart ceased beating.

"Who's there?" she asked in a shrill tone.

There was no answer.

"It's a man, I'm sure," she said. "Mebbe he's druffen."

What she saw was two long arms stretched out in the glittering moonlight, and two huge hands, which had grabbled at the soil, but stiffened in the act; less distinctly, because the shadow of a tree fell there, did she make out a heap like a human body, to which the arms belonged, and a drooping head on the pile of iron dross.

Timidly, with bated breath, she stole up to it. Then she distinguished a pair of short legs, one extended at full length, the other with the knee up and the foot on a large glazed block.

[3]narrow path between walls

She could see the white line of the stocking between the trousers and the boots. Creeping further, she saw the head slung back over a rib of stone, the eyes and mouth wide open, the face inverted as she looked down on it.

She stooped, with the pulses in her temples throbbing violently and her breath coming by jerks.

"It is Richard Grover," she said to herself. Then aloud, "Mr Grover!"

There was no answer.

"Mr Grover!" Still no answer.

Then she touched the head, and it swung in a manner strange to her. She put her hand to it to lift it, but was frightened and let go, it felt so heavy, and it dropped back like lead.

She fled up the lane, ran into the road, paused one moment at the junction and turning towards Askroyd, made the best of her way to the house of her employer, the nearest human habitation.

She rang the front door bell violently, and stood trembling till the door was opened. Hugh, and his uncle and aunt, and Mr and Mrs Jumbold, who were spending the evening with the Arkwrights, stood in the passage. They had rushed out to see what was the matter; a violent ring at the bell being a rare occurrence there at night, unless there was anything the matter at the mill.

"What is it?" asked Mr Arkwright anxiously.

"Oh, sir!" cried Martha, panting for breath; "oh, sir, come quick! there's a dead man i' t' lane." She waited for breath. "I think it's Richard Grover, sir!" She paused again. "I fancy his neck's broken."

Yes, the man-monkey lay straggling over the vitreous prongs and hummocks, and over the road, with his neck snapped, and from his coat-pocket protruded the heading of a tract, legible in the moonlight: —

"JUSTIFIED BY FAITH ONLY."

Book Two

Flame

Mr Furness had been thirty years vicar of Sowden. He was now an old man, with hair nearly white. A small, slender man with a bright face, and a calmness of manner which spoke of peace within. He was unmarried; lived in an old-fashioned vicarage on the south side of the church, in the bright sun, with the door opening on the churchyard. The house was partly of stone, partly of brick, and destitute of the slightest architectural ornament. His predecessor had added to the original stone vicarage a red-brick block of rooms, and Mr Furness had thrown out in addition a long room for parish business, class, and choir meetings. The garden was a grass-plot, the grass exceedingly coarse and wiry, and the flowerbeds empty of all but perennials. In it was a greenhouse containing vines, but the grapes seldom found their way to the vicar's table, being generally distributed among the sick poor. When Mr Furness came to the parish, thirty years ago, there was no church-school; the church was in a ruinous condition, unwarmed, and deserted except of a few old people; dissent was flourishing, and Sowden was in the condition of a manufacturing place in which is no element of religion to season the lump.

The vicar was a man of good family, and had inherited valuable paintings and furniture. He sent furniture and paintings to the auctioneer, and with the money thus raised, built his schools. Such furniture as was absolutely necessary he reserved, and family portraits he retained; the latter adorned his bedroom, the former was scantily spread over the whole house. Two rooms he occupied himself, two rooms he surrendered to the curate, and one to the schoolmaster, till a dwelling for the latter could be built.

The value of the living of Sowden was three hundred. One hundred went to the two curates, fifty was spent on the church and the poor, and one hundred and fifty the vicar reserved for the maintenance of his house and his own requirements.

The services in the church were made more frequent and more attractive, not without the bitterest opposition. The dissenters, finding the Church becoming a living spiritual agency, exerted their utmost endeavours to oppose the vicar in everything he undertook, and as the manufacturers and men of means in Sowden were all of the Methodist persuasion, he had to fight his battles single-handed, without money, in the face of odds which would have made most hearts fail. But he held on through contumely, slander, and poverty. Then came the great battle of the pews. Mr Furness was convinced that the only chance of getting the Church to be regarded as a home by the people was to throw it completely open to rich and poor. The battle was fought, when a faculty was applied for, by a leading dissenter of fortune in the place, who claimed a pew in the parish church which he never occupied, but kept systematically locked. The legal expenses were great. Mr Furness sold all his family silver and a cabinet of coins, to pay his lawyer. He gained the day, and from the moment that the parish church was thrown open to all, the Church went forward conquering opposition and establishing herself in the hearts of the people.

The re-pewing was not a work of a day. The forks and spoons and coins had gone into the pockets of the solicitors, and Mr Furness rightly judged that the rest of the work was for the people themselves to do, and that they would execute it in proportion to their appreciation of the advantage derived from a free Church. The re-pewing was carried out in this manner.

The schools had been in operation many years before this new move was made; and in them had been educated the present generation of workers in the numerous mills of Sowden. It is the custom of travellers when giving orders at any house, to tip the clerk and other officials, not unhandsomely. Also, when visitors see over a manufactory, the overlooker receives half a crown or five shillings. For some years a number of these clerks and overlookers, instead of appropriating this money to themselves, laid it aside for the re-pewing of the church, and the sum thus realised was so considerable that it paid in great measure for the execution of the new work.

Sowden parsonage was what a parsonage ought to be, and what one rarely is — a house open to all. No parishioner thought of ringing at the front door, but walked into the passage and tapped at the door of the vicar or his curates, according as he wished to see the one or the other. If they were engaged, the visitor sat in the hall till the clergyman was disengaged. Of an evening it was not by any means exceptional to see all the chairs in the entrance passage occupied by millgirls; some in their shawls, others "fettled up a bit" and clerks and men who had worked all day in cloth manufactories, sitting or standing in some numbers, till they were admitted in turn to the vicar or his curates.

Among the mill-people there were religious societies formed, the vicar being chaplain to that of the men, and the senior curate to that of the women; these societies met once a month, or oftener, for discussion of religious topics of the day, and for prayer. They were subject to rules for the government of the lives of the members, and once a year assembled for a service and sermon special to them in the church, and then for a picnic among the hills. A perfect *entente cordiale* existed between the priest and his people. The former was careful not to interfere in other than spiritual matters; he exhibited his confidence in his flock, did not ask for deference and exact homage, and they gave him deference, homage, confidence, love and devotion, in good measure, pressed down and running over; they flew to him in doubt and difficulty, following his advice, submitting with alacrity to his wishes, trusting him with confidence, and loving him with their whole hearts.

It is impossible to calculate the amount of good effected by this man. He was not what is generally called a powerful preacher; if he had been, he would have probably trusted to the pulpit rather than the closet. Sermons exert far less influence than people suppose, however eloquent the preacher, and excellent the discourse. Sermons are listened to as institute lectures are listened to, to while away a half-hour, which would otherwise be spent in ennui. What tells on the moral and spiritual character of the people is the private intercourse between the pastor and his flock, and that is a means for good not to be over-estimated.

The vicar of Sowden had it not in his power to purchase the poor. It is supposed by some that the Church can only hold her own by bribery and corruption; and that the parish priest is of necessity a relieving officer. Pastoral visits cost many clergy a shilling a cottage, and begin with prayer, which is patiently endured by the poor person in expectation of the tip which follows the concluding amen. This course demoralises the people, for to receive a charity self-respect has to be sacrificed. Mr Furness was exceedingly cautious how he gave, and to whom he gave, charity. He rarely was the dispenser, he generally made some of the laity attend to the bodily necessities of the poor, whilst he confined himself to their spiritual requirements. Where he was satisfied that there was real want, he communicated the fact to his district visitors and well-to-do parishioners. The result of this treatment was that the poor appeared to him in their true colours, and that the detestable hypocrisy which is encouraged all over England among the needy was discountenanced and stifled in the birth. It may be questioned whether the clergy of the Church of England are not, with the best possible intentions, and with the kindest hearts, doing an irreparable damage to the moral character of that class which is daily assuming greater power in the land, by their indiscriminate charity. Among the poor, that only is valued which costs them trouble and money. The sun, the moon, the stars, they do not charge for shining, they do not cost an hour's toil to make them burn; but oh for the pig! dear object of creation, dearer than all the host of heaven, exalted above stars and moon and sun. Sweet pig! cherished pig! Hast thou not consumed many stone of bran to fatten thee! Hast thou not cost much labour in cleaning out thy sty! Perish sun, moon and stars; God save the pig! Mr Furness never forgot a bit of advice given him by a rough, long-headed operative, thirty years ago, when he first came into the parish: "I tell thee, if thou'rt boun to mak' folks chu'ch, thou mun mak' em pay for 't, and thou mum mak' em work for 't."

And, carried out on this principle, there was not in the end a more popular, active and energising power in the district than the parish church. Savings-bank, night-schools, choir, committees for this and societies for that, kept the young men in constant employ; the girls washed and cleaned the church, worked for bazaars, taught in night and Sunday-schools, made decorations and were never without something to do, never expecting the least remuneration, and generally working at cost of time, labour and money to themselves. And these young people were, for the most part, factory-hands.

Annis, when she fled from the man-monkey, instead of returning to Mrs Rhodes, went straight to the parsonage. She

194

was hurt at the trick which had been played upon her; the deception she could not forgive, certainly not forget. If she had been resolved before to leave the place, she was now determined to leave it at once. Her only relative there had behaved to her with treachery, and she could no longer trust her. The poor girl was so troubled and uncertain how to act that she went where she knew she would meet sympathy, advice and support. She opened the vicarage door, passed through the gas–lit hall, and tapped at the vicar's room door.

"Come in."

Annis walked in. Whoever entered. at whatever time, found Mr Furness writing letters, with his spectacles on his nose, a cabinet of correspondence answered and unanswered before him, a clock with a noisy tick and a harsh tingle at the hour, above his head, and surplice and stole on a peg beneath it.

"Well, Annis, my child," he said, looking up and signing a letter. "Sit down there, near the fire. Let me seal up and direct this envelope, and I shall be at your service."

One of the vicar's remaining luxuries was a bunch of seals which had belonged to his father, and, perhaps, his grandfather. They were engraved gems of antique workmanship, set in gold; one of them bore his arms, and with that he generally impressed his wax, as more appropriate than a Venus or a Cupid or a Psyche.

"Now then," he said, jumping up, twisting his chair round to the fire and reseating himself. He was a gentleman of the old school, courtly and polite in his manners, perfectly able to be familiar and agreeable to anyone, without in the slightest degree losing his dignity. When he went out, he wore a neat black dresscoat and a very good hat; when he sat at home, he was in his cassock, — partly, no doubt, to save his coat–sleeves.

"Now, Annis," he said with a smile, "I have been wanting to see you for a few days, but you did not pop in; you have had other things to think of, poor little heart!"

"Please, sir," Annis said, simply, "I wish to speak to you very much."

"Well, what about? You have caught me quite disengaged."

"You've heard about — " she hesitated.

"Yes, I have heard about your love affair, if you mean that." Annis nodded.

"And you want my advice as to what had better be done?"

"Oh, Mr Furness! I'm boune to leave."

"What! To go away from Sowden?"

"Yes, sir."

"I think that is decidedly the best thing you can do. When are you going?"

"Please, sir, I don't know. I'd like to go soon."

"The sooner the better. Now, tell me. Have you made up your mind to give up Hugh?"

Annis's fingers worked uneasily at the creases of her gown: she said, after a while, very low, "I must try."

"Yes, you must try. As things are at present, you cannot be Hugh's wife. That is quite impossible. I have seen Hugh, and have had a talk with him."

Annis looked up sharply at the old man's face. Her lips quivered and the light flickered in her eyes, as she asked faintly: "Did he say he would give me up?"

"No, Annis, I am bound to say that he did not. But what can he do? He is dependent on his uncle, who will cast him adrift if he marries you, and if you were his you would not be able to assume the position which would be required of you. Annis, you would drag him down, and that you must have courage not to do."

"I cannot forget him."

"I do not suppose you can, but you may learn to be happy, with only the remembrance of the past. Have you never loved anyone else before Hugh?"

"No, no, none; and I can love no other."

"Sometimes," said the vicar, "these sudden and strange affections are only the result of fancy, last for a little while, and then fade away. Sometimes they come of God, and then they last. If you and Hugh are parted for a few years, you will both be able to realise whether the love you now feel for one another be fancy or real, lasting union of heart. If it is fleeting, you and he will always be thankful that you were saved from acting in a headstrong manner, on passion, a course which would have embittered after life."

"Oh, please, Mr Furness," she said, sadly and slowly, "I think my life about like to be as bitter as gall, with never seeing him no more. It is just like having to live in a cellar, and never get a peep o' sun, or be in prison, and never have no hope of being free."

"There is no reason why you should not have some hope," the vicar said kindly and gravely. Annis looked in his face and brightened. "You may be sure, my little girl, that this will lead to good."

"That's what Mother said of everything that happened."

"Leave Sowden, and do your best to make yourself worthy of Hugh, — stay, worthy is not the right expression, that I hope and believe you are already, but I mean fit, — fit, that is, to be his companion. Go and improve yourself, get instruction, allow your mind to be developed, your habits to be moulded; do not set Hugh ever before you as the aim and object of your life, because if you do, he may disappoint you and destroy your happiness forever; but let yourself be educated and trained, trusting the future entirely in God's hands. If, in after years, Hugh finds you a meet companion for himself, if his affection for you has lasted unimpaired, and your heart has remained true to him, then, never fear, God will bring you together again. But if, after a while, he changes his mind, and you cease to care for him, no harm is done, education is never thrown away."

Annis was trembling with eagerness and delight. A future was open to her, and hope revived. "Oh, Mr Furness! where can I go? I was thinking of seeking my mother's brother, at Keighley; he's a farmer."

"No, Annis, you must not go there. Hugh would find you out directly. You must go where he will not know of you. You must be a brave, good, true little girl, as I am sure you are, and keep quite away from him, lest you ruin his prospects with his uncle."

"I'd die, rather than that."

"Well, you must promise me to hold no communication with anyone here till I give you leave, and not to tell anyone here where you are."

"Yes, sir, I will promise."

"Then you shall go to my sister at York; sit still, and I will give you a note."

He twisted his chair round to the table again, and wrote a letter to Miss Furness.

I send you a nice little girl, an orphan, to take care of, instruct, clothe, feed and bring up in her duty to God and man. In return, she will wait on Mother and you, and make herself generally useful. A young gentleman here, of education and good character, has lost his head to her, and I think the poor little body has lost head and heart to him in return. Of course I must do what I can to stop this, or rather, direct it. Bessie, you see to her. If they forget one another, well and good. If God has joined them in heaven, man must not put them asunder, and your kind offices to the girl will have smoothed the way to the final pleasant settlement. Give dear Mother my love, etc.

"Here is the note, Annis," he said, when he had directed it; "show it to no-one in Sowden, lest it should be known whither you are going."

"When am I to go, sir?"

"As soon as you possibly can."

"And I may think of Hugh?"

"I do not say that, Annis. What I will say, is this. Make the most of those opportunities which are afforded you in improving your mind, manners, speech, and so on. Take my sister as a model, and endeavour to form yourself on her type; she is a good woman and a perfect lady. Whatever may happen, it can never have been amiss that you should have copied a good exemplar. Leave the future entirely in God's hands. Trust Him. If He thinks best that you and Hugh should see one another no more, it will be for your mutual advantage; but if He wills that you should make one another happy, He will find means of bringing you together again."

There was a hasty rap at the door. "Come in."

And Hugh entered the room. The moment he saw Annis, he sprang towards her and caught her hands in his, and looked into the bright, dazzling, uplifted eyes, perfectly oblivious of his purpose in entering the vicarage. He saw neither Mr Furness nor his room; he saw Annis alone, and in that moment also the girl's soul leaped up into her eyes, filling them with brightness, like the sudden illumination of dark windows.

The vicar looked at them, gravely smiling. "Well, Mr Hugh

Arkwright," he said.

"I really beg your pardon, sir," the young man answered, starting and letting go one of Annis's hands, but keeping firm hold of the other.

"Nay, no pardon is needed," said Mr Furness. "It is very well that you are here to take leave of Annis. She is going away from you and you will not see her again for years."

Hugh's countenance saddened; he pressed the little hand he held and looked down at the girl by his side.

"Yes, Hugh," the vicar continued. "And now listen to what I am going to say. The love of two hearts for one another is a very sacred and solemn thing. It is enduring, true, patient; it suffereth long and is kind; it doth not behave itself unseemly, seeketh not its own, is not easily provoked, thinketh no evil, beareth all things, believeth all things, hopeth all things, endureth all things and never faileth. It is an earthly reflection of that Divine charity of which the apostle speaks. But there is a false love which is often mistaken for that which is true — a love which is but for a while, growing up but having no root an no depth of soil, and therefore withering speedily away. If you two love one another really, then God forbid that you should not be united according to His law. But this love must be proved. When you are far removed from one another, when you are tempted and tried, you will be able to ascertain for your own selves whether you have the all-bearing, all-believing, all-hoping, all-enduring, never-failing love, or only the fictitious passion which lasts but for a day. Take now that step which you know is right. It is right for you, Hugh, to stick to your business. It is right for you, Annis, to go away from Sowden. And it is right for you both to leave the future entirely in the hands of God."

Then he left the room for ten minutes.

For the greater part of the while neither spoke. Perhaps their hearts were too full, perhaps in mutual love there is an internal voice which speaks and answers, without requiring the lips to form the words. But at last Hugh said, holding the little head to his shoulder, and with his voice scarce raised above a whisper: "What letter is that in your hand, Annis?"

"It is one for the place to which I am going, dear."

"Put it in your pocket, lest I see the address."

She looked up at him and said: "If you were to see it you would not follow me, I know."

"No, Annis, I would not."

Then she put her arms round his neck and kissed him.

Mr Furness came in. "Well, Hugh," said the vicar, "what did you come here to see me about? You had not tracked this poor lassie down, I hope?"

"No, sir, I came to tell you of a startling bit of news; and in the excitement of seeing my little girl here, I quite forgot it; but it is no matter, nothing could be done."

"What is it, Hugh?"

"That man—monkey fellow —"

Annis started.

"That man—monkey who has been preaching here, you know, has been found dead in the lane leading to the sandpit; his neck is broken."

"Good heaven!"

Annis turned white and faint; her large eyes gleamed with horror on Hugh's face as he told the vicar the circumstances.

"He was found lying on a heap of slag. Martha Rhodes was the one to discover him. He was still warm when we moved him to our house, where he is now lying; but life is quite extinct."

"How did this happen?"

"I am sure I don't know," answered Hugh. "Probably the man was drunk and tumbled over the heap in the dark: those piles of sharp glassy fragments are awkward things to light on, or he may have been getting over the hedge and jumped into the road, as he thought, and tripped upon the blocks."

"Then there is no suspicion of foul play?"

"I should think not; but, you see, the thing has only just happened. There can be no—one in the place who bore sufficient ill-will to the wretched creature to kill him, unless it were you, vicar."

Mr Furness smiled. "As to that, I can provide an alibi; for Annis here has been with me." Then, more seriously, "No, it must have been an accident."

"I came to tell you," said Hugh, "as I thought you might like to know, though, as the man is dead, nothing can be done." Then, turning to Annis, he said, "You look frightened."

She shuddered and averted her white face. She shrank from

her thoughts. She remembered Joe Earnshaw catching the man in his powerful grasp, and shouting to her to run. Had there been a struggle between these two men, and had it ended in the death of her tormentor? Probably Richard Grover had been killed unintentionally; but it must have been in the watchman's attempt to save her that the man-monkey had been killed. Annis knew of no motive which could have impelled Earnshaw to commit murder. The watchman had saved her; she felt it was her duty to screen him by keeping silence.

"Please, sir," said Annis to the vicar, "I think I must be going."

"Indeed, yes, it is getting late," he answered.

Hugh stepped forward and said, "I may see her home, as it is to be the last time for some years, may I not?"

Mr Furness hesitated. On consideration he remembered that it was not many yards to the Rhodes' house, and that Annis was evidently frightened by the account of the death of Grover, so he said, "Yes, and then come back to me."

"Very well, sir"; and they went out.

When Annis was at the parsonage door she stopped, looked up at Hugh timidly and said, "Is there a train Normanton way tonight?"

"Yes, at five minutes to ten."

"I will go by it."

"What!"

"Hugh, dear, I will not go back to the Rhodes' no more. I'll go away at once."

"Nonsense; stay the night at your cousin's and go tomorrow."

"I will go tonight, it is better," she said. Then, pleadingly, "Will you come to the station with me, and see me off?"

"Yes, that I will; but —"

"Nay, I'm set on it. Now, Hugh, when I'm off, just go to the parsonage and tell Mr Furness, and then he'll let Mrs Rhodes know, or they'll be seeking me."

"Very well."

He saw her to the station, but did not volunteer to take her ticket for her; and she left without his knowing for what station she was booked. She was on her way to York, whilst he was toiling sadly up the hill towards Sowden.

Suddenly, a hand was laid on his shoulder. He turned round

and saw a dark figure with a slouched billycock and a comforter over his chin. The road was lighted at long intervals by gaslamps. He could distinguish sufficient of the man by the light from the nearest lamp to feel convinced that the figure was that of Earnshaw.

"What do you want?" he asked.

"Where is she sent to?"

"Who are you speaking of?"

The watchman stamped, shook the lanthorn in his hand violently and growled furiously: "You know. Where have you sent her to? How long before she comes back?"

Hugh doubted what to answer.

"Do you think I did not see you?" said the watchman. "Eh, I watched you on the platform putting her into the carriage. Where have you sent her to?"

"I cannot tell."

"When will she be back?"

"Perhaps never."

A growl like that of a wild beast issued from the throat of Earnshaw. "Answer! When is she coming back?"

"I tell you, Joe," Hugh replied firmly, "she is not coming back at all; she has left Sowden till" — he raised himself — "till I bring her here as my wife."

The great frame of the watchman rocked with passion.

"Where have you sent her to?"

"Whither she is gone I do not know, nor will anyone in Sowden know, excepting one."

"Yourself?"

"No, not myself."

"It's a d----d lie."

Hugh raised his hand to strike, but instantly lowered it again; he would not add a blow to that fearfully maimed face.

"It is perfectly true," he said, composedly.

"Do you remember," muttered the furious man, and as he spoke bubbles foamed and were spluttered from his lips — "do you remember what I said?"

"I forget," said Hugh, turning away. The watchman caught him by the arms, mumbling and muttering, and crouching as a tiger about to leap on his prey.

"Let me go!" Hugh exclaimed, struggling to release his arms, but struggling in vain. In the tussle the man's hat fell off; and by the lamplight Hugh saw the wild blazing eyes glaring at him, with the ferocity of madness.

"Do you remember?" with a mocking laugh.

Then there burst on his ear a tramp of feet, accompanying a loud and measured strain: —

"Have you not succeeded yet?
Try, try again:
Mercy's door is open set,
Try, try again.
Yours is not a single case,
Others have the same to face;
If you'd gain your proper place,
Try, try again!"

It was the hymn of a Glory Band beating up recruits for Paradise. In a moment Hugh and the watchman were in the midst of a number of men intoxicated with spiritual excitement, pulling at them, screaming in their ears, and dancing around them with frenzied vehemence. Hugh struck out left and right with his fists, fought his way through them, and fled up the hill to Sowden, leaving the disconcerted rout to form line again and rush downhill after the watchman, roaring at the top of their voices: —

"Have you not succeeded yet?
Try, try again:
Mercy's door is open set.
Try, try again!"

Chapter Twenty-Two

Directly that Mr Furness heard of Annis's abrupt departure, he went to the house of John Rhodes and communicated to him the fact, saying that he had found her a situation where she would be comfortable, but deemed it advisable not to let anyone know where this was, lest it should reach Hugh Arkwright's ears. He said that her precipitate departure had somewhat surprised him, but that he hoped to hear of her safe arrival by an early post. John Rhodes was quite satisfied. Mr Arkwright had told him the girl must go elsewhere for a while, and Mrs Rhodes was more than satisfied, for she had been in a condition of confusion and terror ever since she heard of the death of the man–monkey, lest it should transpire that she had sent Annis to meet him in the lane that very night. She was only too well aware that gossips would impute to her evil motives. She was perplexed at Annis's non–return, and in no little trepidation, till Mr Furness came in, and his statement that she had been with him for some while that evening greatly relieved her. Evidently the girl had not been to Sandy–pit Lane at all.

The inquest on the body was held at the tavern whose sign was "The Spotted Dog". It excited unusual interest, and the room was crowded. Martha Rhodes had to give evidence, and this evidence was curious, for, though perfectly true, it led the coroner and jury to an entirely wrong finding.

"What is your name?"

"Martha Rhodes."

"What is your profession?"

"I make up."

"In whose mill?"

"Arkwright's."

"You found the deceased on Friday night, I understand?"

"Ay, I found him."

"Be so good as to narrate the circumstances."

"Why, thou sees, I went down t' lane about half after eight, I reckon, but I'm not very sure, for I didn't notice time partick'ler, and there I found Richard Grover."

204

"I should like to know where you live?"

"I' Kirkgate."

"Then what took you into Sandy-pit Lane at that time of night?"

"That's just nowt to thee."

"Yes, it is. I must trouble you to tell me."

"Weel, I were seeking some 'un."

"The deceased?"

"Nay!" with ineffable scorn. "As if I'd go seek a Ranter parson!"

This exclamation produced laughter through the room and one or two men who knew the girl's strong predilections for Church, clapped and said, "That's Martha all over."

"You have no love for that ilk," said the coroner, who saw which way the wind lay, and was fond of a joke.

Martha looked her answer.

"You are not fond of Ranter parsons, then?" continued the coroner, pressing the point.

"I've seen ower much on 'em," answered Martha. Another general laugh.

"You'd not be sorry to see them all dead?"

"Happen I'd get ower it."

"Perhaps you killed this man," said the coroner, convulsing the whole assembly by this sally.

"If you've done wi' me, I'll be off," Martha observed; "I'm not going to be made game of."

"Order!" shouted the coroner, rapping the table; and silence was produced. "Now, girl, I insist on knowing whom you went to meet, by night, in Sandy-pit Lane."

"I didn't go to meet nobody."

"You said you did."

"Nay, I said I went seeking some 'un."

"Other than the deceased?"

"Ay."

"Of course a sweetheart?"

Martha looked the coroner straight in the face, and said: "Do you think I'd run after a man? They ain't so precious as all that, I reckon."

Laughter and thunders of applause. Martha spoke calmly,

without boldness.

"Silence! Order there!" from the coroner.

"Then it was not a sweetheart?"

"I han't got one."

"Was it a man you were seeking?"

"It was not a man."

"Who was it then?"

"I went seeking my cousin, Annis Greenwell."

"What made you seek her in that lane?"

"Well, I'll tell you," said Martha. "Mother sent me down to owd Bessy Fawcett for a sup o' yeast, and I met Mary Brierly, and she told me she'd seen our Annis taking along t' Askroyd road. I were a bit mazed to think she was there, and I went after her."

"Stay, you went down the lane?"

"Why, thou sees t' road is like a letter Y. There's a long bit o' road as goes into Sowden, then there comes a branch, and one road goes off to Askroyd, and t'other leads down to t' sand–pit. But they call all t' road, as far as to t' fork, and lane that's along by t' right, Askroyd road. And just afore you come to t' branch there's a bit o' a lane runs down t' hill to t' station and milns. That's to t' left hand, afore you turn down Sandy–pit Lane. Weel, I came along t' road, and I went up right hand turning, that's t' Askroyd road, thou knows, and I didn't see her noways, so then I went back, and I ran a bit down t' lane at left hand, that's Sandy–pit Lane, thou sees, and there I fund t' man–monkey."

"Did you see no signs of any other human being?"

"Nay, there were no one there. It were as still as owt."

"And where, then, was your cousin? She must have been on one road or the other."

"You're out there," answered Martha; and here she made a mistake, which led to the wrong finding by the jury. "She hadn't been along neither one nor t' other, for she'd gone down to t' station by t' little way on t' left hand I told thee of."

"What was she going to the station for?"

"She wor goin' by t' train. She'd gotten a situation and wor off that neet. But she'd told me nowt about it, so I didn't know. I knowed she were going, but I didn't know she were boun to flit that neet."

Annis had acted on that mysterious feminine instinct which takes in her sex the place of reason, when she resolved that night on leaving Sowden at once. By so doing she saved Joe Earnshaw. Had she remained, Martha could not have fallen into this mistake; the coroner would have questioned Annis, when he had learned from her cousin that she had been in or about that lane, and then Annis could not have withheld, in cross-examination, the fact that the night—watch had grappled with the man—monkey and that she had left them struggling with one another on the spot where, a few minutes later, the corpse was found.

Mr Jumbold, the surgeon, having viewed and examined the deceased immediately after its removal to the house of Mr Arkwright, was examined, and gave his opinion that the fracture of the spinal cord might have been the result of accident. He believed that the injuries which had been observed on the deceased might have been caused by the deceased falling backwards on the heap. On being asked whether he thought a man ascending the pile of vitreous slag and slipping could break his neck, he replied that it was not only possible but probable, especially if he fell backward instead of forward. The deceased had been found lying on his back. There were wounds and bruises on other portions of his body, but all behind. Mr Jumbold believed these were caused by the fall. The deceased was a heavy man, and a backward fall was always severe, as the arms could not be employed to arrest it. When asked whether he thought the deceased was in liquor at the time of the accident, the surgeon replied that he had no doubt he was so; there was a smell of gin about the mouth when he examined the corpse, and the saliva on the stones bore a faint odour of that spirit. It was ascertained that no suspicion rested on anyone of having borne ill—will against Richard Grover, who was a stranger in the neighbourhood, and not likely to have made enemies. Money was found in his pocket, his watch and chain were undisturbed; so that no theft had been committed.

Finally, a unanimous decision was arrived at, that the death was accidental, which was about as near the truth as are the majority of coroner's findings.

Richard Grover was buried in the chapel graveyard; the occasion was improved, and the man-monkey was canonised, the preacher observing the suitability of the last hymn sung by the departed saint:

"I am coming, I am coming
Unto Zion, unto Zion,
Faster, faster, faster, faster!"

"Indeed," said the eloquent panegyricist, "he went there a deal faster than ever he reckoned he would. Solemn thought! those words — so full of hope, of courage, of assurance — may have been the last —mark me! O Christian brethren! — the very last uttered by lips which were to open again in heaven to sing the song with angels." This is quoted to show how dangerous it is for people to make these sort of rash suppositions.

If these had been the last words of the blessed saint and elect servant, the coincidence would have been curious; but as a fact they were not; for after having sung that song — hymn, we mean — he had asked for gin at the "Peal of Bells" on Askroyd road, and the last words actually spoken by this vessel of glory ere he spread his wings for realms of light were these, the religious tendency of which is unmistakable: "I'm damned!" uttered in the grip of his murderer.

Chapter Twenty-Three

Annis reached York in the small hours of the morning. The sky was beginning to whiten in the east, and the Minster towers to stand out darkly cutting the wan sky. She left the station, and crossed the new iron bridge, supposed to add beauty to the old city, but actually disfiguring it with its coarse and vulgar affectation of Gothic. The streets were deserted. She wandered round the Minster, then sat down on the flight of steps leading to the south transept door, and waited, counting the quarters as they tingled on the tower bell.

Hungry and chilled, she rose at last and strolled along Coney Street. A few sleepy servant-girls appeared at the doors and windows. A policeman stood impatiently waiting the hour of his release from the arduous task of doing nothing; a market-gardener's cart rattled along the pavement.

The Minster clock struck seven, whereupon that of St Sampson's said seven with *empressement*, and that of All Saints added its assurance that seven was the hour: with a flutter St Michael's suggested seven; seven said St Mary's with decision; whereupon St Olave's, St Saviour's and St Cuthbert's spoke together, making such a jingle that it was difficult to discover their opinions.

Now when all the church clocks had said their say, a little tingling clock in a baker's shop added its testimony; that in a neighbouring grocer's was not much behindhand; and the assertion that the hour was seven came in muffled tinks from several areas.

Annis entered a baker's shop, and bought a couple of biscuits, which she ate in the shop; then she looked at the direction on the letter given her by Mr Furness and asked her way. The baker's girl who had served her, good-naturedly accompanied her down the street and pointed out to her the proper turning, giving her at the same time directions only comprehensible by those perfectly familiar with York. After advancing a little way, Annis went astray, but was put right by a newspaper-boy. After a few divergencies from the direct course, she reached the house occupied by Miss Furness, and, as the clocks struck eight, she rapped at the door.

The lady had not as yet left her bedroom, so Annis waited in the little breakfast chamber. There was much therein to arrest her attention and amuse her till Miss Furness appeared. It resembled a museum. A japanned cabinet against the wall was surmounted by a case of humming-birds of the most brilliant colouring; on the chimney-piece were nondescript ornaments in soapstone from Penang; against the wall were suspended Chinese hats and shoes; between the windows was an Esquimaux canoe; on a bracket against the chimney was the most hideous and grotesque idol from a New Zealand paah. Annis had observed in the passage stuffed sunfish, sharks, walrus' teeth, corals, Indian weapons and bottled sea-mice.

Annis had sent Mr Furness's note up to his sister in her room, and a message had come to her to wait in the breakfast apartment and that Miss Bessie would be down in ten minutes. Annis prowled about the room, wondering over the curiosities displayed at every turn, and longing to know all about them. In after-times, when she was settled into the house, they formed an inexhaustible store of interest and delight to her. She had hitherto regarded the glass walking-stick, which her mother had so persistently cherished as the *ne plus ultra* of curiosities, but what was a glass walking-stick to a tomahawk which had scalped living men — to a mandarin who wagged his head, rolled his eyes, and protruded his tongue, and had been made in China — or to a sawfish which could actually sink a vessel with a thrust of its nose!

How had Miss Furness become possessed of all these objects? When quite a child she had formed a childish attachment to a young midshipman in his Majesty's navy. When the midshipman became a lieutenant he visited the family pretty frequently and asked Bessie to be his wife. She was then twenty-one. She was left by her father in charge of her mother, and she refused the sailor. Though she refused him, she loved him truly, tenderly, devotedly. None knew how she had sat hour by hour at her window hoping to see the light-haired, tall, open-faced officer come towards her door. But duty was dearer to Miss Furness than her own wishes, and she sacrificed herself to her sense of duty. Her mother was a sacred charge which she must not neglect.

After a voyage round the world and an absence of three years, one morning the silver poplar — as the lieutenant was called by those who knew him, from his light hair and height — appeared again before Elizabeth Furness, and again did he ask her to be his. She replied that as long as her mother lived, she could not leave her.

"Let her home be with us," pleaded the silver poplar; but Bessie shook her head. She knew that with marriage came other interests and cares, and that her whole attention would not be directed to her mother.

"I will not conceal from you that I love you," she said; "but, William, whilst my mother is on earth, I must devote myself to her comfort alone."

"Well, Bessie," the sailor said, "then we will wait."

Years passed, and he came again, this time as captain, to seek his wife. Elizabeth Furness was still unmarried, still carefully watching and waiting on her mother. There was a whiter silver in the poplar's hair and there was grey in that of Bessie.

"We must wait a little longer," he sighed.

He came again and found her quietly, dutifully, patiently, attending on her mother. Her hair was grey and there were furrows of age on her brow.

Once more the silver poplar came for his Bessie, truly silver now, with glittering white hair and a beautiful old face, full of the light of an honourable, brave and humble spirit; he was an admiral when he came that last time. Bessie was, as of yore, with intense devotion, cherishing Mrs Furness, now in her second childhood, an old woman of eighty. Bessie could not be his yet.

"I will come once more for you and take no refusal then," said the silver poplar, holding her hand as he parted from her. She did not see him again; he died on the blue seas, leaving the loved one of his life his collection of curiosities gathered by him from all parts of the globe, with intention of therewith ornamenting and furnishing his house when Bessie became his wife. Each of these articles had been purchased and laid by with this one object, and now he left them to her, along with his sword and uniform, his quadrant and sextant, and all the savings from his pay laid by for his marriage, the savings of many years of patient waiting, amounting to a considerable sum. Will he keep his promise and come again for his Bessie, when she can no more refuse to accompany him? We cannot tell.

Above the chimneypiece in her bedroom was a little medallion portrait in ivory of the silver poplar, with a high-collared blue coat, and a white waistcoat and fair youthful face with clear skin and pure colour, with blue eyes and a high head covered with very pale hair. It was a portrait of the young lieutenant as he came courting Bessie forty-five years ago. And under the black frame hung a decoration which the admiral had won and worn upon his breast, and bequeathed to her to whom he had been true in life and death, and who had never been other than true to him.

Miss Furness swept into the breakfast room in that soft, cool, noiseless manner belonging to some women; turning the handle quietly without letting it squeak, opening the door without its creaking, having descended the stairs without the banister rattling, and crossing the hall without her footfall sounding. Her entrance was like the breath of cool air wafted into a conservatory when the windows are thrown open. She was dressed in a silvery grey, matching with her hair; on her zone was a little autumnal rosebud of the delicate hue of her cheek. Every movement of Miss Furness was full of ease and grace. Her features were very delicate and refined; she had been a very pretty girl, a handsome woman, and she was beautiful in her old age. It mattered little whether the nose and mouth were, from an artistic point of view, well moulded, for in looking in Bessie's face no one thought of the features, but of the light and beauty of self-sacrifice which had glorified and perfected her. Patient continuance in well-doing and hope deferred and never abandoned, exert a wondrous power in moulding and developing expression in the plainest face, an expression of unearthly beauty, to be discerned spiritually.

Miss Furness was very like her brother, not only in features, but in expression; their features they owed to common parents, their expression to a common schooling. Both had been trained in self-denial, self-devotion and self-sacrifice. The brother had sacrificed his life to his parish, the sister hers to her mother. The best people in the world are least known. Mr Furness was not spoken of out of his own immediate neighbourhood, nor Miss Furness beyond her own family. But there is a roll wherein their names are written, and there will dawn a day when those who have been accounted last shall be first, and the first last.

When Miss Furness entered, she glided up to Annis with a beautiful welcoming smile on her bright face. "My dear," she said, "thank you for coming."

Then she removed Annis's bonnet with her own slender fingers, contemplating her kindly and reassuringly as she did so.

"My dear, you have come very early. When did you leave Sowden?"

"Please, miss, it was nigh eleven last night." Annis spoke with perfect confidence. She felt, the moment she saw Elizabeth Furness, that she was not with a stranger.

"And when did you reach York?"

"About four o'clock this morning. We waited a very long while in Normanton."

"Why, my poor little pet, what have you been about these four hours since the train came in?"

"I have been walking about York, miss! I didn't like to come earlier; I fancied no one would be up."

"And you have had no sleep?"

"Yes, miss, I got a wink in the train."

"Nothing to eat?"

"I bought some biscuits in the baker's shop."

"Come along with me," said Miss Furness. "Come to my room and let me put you to rights and make you comfortable for breakfast. You shall have something to eat, and then you shall go to bed, and not get up till dinnertime."

"Oh, Miss Furness!"

Elizabeth slipped her arm round her and drew her lightly with her out of the room and upstairs. There she made her wash her face and hands, smoothed her hair down with her own comb and brush, dashed a little eau de Cologne over her brow to refresh her; selected a little white rosebud from her nosegay on the toilette table, fastened it with her own fingers by the jet and crystal brooch to the girl's bosom, kissed her, telling her she was

213

charming and looked quite fresh, and then brought her back into the breakfast room.

Annis's childish heart began to overflow, and the tears to form in her eyes.

"Oh, Miss Furness," she said, "may I tell you all?"

"Not now; I know a good deal from my brother's letter. My dear, sit down. I am going to fetch my mother, and then we shall have prayers and breakfast." So saying she slipped away, but put her head in again in a moment, asking, "Would you assist me, Annis? I cannot bring Mrs Furness down without help."

Elizabeth knew that the best way to make a stranger feel comfortable and at home, was to find that person employment.

Of Mrs Furness little need be said. She was, as has already been mentioned, in her second childhood. Second childhood! — old age, the infancy whose maturity is eternity.

She was a white-haired, clear-complexioned old lady, with a smile generally lighting up her face, with a sharp nose, rendered prominent by the absence of cartilage to her nostrils. This made necessary the insertion of small tubes into her nose when she slept, and these tubes were the constant worry of her life. She felt so much greater facility in breathing when these were inserted in her nostrils that she was constantly asking for them, and had to be diverted from wanting them by the ingenuity of her daughter, for the apparatus could only be used occasionally, lest it should fret the skin and produce a sore. Mrs Furness had lost her memory, to a considerable extent; she had not forgotten her son, nor did she forget those who were constantly about her, least of all did these "pipes" as she termed them, drop from the chambers of her reminiscence; but she entirely forgot that she had asked for them ten minutes ago, and had been put off; she forgot the reasons alleged; she forgot whether she had taken her meals, and a quarter of an hour after dinner she would be wondering why the bell did not ring to announce that it was ready. She forgot that she had gone through the religious exercises of the morning ten minutes after their conclusion, and could not be satisfied unless they were recommenced, so that the morning was often spent in a succession of "Psalms and Lessons" for the day.

The constant attendance required by Mrs Furness was excessively trying to Elizabeth, and, of late, her loss of memory had greatly increased the labour, so that it had become necessary for Miss Furness to have someone whom she could trust to relieve her. At present she was with her mother night and day; she fed her twice during the night, and dressed her, read to her and argued the question of the "pipes" throughout the day; cut up her food for her, took her out in a wheeled chair when the weather was fine and remained in with her when it was inclement. If she left her mother for half an hour to do some shopping, or make a call, or go to church, the old lady became restless and exceedingly fretful and cross. The servants did not understand how to manage her, were rough or clumsy, and generally exasperated the aged woman, so as to render it difficult for her daughter to pacify her on her return.

Mr Furness, having been told by his sister that she was in want of an assistant in the charge of attending to his mother, had sent Annis to her to occupy this post, one for which he considered the girl qualified, and one in which she would derive great benefit to herself.

When Miss Furness and Annis went upstairs, they found the old lady impressed with the idea that it was bedtime, and calling out for her daughter to unhook her gown behind.

"My dear mother," said Elizabeth, "you have only just got up; you can't go to bed again."

"But I've my pipes in my nose," protested Mrs Furness.

"Yes, dear, because I have not taken them out yet."

"But they are not taken out at night," argued the old lady.

"It is not night now, dear, you know."

"Yes," retorted she, "I always have my pipes in at night, and I have them in now, so it must be night."

"I must remove them, however;" and Bessie extracted the apparatus, regardless of the old lady's remonstrances and struggles to retain it.

"They must be cleaned, you know, and oiled, and made all soft and nice for next time."

"I want my pipes," wailed Mrs Furness.

"Come along, darling Mother; it is breakfast time."

"My pipes!"

"Annis!" said Miss Furness; "you take one arm and I will hold the other. Let her lean on you and take care she does not slip in descending the stairs."

At breakfast the old woman had fancies about first one thing and then another. The egg was stale, there was a young bird in it, and Miss Furness had to smell it and assure her mother it was quite fresh. The tea was too strong; there was green in it, the good lady thought, and she could not bear green — it affected her nerves. Bessie very patiently produced the tea-caddy and showed her mother that the compartment for green tea was empty. Then, suddenly, Mrs Furness insisted upon being set upon her feet and after having been so placed, she very solemnly said: "For these and all His other mercies," and then subsided into her chair again. "You forgot to say grace when we began," was her rebuke. Bessie had not forgotten, but she did not tell her mother so.

Presently a crumb went down the wrong way and the old lady coughed, and had to be slapped on her back. Then she upset her cup of tea on her lap and her daughter was obliged very carefully to wipe her mother's black silk dress, lest it should be stained.

Five times during the meal was Bessie asked, in a whisper, who Annis was. Not once, however, were the nasal tubes referred to, to the indescribable relief of Miss Furness.

When breakfast was over, Annis was taken to bed. "Where is your box, my dear?" asked Elizabeth Furness.

Annis explained that she had come away in a hurry from Sowden without it.

"Never mind. I will write to my brother by today's post and ask him to forward it. Meanwhile, I will lend you what you may want."

She undressed the little girl herself, put her to bed, like a child, drew the sheets about her head, then shut the shutters and closed the curtains, darkening the room to a dull twilight. Then she glided to the side of Annis, bowed over her, put a hand on each temple, and said in a low dove-like tone, with her soft eyes distilling love and compassion: "Sleep soundly, poor little heart! and do not think over your troubles. God will order all things as He sees best. Kiss me, and promise me not to rise till

216

I call you."

Annis folded her arms round the old maid's neck and kissed her, and promised as required. Then Miss Furness stole from the room, shut the door, and left Annis in stillness as that of night.

She soon fell asleep, and did not awake till noon, when she opened her eyes on a grey figure standing by her, smiling brightly upon her. Bessie, seeing she was awake, moved to the window, and let in on her the golden mid–day sun.

Chapter Twenty-Four

There can be little doubt that the line adopted by Mr Furness in dealing with Hugh and Annis has greatly shocked the majority of readers. The vicar ought to have rebuked Hugh for having fallen in love with a poor mill-girl. He should have stood forth the champion of outraged society, and have clearly represented to him that an unequal match is a heinous crime in the sight of the world. He should have made him aware that society imperatively demands of a man who marries, that he should choose a partner who is his equal in birth, or, at least, is richly furnished with a golden dower. Society does not ask whether there is mutual love, nor does it require that there shall be congruity of natures, and congeniality of souls; it does not expect the woman to be selected for her domestic virtues, certainly not for her moral qualifications.

All this ought to have been insisted on by the vicar. But of this he said nothing. He knew that the voices of society — very many and very loud — would make themselves heard, and ring in Hugh's ears all day long; that his uncle would sound the loud note, and that the echoes would pass from mill to shop, and be repeated from the kitchen. On this point, therefore, he did not speak. Possibly he did not hold altogether with society.

Once, when a boy, he had been taken to the Surrey Gardens, and had there seen Mont Blanc illuminated with fireworks. He had strayed from the crowd which gazed, enthusiastic and applauding, on the snowy slopes and the icy spires lighted up with Bengal flames, and strontian fires, and ringing with the pops and snaps or squibs and crackers, and had made his way to the rear, where he had contemplated with amazement and disgust, the bare canvas, the pulleys, the gaunt ribs, the smears of oil, the baulks shoring up the mountain, the concealed barrows and picks and levers, the planks on which stood greasy mechanics with fusees, exploding the rockets and firepots and Roman candles. As a priest he had been for thirty-five years behind the great white mountain of conventionalism, seeing its bones and bolts and framework, and the stitches which held together its rents, and he had observed the construction and apparatus which produced the most startling effects that gratified the open-mouthed public. He knew that the pure snow was only white lead, that the grim rocks were but dabs of burnt siena, that the prime ingredient of the coloured lights was brimstone, that the vivid lightning flashes were only ignited rosin dust, and that the thunderclaps were vibrating sheet-iron.

The vicar of Sowden had studied human nature. He knew that it was a law of the universe that no force can be permanently checked. It may be directed, but it cannot be brought to a total standstill. It must either resume its course or produce ruin. If the smallest rill be blocked, it may appear to have ceased to flow, but in the end it will reassert its onward tendency, probably bursting the barrier and producing desolation. The action of the pores may be impeded, but the result is fever and perhaps death. The passions in man are forces as powerful as those of nature. Society is ever casting up embankments to hinder them from taking their legitimate course, and is ever thereby producing stagnation or devastation. If they are to be directed to the use of mankind and to the wellbeing of the world, the sluice of hope must be kept open, and they will remain sweet and flowing.

The vicar had to deal with facts. Society loves to cast a veil over facts or to stamp them out. The vicar preferred recognising and utilising them. It was a fact that Hugh and Annis loved one another. In this he saw nothing opposed to the law of God and of nature, though it was repugnant to the law of conventionality. Society allows that such facts do occur as love beyond the limits of social position, but it likes its sentence against a union of those who thus love to be carried out at the expense of God's law. It will not tolerate legitimate union, but it will wink at that which is against the eternal principle of morality and honour.

Love is the master passion. It is a force which cannot be nullified, it must expend itself on something; no barrier of human construction can stay it. The vicar knew that if he and Hugh's relations united in attempting to stifle the young man's passion, it would burst forth with an ungovernable violence in a lateral direction and ruin him. It would either precipitate a marriage in opposition to his uncle's wishes, and to the destruction of his prospects in life, or it would lead to sin. By giving the young man and the girl a hope, though that hope was remote, he directed the power within each into health–giving channels. Hugh would apply himself with enthusiasm to his avocation, in hopes of acquiring a competency on which to marry, and Annis would labour with diligence to qualify herself for a position above that in which she was born. And by showing that he trusted the young people and that he sympathised with their romance, he made them desirous to prove themselves worthy of his confidence and sympathy. The vicar had learned by experience of the world how much evil and misery is caused by the ignorance of parents and guardians in their dealing with the young when attached to each other. He had seen marriages forced on where the hearts were engaged elsewhere, and these had resulted in the destruction of happiness and moral ruin. He had seen too much of the lightning and heard too much of the thunder of society to dread either. He knew that neither could kill or seriously injure. He remembered the rosin dust and sheet–iron.

It was probable that years of separation might render the young people indifferent to one another, or they might be thrown amongst others who would make them forgetful of their first passion. Should they remain true and loyal to each other, then, the vicar thought, no harm had been done. He knew Annis well. He was convinced of her goodness, simplicity and natural refinement. And Hugh he also well knew, and believed that he had courage and strength of character to face the rosin flashes, and listen unmoved to the roll of sheet–iron.

The following letter reached Mr Furness by post on Monday morning:—

DEAR WILLIAM

I am so much obliged to you for sending me the little girl, Annis Greenwell; I know that I shall be very fond of her. I like her little, fresh, dewy face already, and I can see that she is a good, truehearted child. I have not the least doubt that Mother will take to her. Annis is evidently sympathetic, and not at all likely to be irritated by the dear old lady's ways. She has come not a moment too soon: I do not think I could have gone on by myself much longer, as I am obliged to be in town occasionally, and none of the servants understand Mother. Some indulge her with her nose-tubes to keep her quiet, and others worry her by their well-intentioned scoldings, and these she cannot bear. I wish you would come over to York and see us oftener; but I know what you will say — there are parish matters to attend to. Well, you are right, of course, dear brother. I have made a discovery — by reading any book to dear Mother, she can be kept quiet. I read *Les Miserables* to her last week, and she listened with great attention, solemnity and patience, believing that she was undergoing the Psalms and Lessons for the day. Of course, William, I read the latter immediately after breakfast, by Mamma forgot ten minutes after, and asked for them with such pertinacity that I took up *Les Miserables* and found that it answered quite as well. Do you know, William, when I read about Monsieur Bienvenu, I could not help thinking of you. If I had not known you I should have thought the character overdrawn. But though he resembles you in many points, in others he is unlike you: I do not think he possessed that knowledge of the world that you are gifted with, and, on the other hand, you are not as charitable, I should rather say, as injudiciously reckless as he was. I wished, when I read the book, that I could have lived with you, and kept house for you, like Mlle Baptistine, but God has seen fit otherwise.

And now, brother, what about Annis? The poor little soul has poured out her story into my ear. I saw she could not rest till she had told me all, so I brought her into my little dressing-room and then she gave me her history — told in such a simple, candid way that my heart quite dissolved within me. I am sure she is a very good girl, very natural and free from all affectation and conceit. Her heart is evidently full of the Hugh she told me of. As she spoke to me, my mind ran back unconsciously to the dear old days when the Silver Poplar visited our house. I cannot tell whether with Annis her love is a transient feeling or not. I think when women love, they love forever; at least, I am sure that when once my affections are engaged, I cannot divert them to another object; it is an impossibility, it would be a violation of my instincts and I doubt not that what applies to me applies to my sex generally. As for time effecting a change in the feelings, that I do not believe in; my impression is that time only deepens the channel, and thereby fixes the direction of their course into permanency. Of the young man I can say nothing, as I do not know him. Some men, I believe, are volatile, but others are not, as I am thankful to know.

I have not had time to examine Annis on the amount of her knowledge, but I do not suppose it extends very far. I shall do my best by her; by setting her to read to dear Mother, and selecting suitable works for the purpose, I hope to develop her mind; and it will be quite an amusement to me to help her on in other little matters.

Please to send her box as soon as convenient, as she arrived without anything.

I remain,
Your affectionate sister

ELIZABETH FURNESS

Hugh, for some days, felt the discomfort of being closely watched. When he went to the mill of a morning, he was aware of a figure loitering about the yard. The same person was there when he left at night. Once or twice he saw him waylaying him in the lane leading up the hill, and if he had not been in company with Mr Arkwright, an unpleasant meeting might have ensued. This person was Joe Earnshaw. The mill people observed that now, instead of concealing himself during the day, he was continually about the mill. He had taken lodgings in a cottage which stood on the roadside, commanding the mill-gate. It was ascertained that Joe had paid the woman of the house a visit, and had offered a somewhat extravagant price for the use of her upstairs apartment; for she boasted that the watchman paid like a gentleman, or else, she said, she wouldn't have taken him in, as she was inconvenienced by the loss of her room and the children were frightened at the watchman's appearance.

One day Earnshaw stopped Martha on her way home.

"What do you want with me?" asked the girl.

"Step aside," answered the man curtly.

222

"I'll not go very far," answered Martha; "you're so queer. I'm flayed of you."

"You need not be afraid of me," said the watchman. "I will not hurt *you*." He placed a decided emphasis on the final word.

"Well, I cannot stop long speaking with you, and what is more, lad, I'll not be seen talking wi' nobody i' a dark corner; so there now. Say your say and ha' done."

A group of mill-girls was not far off, watching. Joe Earnshaw had not been seen talking to a lass before. Martha had no wish to become a butt for their jokes.

"Let go," she said sharply. "I'm boune home."

He held her arm firmly so that she could not stir. "No," he said; "not till you have answered me."

"I will not speak to you except here i' the middle o' t' street."

"Why not?"

"I tell you, lad, I'm flayed of you."

"I tell you, I will not hurt you. Now come with me yonder. I cannot say what I want here."

"Well, I will go with you to the railway bridge, where no-one can hear, but anyone may see."

"Come then."

He drew her with him. Martha could hear the girls laughing, and her colour rose. If she had not promised, she would have wrenched her arm from his grasp and have run away. She called to the girls to wait for her; she would be with them directly.

When she reached the centre of the bridge which carried the road over the Lancashire and Yorkshire line, close above the station, she resolutely planted her feet against the causeway and said: "Joe, I'll not go an inch further. What do you want?"

He relaxed his hold of her, and turning towards her, leaned his elbow on the parapet and eyed her strangely. "I wish tha'd keep thy glances to thysen," said Martha; "I'd thank thee to be sharp about speaking, and ha' done wi' staring."

"Martha, where's Annis Greenwell?"

"Eh! Is that what thou'rt driving at?"

"Where's Annis Greenwell?"

"That's no concern o' thine, Joe."

"I will know," he growled between his teeth. "Tell me at once!"

223

"Nay! I cannot."

"You will not, you mean to say."

"I'd like to know what it matters to thee, lad, where our Annis is. I reckon it don't concern nobody but me and Father and Mother —"

"And Hugh Arkwright," he threw in with a roar.

"Ay," she answered frankly; "and Hugh Arkwright, in course, because he's axed her to be his wife, tha knows."

Flashes of lurid fire shot through the gloomy eyes of the watchman. Martha shrank from him, saying: "Joe, I reckon thour't a bit mad."

"I'm altogether mad," he howled. "Tell me, I say, where is Annis Greenwell?"

His tone, his look, the frightful passion which worked in his muscles and features startled Martha, and she answered harshly: "I do not know."

"Find out and tell me."

"I cannot."

"Ask your mother."

"She does not know where Annis is."

"Ask your father."

"He does not know, neither."

"Then who does?"

"There is no but one i' all Sowden as knows."

"Who is that?"

"Nay! I will not tell."

Earnshaw leaned over the parapet. The platform of Sowden Station extended to the bridge, against which was erected the signal post, and the chimney of the little office of the clerk of the luggage. The platform was perfectly visible from the railway bridge. The watchman snorted, pointed to a figure waiting for the train, in front of the ticket office, turned his blazing eyes to Martha with a mingled air of rage and triumph.

"There," he hissed. "He."

The girl ran her eye in the direction indicated and observed Hugh. "No," she said calmly; "Hugh Arkwright does not know where she is." Then she slipped away, ran along the road towards Sowden, and rejoined her companions.

"Eh, lass! Thas't gotten a rare sweetheart!" was the mocking cry of one.

"What did he want wi' thee?" asked another.

"Who ever'd ha' thowt o' Joe and thee bein' thick!" from a third.

Martha shrugged her shoulders and smiled. "Poor lad," she said. "He's about ravin' mad."

"What did he say, lass?"

"He'd some long nomine, but I gave no heed to 't. He's daft."

Hugh had been annoyed with being so constantly watched by Earnshaw, and he had alluded to it in conversation with his uncle the day before. He had said to Mr Arkwright, "I cannot see how you can retain that extraordinary man called Earnshaw as your night-watch. He seems to me mad."

To which his uncle had replied, "There is a great deal of madness in this world. If we cleared all cracky people out we should depopulate it."

And Hugh had quoted Horace:—

"Nimirum insanus paucis videatur, eo quod
Maxima pars hominum morbo jactatur eodem."

Whereat his uncle had laughed without in the least understanding the passage, but imagining that a joke lay concealed beneath it.

"My boy, it is rather rich your crying out against that unfortunate man, when you have exhibited the strongest symptoms of insanity of any man in Sowden."

"How so?"

"By your romantic and absurd attachment."

"On that point," Hugh had answered, reddening, "I am in my right senses. But I do think your watchman is mad. He dogs me everywhere, watches me when I go to the mill, and watches me leaving it."

"Psh!" his uncle had said. "A cat may look at a king."

And now as Hugh stood on the platform, he saw Earnshaw with his face muffled in a comforter, and his cap drawn over his eyes, run down the flight of steps from the roadway to the station, and take his stand close to him, leaning against the wall of the booking office. Hugh moved to the further end of the

225

platform. The watchman followed him. He paced up and down. The night-watch paced after him never removing his eye from him. Hugh was irritated; he turned sharply on him and asked: "Do you want me?"

"No."

"Then I will trouble you not to follow me everywhere." And he walked under the roof of the shed and sat down on the bench, near a pile of boxes.

The watchman came after him. Suddenly he stopped. "Hst!" he said, fixing his eye on a trunk covered with mottled purple paper, with two black tape handles nailed to the extremities. Earnshaw stooped, removed a hamper which was upon it and read the address: —

MISS FURNESS
MINSTER YARD
YORK

Then he chuckled; replaced the hamper and seated himself on the bench beside Hugh.

At this moment the glass booking-office window opened noisily and the young man, starting from his place, in Earnshaw's hearing, took a return ticket to Bradford. The watchman remained on his seat, laughing to himself with low gurgling gulps, and did not move from it till the train came up, and Hugh had taken his seat near the door, when he rose, strode across the platform, took off his hat, and thrusting his horrible face in at the window, so as almost to touch Hugh, shouted: "Do you think I don't know where you've hidden her? I do."

Yes; the secret was now known to two persons: the vicar and the watchman.

Mr Furness had made John Rhodes send up Annis's box packed to the parsonage, where he had directed it to his sister, not to Annis, and had sent it down by the railway van to the station, where it was waiting to be forwarded on the arrival of the train for Normanton. Earnshaw, from having lodged in the Greenwells' house, recognised the box at once, and by looking at the address on it, had ascertained where Annis was concealed.

Chapter Twenty-Five

Hugh was engaged on business in Bradford during the afternoon, and it was dusk when he came to the station, but not dark enough for the gas to be lighted. The platform is long. He was early, and had a quarter of an hour to wait.

Two mill-women, in dirty gowns, with grey shawls over their heads, were wrangling and abusing one another on the platform. Their faces were worn and haggard; one, if not both, had been drinking. The subject of their quarrel was not very clear, but their mutual animosity was sufficiently apparent. The language they used was not choice, nor was it delivered in low tones. One of the porters made an ineffectual attempt to expel the women, but beat a precipitate retreat when he found himself the object of attack from both.

"Thour't an owd cat!" yelled one.

"It's thee as has t'claws," retorted the other.

"Thou can brazen it out right grand."

"It's thee is as bold as a bad lass."

"Say that again!"

"Ay, I'll say't and never fear."

"Mucky-fa-ace!"

"Foul-mouth!"

"Now then! now then!" from the station-master, in a voice of authority. "No squabbling here."

The women started apart and the officer drove one to each extremity of the platform.

"Keep order here," he said, "or I'll turn you out." Such scenes were not uncommon.

They were quiet for a while, being some hundred yards apart. The station-master was satisfied and retired to his private apartment. Presently the two females began to walk up and down the platform, in opposite directions.

The first time they passed one another, they contented themselves with making grimaces expressive of contempt at one another. The second time they passed: "Mucky-face!" said one.

"Dirty fingers!" retorted the other.

The third time, one turned and spat at the other. This was distinct proclamation of war *à l'outrance*, and the aggrieved woman, with a scream of rage, sprang at the other with her nails, and a fight began. Shawls were torn off, hair flew about, combs gave way, blood flowed from scratched faces, mingling with oil stains; the yells and curses of the infuriated creatures became deafening, and attracted all the passengers waiting on the platform, who seemed, for the most part, to derive entertainment from the scene.

Hugh, who had kept away from them whilst they quarrelled, and had amused himself examining the advertisements that adorned the station walls, came suddenly up, laid a hand on each of the battling women, wrenched them apart, and drew them violently out of the station.

"Keep outside these rails," he said, "or I'll give you in charge of the police."

At the same moment, he noticed a figure leaning against the bars, with his back towards him; this man was thickset, wore a broad–brimmed hat, a high–collared greatcoat and a blue muffler. Hugh started. The figure and dress belonged to the night–watch. The face he could not see.

Up came the train at this moment, and Hugh left the railing to cross the platform and secure a place.

He had a second–class ticket. He took his seat in a carriage occupied by two men, one old and bald–headed, the other a middle–aged mechanic, with a basket of tools on the seat beside him.

Hugh caught a glimpse, on entering, of a thickset muffled person passing behind him into the next compartment of the same carriage.

"Fine evening," said the bald–headed man.

"Beautiful," responded Hugh.

"Bit of frost i' t' air," added the mechanic.

"Trade's slack," said the old man.

"Middling," remarked the artisan in reply.

"Might be worse," quoth Hugh.

"Do you mind the window being closed?" asked he with the bald head. "I'm subject to stuffiness in the nose if I inhale night air."

228

"Not in the least. Let me draw up the glass," said Hugh, suiting the action to the word.

"Tickets!" from the collector, putting his head in.

"Brighouse," said the old man, producing his blue card.

"Change at North Dean. Now, then!" to the mechanic.

The man produced a pass.

"Get out! You're in the wrong train; next behind."

So Hugh was left with the old bald-headed man. He rose from his seat and leaned out of the window, to look after the artisan. Then a man on a ladder applied a light to a gas jet in the station, and a yellow blaze fell over the platform and struck a ghastly disfigured countenance which peered out of the window of the adjoining compartment.

"By Jove," said Hugh, reseating himself as the train moved; "the man is Earnshaw."

"Did you address an observation to me?" asked the bald man.

"No, sir; I was speaking to myself."

"May I trouble you to raise the glass?"

At North Dean the old gentleman left the carriage, wishing Hugh a very good evening.

"Will you oblige me by handing me that bag? — Thank you — And I think you will find a small portmanteau under the seat — Much obliged — Is there an umbrella on the seat? — Ah! Thanks! —That newspaper, I think, is mine."

Hugh was alone.

"Any more going on?" loudly from the station-master.

The bell rang. The wheels turned and the train moved, and the gleams from the station lamps changed direction in the carriages. Then a shout, angry or indignant: "Now then! What are you after there?"

The door suddenly opened, a man sprang in and took a seat opposite Hugh. By the dull light from the lamp in the carriage, the young man ascertained that his companion was the night-watch.

Hugh calmly contemplated the prospect from the window. The evening sky was cloudless and green. Venus, like a silver lamp, hung in the west, where the moon was just setting, not white and pure, but scarlet, like a glowing furnace. A soft light still lingered over the hills above Riponden, but the vale was steeped in purple black. A white mist hung along the bottom, following the courses of the Rye burn and Calder. Little whiffs of foggy air rushed in at the window, which Hugh had lowered, but, for the most part, the mist lay so low that the line was above it.

Sowerby was lighted up. The factories presented lines of illuminated windows, showing that work was not slack there, for the mills were running by night as well as by day. The river caught and reflected them where the railway bridge spanned the water, and the draught descending the valley swept the fog away.

From a church on the hillside sounded a bell for prayers — a single bell rung slowly, clinking like a smith's hammer on the anvil.

Hugh was conscious, all the while that he watched the shifting scene from the window, that the eyes of the watchman were fixed upon him. He did not look towards Earnshaw, but resolutely directed his gaze without, yet he felt that those gloomy eyes were riveted on him. Probably, everyone is aware when another is observing him. A peculiar uneasy sensation creeps over one, and constrains him to look at the eyes which are upon him.

The fog became denser, lying white upon the water and meadows. Above it stood black trees, whose roots and trunks were steeped in the vapour, and the upper windows of cottages that had their doors immersed. The train roared over a bridge, past a lamp flashing crimson, then green, and plunged into mist, which suddenly obscured the sky, obliterated Venus, shut off the prospect of the hills, chilled the air, and clogged the lungs of those who inhaled it.

Hugh, leaning against the door, was aware that the handle was not turned, for, in entering the carriage, the watchman had not troubled himself to secure the fastening. Hugh with his hand kept the door closed. He might have put his arm out of the window and turned the handle, but for some reason for which he did not account to himself, he preferred to leave it as it was. His destination was not far off, and he would jump out all the more rapidly if the door were unhasped.

A rush of sparks went past the window, and a fume of

smoke from the engine entered and pervaded the carriage. The practice of burning coke on the Northern lines has been abandoned and, in defiance of law, coal is invariably consumed.

The train shot past a barge lying in vapour on the canal, with a little scarlet fire on board, illumining the fog, which dispersed the light as ground glass spreads that of a lamp. A shadow figure of a bargeboy in the fog, gesticulating at the train and a muffled shout was audible. The canal was apparently running alongside of the line of rails, so that a stone cast from a window of the carriage would splash into the water.

Crash!

Hugh turned his head.

Earnshaw had shattered the glass of the carriage–lamp with the handle of his large pocket–knife. He then blew the light out. A whistle, distant, timorous, shrill, waxing shriller, bolder and approaching nearer every second, answered by that of the engine of the train in which was Hugh, high–pitched, piercing, pealing and thrilling as if agonised with fear, rising in pitch, increasing in volume, jarring with that of the approaching engine; then a roar and throbs of thunder, as the trains passed one another. Suddenly, Hugh felt himself in the grasp of the watchman, whom, in the darkness, he could not distinguish, and hurled against the door. The action was so sudden and unexpected, that the young man was unable to gather up his strength for resistance. He had been caught by the waist, lifted, and dashed backward in a second. He felt the door yield behind him, but he caught at the jambs, and planted his feet against the step. The violence with which he had been thrown, sent him out of the carriage, and his body swung over the flying road, with its sleepers darting by.

He heard the harsh laugh of the night–watch above the throb and rattle of the wheels and the rush of the departing up–train. He endeavoured to recover his balance and swing himself into the carriage again.

"Off with you!" bellowed the madman, grasping his arms and trying to wrench them from the door–jambs.

Hugh clung with desperation. If he let go, he must fall. If he fell — !

The watchman kicked at his feet, where they rested on the

231

ledge of the carriage floor; he thrust one from its place, but it was planted again instantly. Next, he leaped on them, and stamped, yelling with rage and fury.

Then they slipped. But before they yielded, Hugh caught the window and clung to that.

He hung to the door, as it swung forward and backward, wide open, clasping the panels with his knees and his hands about the bar.

Then the maniac looked out at him and laughed; and, laughing in a gulping jerky manner, opened his great pocket-knife.

It is said of people who hear with difficulty that in a noise their ears become capable of hearing what in a hush they could not catch. In the roar of a street, they can follow a conversation which would sound as a confused murmur in a chamber.

Something of the same description must have influenced Hugh's hearing, for the click of the opened blade came sharp on his ear, through all the rush and clatter of the train. His peril concentrated his powers of eye. He observed nothing but what concerned his safety. It had been dark in the carriage, it was clearer outside, the white fog caught and entangled in it some of the lingering light. Hugh could not make out the face of Earnshaw, but, partly through his sight and partly through an undeveloped faculty within, residing in the nerves, he was conscious of his every movement.

He saw and felt him catch at the latticed ventilator over the doorway, and sling himself out and strike at him with his feet, and, failing to reach him, lay his hand on the window, lean outwards and stab at his knuckles with the knife.

And then the train whirled past a tuft of furze which had become ignited, either by some sparks from the funnel, or by children in sport, and the flickering light kindled the hideous face which leaned towards him, the eyes glaring with demoniacal hate, the flesh scarlet, blotched, seamed; the glittering white teeth exposed, the arm uplifted with the knife to stab again.

The first blow had missed. Before the second fell, Hugh caught at the iron handle which is affixed to each carriage, and set his foot on the wooden rail which projects above the wheels.

With a little caution, he might now proceed the whole length of the carriage and find a compartment where he might be safe.

He looked before him. He was disappointed. The compartment he had been in was the first of the carriage.

Earnshaw seemed to have detected his intention and subsequent disappointment, for Hugh heard the wild mocking maniacal laughter again.

The handle could be reached from the window. Earnshaw leaned out and made a downward slice at the fingers which grasped the iron. Hugh felt a cut and then a gush of blood. No tendon had been severed, for his hold remained as firm as ever. The jolting of the wheels over the sleepers had prevented the watchman making as effectual a stroke as he had intended.

With his disengaged hand, Hugh grasped that of the madman which held the knife above the wrist, and swung it against the handle and crushed it upon the iron, till the weapon slid from its grasp and was lost.

Then he let go. Howling with rage and pain, Earnshaw stepped deliberately down to the rail on which Hugh stood.

The young man felt confident of escape. The speed of the engine was slackening. Through the fog he saw the light of Sowden station, still distant, but becoming momentarily nearer. He heard the bell ringing on the platform, for passengers to prepare to take their seats. He had but to retain his position for three minutes and he would be safe.

The brake was put on. He felt the jerk and quiver. Earnshaw also saw that in a little while his enemy would be beyond his reach.

"I'll have you yet!" he roared.

Then he made a leap, caught Hugh, wrenched his hand from the hold, his feet from that on which they were stayed. For a throb of the pulse they were grappling in the air, then they struck the ground, rolled, still grappling, one falling over the other, and plunged into the ice-cold water of the canal. They went down together, and touched mud.

They rose apart.

"Halloo, there!"

They were close to a barge, and the man on it had seen the fall and now shouted.

"Help!" cried Hugh; and he and Earnshaw struck out. The watchman was the first to reach the side. He did not climb into the boat, but waited, clinging to the gunwale and turning his face towards Hugh.

"Here, lad! Up wi' thee," said the boatman. Earnshaw made no answer.

"Come; one at a time," he said again. "Tha don't seem ower fain to get out o' t' water."

Then Hugh touched the side, the bargeman knelt in the heavily-laden boat and put forth his hand to assist the young man. The watchman raised himself, turned and deliberately kicked Hugh in the chest. And the young man sank.

Then, after a prolonged laugh, Earnshaw loosed his hold and vanished.

Chapter Twenty-Six

"Five foot seven and a half," said Mrs Doldrums; "I think, Sally, that we have one as'll suit. Maybe must screw up his legs a bit, but it'll do."

The stout lady was applying a tape to the body of Hugh Arkwright as he lay on a bed in her house.

"That's two yards, all but four and a half," said Sally.

"Mother, mother!" cried Miss Doldrums; "he is not dead yet!"

"Sally," ordered the stout lady, "bring the bigger-sized coffins down, will you."

Hugh was not dead. When Earnshaw kicked him in the chest he sank, but the boatman caught him by the hair before he went to the bottom, otherwise he would not have risen to the surface till decomposition had set in.

The bargeman had at once carried him to the nearest house, which was that belonging to the Doldrums' family, the garden of which extended to the water's edge. Having deposited his load there, the man had gone in quest of a doctor.

"Sally," said Mrs Doldrums, "fetch a big book, and put it on his stomach. Yonder is one as'll do. *Pinkerton's Geography.* Clap it on his belly, lass."

Sally, the venerable confidential servant, obeyed.

"Clap on the other volume," added Mrs Doldrums. This was done with alacrity. "Now, Sally, just you get a straddle on them, and sit you down on the books for about half an hour and I fancy you'll squeeze all the water out of his lungs."

"Mother! For heaven's sake, don't. Sally, keep off!" cried Laura.

"My dear," said Mrs Doldrums, "it's the way corpses are plumped."

"Mother!"

"Ay. Your dear father was plumped with that *Pinkerton's Geography* and Sally a-straddle on top of it. Wasn't it so, Sally?"

"Sure enough, mam."

"I told you so, Laura. Your father was a terrible sufferer, and a man can't suffer and keep his flesh. It is not reasonable that he should. No—one can do two things at the same time. Ah! Doldrums' groans were dreadful, were they not, Sally?"

"They were, missus."

"He fell away shocking towards his end, Laura. We fed him up with chicken—broth, and beef—tea, and calf's—foot jelly; but we might as lief have put the bellows to his mouth. And no man can live on air, Laura, it isn't to be expected; so he lost flesh and shrunk away till I was quite ashamed to let the corpse be seen. I fair blushed to the roots of my hair when the undertakers came to measure him; he looked skin and bone, as if he'd been famished. So I said to Sally — Sally, whatever shall we do, that Doldrums may be a credit to us? And Sally proposed we should plump him; and we did so, always hoping as I did to others I may be done by."

"He looked beautiful, missus, when his face were puffed out," said the servant.

"Sally," said the stout lady, "loosen the young man's collar and take off his cravat."

"Yes mam."

"Undo the buttons of his waistcoat and expose his bosom, so as to give play to the lungs."

"Lor, mam, what's this?"

"A red cotton handkerchief," exclaimed Mrs Doldrums. "How odd."

"It's like one them mill lasses wear on their heads," observed Sally.

"I see it all!" cried Laura, with enthusiasm. "Good, dear fellow!"

"My love!" exclaimed the stout mother staring at her daughter.

"It is a memorial of his poor little vanished girl," said Laura.

"Now, Sally," ordered Mrs Doldrums, "put the third Pinkerton on and then up with you, and get a—straddle."

Hugh sat up, opened his eyes and looked round.

"Well, I never!" exclaimed the fat lady.

Laura, who had been in distress and terror whilst he lay motionless on the bed, now flew to him with a cry of joy, and clasping his hand, exclaimed with earnest sympathy: "You are not dead! Oh, say you are not dead!"

It was some minutes, however, before Hugh was sufficiently recovered to give her the requisite assurance.

And when the colour returned to his cheek, and he spoke, the good-natured and lively girl danced with delight. "What can I bring you? Oh, only tell me!"

"I think," Hugh answered faintly, "I should like my trousers."

"Why bless my soul!" exclaimed Mrs Doldrums, "he thinks he's waking of a morning. I say, young man!" in a loud tone into Hugh's ear.

"Eh!" with a dim look, for consciousness had only partially returned.

"You are dressed, I tell you. You are not in bed, though you're on it. Do you know where you have been?"

"No."

"You've come from the bottom of the canal, and you're full of water."

At this moment the surgeon arrived. He at once silenced the women, and cleared the room. He had some difficulty in picking his way among the coffins. "What are all these for?" he asked with amazement.

"Oh, they belong to missus," replied Sally; "she thought one of 'em might come in useful."

"And this?" asked the surgeon, taking a long white linen vestment in his fingers.

"That's missis's shroud; she thought she'd be so good as lend it to the young gentleman."

"And, pray, for what purpose are these huge volumes on the bed?"

"Lor, sir! Missis and I was boune to plump him."

"Remove the books at once."

The medical man spoke with authority and decision. Sally obeyed in trepidation. "Now, away with the shroud!"

"Missis is so considerate —," she began, but was at once cut short by a stamp of the foot, and a peremptory "Off!"

The shroud was accordingly folded up and replaced in its usual drawer.

"Remove these coffins immediately."

Sally shoved one under the bed and shouldered another.

"Now, let us see to the patient."

Laura and her mother remained outside, in anxiety.

"Oh, Mother! If he were to die!" moaned the girl.

"If he were to die, my dear," said the old lady, turning towards her slowly, "why, I hope we should be able to make a nice corpse of him, such as would do us credit."

"How can you talk so, Mother?" Laura said, piteously.

"And then" pursued Mrs Doldrums, "one of the smaller coffins would come in handy."

"I do hope he will get well."

"Of course; but it would be a pity, too."

"Mother!"

"I say, Laura, it's a pity to have them coffins unused; they cost some money, which might for all the good they have done, have been cast into the river."

"Why did you have them then?" she asked impatiently.

"Because I've fattened out and overlapped 'em. One after another's gotten too small. Never mind. I'll keep apples in them."

The door opened and the surgeon came out. "Well?" Laura asked, with uplifted hands and fluttering colour in her cheeks.

"He must have a good sleep tonight, and I hope he will be all right tomorrow."

"Thank heaven!"

"Sally, put the winter apples in one of the coffins, and the preserving pears in the other."

After a pause, during which the old lady gathered up her breath, she asked: "And pray, doctor, what about his victuals? And, if you please, what is he to drink?"

"Give him a stiff glass of brandy and water."

"Would rum do as well?"

"Yes."

"Or whisky?"

"Yes."

"Or oil of peppermint, which is very comforting? I have all four."

"Then the brandy, please."

"And what is he to eat?"

"Oh, anything."

"Will a mutton chop do, think you?"

"Admirably."

"Or a beefsteak?"

"Just as well."

"What do you say to a veal cutlet and tomato sauce, Mr Jumbold?"

"Anything he takes a fancy to, madam."

Then, after a little preliminary meditation, Mrs Doldrums inquired, with hesitation: "When my husband was ill, you see, it was wind with him, and we gave him a deal of charcoal biscuits. They say charcoal absorbs the wind, but I can't say we found it so. However, as they were supposed to do good, I've been thinking that perhaps some sponge cake would be nice and suitable for Mr Hugh Arkwright. It might sop up the water, you know. What is your opinion, doctor?"

"Oh, certainly, give him sponge cake, if he likes it."

Reassured by finding her suggestion accepted, she ventured on another, with more confidence.

"I've thought a couple of volumes of *Pinkerton's Geography* clapped on his stomach, and Sally a–straddle—"

"On no account," interrupted the surgeon; "I could not answer for the consequences."

Mrs Doldrums mused. "I see," she said meditatively. "It might send the fluid into his head, and result in water on the brain."

"It might lead to Sally and *Pinkerton* being pitched out of the window," said the surgeon.

The next to arrive was Mrs Arkwright, pouring forth a torrent of German, thinly diluted with English. The report had reached her that her nephew was dead, and dressing, or being dressed, for his funeral. This report had been brought her by Mrs Jumbold, who had heard the account of the bargeman, when he came in quest of her husband.

When Mrs Jumbold called, Mr Arkwright was out, his wife did not exactly know where, so the little lady left a message for him to come on to the Doldrums' mansion immediately on his arrival, as something had happened to Hugh. Sarah Anne, awaiting her master's return, with the message in her keeping, formed her own opinion of the cause of the catastrophe. Hugh had committed suicide, on finding that his little girl was taken from him, so Sarah Anne opined; and, consequently, on the arrival of her master, she conveyed the message in this somewhat altered form:

"Oh, please sir, Mr Hugh's gone and done it."

"Gone and done what?"

"Drownded hissen, all about that lass Annis."

"Fiddlesticks!"

"It's ower true," said the girl, sobbing. "And missis be gone off wi' two pennies i' her pocket to put on his eyes and keep t' lids shut."

"Where is he?" asked Mr Arkwright in great alarm.

"Mrs Doldrums has t' corpse," between the sobs. "And Miss Laura's been a-washing it wi' t' mop."

"Is your mistress there now?"

"Ay, sir, wi' them two pennies. Mrs Jumbold came and fetched her away. Eh! poor lad, poor lad!"

"Does the information come from Mrs Jumbold only?"

"Yes, sir; she came over at once when t' doctor were sent for."

"And she left the message that I was to follow, I suppose?"

"Ay, sir, she did; and you was to send to t' undertaker."

Mrs Jumbold on her way home called in Kirkgate, at Mrs Rhodes' shop, to buy some ribbon.

"I suppose you've heard?" said the doctor's wife.

"No, mam; what?"

"Shocking; isn't it?"

"What, mam?"

"Mr Hugh Arkwright's decease."

"Decease!" with a stare and blank face.

"Yes, Mrs Rhodes. Your niece, or cousin — which is it? — Annis Greenwell, may be relieved from apprehension of pursuit. Her lover has perished miserably in the canal."

"You don't mean to say so?"

"It is quite true."

"I've always thought," said Mrs Jumbold, thrusting her nose forward, "that Annis Greenwell disappeared because, you know, she had expectations of — you understand."

Mrs Rhodes stood still, aghast.

"And of course she would have come down on Mr Hugh Arkwright for its support."

"Its support!" echoed Mrs Rhodes.

"But now she can't. You can't come down on a corpse, you know. I put it to you as a woman, can you?"

"What for?"

"When a young woman goes into hiding for a bit, we all know what that means," the doctor's wife pursued. "Of course it is generally accepted that there were reasons which made it advisable for Annis Greenwell to retire into privacy for a while. Now her lover is dead, drowned, mysteriously, I can't say how, and so the expenses of its support will fall on her alone — or, more probably, on you."

"Mr Hugh Arkwright's dead!" gasped Sarah Rhodes.

"And lying in Mrs Doldrums' house," added Mrs Jumbold. "How he came by his death I won't say, but there are suspicions — ahem!" and winking and nodding her head, she left the shop.

Mrs Rhodes put on her bonnet in the back parlour. Martha and Susan were there. The woman fixed the former with her eye, and said: "This comes o' church-going."

"What, Mother?"

"Yond Hugh Arkwright is dead."

"Dead!"

"Drownded and lying a corpse at Mrs Doldrums' house. So much for church-going." Then she hurried into the street.

At a corner near the apothecary's shop was the bargeman who had rescued Hugh, dilating on his adventure to an admiring audience.

"Thou sees, lad, if I hadn't a gotten hold on him at t' right moment, he'd a never comed up no more. As for t'other on 'em —"

"What other?" asked Mrs Rhodes, stopping.

"The man, missis, as were with him."

"Were there two, then?"

"Ay, I reckon, they seemed as if they'd been a quarrelling, and had jumped i' one another's arms, fighting like owt, into t' canal."

"Who was the other?" asked the woman.

"Nay, lass, I cannot tell."

"Do you think he might ha' been a policeman?"

"He might ha' been, for aught I know to t' contrary."

"Yes," said Mrs Rhodes, "he must have been a policeman, and now I see the whole case clear."

"You do!"

"Ay, I do. Our Annis has been murdered."

"Never!" from three or four.

"Ay, but she has. Murdered by Hugh Arkwright; and yond policeman was boune to take him up on t' charge of murder, but he jumped into t' canal to be shut of him."

"It can never be."

"Eh! but it can. Why, lads, it is as clear as day. Hugh Arkwright had rather drown hissen than be ta'en up by a peeler, and have the shame of being tried in court, and of being sent to prison and then of being hanged in front of Wakefield gaol. When he saw that he must be ta'en, he threw hissen into t' river. I see the whole affair."

"And where's your Annis?" asked a man.

"Nay! How'm I to know? Maybe he's cast her, with clock-weights round her neck, into the river; maybe he's cut her throat wi' a jack-knife, and buried her in some dark wood. Maybe he's hacked her blessed limbs one from t'other wi' a meat-chopper, and then burnt 'em to ashes i' a kiln. Dost thou think he'd tell me how he's done it? That's likely! eh! it is a wicked world!"

Mr Furness was writing letters that evening with his spectacles on his nose, at his little side-table, when his housekeeper came in, with pale face and uplifted hands.

"Lord, sir, it's awful!"

"What is the matter, Mary?"

"Matter, sir! enough to make us think the world is at an end. It's awful, master."

"Another *aurora borealis*?" asked the vicar, remembering that the last exhibition of the northern lights had called forth a similar expression of belief that the term of the world's duration was expired.

"No, sir; but poor Hugh Arkwright and Annis Greenwell."

"What of them?" he inquired sharply, and with a start.

"They've been dredged up from the bottom of the canal, sir, tied together with a bit of rope — dead, in one another's arms. Ain't it awful, sir, awful!"

244

"Mary, this cannot be true."

"And they say," continued Mary, "that a family of eels had made a nest in her head and there was a lot of frog-spawn in his."

When Mrs Arkwright arrived at Doldrums Lodge, Hugh was sufficiently recovered to come downstairs and talk and eat. Of the circumstances attending his accident he could or would give only a confused account and was glad to acquiesce in Laura's arrangement that he should not be asked about it till he was quite well.

"If you wouldn't mind," said Mrs Doldrums, "I think, Mr Hugh, we might get the water out of you in a simple and effectual manner."

"I shall be much relieved if you could."

"Then you will perhaps allow me to have you stuck up against the wall, with your legs in the air, and your head downward. Thus the water will all trickle out, and you needn't mind for the carpet, as it's an old one."

"I should prefer digesting it," said Hugh.

"Or you might swallow a packet of blotting paper," pursued Mrs Doldrums; "and then with a dose of ipecacuanha get rid of it when it had sopped the water up."

"Don't you think, Mamma, that the sponge cake would be a more agreeable remedy?" asked Laura, intercedingly.

"Perhaps it would, and then there'd be no need for the ipecacuanha. I'll send Sally for some cakes."

"I should infinitely prefer a mutton chop," said Hugh.

When his uncle arrived in a cab, he found him engaged in discussing a mutton chop, and drinking hot brandy and water.

"Well!" said Mr Arkwright, "doing pretty well for a dead man."

A rap at the door. The vicar arrived with anxious inquiries.

"Oh!" as he entered the room. "The deceased looks hearty; and the frog-spawn turns out to be mashed potatoes."

Presently a ring at the bell. Then some words in the hall. A tap at the door. Sally looks in and says, "The police inspector!"

"I've thought it my duty to call," said that official, bowing and standing in the doorway, "to make some inquiries touching the very painful circumstance that has occurred."

"Quite so," from Mr Arkwright.

"I think it would be advisable that I should inspect the corpse, and see if there be anything about it which might help lead to the detection of the person or persons implicated in this most dreadful crime."

"You wouldn't object, now," said Mr Arkwright, "to drink the corpse's health, I suppose."

"Certainly not, sir," replied the inspector; "though I may observe, sir, that such a proceeding would be unusual — not the drinking an 'ealth, sir, but the drinking an 'ealth to a corpse."

"Nor would you feel a repugnance to having the glass mixed for you by the corpse."

"It would be unusual, sir — very. Not, understand me, the having a glass mixed; but I allude to the mixer."

"I suppose you would have no aversion to having your good health drunk by the corpse?"

"Most unusual, sir. Not, I mean, that my 'ealth should be copiously and enthusiastically drunk, but I refer to the drinker. May I ask where I shall find the defunct?"

"In this room."

"Rather unusual, is it not? — in the presence of company, and company at supper, and supper of a convivial nature."

The inspector looked round the room in expectation of seeing the body.

"Gentlemen and ladies," he said, "where may it be?"

"Here," answered Mr Arkwright, pointing to Hugh. "At the present moment engaged in preparing for you a stiff glass of whisky and water."

Then was heard an altercation at the front door. The cabman had looked in, and was inquiring of Sally where he was expected to convey the deceased, because he would prefer not to do so; his vehicle was not calculated to serve the purpose of a hearse. The conveyance of a corpse, he urged, might impart an odour to the cushions which it would be difficult to remove; and he averred that his cab was not licensed to carry dead people, but, as he expressed it, "them as was wick."

"Come," said Mr Arkwright, "I think, Gretchen, we had better be off. I suppose we must leave Hugh in your care, Mrs

Doldrums, for this night, but we shall transport him to his office duties on Monday."

"I am sufficiently recovered to go with you, sir," said Hugh.

"I will not allow it," exclaimed Mrs Doldrums. "Here you stay. I have given orders for your room to be got ready."

"But I am not provided with the requisites," said the young man, smiling.

"We can send for them," Mrs Arkwright assured him.

"Oh," said Mrs Doldrums, "never bother about that, my dear. There is my poor husband's nightshirt — who is now mouldering in his grave — and comb and brush, and there's the lather-brush and razor that were used to shave him with, before they put him in his coffin. You can have them and welcome; they have not been used since then, so I know the razor must be sharp. Besides, razors, they say, always improve by keeping."

"Yes, you must stay," Mr Arkwright ordered, "and we will see what the doctor says of you tomorrow, before you stir out of the house."

"Of course you will stay," Laura urged. "We cannot afford to part with you yet."

"Thank you," said Hugh. Then to his uncle, "May I accompany you to the front door without running some frightful risk?" And he led his aunt into the hall.

As the front door opened, the light from the gas chandelier in the hall fell over the figure of a girl with a shawl round her head, standing on the doorstep. Her cheeks were glistening with tears.

"Martha!" exclaimed Hugh. "My dear girl, what brought you here?"

"Oh, sir!" she answered, "I heard you were dead. It is not true. I am so thankful. I could not rest till I knew all and I was afraid to ask."

She clasped his hand and wrung it, in hearty Yorkshire style. "I was sick with fear," she said; and then in an undertone, that Hugh alone could hear, she added, "For our poor Annis's sake."

Chapter Twenty-Seven

For a few weeks Annis felt the difficulty of falling into a position which she had been unaccustomed to occupy, and to find entire ease in the society of Miss Furness. There was something in that lady which filled her with awe, at the same time that she was attracted powerfully to her. Miss Furness was different from those ladies with whom she had hitherto been brought in contact. There was in her a repose, an inherent dignity and grace, which was new to Annis. She possessed qualities which the girl had never observed among the well-to-do manufacturers' wives and daughters in Sowden. This aroused Annis's wonder. She watched her intently, to find out what was the exquisite charm in her, that she might acquire it herself. But that same charm she herself unconsciously possessed. It was naturalness. In Miss Furness there was no affectation, no self-assertion, no effort to appear other than she really was. All her acts were spontaneous, springing from the impulses of a disciplined heart and a refined head.

She drew Annis towards her and unconsciously impressed and moulded her. The girl continually and involuntarily contrasted the monied aristocracy of Sowden with the lady whom she now daily saw. They wore their gentility as though it had been made by a bad tailor and did not fit; they were constantly engaged in looking it up, and asserting it; in proclaiming it by their expensive dress, in announcing it by costly plate, in forcing it into notice by their dashing equipages, in repeating it in their gilded furniture, in assuring people of it in their conversation. Their gentility had no braces to keep it up. It slipped down, and had to be pulled up with a jerk, and then directly after was descending, to be again hitched up; it was never stationary, it was always in process of slipping down or of being brought up with an effort.

Annis's life in York was very calm and monotonous; one day passed much like another. Mrs Furness had to be dressed every morning, to be fed, to be argued with touching her nose-tubes; had to be given her course of psalms and lessons, and amused till the early dinner hour at half-past one. In the afternoon, if the weather were fine, the old lady was wheeled in a chair round the Minster yard and close. At four, Miss Furness and Annis went to service in the Cathedral, and at six had tea. Then the old lady was put to bed, supplied with her tubes and sent to sleep with a chapter.

During the evenings, Annis worked with Miss Furness, reading to her or being read to: these evenings she thoroughly enjoyed.

The girl was happy. She was fond of both the old woman and her daughter, she enjoyed the quiet of the little house, the solemnity of the great Minster standing before the windows, sending its mighty shadows over the houses, its great bell booming at the hours, the organ thundering within, and heard indistinctly without. The gravity of the cathedral town, after the stir and noise of a manufacturing village, impressed her; and the numerous vestiges of antiquity around her opened up to her peeps into long vistas of history of which she had no conception before, and which awoke her liveliest interest and kindled her enthusiasm.

She never tired of the Minster. Whenever she was able, she ran into it, or wandered round it. The battered pinnacles, the corroded tracery, the disfigured statues, were full of charm to her. She watched the birds fluttering about the parapets, and soaring to the towers, with a longing to be like them, prying incessantly into the mysteries of stonework of that cast fabric. Within, the screen of the kings delighted her beyond expression, and she was convinced that each statue was a portrait. She loved to unravel the confusion of the venerable stained windows, and pick out a bishop here and an Adam and Eve there. The great dragon in the triforium of the nave, stretching its gaunt neck over the passersby, filled her with awe; the little sparrows on Archbishop Grey's tomb delighted her continually. The numberless heads in the transepts, grinning, yawning, crying, proved of inexhaustible interest; so too was Delilah clipping Samson's hair, whilst the strong man rent the lion over the aisle door. From the ghastly emaciated John Haxby, lying behind a grille, she ever shrank with horror.

In Mrs Furness's house Annis found abundant matters of

interest. The curiosities which had been collected by the Silver Poplar seemed to her never to exhaust themselves. When she thought she had seen all, Miss Furness would open a drawer, and display exquisite tropical shells and seaweeds, which she had not hitherto cast her eyes on. Or the lady would unlock a cabinet and produce a collection of Egyptian idols and fragments of a painted mummy case. The admiral's library was also there, consisting of voyages and travels to all parts of the globe, full of pictures, many coloured.

The little girl often thought of Hugh and Martha. Sometimes a feeling of longing came over her to be back in Sowden at the factory, reeling, but then the remembrance of the misery of that last day there returned and stifled the longing.

Mr Furness often wrote to his sister and sent her kind messages, telling her news about Sowden, and her cousin, but never mentioning Hugh. And now and then Martha put in a little note, hoping that it found Annis as it left her, in good health.

So time passed by. Christmas came, and the streets of York rang, like those of Sowden, with the strain

"Christians awake, salute the happy morn!"

chanted by a choir, bellowed by schoolboys, whistled by carriers, ground from a hand-organ, played by a German band, trolled out of tune by drunken men, till every soul in York was sick of being bidden "awake, and salute the happy morn," not in the early part of the day, but, more especially towards dusk of evening, and vociferously at night.

Christmas in Yorkshire is a time for noise and merriment. Then the streets are thronged with parties of mummers endeavouring to obtain admission into peaceful households, where they may cause uproar; or sword dancers seek turfy lawns on which to perform the play of St George; or the yule tup bursts into kitchens, frolicking and kicking, and only to be pacified with cake and ale. Then by night and by day children prowl about with "milly-boxes" containing a Virgin and child, surrounded with oranges and coloured bows, craving a little offering to adorn the box, in the pretty words of a pleasant carol:—

250

"We go a wassailing
Among the leaves so green."

And after the round of "milly-boxes" is over, comes the more serious round of Christmas boxes; boxes for coals, boxes for ringers, boxes for lamplighters, boxes for water-carriers, boxes for porters, boxes for errand-boys, boxes for milkmen, boxes for butchers' men, boxes for bakers' men, boxes for everyone. Indeed, any person for whom a job, however trifling, has been performed during the past twelvemonth, a job which has been paid for and is fondly deemed done with, is boxed. No-one with a little money at his disposal escapes being boxed; ladies suffer most, being boxed without the smallest compunction, boxed in their own houses, boxed on their doorsteps, boxed in the street, boxed even in church.

Christmas is unquestionably a joyous time — to the boxers; but it is a season of trial of temper and emptying of purses to the boxed.

There is little fear of those old English customs dying out which give opportunity for extortion of money.

One beautiful day after Christmas Miss Furness and Annis were walking on the city walls, which at York form a delightful promenade for two, but an aggravating one for three. After having made the circuit of the lower part of the town, they stood leaning on the parapet and looking at the turbid Ure.

"I miss them mountains and hills we had at Sowden," observed Annis.

"Do not say them," Miss Furness said; "say those, instead."

"Those mountains," the little girl repeated.

"I dare say you do feel the want of them, my dear," Miss Furness now answered. "The neighbourhood of York is very dull and flat. But then it has its charms. There is the river Ure."

"There is a river at Sowden," said Annis; "it is not quite so big as this one, but it is a fair-sized river for all that."

"It is black or blue with dye."

"Ah, Miss Furness, and this is brown with mud."

"Well, if you have a river at Sowden, you have not got a Minster."

"No," answered Annis; "that indeed we have not. I never

thought I should see so bonny a building — may I say bonny?"
she suddenly asked, looking cautiously up.

"Yes, by all means. It is a beautiful word, and far more
expressive than 'pretty'. I do not think you will venture to
compare your Sowden factories with the cathedral."

"No, I should not think of doing so. But I do miss the hills."

"My dear," observed Miss Furness, "you will find, all through
life, that you are losing some things and gaining others.
Remember, that if we are to be happy, and to profit by what
falls out, we must not repine over those things which are lost,
but keep a lookout for the things we are to gain. I hope you are
not fretting over your removal from Sowden."

"Oh, no, no, Miss Furness!" answered Annis, flutteringly. "I
hope you have not thought that. You have been so very, very
kind to me and I am so happy and comfortable. I would not for
the world have you think I was fretting."

"Dear child, I know that your heart must turn at times to the
old friends, old scenes, to memory dear; it is only natural."

"I did love Sowden," said Annis, musing.

"And those there," added Miss Furness.

"And *some* of those there," was the girl's correction.

"Of course, you could not love all," said the lady, laughing.

"Oh, Miss Furness!" Annis began. "I do wish my cousin
Martha knew you, and you knew her. She is one of them
girls—"

"Those."

"Of those girls who never do aught but what is right. Martha
always knows what is best to be done, at any time, choose how
great a difficulty —"

"One moment. That expression 'choose how' is peculiar.
Suppose you alter the wording a bit. There, Annis, you will
think I am always catching you up."

"Thank you for doing it. I want to speak right."

"I think you had better alter that sentence into 'however great
a difficulty she may be placed in'."

"Very well, Miss Furness. Now I will say it— " She suddenly
paused.

"What is the matter, dear?" asked Elizabeth Furness after a
while.

"Oh! Do look yonder. Do you see that strange figure?"

"Yes," answered Miss Furness, looking in the direction indicated. "I suppose you mean that stoutish, thickset woman."

"Do you see her veil?"

"She has her head turned. Yes. A red veil."

"I have seen that woman in the street, and in the Minster, and she always wears her veil down. And, besides, it is such an odd colour for a veil — is it not?"

"It certainly is an unusual colour."

"Have you observed her when she walks?"

"No, I did not notice her before this minute."

"Her walk is strange. She is queer altogether. When she is by, I cannot take my eyes off her, and—" Annis dropped her voice, "I can't but think she is looking at me through her red veil all the time of service at the Minster. I fancy I see her eyes glitter. And when I pass her —"

"Nonsense, Annis."

"Please, Miss Furness, I can't help it, so don't be angry."

"I am not angry."

"No, but I am afraid you will be when I say something. But I must say it. I am frightened of yon woman."

"Has she spoken to you?"

"No, but I think she follows me."

"Perhaps she wants assistance; she is evidently poor. Shall I go up to her and speak?"

"No, no, no!" anxiously catching Elizabeth's arm. The woman, who had been on the walls, now left them abruptly.

"Why should she wear that red veil always down?"

"Perhaps the poor thing suffers from a complaint in her face," answered Miss Furness.

Annis shuddered. Some memory was recalled by the words. "Let us go home," she said. "I hope I shall never see her face."

Chapter Twenty-Eight

"And now, if you please, let me hear the particulars."

"Of what, uncle?"

"I am clear as to the manner in which you got out of the water, but I am imperfectly acquainted with the manner in which you got into it. One or two facts are obvious. You did not plunge into the canal of your own accord; the man with whom you took the dive must have cast you in, and he must have had some reason for so treating you. Explain."

"You ask me to do that which is entirely beyond my power," answered Hugh.

"How so?"

"Because I am in the dark as to the cause, unless that be the simple one of insanity."

"Who threw you into the water?"

"That raving maniac, Earnshaw, your watchman. He attacked me furiously with a knife. Look at my hand; there are the evidences. Then he grasped me in his arms, and leaped over the bank with me into the canal. Uncle, I told you some while ago that the man was mad."

"It certainly looks as if he were mad; madder, I mean, than the majority of people. Most folk do not job at others with knives. The usual practice is to use the tongue for that purpose, and a much more damaging weapon that is than knife or stiletto. Most folk do not either jump with others into canals. They usually prefer to involve them in some desperate speculation. I want the reasons why this madman singled you out for attack. Why did he not attempt to murder me instead of you?"

"I believe he bears a dislike to me."

"Why so?"

"How can I tell, uncle?"

"Because you must be perfectly aware of the reason of this dislike. Nothing, my dear Hugh, goes on in this world without a reason. No effects are produced without causes. Why did Earnshaw dislike you?"

Hugh hesitated for some while. At last he said frankly — "I

believe he has taken my engagement to heart."

"Petticoats!" with a burst, like the explosion of a gun. "Always petticoats."

"I should like to know," said Hugh, "whether the fellow had turned up, alive or dead."

"No. He has not. The police have been making inquiries. The bargeman saw him sink and is strongly impressed with the conviction that the man is drowned. His body has not however been recovered as yet, notwithstanding that the drag has been used, and that a loaf weighted with quicksilver has been floated on the canal —"

"What, sir?"

"Ah! you do not understand. When a body is lost in a river or canal, it is the custom here for a penny loaf, with six penn'orth of mercury in it, to be launched on the water. Popular superstition avers that the bread will remain stationary over the spot where the corpse lies.'"

"And has this been tried?"

"Certainly. The bargeman conducted the experiment before a great concourse of interested and expectant people, but without result."

"Earnshaw wore a thick, heavy, greatcoat, which when sodden must have weighed heavy, and if he is drowned, will retard his rising."

"That he is drowned I have very little doubt. I shall have to get a new watchman and a fresh set of keys, for Earnshaw has carried down with him those of the warehouse and factory. These are now probably in his greatcoat pocket, in the slime of the canal bottom."

"It will be well to ascertain whether he really is lost."

"That can only be done by letting off the water of the canal, leave to do which is costly, as it retards traffic. To my mind, the negative evidence is as strong as the discovery of the body would prove. For, consider, a man with a face marked in the frightful manner that his is, must be observed wherever he goes. He will need shelter and food, and if he enters shop or lodging, his features at once attract attention; and the police are notified to be on the lookout for a man so disfigured."

"If Earnshaw does turn up alive, he must be put into a lunatic asylum."

"*If* he does. But I suspect he will trouble you no more. Now look in the paper, and see what a muddle has been made of your little adventure."

"Where? I should like to see."

"There. Next to that account of the robbery at Midgeroyd."

"What has taken place there?"

"Oh, only a cottage broken into and clothes stolen from it."

The paragraph in the *Mercury* was this:

SOWDEN. ENCOUNTER WITH A MADMAN

On Friday evening Mr Arkwright, the son of a well-known manufacturer in Sowden, was attacked in a second-class carriage on the Lancashire and Yorkshire line, between North Dean Junction and Sowden, by a maniac armed with a knife. The encounter was of the most desperate character; and Mr Arkwright, having been already severely wounded in several places, threw himself out of the carriage into the canal which adjoined the line of rails, and succeeded in reaching the other side in safety. The madman, however, in springing after him, struck the embankment, as it appears, and was stunned, for, having rolled into the water, he did not rise, though the spot where he had fallen was anxiously watched, both by the gentleman he was pursuing, and a bargeman who happened to be close at hand. As yet, the body has not been covered. The deceased, whose name was Joseph Earnshaw, has long been regarded as dangerous. Mr Arkwright, who was promptly attended by a surgeon, is convalescent, none of the wounds being mortal, though one was within a hair's-breadth of a vital centre.

"I think," said Hugh, laughing, "that the purveyor of information for the *Mercury* in this neighbourhood has been as near the truth as was the wound to a vital centre in me." Then he ran his eye over the next paragraph.

MIDGEROYD, NEAR SOWDEN

On the night of the 30th, a lone cottage belonging to a somewhat eccentric old lady in the hamlet of Midgeroyd was broken into by some ruffians, who carried off wearing apparel, having first consumed the contents of the good woman's larder. The burglars made so little noise that the old lady did not discover her loss till the following morning. It is probable that they anticipated finding money, but were disappointed. The police are confident that the perpetrators of this outrage belong to a band of professional thieves, who have for some while infested the neighbourhood of Halifax, which is their headquarters.

"Do you know anything of the poor creature who has been robbed?" asked Hugh.

"Yes, a little," answered his uncle. "It is old Peggy Lupton, a lone woman who is popularly regarded as a miser, and who is actually a poor creature who has known better days and who finds it a hard matter to make both ends meet."

"I see."

"Peggy is a good woman, and somewhat eccentric withal. She lives quite by herself in a lonely place. But Gretchen can tell you more about her than I can, for she visits her occasionally and gives her a little assistance in the shape of a pound of tea or sugar, and odds and ends of clothes. You may depend upon it, before long Mrs Lupton will be hovering about our door, full of woe, and throwing out hints that she is short of dresses on account of the robbery. I have seen the poor woman equipped in a complete suit of your aunt's old clothes. There was an old familiar green tartan I was very fond of, and to which I had become so accustomed that I looked to see the tartan at tea every bit as truly as I looked for muffins and cake. One day my wife appeared in a different gown. I remonstrated. She assured me she had given away the green tartan; and sure enough, next Sunday, Peggy Lupton turned up in church wearing the identical gown I had grown to love. It was exasperating."

"And now the green tartan is in the possession of the thieves?"

"I should not be surprised. By the way, I wonder whether something else has gone."

"What, sir?"

"Something about which Gretchen and I have had many a

257

joke; indeed at one time, almost a quarrel. She brought with her from Germany a quantity of foreign articles of apparel, which would do well enough in Deutschland, but which are quite out of place in England. Among other articles of this sort was a veil. On the continent people indulge in extraordinary colours. They have crimson and blue umbrellas, whilst we never rise above green. The ladies are not content to veil their faces with black, blue or green, but affect red; and one Sunday, of all days, your aunt appeared in church with a carmine veil. I secreted it on my return home, but she found it again. I protested against its use; she declaimed against English want of appreciation of colour. I vowed I would burn that veil if I found her in it again. She entreated for it, and at last we compromised matters by giving it to Peggy Lupton. Now, Hugh, shut up your book and come along. We must be home early for tea, as the Doldrums are expected."

"I am ready, uncle."

"What do you think of Laura, eh?"

"She is a very nice, unaffected girl, and good-looking as well."

"And she has lots of money. Keep your eyes open. The secret of success in life lies in being always alive to opportunities and seizing them as they occur."

Laura really was what Hugh said, a nice unaffected girl, and she was also decidedly good-looking. She had dark hair, a rich brown skin, with cheeks that glowed warm and luscious as a peach, bright, dancing hazel eyes, full of life and light, a faultless figure and an elastic step. Laura was never grave. She woke with a chirp in the morning and went chirruping to bed at night. Her mother plied her with coffins and she danced over them; she impressed on her shrouds and she laughed behind them; she regaled her with funerals, and they got into her head and made her giddy. Yorkshire people are supplied with an almost inexhaustible supply of animal spirits. In this they are distinguished from the Lancashire folk, whose calm saddened tone is in marked contrast to the exuberant mirth of the good people east of Blackstone Edge. In a Lancashire town you meet pale earnest faces, bowed head and eyes full of intelligence but no sparkle. In a Yorkshire town you are startled by the gushing vitality that boils up on all sides. The "loosing" of a Lancashire mill is a different thing altogether from that of one in Yorkshire. From the former, the hands steal away, silent, thoughtful and depressed; from the latter they burst away in an effervescent palpitating flood, noisy with laughter and song and joke, and glowing with leaping blood and bubbling spirits.

Laura had enough vital energy in her to supply a whole Lancashire family. The day was too short for expending it. She flooded her mother with her vivacity and then plunged down into the kitchen, where she speedily excited an uproar. Then she darted into town, paying visits or shopping, and letting off a little of her spirits wherever she went. This excess of life in one unrefined or uneducated becomes very generally vulgarity. Had Laura not ladylike instincts, and had she not been at good schools, she would have been set down as a giddy boisterous tomboy. As it was, she never degenerated into vulgarity, and never descended to real improprieties.

Mrs Doldrums was a woman of no education or natural refinement: she had few interests, and those few were centred in mortality and smoke–jacks. Deceases and the subsequent interments were the principal subjects of her thoughts; but mortal diseases, as conducing ultimately to death and a funeral, presented subsidiary attractions. Smoke–jacks, as having led to her fortune, were not without their charms in her eyes, and she could descant on the merits of her husband's patent with vehemence if not eloquence. If the old lady was in body with the smoke–jack, then, she was in spirit with the deceased.

But Laura, by having been sent to school, was elevated to a sphere sufficiently removed from the smoke–jack, and infinitely remote from the mouldering Doldrums.

In society the mother was not brilliant. She was wont to sit and smile, and turn her rings on her fingers, and wipe her brow with a handkerchief, perfectly silent, till some casual remark, more or less remotely connected with smoke–jacks, bereavement or decease, fell in her way, when she rose with a rush, burst in on the conversation, expanded, became dogmatic and noisy, then collapsed and settled down to the bottom once more, waiting for another rise.

Mrs Doldrums affected a title. This title was, "The Relict". It was one of which she was proud. Providence, she was wont to say, not royalty, had made her the Relict of Jonathan Doldrums. To circumstances, not to ancestry, she owed this honourable distinction. Some had obtained titles by a career of crime, she by the over–ruling hand of destiny.

Mrs Doldrums was a bad reader, a worse writer, and an abject speller. A consciousness of her defects made her profess ocular debility, which no spectacles could relieve. Accordingly, she shrank from reading, shunned writing and revolted against spelling.

The stout lady's ideas were not harmonised by what the schoolmen call the grace of congruity. They were accustomed to fuse together distinct conceptions into a compound far less valuable than the famous Corinthian brass; and when she did read her newspaper, or when she heard it read to her, she rose from it with a general confusion of ideas as to the localities of the battles, the objects for which armies fought, and the sides on which the generals were engaged. And when the element of Court of Probate and Divorce, and again, that of royal movements, were imported into the news from the seat of war, Mrs Doldrums' conception of the state of politics was one of inextricable confusion, in the midst of which gleamed a single prominent spot of red — General Garibaldi.

Laura Doldrums made no attempt to conceal her admiration of Hugh. The romance attaching to him had invested him with a charm in her eyes, equal to that characterising the conventional hero of a novel. She cared the less to hide her admiration because she regarded him as engaged, and therefore carried beyond the reach of her love. Had he been free, she would have been more cautious in exhibiting her appreciation of him; but as he was secured, she felt as if all necessity for masking her devotion was obviated. Hugh, on the other hand, was flattered. It was impossible for anyone to dislike Miss Doldrums, and when a young man feels he is attractive to a pretty, bright and amiable girl, he cannot fail to be fascinated. Hugh did find pleasure in her society, and he did not object to let his feelings be known.

Young people of opposite sexes are shy of one another as long as there exists a possibility of their becoming united. The girl thinks that the man is struck with her and intends to make an offer, when he shows an approach to familiarity; and he, on his side, is ever on his guard lest she with whom he is brought in contact should suppose, by his throwing aside restraint, that he entertains ulterior designs. But when this cause of mutual distrust is removed, they frankly and readily form friendships of a simple and guileless nature, such as that which exists between brother and sister, beautiful and mutually beneficial, and of which each through life preserves a hallowed remembrance.

Mr Arkwright was highly pleased to notice the regard for one another exhibited by the young people; and he fondly hoped that this regard would ripen into attachment, which would in turn mellow into love. But Laura was not one to whom Hugh could have devoted heart and soul. Her liveliness attracted, but did not captivate him; her elasticity of spirits pleased, but did not fascinate; he was amused by the sparkle of her mirth, but he feared lest it should evaporate and leave flatness behind. He observed in Laura abundance of vivacity, but felt the deficiency of repose.

On the return of Mr Arkwright and his nephew to their house, they found the Relict of Jonathan Doldrums and Laura already arrived. The little German lady had involved herself into inextricable confusion in attempting to make an explanation to Mrs Doldrums of the method of cooking spinach with sugar in her own country. And that lady, believing that the conversation turned on politics, was descanting on General "Garibawldy", whom she regretted to find involved in a sad divorce case, on account of Herr Bismarck's attachment to the infamous singer, Chassepot, an affair which was likely to result in dividends to the ritualist

"Don't, Mother!" deprecated Miss Doldrums.

"My dear, remember my eyes are not what they were. I have consulted the most eminent oculists in Halifax and Bradford, and they all agree that I must mind my eyes; that they want humouring and that I am not to exert them."

"Yes, Mother," persisted Laura; "but surely your eyes did not pursue the General into Austria and bring him to bay in the Dividends."

"My dear, I assure you it was all in the papers. The ritualists are in arms, marching upon Rome, and General Garibawldy is at their head."

"Garibaldi!" exclaimed Hugh. "You amaze me, ma'am."

"Yes, sir. Garibawldy is an eminent ritualist. He wears a scarlet vestment, and if that ain't being a ritualist, I don't know what is."

"And marching against Rome?"

"No, no! You misunderstand me. Count Bismarck of Alipa— Laura, what is it?"

"Oh, Henry," interrupted Mrs Arkwright; "what do you think? I have had one visit, and from whom?"

"I cannot tell."

"Guess, Henry, guess."

"Count Bismarck or the great ritualist Garibaldi?"

"But no. From the old woman, Mistress Lupton."

"Did I not tell you so?" asked Mr Arkwright, turning to Hugh with a laugh.

"It is true she has been robbed."

"Yes, I am aware of that. I saw it in the paper."

"Poor thing. It is *schrechlich*! And she is affrighted all over. The robbers stole the most of her habiliments, and she is quite ill of the fright. They ate up her beautiful pie, and they drank her beer, and they took away her habili—"

"Enough of that word!"

"What shall I use?"

"Clothes is the proper term."

"You taught me of the other. Well, *es geht nichts*! what think you they have taken?"

"The pie."

"Ah! yes, but besides."

"The beer."

"That is very well, but still more."

"Why, the habiliments."

"The clothes, sir. And of them?"

"I never enter into particulars, especially when the articles belong to a lady."

"Why, Henry, the veil, the red veil. That is gone also."

Chapter Twenty-Nine

One evening Annis was standing in the nave of York Minster, listening to the organ voluntary after the service. The gas in lines of light below the triform, and the nine jets above the altar, filled the choir with a soft yellow glare; but outside the great screen of the kings all was dark, except that a flake of light fell through the screen gates, and a subdued twilight hung about the intersection of the nave and transepts. The five sisters were like plates of frosted silver. A faint glimmer stole through the rich tracery of the western window; the nave pillars were scarcely distinguishable.

Annis stepped into the south aisle, where she might stand unobserved and drink in, in silent rapture, the rolling music of St Cecilia's instrument. The organist was playing "Despairing, cursing rage," from the Creation, and he made the old walls quiver with the thunder of the great fugue. Annis was completely abstracted and did not notice the choristers clattering from their vestry to the transept door; nor observe the minor canon stalk past with hat and stick, complacently stroking his light whiskers; nor the blind gentleman feel his way, tapping the pavement with his staff; nor the old women disappear, hawking and coughing. Annis had a genuine West Riding love of music, and the great organ in the Minster excited her daily delight. Hitherto she had only heard the singing of the church choir of Sowden, and its small instrument. There was a magnificence in the great organ of the Minster which overwhelmed her.

The throbbing of the serried waves, the quivering of the walls, and the shiver of the glass suddenly ceased, and the exquisite chant, "A new created world", floated through the dusky Minster and thrilled the little girl's whole being with rapture.

When a hand was laid on her arm she scarcely noticed it, so entranced was she, and it was only when the flutter of a veil before her eyes attracted her attention, that she all at once became conscious that the mysterious woman, for whom she had expressed to Miss Furness her aversion, was holding her and endeavouring to lead her further down the nave aisle.

"Let go," said Annis, startled. "What do you want?"

Then the organ bellowed forth once more: "Dismay'd, the host of hell's dark spirits fly; Down they sink in the deep abyss, To endless night. Despairing, cursing rage, attends their rapid fall"; and it was impossible for her to catch a word of the reply in the vibrations of sound.

But as again the pure, tender melody, "A new created world", swept softly along, she heard a musical voice say, "I am very poor, I am very poor, Miss Greenwell."

"Do you want relief?" asked Annis, compassionately.

"Will you visit me? I am very poor."

The organ had ceased. The voice of the woman with the red veil affected Annis strangely. She looked nervously and fearfully at the thickset female figure before her, with the strangely-coloured veil drawn over the face.

"Where do you live?"

"In Peter Lane."

"I will tell Miss Furness."

"No," said the woman sharply. "You must come. No one else."

"I really cannot. You are mysterious. Why should you wish to see me and not the lady with whom I live?"

"There are reasons," answered the woman.

"All out!" bawled the verger, rapping his staff on the ground. The echoes lumbered down the aisles and muttered in the chapels and vestries.

"You must come. Promise."

"Indeed I will not."

"All out!" again, and imperiously.

"You are hardhearted; surely you will come and see a poor thing who is nigh clemmed."

"Miss Furness will visit you and give you relief."

"I will have no Miss Furness. I must and will have you."

"Now then!" from the verger. "All out! All out, please."

So they were hurried towards the transept door. The white-jacketed bellows–blowers straggled past. Then the organist went out. The gas was extinguished. Down went the verger's staff with a far–echoing stroke. The transept clock ticked the hour; for the last time the verger called, vociferously and ferociously,

"All out!"

All out! muttered the walls about Archbishop Scope. Now the prelate can lie still through the long night, wrapped in contemplation. All out! whispered the slabs about the emaciated John Haxby. Now the moon will flare in on his ghastly face and skeleton limbs, and none will see him turn and laugh and grind his teeth behind his grille. All out! was called from wall to wall of the choir, and alone in the hush of night, the brass eagle will wait poised and expectant till twelve o'clock, when he will rise and sail thrice round the great church, in and out among the moon-streaks from the clerestory windows. All out! went laughing down the dark triforium of the nave, and the dragon will turn his head with none to see him uncoil, and he will hiss at St George, and the Saint will smite him once, twice, thrice.

All out! faintly in the sepulchres below, telling the dead that the time of the living was over, and the time of the dead is come, when they may rise for the solemn mass of souls.

"Annis!" was spoken slowly and distinctly from behind the red veil.

The girl's blood leaped to her heart.

"Annis. I expect you to visit me tomorrow, at three, in Peter Lane."

"I —"

"You will come!" Then down the steps, across the yard, and away into the gloom, went the stranger.

Miss Furness observed that something was wrong with Annis when she came in. She looked up from the book she was reading to her mother and said, "My dear, you look very white."

"Oh, do I, miss? It is nothing."

"You have been standing listening to the organ, have you not?"

"Yes, I have. I could not help it. The music was so beautiful."

"Well, and you have got a chill. Now come up to the fire. There, darling, kneel down on the mat and get the roses back into the little gardens of your cheeks. We must not have winter there."

"I—wish—Annis—you—would—put—those tubes—"began Mrs Furness, slowly, and with great effort to speak distinctly.

"Oh, fudge, Mammy!" laughed Elizabeth; "you know you

can't have them till you go to roost."

Annis knelt before the fire, expanding her hands, and musing on what had taken place. She felt a pressure on her heart, caused by fear; and she asked herself again and again whether or not she should go to Peter Lane on the morrow. She was not in general reserved with Miss Furness, but she could not resolve to tell her her trouble. Bessie had laughed at Annis for being afraid of the red veil, and Annis was too sensitive to incur this again.

When she went to bed at night, it was not to sleep. She turned wearily from side to side, but could not find rest, for the poor little mind was still revolving the same question, Shall I go? It was strange that such a simple matter as a visit to a poor woman should so harass her, but the red-veiled person was regarded by her with a peculiar and inexplicable repugnance. Whenever in the Minster she caught sight of that veil — and if it were in the church at all, she was certain to detect it at once — she could not keep her eyes off it. It fascinated her, with the fascination of horror. She was imbued with a sickening dread lest the veil should be lifted, though for a moment only. Her wakeful eyes looked towards the window where the Milky Way streaked the dark night sky with hazy light. She heard the Minster clock tell the hours, and they seemed to glide along with speed. Then the form taken by the window curtain distressed her; it assumed a resemblance to an antiquated bonnet, over which hung a veil. She turned her face to the wall with a weary sigh, and endeavoured, by counting sheep going through a hedge-gap, to trick sleep into closing her eyelids. But when she had counted till uncertainty supervened, the form of the shepherd appeared standing in the gap, wearing a rough coat and slouched hat, and she was brought to consciousness with a start, by turning mechanically in bed, fearing lest she should see his face.

Then she crept from her place, and going to the washstand, half filled the tumbler with cold water and drank it off.

The clock tolled three. She fled to her bed, thinking that in twelve hours she was due at the house of the Red Veil.

At last a broken sleep came on, from which she woke scarcely refreshed in the morning, and still with the leaden weight upon her heart.

"I must, oh, I must go!" she said, despairingly.

266

Three o'clock in the afternoon sounded as Annis entered Peter Lane. It is an old, wretched, half street in the city, with tottering, unpainted, unplastered houses on either side, their windows dirty and cobwebbed, and many broken and patched with scraps of newspaper. A low public-house stands on one side, with a broad window half obscured by a green gauze screen. Near it is a shop, where is sold ginger-beer in summer, or what professes to be ginger-beer, but looks like the wringings of dishclouts; and in the window are unwholesome pink and yellow drops in bottles, which have adhered and partially dissolved. And on the opposite side in a window are some discoloured eggs, and a plaster cow spotted with flymarks, and a small badly-written label affixed to the glass by various coloured wafers, which must have been moistened to thin pulp before applied: on this label is written, "Fresh milk".

The houses are high, and are apparently inhabited chiefly by children, and children with perennial colds in their heads. Uncombed, unwashed heads of small and big "bairns" appear at the windows of the top storey; on the next below are to be heard children fighting; on the next is to be seen a woman smacking a child on a sensitive part of its body, and the said child running, not at the nose only, but at the eyes and mouth as well.

Peter Lane, having pursued a short career of dirt and disorder, suddenly shrinks into a narrow passage about three feet across, with doors opening into it, but no windows, seeing that it is too contracted to admit of much light. Across the wider, and therefore least reputable part of the lane, in that its width allows greater scope for the exhibition of its degradation, is hung a clothes line, on which are suspended articles of wearing apparel and chamber linen, which have been washed; but these articles are all so much out of repair, as to excite surprise that they were thought worth washing, and next, are so badly washed, that it is only their position on a clothes line which entitles them to be regarded as having undergone soap and water.

Just where the lane contracts is an accumulation of broken crockery, orange peel, carrot tops, and potato parings, round which a lean, yellow, stumpy-tailed tom-cat is cautiously smelling. Near this spot a fetid gutter takes its rise, a gutter which is the principal source of amusement to the children of

267

the lane, for therein, from earliest infancy, they paddle with their feet and dabble with their hands, and over it straddle at a maturer age, and thence derive the major portion of the dirt with which they decorate their persons, and especially begrime their noses. On this, in summer, they float walnut-shells, and in winter slide; into this they pour the slops of the houses, and out of this gather an abundant crop of typhus, cholera and scarlatina seed.

It was into this lane that Annis entered, frightened and looking from side to side. She passed the tavern and the ginger-beer shop, and was about to enter the narrowed passage, when the door of a small yellow-washed hovel, jammed in between two tall toppling houses, opened and in it stood the woman with the red veil.

"I have been expecting you."

"I have come," said Annis, faintly.

"Come in."

The girl looked round and hesitated. The woman caught her by the wrist and drew her within.

'Follow me."

The Red Veil went first down a low passage, leading towards the back of the house, threw open a rickety, wormeaten door, and led her into the room.

"Sit down." The woman pointed to a low three-legged stool near the fire. Annis looked about for a chair, but there was only one, and that the strange veiled female took. She pointed again to the stool, and the girl seated herself on it.

Neither spoke. The woman looked intently at her from behind her veil, and Annis leaned her cheek on her hand.

"Yes, like that," said the woman, shortly; "as of old."

That was the position in which the girl had been wont to sit in the little cottage in the sand-pit.

"You're changed, too," the woman said, after a long pause.

The room in which Annis found herself was very small and low. The house was old. The timber of the floor of the room above showed black, as there was no ceiling. By the side of the fire there was a little one-pane window, or peephole. The main window was in compartments, partly latticed with old smoke-tinted quarries, partly patched with square panes, "bull's-eyed" in the middle. A scanty bit of green curtain was drawn back from the window. The walls were papered with various patterns, in strips, of the most discordant colours, and all dirty, peeling off and tattered.

Before the fire lay coiled up a white cat, very clean, on a shred of rug.

"Totts!" whispered Annis.

The cat looked up, stretched itself and leaped onto her lap; there it coiled itself up once more.

"Do you know me?" asked the strange woman.

"I think I do," the girl answered faintly.

"Shall I lift my veil?"

"No, no, no!" with a cry of distress and a shiver which sent the cat off her lap.

"The same as ever," followed by a deep sigh. The voice had lost its musical tones, and was deep and sonorous.

"Why have you come here? Oh, why did you come?" asked Annis, with her eyes determinedly fixed on the cat.

"Because I am constrained to hide."

Annis shuddered. "You killed that dreadful man," she said.

"Yes, I killed him — him who was insulting you."

"Oh, why did you do that, Joe? But I suppose you did not mean to do it. No, I am sure it was done accidentally, and I have said nothing about it to anyone. I have been so afraid of telling what I know, and getting you into danger."

"You are anxious for me?"

"Yes, Joe, of course I am. You rescued me from that man-monkey, and I feel bound to do what I can to save you from the consequences of what followed."

"Annis."

"Yes, Joe."

"That man was a hypocrite."

"I know it. I feared and disliked him."

"Do you fear me?"

She could not answer with her lips; but there was no mistaking the meaning of the pale cheeks and nervously twitching hand, and look of the distended eyes.

"Do you dislike me?"

"Oh! do not ask me such questions. Please do not. I am very,

very grateful to you for having saved me from the man-monkey. I shall never forget what I owe you for your ready help that dreadful night."

"And you will do all you can to screen me?"

"Yes, indeed I will. I have not spoken to a soul of my having seen you in the lane that night with — Oh! I cannot bear to think of that."

"Did you suspect me in this disguise?"

"I do not know what I thought. No, Joe; I do not think I did, till I heard your voice, and even then I was not sure. But I always felt — " She hesitated.

"Well, what did you feel?"

"I felt frightened when I saw that veil ever down."

"What has made you visit me today, suspecting who I was?"

"I was afraid, if I did not come, that you would be seeking me out at home."

"Home?"

"At Mrs Furness's house. and then there might have been danger to you, as questions would have been asked, and I could not have told lies. And besides —" She broke down and hung her head.

"Go on. And besides."

"I cannot." Her tears burst from her eyes, and she was compelled to give way to a fit of sobbing. Earnshaw did not attempt to interrupt it, till she had herself overcome its violence. Then he said leisurely again —

"Go on. And besides."

"Joe!" She spoke in a tremulous voice. "I should so like to know something about my old home. I hear so very little."

He growled in his strange beastlike manner, and began to pace the room, muttering to himself. She gazed at him in alarm. He must have seen her fear, for he stopped suddenly and asked, "You want to know all about folks at Sowden?"

"Oh, yes; so much. I have been here many months and heard nothing. Tell me something, do, pray."

"I have been here for some months, also."

"But when you left, were all well? — all at the mill?"

"Whom do you ask for especially?"

"Martha and Susan and Rebecca and Jane Foljambe."

"Yes."

"And— Oh, Joe! Is —" She trembled, poor little bird! For four months she had not heard a word of Hugh, or been able to speak of him, and her heart ached to know something about him. But yet she dare not ask.

"Do you ask after Hugh Arkwright?"

"Yes, yes!" glad that the question was put for her.

From beneath the veil proceeded a long low howl. "I do not know," he said at last.

Spots of colour had risen to her cheeks. Now they vanished again; and her head, which had been eagerly raised, sank upon her hand. Earnshaw strode up to her, grasped her by the shoulders, and said, in his deep sonorous tones, "Tell me truly, lass, do you love him?"

The little girl trembled in his powerful grasp, and, without answering, covered her face with both her hands. The disguised man did not relinquish his hold, but shook her gently to attract her attention. She felt that his eyes were fixed upon her with an intensity of interest from behind the veil; she dared not look up and catch their glitter through the red gauze, lest she should cry out in the agony of her horror. But every nerve of her body was excited and quivering, and the pressure of the hands on her shoulders struck through her to the soles of her feet.

"Answer me," said the man.

She clasped her hands, and, looking vacantly into the fire, replied, "I do, indeed I do. I have heard nothing of him now for many months and I am so anxious and troubled, that I cannot feel happy. Do, Joe, do tell me something about him."

"I can tell you no good."

"Joe!" plaintively, tremulously. "What do you mean? Is he well?"

"I cannot say."

"Tell me this, then. Is he alive? I fear such things, sometimes."

"I cannot tell you even that."

"Oh, Joe! I have such an ache here." She laid her hand on her bosom. "I long so much to know something about him. I do not wish to see him, but just to hear of him, to be sure that he is alive and well and happy; and I thought you might have been able to give me some little information. One evening I was on the walls at dusk, looking over the river, and I fell into a sort of waking dream and I seemed not to see anything; but all at once an unspeakable terror came over me, with nothing apparent to cause it. I was not afraid for myself, but I thought Hugh was in danger. I heard the scream of the engine coming into York station, and somehow, unaccountably to me, it mixed itself up with the terror that oppressed me. And then, all at once, as the whistle stopped, I became conscious of the rushing water below the walls, and I was chilled to ice, and there was struggle within me as though I were battling with the flood, then a sharp pain in my chest, just as if I had been struck there. Yet all the while, I did not feel for myself, but for *him*. I could not sleep that night, and since then I have always had a restless fear hanging about me, and a longing to know how he is. Is it not strange, that the very day after I had that waking dream, I saw you standing in your red veil by the Minster door for the first time."

Earnshaw let go his hold of her as she spoke, and recommenced his pacing up and down the room.

"Annis," he said, "you shall know something about him shortly."

"Oh, thank you, thank you. But do not expose yourself to danger on my account."

"I want to know as well as you. But I tell you this, you shall never be Hugh Arkwright's wife."

"I do not suppose that I ever shall," she answered sadly. "I now know better than I did what stands between us. No, I never shall be. But I must think of him still and long to know how he is; and I shall always pray for him."

"Do you ever pray for me?"

"Joe, I have not as yet, but I will."

"Do so."

"You will tell me something shortly about him?"

"Yes, yes. Damn! How you go back to *him* at every moment. You were talking of *me* last. Speak about me now."

"What shall I say? Are you very well, Joe?"

"I am never well with this face." He made as though he would lift his veil, and Annis, seeing the motion, quickly turned her head to the wall. Seeing this, be burst into a loud discordant laugh.

"I am going back to Sowden," he said, when his laughter ceased. "You send me to Hugh Arkwright."

"I would not have you run into any danger. I had rather that you did not go. At all events, do not wear that dreadful red veil. It unnecessarily attracts attention."

"Does it? It suits my complexion."

"Yes, but red veils are not worn now, and people are forced by the colour to notice you, when otherwise they might not give you a thought. Where did you get it?"

"That I will not tell."

"Will you wear this one instead?" asked Annis, drawing a parcel from her pocket and opening it. "I brought this thick dark green veil for you on my way. Give me that other."

"You take an interest in my welfare."

"Indeed I do," said the girl gently. "I could not do otherwise, knowing how grievous are your trials, and how great a service you once rendered me."

"Turn your face while I change veils," Earnshaw said in a softened tone. Annis obeyed. Near the fireplace was a small square pane of glass let into the wall. This commanded the street, the main window of the room opening into a little back yard. Annis looked from the dark room into the dusky Peter Lane, whilst the red silk veil was being untied, and the green one being fastened on the bonnet.

"If you determine on going to Sowden," she said, "remember that the cottage in the sand–pit is mine. It belonged to Mother, and is unlet. I believe that John Rhodes has seen to its being set to rights since the flood. You can go there. Martha would be able to get the key for you; and if you tell her you do not want it to be known in Sowden that you are there, she will, I am sure, be silent. You can always trust Martha. Give her my best love, please."

"I can let myself in without the key," answered Joe. "What are you looking at so fixedly now, lass?"

"I think I saw a policeman pass the little window, and come to this door. Hark! I hear him in the passage."

"He is come for me," said Earnshaw, composedly. "Now, lass, detain him as long as you possibly can."

They heard the voice of the officer making inquiries at the door and the words of the lodger, who occupied the front room on the left, in answer —

"On, down yonder, you can't miss. Door on t' right hand," left them in no uncertainty of the object of the policeman's visit. Earnshaw slipped through a side door into the back kitchen, which communicated with the yard, and Annis was left in fluttering expectation.

The room was nearly dark now, but a glow from the fire illumined the floor, and the puss lay basking in it, on its side, with the legs extended. Annis drew the chair into the gloomiest corner and sat down. She heard each step of the policeman, as he stumbled along the passage, and momentarily expected his entrance.

But just before he came to the door, Earnshaw stepped back into the room, caught up the white cat, and disappeared with it.

The policeman rapped at the door, and Annis called tremulously to him to come in.

"Service, ma'am," with a look round the room, and a nod towards the figure seated in the shadowed corner. "Hope you enjoys middling health. I've come after a little job, you see, and I hope there won't be no unpleasantness whatever."

"What do you want?" she asked in a low tone.

"I want to know all about some articles of clothing, a green tartan gown more partickler, and a red veil, as was taken some few months ago from an old lady's house near Sowden. We ain't bound to suspect you, you know, but I happen to have observed a werry similarity atween your dress and them articles as was taken away by, there's no doubt, a gang of thieves nigh Halifax, and there are a deal of cases where they've been at their carryings on. Now, may happen we may catch 'em through that gown and veil, if you can tell us where you bought 'em. Some slop shop, I reckon; and if you say where they was got, we can easy find out the sort of chaps who disposed of 'em, do you see?"

"Yes," faintly.

"I ain't going to frighten an old woman such as you. You ain't like to be house-breaking of a night, and burgling. That's what men does, it ain't the province of old women. But if men steal

274

female garments, it ain't their province to wear 'em, though some men is over partial to petticoats. If they take 'em, they dispose of 'em to a receiving shop, and the shop sells 'em. And if we can find them as buys 'em, do you see, we can learn where that party bought 'em, and we can discover from the shop as sold 'em whence they got 'em. That's clear as a parabola of Euclid, now ain't it?"

"Yes."

"So now I must know all about where you purchased that tartan gown, and that red silk veil. So tell me, old lady."

"I never got them."

"How can you have the everlasting face to tell such a busted lie? When I see you with my bodily eyes in 'em, coming down Coney Street today and yesterday, and the day afore that. It's a wonder to me I never observed 'em before. But we're bidden look alive over those eternal thieves, and I saw the identical articles specified in the 'Hue and Cry', which you wear every mortal day."

"I do not wear them. You have made a mistake."

"Me make a mistake! Not if I knows it, missis. That ain't my province, no more nor wearing a glazed hat ain't yours. I'll just do myself the favour of showing a light."

He lit a twist of paper at the fire, and applied the flame to a tallow candle on the mantelshelf.

"There now. I'll take a good look. Ginger and treacle! But who are you?" staring at Annis.

"I am visiting the old person who lodges here."

"A visit of charity?" examining her from head to foot.

"Yes," answered the girl; "I suppose you may call it so. The woman lodging here told me she was very poor, and in want, also I came to make inquiries."

"Who are you, miss, may I ask? I'm dumbfoozled with having made such a mistake."

"I live with Mrs Furness in the Minster yard."

"And where is the old woman?"

"She is out."

"And are you waiting for her, miss?"

"Yes."

"Where may she be? Have you been waiting long?"

"Not very long. What time is it?"

"Half after four o' clock."

"She generally goes to the Minster at four."

"You're right. But ain't you seen her?"

"Yes, I have seen her."

The policeman shook his head, and opening the door into the back kitchen, peered in there. The door to the yard was locked on the outside.

The moment that the man's back was turned, Annis rose from her chair, crossed the room, and thrust the red veil between the bars into the fire.

"There's a smell of burning; you're singeing yourself," said the policeman, on his return. "You shouldn't ought to stand so close to the fire; you'll turn your gown rusty, you will."

"I suppose I need wait no longer," said Annis, nervously.

"There's no occasion, miss. I'll make myself comfortable here till the old lady comes back from the Minster, and I'll tell her you kindly called. Miss, you *are* burning." He came over to the fire with his candle, stooped and picked out of the grate a fragment of smouldering red silk gauze.

"I may say," said the policemen, "that this is a rum go. I believe this is a bit of that identical veil. I never saw a rummier go. I may assert, miss, without fear of contradiction, it's the very rummiest of rummy goes."

"I will say good evening." Annis made a slight bow as she glided towards the door.

"Stay a minute, miss. When did you see the old lady last?" Annis hesitated.

"I don't mean particular as to the minute."

"A short while before you came in."

"And you was waiting her return?"

"Yes."

"What made you think she was gone to the Minster?"

"I did not say she was. I said I thought she generally went there, and that is perfectly true."

"Which way did she leave the house?"

"She went through the back kitchen. I only saw her go in there."

"The door into the yard is locked from the outside," mused

276

the policeman. "By Ginger! I have it, she locked the door against me. Why, miss, will you believe it! No, you hardly can, but I see right through it, from one end to t'other. She must ha' seen me coming and guessed what I were a coming after. She's deeper not I thought for, and we're diddled both of us. You'd better go home, miss, for I must make a search. Odd, ginger alive! To think I should have missed her. As I came in at one door, she hooked it out of t' other. Hold hard!" this to Annis. "Will you tell me how long this party has been in York?"

"About four months."

"You are sure?"

"Yes. I first observed the person on the last day of October."

"Ginger!" he exclaimed. "To think that Me, Me, Mr Physic, is diddled."

Chapter Thirty

The cold damp of the morning had taken the stiffness out of Mrs Jumbold's curls, and they depended on either side of her face in elongated screws. The cold had given a dull blue tinge to her nose, and had purpled her lips, and reddened her knuckles. Mr Jumbold was supplied in the person of his wife with a barometer and a thermometer in one. When the weather was dry, her ringlets were short and crisp; when moist, they uncurled and draggled to her shoulders. The hue of her nose, lips and knuckles was also a sure indication of the temperature.

A cold spring rain had set in, and Mrs Jumbold's ringlets were faithful witnesses to the downfall, and her nose, knuckles and lips to the chill. She tramped about Sowden in goloshes, with a black umbrella expanded over her poke bonnet, her gown drawn up to a somewhat unnecessary height, displaying a pair of exceedingly thin stocking-encased props, which described segments and curves and straight lines and angles, about the causeway, in avoidance of little water-filled hollows. Mrs Jumbold affected rainy days. When the sun shone and the sky was blue, she kept much at home, but as soon as the clouds burst and the day gave tokens of an intention to be disagreeable, the doctor's wife emerged from her door, in goloshes, umbrella and white props, to make charity visits, to call on her acquaintances, and to do her shopping.

She was not unwont to combine the visits to the sick and poor with those to her equals in position in one expedition, bringing, with the goloshes and umbrella, dirt and water into whatever house received her.

If she had visited a cottage in which was scarlatina, or better, typhus, best of all, smallpox, she made a point of next visiting a friend who had children. "I never take infection," she said to herself, "and I do not believe in it. If there be such a thing, then I am only making work for my husband."

On the day, the events of which are now being recorded, this lady called on Mrs Tomkins, an intimate friend.

"Come, Sissy; come, Gussy," croaked Mrs Jumbold,

addressing the little daughters of Mrs Tomkins. "Come and give me a kiss."

Then, holding the children in her arms, she said, fixing her eyes on the mother, "Do you know that poor thing, Mrs Bowers, in Westgate? She has four children down with measles. I have just been sitting with them. The room was so stuffy. Now — another kiss, darlings."

"Run away, run away!" ordered the horrified mother. "Gussy! Sissy! out of the room with you."

"Ha, ha!" laughed Mrs Jumbold. "You are afraid of infection, are you? That is silly; scientific men don't believe in there being such a thing as infection. It is a superstition of the past. You need not be afraid for the little things. Even if they were to catch measles from me, why, it is a complaint all must have, sooner or later, and the spring is as seasonable a time to be having it as any. I always think it a good thing to get these diseases over and done with; then you know what to expect with children. You know they have good constitutions. If they are to die, let them die early, is what I say; then they're more sure of going to heaven, and there is not such an outlay in clothes, victuals and education. Now there was young Mr Hall cost his father a great amount. He was sent to a first-rate school and then to college; and what did he do there? He caught scarlet fever and he died. That was a pity. If he'd had it when a baby, and he'd died then, and not have cost so many hundreds of pounds in learning Latin and Greek, which could be of no use to him in the other world. I'm sure, if I had children, I'd expose them early to all the diseases they would be likely to have, and then I'd know their stuff. I'd know whether they were likely to live or not, and regulate expenditure accordingly. If I had a girl who was weakly, and who nearly died through measles, probably she wouldn't survive scarlatina, and if she did, whooping cough would be the death of her. Now, such a girl as that. Do you think I'd send her to an expensive school and dress her in silks and satins? Not I. She should pick up what learning she could from her sisters, and wear her sisters' old dresses — that is supposing the sisters were able-bodied and vigorous, and had got through the customary complaints without dying."

Another of Mrs Jumbold's visits was to Mrs Arkwright. That

little lady had just new carpeted the drawing-room with a delicate white Brussels, powdered with flowers. The doctor's wife came in without removing her goloshes and with her dribbling umbrella still in her hand.

"Ach, weh!" exclaimed the little German woman, after the departure of her visitor. "What a horrid mess she has made. The great brown footmarks, and the slop where she poked the end of her *Regenschirm.*"

She also made a call on Mrs Hawkes, a bride. "Where do you suppose I have been?" asked the doctor's wife. "I have been to see that old Betty Coltman."

"We are going to have an early lunch," said the bride. "Will you take some with us? It is ready in the other room."

"Thank you," answered Mrs Jumbold; and taking her seat at table she began again. "Poor Betty Coltman's leg is very bad. A sort of abscess has formed on the shin below the knee. It looks —"

"Will you have some chicken?" interrupted Mr Hawkes.

"It looks very angry," continued the irrepressible woman; "and there is a livid ring of purple —"

"Some wine, Mrs Jumbold?"

"Thank you. I assure you the discharge —"

"What is the matter with you, dear?" asked Mr Hawkes of his bride.

"Nothing, Henry; only I have completely lost my appetite."

She also paid a visit to Mrs and Miss Doldrums, taking in Ezra Poulter, the bedridden miser, on her way.

"You have no notion," began Mrs Jumbold to the Relict of Jonathan Doldrums, "I am certain you have no conception of the filth of Poulter's hovel. The floor is ingrained with dirt, the ceiling is black with smoke, the windows cobweb-covered and the furniture broken. I have only this moment come from there. Do you know? I seldom or never visit that cottage without bringing away— " she dropped her voice — "vermin."

"What!" with horror. "F...?"

"No," with solemnity, "B..."

"Good heavens!"

"Fact. Awful, isn't it?" shivering and shaking her dress about the floor. "I may have them about me now."

"You really mean B...?"

"I really do mean B... I should not mind F so much, but B!"

As soon as Mrs Jumbold was gone, Mrs Doldrums rang the bell. "Sally, I must have the carpet examined and swept all round that chair. I wouldn't have one — Laura!" with a cry.

"What, Mamma?"

"I think — I think —I think —"

"What, what?"

"I am sure— yes, I am sure —"

"Oh, for heaven's sake, what, what, dear Mamma?"

"I— I feel one now."

"A what, Mamma?"

"A B..."

A pause. Laura stared at her mother. Sally, with her broom in her hand, stared at both.

"So do I!" cried Laura, turning white. Another pause.

"So do I!" screamed Sally. Down went the broom and all three fled to their respective bedrooms.

On her way home from Doldrums Lodge, Mrs Jumbold stepped into the shop of Mrs Rhodes.

"It is very wet, ma'am," observed that person, coming from the little kitchen at the back, into the shop.

"I should not mind the wet, but that it splashes," said Mrs Jumbold. "I can keep it off with my umbrella when it comes down, but I can't keep it off when it splashes up. I think the paving of the town, and the laying of the causeways, is shameful."

"It is not so good as it might be," said Mrs Rhodes. "What may I serve you with today, ma'am?"

"It is seldom I do my shopping in Sowden," observed Mrs Jumbold. "I generally make a point of going into Halifax for what I want. I get things there a deal cheaper and much better than I do here. You stick on the prices in these little places and your articles are very inferior."

"Indeed, ma'am, I think you are mistaken."

"No I'm not. I know what I'm about, and I wouldn't be shopping here today, only I can't get in to Halifax conveniently, and I want a penny skein of black silk."

"Anything more, ma'am?" when this was given.

"You may let me look at your ribbons."

The drawer of dark colours was exhibited, and the lady examined them contemptuously. "Let me see the coloured ones, the pink and violet tints." The drawer was produced and its contents criticised. "Haven't you some rather wider ribbons?"

"Yes, ma'am."

"Oh, these are too wide. Any intermediates?"

"I don't think that an intermediate width is made."

"Don't tell me that. I know better. I have seen them at Halifax of all widths. I wanted a mauve spotted with black. I see you have got none."

"Here is one, ma'am."

"Ah, but that is too wide. No, there are none that will suit. Let me look at your silk fringes."

One after another was brought out and unrolled, but none satisfied Mrs Jumbold; some defect was sure to become apparent, or the depth or shade was not to her liking.

"No," she said. "It's always the way with your little country shops; there is never anything in them that one wants."

Mrs Rhodes could hardly contain her indignation. She would probably have given noisy vent to her wrath, had she not suddenly discovered a method of causing annoyance, in turn, to the person who had been aggravating her.

Mrs Jumbold had put down her penny in payment for the skein of black silk and was about to leave the counter, when Mrs Rhodes said blandly, with a grim smirk on her face, "Would you be so good, ma'am, as to let me look at that umbrella?"

"Oh, certainly," answered the lady precipitately, a flash shooting into her eye. "Please to examine it. You will find it very wet. Take care; I saw one drop fall among the ribbons."

"May I ask where you got this umbrella?" asked Mrs Rhodes with some asperity.

"Do you happen to trace any resemblance between it and one you know?" was the return question.

"I know the umbrella," answered Mrs Rhodes, roughly. She felt that now was her moment of triumph, and she cast aside her obsequious shop manner.

"And would you like also to claim my bonnet, my gown or

282

my goloshes?"

"No, ma'am. But I am pretty positive that this here umbrella belonged to us."

"Could you swear now?"

"Yes, I am sure I could swear to it. Why, bless you, it came out of the shop; it was the only one left."

"You never sold it to me."

"No, ma'am, that I'm very certain of."

"And I shouldn't think of buying such an article as an umbrella in a little poking country village."

"No, nor buying one at all when you could have one for the taking, I fancy." Mrs Rhodes looked triumphantly at her customer, who however returned the glance in an equal spirit of elation.

"And pray, whose umbrella do you assert this to be?" asked the doctor's wife, with a snigger.

"I know it very well," answered Mrs Rhodes. "It belonged to our Annis, that is, Miss Greenwell."

"Indeed!" with an expression of delight which staggered her antagonist.

"Yes, this was the last black umbrella we had in stock. And after the death of Mrs Greenwell, Annis wanted one, and we let her have it. I could swear to it because Mr Rhodes marked an A with a hot skewer on the handle."

"There is the A!" said Mrs Jumbold.

"And I should like to know where you found the article, or how you got it."

"Haven't you seen a bill put in the shop windows, to the effect that an umbrella has been found, and that anyone who had missed one, might recover it on applying to me and describing the article?"

"Yes," answered Mrs Rhodes, somewhat discomfited. "But that was some months ago."

"Why did you not apply?"

"Nay, I did not know that our Annis had lost her umbrella till I saw it and recognised it, in your hands. And you see she couldn't apply because she was not in Sowden. When did you find it, ma'am?"

"I found it the night that she left Sowden."

"Where?" with a start.

Mrs Jumbold leaned on the counter, fixed her eyes on Mrs Rhodes and said, in a low hissing whisper, "I found it close against the heap on which lay the corpse of Richard Grover."

The woman of the shop recoiled, her face losing all its colour, and a ghastly glitter of horror appearing in her eyes.

"I was at tea that night with Mr and Mrs Arkwright. And when your daughter Martha came to the door, to say what she had found in the lane, I ran to the spot with the others. Whilst the body was being removed, I found this."

"Martha must ha' had it," gasped Mrs Rhodes.

"No, she had not," answered the doctor's wife; "for I asked her, before she went away, whether she had brought an umbrella with her, and she answered that she had not. You look alarmed, Mrs Rhodes. You really do. Come now, suppose you explain to me how it was that I came to pick up in Sandy-Pit Lane, near the body of the man-monkey, this article that you have identified as belonging to the person Annis Greenwell."

"Oh dear, oh dear! That it should ha' come to this, and I intending all for t' best," moaned the terrified woman.

"I think your best course will be to offer an explanation, or I shall feel it my duty to place the matter in the hands of the police."

"Pray don't call them police in. It'll be the death o' me if they comes here, and I a regglar chapelgoer, and known to be one of the elect. I wish I'd never listened to what Richard said, and then it 'ud ha' never come to this. Step inside to the parlour, ma'am, and I'll make all clear, as far as I can. Whatever shall I do?"

Mrs Rhodes was completely thrown off her balance. The tables had been unexpectedly turned upon her, just when she was most sure of being able to discomfit her irritating customer. She now drew her out of the shop, fearing lest what she said might be heard. The poor foolish woman was possessed with terror lest she should be brought in any way into court, and be subject to interrogations by magistrates or police. She feared lest she should lose caste in her society by such an event; for to her narrow mind the witness was every whit as bad as the criminal.

How Richard Grover had come by his death she did not

know; she was aware that Annis must be acquainted with the circumstances, as the girl had not returned to the house after having been sent by her to meet the man in the lane. She had sufficient instinct of right and wrong to feel that the opinion of the public, and indeed that of her own husband, would be strongly against her for having acted as she had towards the poor girl, and she feared the exposure which would bring down condemnation on her head. This fear had even stifled her curiosity to know how Grover had come by his death.

"Oh, ma'am! I'm in a proper mess," began Mrs Rhodes; "and if I tell you, you must never breathe a word to nobody." She paused for breath and then continued: "You see Richard, he were fair smittled wi' t' girl, and he would have her brought to t' Lord. He'd ha' converted her here, but my master came in just as he were agait, and stopped t' proceedings. So Richard — eh! he was a man o' God! — he asked me to let him meet her somewhere, where there would be no interruption, and he fixed on Sandy-Pit Lane and I sent her there to meet him. Eh! but Richard was mighty in the spirit, and a powerful preacher."

"Well!" exclaimed Mrs Jumbold, "this beats everything I ever heard. Where is your conscience, madam?"

"I did it all for t' best. I was longing to see Annis a child o' grace, and there was no other way of fashioning it. I couldn't get her to chapel, no road."

"And what took place when they met?"

"Nay, ma'am, how can I tell? I never saw our Annis from the moment she left our house to meet Mr Grover. She never came back no more, from that day to this."

"Did she go of her own accord to see the man?"

"Nay, not altogether."

"Are you sure she went there?"

"Ay, I think I may be sure o' that. I made as though it were Mr Hugh had asked to see her once more. And she was keen enough to meet him, I reckon."

"And do you mean to tell me that she never returned?"

"She never came back. And where she is now I do not know. My master, I fancy, does, but he won't let it out to me. The vicar told him; but I haven't been able to screw it out of him anyways and I've tried a deal o' times."

Mrs Rhodes, who in the shop had spoken fair English, in her agitation had fallen into broad Yorkshire brogue.

Mrs Jumbold was much surprised at the revelation that had been made, and great was her internal exultation, but now she carefully refrained from exhibiting it. She had kept the umbrella by her, and had used it continually, in the hopes of its attracting someone's attention, and of her being led to some discovery thereby; and now that the discovery was made, it was imperfect, but such as it was, it surprised her beyond measure, so utterly at variance were the disclosures with her own anticipations. She had not produced the umbrella at the inquest on the body, partly because it was a very good new umbrella, and would be serviceable to herself, but chiefly because she thought it would be more likely to lead to results in her hands than in those of the police, who would advertise the discovery as suspicious, and put the owner of the article upon his guard. She had caused a notice to be printed and put in shop windows, announcing her having a found umbrella in her possession; and when months passed, and these notices had produced no claimants, she had given up hopes of making discoveries and she had contented herself with the use of a very capital umbrella, which had cost her nothing.

"I see this very distinctly," said Mrs Jumbold, musing; "Annis Greenwell, and probably she alone, can solve the mystery of the death of Richard Grover."

"I reckon so, too," threw in Mrs Rhodes.

"And it is essential that she should be seen, questioned and made to relate what took place."

"Oh, ma'am! for mercy's sake, let me not be brought into it."

"It is impossible for me to say whether you can be kept out of it. It is certain that the whole case must be put in the hands of the police, and it is a matter of felicitation to myself that Providence should have enabled me to unravel a mystery which the police were powerless to solve. I will take the umbrella with me, Mrs Rhodes, of course. You will hear further, shortly, I have no doubt in the world. I wish you a very good afternoon."

But once before in her career had Mrs Jumbold experienced happiness such as that which uplifted her now. That former occasion had been the discovery made by her in Whinbury Copse.

Chapter Thirty-One

"I look toward you, sir," said the York policeman, whose acquaintance we have already made.

"And I, sir, catches your eye," responded the Sowden policeman, with promptitude.

"This, sir, is the tenth anniversary of my union with Mrs Physic. Ten years of matrimonial felicity have left me, not what I was once, sir, no."

"Your wife's health and many of them."

"The children that have accrued to me since that union are awful to contemplate."

"Personally or numerically?" asked he of Sowden.

"A little of both, sir. My spouse has a knack of bringing twins into this world of woe, where units would prove more acceptable. Once we dreaded trins[1], sir, but it proved lusty male twins. So much for them numerically. Personally they are a caution — not, understand me, in their natural condition, but as modified by civilisation. Most of my sons are boys, sir, and boys require attention at three points, the elbows, the seat and the knees. Between the periods of my wife's confinements, which are annual, she lives in a state of patch. At one moment the knees are through, and by the time she has patched the knees there is a cleavage at the seat, and when the seat is mastered, the elbows break out. Would you believe it, sir, no sooner has she grappled with the elbows, and mended them, than the knees are at it again. Thus she spends her unconfined life, in revolving from knees to elbows, with the seat intermediate."

"It is shocking. I'm an unmarried man, I'm glad to say."

"Well, marriage is not to be enterprised, nor taken in hand, unadvisedly or lightly; for it leads to two necessary results which are alternative —doctors or babies. And a man before he marries must make up his mind as to which he prefers, or, more

[1]triplets

287

strictly speaking, which he abhors least, and make his choice accordingly."

"How do you mean?"

"Let him take a sickly woman to be his partner, if partial to doctors; but if his tastes lie in the way of babies, then let him look out for a female with a vigorous constitution."

"It is most unusual to drink a health in unfermented liquor," said the Sowden policeman, raising his cup of coffee to his lips; "but may I wish your life to be as agreeable as is this cup, with the coffee and the milk combined in harmonious proportions, and the sugar evenly sweetening both."

"Thank you, sir. You observe the unusuality of toasting in unfermented liquor. I regret to learn that you are beerbiferous. I am a teetotaller, otherwise I should have offered you spiritous beverages; but I do not on principle. Since the illustrious Duke of Clarence inaugurated self-immolation in liquor, the number of victims to drink has been truly appalling. It is now nine years and a half since I took the pledge, and I have kept it ever since. Had I been a teetotaller ten years ago, I might not now be a married man, and the father of — one — two — three — four — five "

"What are you counting on your fingers, Mr Physic?"

"My children, sir. I can seldom keep them all in my head. One or two are constantly slipping out. Let me see, where was I last? Five, I think; that was Georgianna. Six and seven in a lump."

"Lump, Mr Physic?"

"I mean twins. Eight died in teething. Nine — sharp lad, that. Ten and eleven in a lump again. Twins I mean. Twelve, the present hurdygurdy. I have been for ten years constrained to dwell among those who are enemies unto peace, and all along of liquor. I was in liquor when I first saw the present Mrs Physic, I was fresh when I proposed, and I was drunk when I married her."

Mr Physic shook his head, the Sowden policeman shook his. Then each raised his cup to his mouth, and looked at one another over the rim, whilst drinking. The York officer withdrew his mouth from the wholesome, but not exciting, beverage, for a moment, to sigh. The Sowden officer sighed responsively.

288

"And may I ask what has brought you here?" asked Mr Physic, replacing his cup in the saucer.

"I'm after a lady," answered his friend.

"Not in a matrimonial way?" sympathetically.

"No, in a business line."

"And who may she please to be, sir?"

"A young lady who lives in the Minster yard. I'm not a—going to nab her, you know. But I want to speak with her a bit, along of something."

"What young lady, if I may be so bold as to ask?"

"Miss Greenwell; her as lives along of Mrs Furness."

"By ginger!" exclaimed Mr Physic. And then, apologetically: "I teetotal my oaths, sir. I generally swears by treacle, but when I'm much decomposed or enraged, I rise to ginger, as pungenter. But I never overstep that limit. I said, By ginger! for you surprised me. I have had some acquaintance with that lady, along of that theft in Midgeroyd, in your neighbourhood."

"Indeed."

"I found a party who wore those articles that were stolen, sir, or some very like them; and I went to the house in which the same party lived, and there I found Miss Greenwell, the party you're after; and the party I was after had hooked it. It was a rummy go."

"Did you make any inquiries of Miss Greenwell?"

"Of course I did. You don't catch a weasel asleep in an ordinary way, do you? But she knew nothing of it."

"What has become of the party who had the stolen articles?"

"My party, as I said, has hooked it. When she—"

"She! A woman!"

"A woman certainly. When she ascertained that I was coming, she made off, and has not returned since. This leads me to suppose that she was privy to the theft."

"And what had Miss Greenwell to do with her?"

"Nothing at all. She went there to visit her on charity."

"And whilst visiting her the party made off."

"I suppose so."

"It almost looks as if Miss Greenwell must have been a party to her escape."

"If you mean to say that your party was a party to my party's hooking it, I cannot say that I agree with you."

"There are some coincidences which seem to need a clearing up, Mr Physic."

"I quite agree with you. As I remarked on the occasion, of all rummy goes, I had met with none rummier, and I considered this as the ne plus ultra rummiest."

"Miss Greenwell comes from Sowden."

"Indeed, sir, I am glad to hear it."

"The theft took place in Sowden, or adjoining it."

"I am aware of that also, sir."

"And Miss Greenwell allows the party wearing the stolen articles to escape."

"It is remarkable also," said Mr Physic, "that your party observed to me, in answer to close examination, that she had first observed my party on the very day after the burglary took place. Have you come to see your party relative to the same affair?"

"No, on quite another. But I think we two might call together, and prosecute our inquiries conjointly."

"I am all agreeable," replied Mr Physic.

Annis was labouring through the voyage of La Perouse when the servant told her that there were two "gentlemen" to see her.

"Who can they be?" asked Miss Furness, looking up from her needlework.

"I think they're policemen, Miss," replied the servant.

"Police! What can they want with you?" Annis dropped her book and turned very pale. She had dreaded lest further inquiries should be made about the red-veiled woman, and had been for a couple of days in nervous apprehension of a visit of this kind. She feared interrogation, lest she should be forced to yield up the secret of who the wearer of the veil was. Now she saw clearly what Earnshaw had done. He had stolen the articles of female clothing he had used for his disguise. If her evidence led to his conviction for this offence, in all probability there would be drawn from her sufficient to bring against him the more serious charge of having caused Richard Grover's death.

She remained seated, with her hands on her lap, looking blankly before her.

Miss Furness ordered the servant to show the officers into the dining-room, and to tell them that Miss Greenwell would be with them directly.

"Now, Annis, dear," she said, "what is the matter?"

"Oh, Miss Furness, I wish you would come down with me, I am so afraid of those men."

The lady promised to accompany her, and then asked again what was the reason of the visit.

"Nothing concerning me, exactly," answered Annis; "but you shall hear. Only tell me first if I am bound to answer every question put to me?"

Miss Furness looked at her with surprise. What could the girl be so anxious about? She replied, "Certainly not, unless put on your oath. But when you do speak, let it always be the truth."

"You may trust me," Annis said.

"Yes, dear, I know I may. Now, come along, and let us find out what these men want. You have quite perplexed me, I assure you."

They found the policemen examining the marvels of nature and curiosities of uncivilised art which adorned the room. With the origin of each Mr Physic had been professing his acquaintance to his brother officer; and before the arrival of the ladies he had been indulging the Sowden policeman with an account of swordfish, Chinamen, nautili, and idolatry in general, according as his eyes rested on the thrusting weapon of the fish, the hat and shoes of the Celestial, seashells, or images of Buddhist deities. It was difficult to light on a subject with which Mr Physic was not fully conversant. The variety of object in the room gave ample scope for the exhibition of his knowledge, delivered with gravity and solemnity, in an undertone.

And then, just before the entry of the ladies, he of York had poked him of Sowden in the ribs and said, "You may take the word of John Physic for one thing, sir. He is a judge of female beauty. You can't mislead him in that. He is a perfect connoisseur. And he'll tell you this — your party is a tip-top stunner."

The tip-top stunner was in a thick black woollen gown, very neat and quiet, with white cuffs and a narrow white collar edged with black, a little silver cross suspended to her neck, her complexion beautifully clear, like a delicate camellia leaf, with the faintest tinge of colour in the cheeks. Generally it was lighted with the most glorious flush, like the afterglow of an autumn sun on snowy heights; but anxiety had momentarily blanched her. Her profusion of burnished hair, braided and plaited behind her head, was the only colour about her. Her eyes were of a saddened depth, that they had lately acquired; they sank before the stare of the two officers, as they bowed stiffly and eyed her curiously, and regretting the interruption, expressed a hope that their intrusion would not be for long, but there was a little matter, etc.

"What is it?" asked Miss Furness. "Will you take a seat?"

"Thank you, ma'am," said the Sowden officer.

"Thank you *miss*," said Mr Physic, looking at his brother officer with indignation.

"There is not much to detain you, ladies," began the Sowden policeman; "but I have with me an umbrella, which is thought to belong to one of you. Is it yours, miss?" offering it to Miss Furness.

"No," answered Bessie. "I have not lost one. Do you own it, Annis?"

"May I look at it?" She took it in her hand, examining it carefully, and said, "Yes, this is certainly mine. I left it in Sowden."

"Do you remember where you lost it?" asked the country officer.

"No, I really cannot remember. I did not have it long, and I did not know that I had left it about anywhere."

"On what day did you come to York, miss?"

"She came on the morning of September 11th," replied Miss Furness.

"And it was found on the night of September 10th," said the man, looking fixedly at Annis. The girl lifted her eyes, startled, and met his eyes.

"Where did you find it?"

"It was found in Sandy-Pit Lane, Did you go there that night?"

"Yes, I did."

"There was an unfortunate little affair took place on the night of the 10th, and as you were on the spot where it happened, much about the time, it is thought that possibly you may be able to give some evidence which will clear up what is at present shrouded in uncertainty."

"What little affair was it?" asked Miss Furness.

"Merely the death of a man under extraordinary circumstances," was the reply.

"Annis," said Miss Furness, "do you know anything about this?"

The girl hung her head, folded her hands and made no answer.

"Of all the rummy goes," began Mr Physic.

"Presently, if you please," said the Sowden officer, turning on his comrade and silencing him. "It would be satisfactory if you would give us an answer," the policeman said.

Annis looked up, and said in a scarcely audible voice, as she caught Miss Furness's arm for support, "I should prefer not to give my evidence now. I can say something, but I will not, till put on my oath."

"Very well, miss," said the officer. "You will come to Sowden today or tomorrow please; this matter must be investigated."

"I will go there today," she answered, "that is, if Miss Furness will spare me."

"Yes, that will be best," said Bessie. "Get it over, dear, and be back as soon as possible."

"And now, please," said Mr Physic, ill at ease at not having been brought into sufficient prominence in the foregoing conversation, "I should like to put a few questions, miss."

"I am ready," answered Annis.

"That was a regular conflustercating affair that, the other day, now wasn't it? And I taking you for the old lady, with you sitting in the dark! I'm gingered, but it was almost comical, and it must have dumbfoozled you a bit, miss, with me putting you through a cross-examination about that you knew nothing at all. Wasn't it, now?"

"I do not exactly know what to answer. What is your question?" Miss Furness looked indignantly at Mr Physic, and the Sowden policeman seemed provoked.

"Didn't I state my views about its being, of all rum goes, about the new plus ultra rummiest?"

"I will trouble you to put proper and intelligible questions to Miss Greenwell or to leave the room," said Miss Furness, haughtily; and then turning to the other officer, asked whether he could not put the inquiries instead of Mr Physic.

"You be easy, miss," said the York functionary. "I'm coming to the point, right on end. Now, Miss Greenwell. About that woman. When did you see her first in York?"

"I told you the other day, the thirty-first of October."

"Can you be sure of this, Miss Greenwell?" asked he from Sowden.

"Yes, I can," she answered. "I think I could swear to the day."

"Now, then," began again Mr Physic, "I want to know, was the woman in the house when you called?"

"Yes, she was."

"Did you know she had stolen the articles? You'll excuse me for asking, miss. But professional duty requires it, and it's a painful obligation imposed on us officials, to discharge our duties at the expense of our personal feelings, and I may add, of our genteelness."

"I certainly did not."

"No, I did not suppose it for one moment. You will excuse my asking the question which implied a suspicion. You did not observe her destroy the veil, did you?"

"No, I did not see her burn it."

"I should think not. She was a vast deal too dodgy for that. But though she might escape your observation, she couldn't evade my penetration. And you had not been to her house before? And only this time you visited her in charity, according to her wish?"

"Yes, she asked me to go and see her, as she was in want."

"One moment, Mr Physic," said the Sowden officer. "Allow me to put a question to the lady. Miss Greenwell, had you known this said party before?"

"Before what?" nervously, evasively.

"Before that party came to York."

Annis made no reply.

"Not likely; don't insult her, sir. There are bounds which even professional exigencies should not force a man to overstep," said Mr Physic, with stateliness and a deprecating look at his comrade.

"Miss Greenwell," said the country officer, "do you reserve the answer to this, as well as that to my former question?"

"I do."

"I think, Mr Physic, we need trouble the ladies no longer."

"Certainly, certainly. Ladies, a good morning."

"You have promised, miss, to be at Sowden this afternoon or evening. There is a train leaving York at 3.25, another at 4.20, a third at 6.50. Probably you will not go by a still later train. I may rely on your being in Sowden by tomorrow, may I not?"

"Yes, you may expect me."

"And where shall I find you, miss?"

"At Mrs Rhodes's, Kirkgate."

When the policemen were gone, Annis sank into a chair and covered her face. Miss Furness was surprised immeasurably by the questioning of the officers and the answers of the girl. She could not in the least comprehend the drift of the latter part of the inquiry. That with reference to the death in Sandy–Pit Lane explained itself.

"What is all this about?"

"Oh dear, Miss Furness, do not ask me now; it will all be cleared up shortly. Perhaps you will trust me when I tell you, in confidence, that one in whom I am thus far interested, that he is a great sufferer, and that he once rendered me a great service, is now in danger; and that had I spoken I should have endangered his life. Even now, I shall, I know, have to speak what, if he does not escape, will bring him to the gallows."

Chapter Thirty-Two

Small idea had Hugh, as he sat joking with Laura in his uncle's drawing-room, that his little Annis, whilst he was thus engaged, was approaching Sowden.

The Arkwrights and the Doldrums saw a good deal of each other now. Hugh's accident had been the means of drawing them together, and a week rarely passed without an evening being spent by Mrs and Miss Doldrums at Belview Cottage where lived the millowner, or by Mr and Mrs Arkwright and Hugh at Doldrums Lodge.

Laura had persuaded the young man to make of her a sort of confidante, or, more correctly speaking, she had burst in on his confidences, and taken them by storm. One the very first opportunity of speaking to him in private, she had insisted on knowing something, nay, everything about Annis, and had not rested satisfied till she was made acquainted with the leading circumstances of Hugh's "charming romance", as she termed it. Having acquired the requisite information and taken violent possession of Hugh's secrets, she became his most zealous champion. She would not hear a word spoken in disparagement of him or Annis, she upheld his right to make his own choice, lauded his good sense in having broken away from the usual run of engagements, asserted her conviction that his judgment was to be relied on, and proclaimed her opinion that so long as a girl was good and true and honest, she was worthy of any man. One forcible argument in favour of Annis, Laura invariably fell back upon.

"You know, if it hadn't been for that blessed smoke-jack, I should have been a factory-girl myself. People would not be shocked or scandalised if Hugh Arkwright were to propose to me; but the only difference between Annis Greenwell and myself is that my father patented a smoke-jack and hers didn't."

And then her mother would add, "It's quite true, my dear. We was only in a very small way, when Doldrums, who is now mouldering in his grave, with room beside him for me, and some inches over, discovered the patent smoke-jack, the

296

contrivance of which is simple and yet marvellously efficacious, which has been extensively used and largely patronised, and which continues to give general satisfaction."

Hugh was not reluctant to make Laura to a certain extent, and within certain limits, a confidant. She was sympathetic, and of a kindly, affectionate disposition, which led him to trust her. He was glad to have someone to whom he could speak on the subject uppermost in his thoughts. It had become almost intolerable to his frank nature to have a matter concerning him most nearly tabooed at home. His uncle never alluded to the absent girl, and Mrs Arkwright had been given a hint by her husband not to speak upon the past. Martha, he had few opportunities of seeing, and he shrank from seeking her out, lest he should cause his uncle annoyance. Mr Furness was resolutely silent on the subject. Hugh saw a good deal of the vicar, and occasionally approached the topic, but Mr Furness invariably turned the conversation.

Mrs Jumbold, however, was ready at any moment to give him her mind on the "Scandal" as she insisted on designating it to his face; but when she did, it was to throw out such odious insinuations as to the reason why the girl had been removed from Sowden, that Hugh would never allow her to speak on the subject.

But Lauara was very different. Her heart overflowed with sympathy towards the young man in his solitude, and she used her best endeavours to relieve his desolation, by giving him the opportunity he desired of speaking about her, who was ever present in his thoughts, to one who could enter into his feelings. She made him describe the absent lassie to her, and listened to his glowing descriptions with pleasure that she took no pains to conceal.

"And then," was Hugh's usual conclusion, "Annis is so good."

"Ah, there! Goodness last of all."

"Not a bit. If she were other than good I could not love her."

"And pray how do you know she is so excellent? Have you had much opportunity of conversation with her?"

"A woman carries her character in her face — in her eyes," answered Hugh. "It is legibly written by Nature or Providence, I cannot say which, and he who chooses may read it."

"Indeed! And is my character inscribed in my face?" asked Laura.

"Distinctly."

"And so you judge of a woman's soul by her looks."

These confidences did Laura much good. They opened her eyes to the reverence and devotion that the true, honourable man feels for what is womanly in woman. It startled her to find that a man could so entirely penetrate through all the disguises which artifice puts on, that he could brush aside all that was acquired and irrelevant, and detect at once what was genuine and noble and pure. She began to realise that there were elements in woman's nature which exactly met the cravings of man's nature, elements which are inherent, and which education does not always succeed in developing. She began involuntarily to contrast herself with the ideal woman, and to feel how false much that was in herself proved to be. Slowly she awoke to the consciousness that she herself was not true to her own nature, and that there were in her germs of good which had not been given room for expansion.

On the evening that Annis arrived in Sowden, Mrs and Miss Doldrums had come to Belview Cottage to tea and supper. On similar occasions, and these occasions were, as has been already intimated, pretty frequent, Mr Arkwright amused himself with the Relict of Jonathan Doldrums, making an occasional sally upon his wife, drawing her into the conversation, bewildering her, covering her with confusion and dismissing her with a laugh. Laura's mother in no way interested him, but he bore with her company, and relieved the load by making a fool of her, so as to give Hugh opportunities of cultivating Laura's society, and forgetting his past delusion. Mr Arkwright was convinced that his nephew was slowly, yet surely, coming round to his views. He had not made an attempt to find out where little Annis was hidden. He had not spoken to him of her, and above all, he displayed an unmistakable liking for Miss Doldrums, and took no pains to conceal the pleasure he found in her society. This, poor simple Hugh never thought of doing. The possibility of his breaking faith with Annis did not for a moment enter his head, and he scarcely considered whether other people might form a different opinion. It was talked of in Sowden, however, as probable that Hugh would think better of his engagement to the mill girl, and would eventually propose to Laura; and people generally thought that this was the best thing he could do. Miss Doldrums had a fortune, Annis had none; the former occupied a good position in the social world of Sowden, the latter held none. Advantages manifold would accrue from a marriage with Laura, but only disadvantages from a union with Annis. As for such trifles as honour, plighted troth, and disinterested love, public opinion took no account of them; they were not palpable facts of monetary value.

Mr Arkwright heard it whispered that Hugh and Laura were attached to one another, and he chuckled to himself, and gave no denial to the rumours. Mrs Jumbold made it a text for expounding her views on the indifference to morality distinguishing the present generation from that to which she herself belonged. "For my part," said she, "I can't think how a young lady like Laura Doldrums (with her means) can associate with a young man of smirched character. I'm sure when I was young, if I had had a suitor whose morality was half as bad as that of Mr Hugh Arkwright, I would not have tolerated his presence. I always thought Miss Doldrums a decent girl with some propriety — and she has a considerable income — but I suppose the old proverb is true, 'Birds of a feather flock together'; and if she is so ready to wink at the licence of her follower, her own character may be a little blown upon; there is no knowing."

Of course Mrs Rhodes had also her little say on the matter; she took a different line. She thought Mr Furness ought never to have huddled Annis out of the place; that it was like "them church folk, always to stick up for the rich and take no account of the poor." That if she had had her way, Annis should not have been allowed to go till Mr Hugh had been brought to sign a paper, swearing that he would marry her, and that if he did not he would pay heavy damages.

"And now," said Mrs Rhodes, "we'll have to go to law about it, and try our best to get brass out of him. But them lawyers will swallow half."

To which John replied, "Hold your tongue, missis. No one will be better pleased than I, if it turns out as folks say. I never thought well of them young folks getting together, and I shall be glad if they forget one another, and get suited according to their stations."

"And ain't you going to law, to get damages? They always do in a case of breach of promise of marriage. And big damages they get sometimes, I've read i' t' paper."

"Certainly not," answered John. "And I will trouble you, missis, to hold your tongue about this business; it is no concern of yours."

But Martha felt troubled and disappointed. She had believed in Hugh. She had promised to trust him fully, unreservedly, that day she waylaid him at the stile; and she had conscientiously kept her promise. She agreed with her father that if Hugh should prove unfaithful, no notice should be taken of it; the young man would be unworthy of a thought, unworthy of Annis, and it would be a matter of rejoicing to her to know that her cousin had not fallen into the hands of one undeserving of her. But her great, noble soul refused to disbelieve in Hugh. She observed him at the mill, she watched his face in church, and felt comforted; it was the countenance of an honourable man who would be true to his word, and better still, true to that love which, when real, is enduring.

One evening Martha slipped into the vicarage to consult Mr Furness on the point.

"My dear Martha," said the old man, "do not trouble yourself. Leave all in God's hands." And she was comforted.

Martha could not but believe in good, and believing, have trust. However often unworthy and mean motives were brought before her, as influencing her mother and sisters and friends, she put them from her, and went forward in her confident silvery course, unaffected by them. She saw what was evil, but took no impression from it; her own clear sense of right she supposed must actuate others; and when their conduct appeared to her opposed to such a sense, she shut her eyes. Indeed, her life, like that described in Talfourd's "Ion", flowed...

> "From its mysterious urn a sacred stream,
> In whose calm depth the beautiful and pure
> Alone are mirror'd; which, though shapes of ill

300

May hover round its surface, glides in light,
And takes no shadow from them."

"You don't happen to have heard of the convertible coffin, have you, Mrs Doldrums?" asked Mr Arkwright after tea.

"No; a coffin, and convertible!"

"Yes. I have ordered one for Mrs Arkwright."

"Oh, Henry!" from the lady, alluded to. "What about coughing. I'm very well."

"It's the thing they put dead people into, you know," said Mrs Doldrums, with a confidential nod.

"You have not seen the convertible coffin, then?"

"Certainly not. If I had, I'd sure to have made a note of it; that's if my eyes would have permitted. What is it like, may I ask?"

"It is useful for various purposes. It makes a very good bed. Also, inverted and expanded, it serves as a dinner-table."

"A rather small one," observed Mrs Doldrums.

"Not so very small as you would think, madam. The sides and ends are made to lift up, like the leaf of a table, so that the size is by that means doubled; and then again it opens down the middle, and the lid can be inserted, so as further to increase the surface."

"I don't quite see how the shape would permit," objected Mrs Doldrums, all in good faith, and exhibiting a profound interest in the subject.

"That can only be understood by personal inspection. But I have not done with the convertible coffin yet. It makes a charming cradle for a child. Again, it is adapted to serve as a portmanteau. The sides are fitted up with pouches, to contain, on the one side, soiled linen, and on the other side, razors, lather-brush, strop, combs, and hair-brushes. Then the lid internally is crossed with red tape, for the insertion of collars, or note-paper and envelopes."

"And may I ask who are the patentees?"

"Hearse, Mould and Company."

"Would you kindly write down the address. My eyes are not what they used to be or I would not trouble you."

"Do you hear what nonsense my uncle is talking to your

301

mother?" asked Hugh, aside to Laura.

"Yes," she replied. "He delights in making game of her and she swallows all he says. Tomorrow she will be insisting on my writing for one of these new coffins, and I shall have to pretend that I have done so."

"It is a curious hobby for an old lady to have," said Hugh.

"It is a very harmless one," answered Laura; "but it is tiresome at times, especially when she insists on being laid out and gives full instructions how the funeral is to be arranged. She actually, one day, had the napkin put over her face, and taught me how to lift it, so as to show her features to any sorrowing friend who might wish to have a look before she was screwed down. Hark! Mr Arkwright is at it again. Look how bewildered your aunt seems. Oh, Hugh!"

"Yes, Laura."

"I want to say something to you quite privately. I am afraid of speaking here, lest Mr Arkwright should overhear me. Could you manage to show me the greenhouse? What I have to say is something very particular and very private."

"Come along, then. There is a lamp in the conservatory, and the flowers — the camellias — are well deserving of inspection. My aunt is very fond of them, and Mr Arkwright likes to use the greenhouse as a smoking-room."

A door led from the drawing-room into the conservatory, which was small, but in good order and well stocked. The care of this little place devolved on Mrs Arkwright, and in it was spent all the spare time she could afford. The flowers were not rare and expensive, but showy. At the present time there was but little to enliven it except white and crimson camellias in great abundance, and rows of blue, pink and white hyacinths, exhaling a delicious odour. In these hyacinths Mr Arkwright took great pride. He had a business acquaintance in Hamburg, who supplied him annually with bulbs, and he pretended to be able to distinguish the varieties with the precision of a connoisseur. A few pots of cyclamens and narcissuses completed the show.

The conservatory looked bright and cheerful, as it was snug and warm. The floor was boarded and covered with a felt carpet. There were two or three chairs inviting occupants not garden chairs of dismal green painted wood, hard to sit upon, and with uncomfortable backs, but cushioned. From the roof depended a lamp, which lighted the house sufficiently, and brought out the rich colours of the flowers. The temperature was high; white linen screens drawn over the roof shut out the black night sky, prevented the upward radiation of the heat, and reflected downwards the light of the lamp. Only at the side facing the garden was the greenhouse open to the outer darkness.

"It is quite a snuggery," said Laura. "Our conservatory is three times as big and not one quarter as comfortable or as pretty."

"Do you notice the supports and ribs?" asked Hugh. "They are coloured blue and red, and a painted cornice runs along the three walls. This little amount of colour has a wonderful effect in giving finish and the carpet and chairs add their testimony to the comfort."

"So they do," said Laura. Then, with a little change in her face and an alteration in her tone, she asked, "Do you know what I have to say to you?"

"I have not the remotest conception," answered Hugh; "but I am sure it will be something agreeable, for whatever you say is pleasant to me."

"You flatterer!" she exclaimed, for an instant recurring to her former manner. "Now, I assure you, I have something very particular to tell you of, which others — your uncle, for instance — know, but which I have no doubt is kept from you." She spoke earnestly, and with a tenderness in her manner such as she always assumed when speaking with Hugh on The Subject. The young man noticed this change, and divined at once that she was going to say something about Annis.

"What is it?" he asked, with roused interest.

"Do you know that either tomorrow or Monday your little friend will be in Sowden?"

The colour rose into Hugh's face, and his eyes sparkled with delight. "Laura! Is this true?"

"I have heard it. Indeed, circumstances have rendered it necessary that she should be sent for. Have you heard nothing of them?"

"Not a word. No one except you speaks to me of — of — *Her*."

"No, and they might refrain from telling you this. Be

303

composed, Hugh, there is a good fellow, and I will tell you all."

"Is it anything to distress me?"

"No, I think not. But there is something odd and inexplicable in the matter, which I do not understand."

"Tell me all about it."

"You remember how that a horrid fellow, a man-monkey, or something of that sort, was found dead last autumn in Sandy-Pit Lane."

"Yes, I remember the circumstances very well. A girl, Martha Rhodes, came to the door here one night, to tell us that she had found a corpse, and my uncle and I went at once to the place where it lay. It was that of the converted gorilla. It was a nasty sight. Why do you allude to this?"

"Was it not on the same night that Annis Greenwell left?"

"Yes, it was so; on September the eleventh."

"Well, it seems she was in the lane that night."

"That cannot have been. I saw her at the vicar's,. and walked with her to the station."

"What, before you found the body?"

"No, just after. I ran from home to Mr Furness, to tell him of what had taken place, and found Annis in his room."

"She must have been there, however, for her umbrella was discovered near the spot where the corpse lay."

"Who found it?"

"Mrs Jumbold. It seems that she sallied forth, directly her husband was sent for, and went at once to the place and there, at the side of the lane, lay the umbrella. She said nothing about it at the time, lest the owner should take alarm, and not identify it; but she waited her opportunity, and one day, Mrs Rhodes seeing her with it, claimed the umbrella. Off went Mrs Jumbold to the police,. and I believe one has been sent in quest of Annis. The vicar told them where she was."

"This is very odd. Martha must have had the umbrella."

"No, she had not. Mrs Jumbold taxed her with it being hers that same night, and she declared she had not brought one from home with her."

"You have not got the story quite correctly," said Hugh. "Mr and Mrs Jumbold were at tea at our house that evening, so that the surgeon was on the spot as soon as I was. I remember that

304

his wife persisted in coming also, notwithstanding my aunt's remonstrances; and I remember her asking Martha, in a casual sort of way, whether she had an umbrella. I thought at the time it was an odd question for Mrs Jumbold to put to the girl, but it passed out of my head. I have no doubt now that Martha had taken the umbrella with her, but had forgotten it in the alarm and flurry of the discovery."

"No, you do not know all. Mrs Rhodes confesses to having sent Annis to meet Richard Grover in Sandy-Pit Lane that night."

"You do not mean it? Did Annis go?"

"She did, supposing that you wanted to see her."

"I!"

"Yes. Mrs Rhodes sent her out, having led her to believe that you wished to say goodbye to her."

Hugh paced up and down the conservatory in the greatest agitation. "Poor little lamb!" he muttered, and almost sobbed.

"But I met her directly after, at the vicarage," he said, abruptly stopping, and recovering himself. "I cannot understand this. The whole thing is a puzzle to me. She had come by no harm; she was pale and agitated when I saw her, but that was all; and she certainly knew nothing of Grover's death, for she cried out with horror when I mentioned it to the vicar. It will all come right."

"It will all come right, certainly," said Laura.

Then Hugh went up to her and took her hand between his. "Thank you, good kind girl; thank you for telling me this. I had rather have heard it from you than from anyone. All this has been kept from me, as if I were not of all people the most interested in it. Now, will you do something else for me?"

"Yes, anything, almost," frankly and looking up with a bright smile into his face.

"When Annis comes, will you see her and be kind to her?"

"She shall come and stay at our house. She must not go to the Rhodes's after the vile way in which the woman there behaved to her."

"Thank you, Laura."

"And I will do all I can to make her happy and comfortable; and" — in a low voice, accompanied by a twinkle in the eyes

305

— "I will talk to her about you, and tell her how true you have been, and of the many chats we have had together about her. Will that satisfy you?"

He pressed her hand and lifted it to his lips. When he raised his head, his eyes fell on the surface of glass commanding the front garden. There, looking in on him, was a face.

A face once seen in the combing–shed, once again in the train, now, for the third time, and always by the light of flame. Once at the time of that awful flood, once before that plunge into the black canal, now — what did it signify?

There it was, scarlet and purple, with the glittering white teeth, with the nose flattened against the glass, the thick patches of eyebrow, the seams and warts horribly distinct; with the great glaring dark eyes fixed on him — the whole standing sharply out of a blue–black night.

"Good God!" Hugh gasped.

"What is it? asked Laura, startled by his tone, and by the expression of his face.

"He is not dead after all."

Laura followed the direction of his eyes, and saw nothing. The face had disappeared into the night.

Chapter Thirty-Three

When Annis arrived at the Sowden station, no one was there to meet her. She had not expected anyone, for she had not told the policeman by what train she would come. Yet it struck her with a sense of loneliness when she left the station, that on returning to the place which, after all, was home to her, though all that really constituted home was gone from it, she should find no one on the platform to take her hand and greet her with words of kindness and welcome. She gave the little portmanteau Miss Furness had lent her to the care of the porter, promising to send for it, and then she left the station.

During the journey she had considered what was best to be done, and had resolved on going at once to her old cottage, where she expected to find Joe concealed, and warning him to escape, as her evidence must be given on the morrow, and then search for him would ensue as a certainty.

She took the way by the river, which, she expected, would be the least frequented, and met no one.

A few stars were shining, and by their light she was able to see her path. They were reflected in the sluggish river. A gaunt skeleton of a barge which had been washed up on the bank at the flood, and had gone to decay out of its element, was the only novel feature on the well-remembered way. The old familiar sights and sounds were there; the ruddy light beyond the hill over Halifax, the pulsating reflections of the iron furnace, the rows of illuminated windows of a cloth mill running all night, the fretting of the river over the weir, the noises of the railway, the evening bell of Sowden Church.

The wind was chilly, blowing down the narrow valley, and tracking the course of the water. She had a knitted shawl round her, crossed over her chest, and tied by the hands of Miss Furness behind her back, and over that a black silk mantilla, which flapped, with the harsh sound silk always makes, in the cold rushing air. She had a pair of black woollen gloves on; she was glad of them. She did not wear a bonnet, but a black straw hat, and she had no veil, so her face was very cold. Glad was she when she heard the babbling of the beck which flowed into the river and trod the plank bridge over it and stepped over a stile, and saw against the grey sky the outline of the sand rock, and the gable of the cottage in which she had spent so many quiet happy years. Often of old had she come briskly along this path towards it, singing and rattling her little dinner can, with the ends of her red handkerchief, or grey shawl, flying behind her, as she quickened her pace on seeing the saffron glow from the window of the kitchen parlour, that she might meet her mother, and sit down to a comfortable tea by the ruddy fire. But now those days were over forever. The little red flapping kerchief had been given away and with it had gone the blithe dancing heart. The mother was departed from earth, the windows were all dark and the hearth was cold and black.

The girl sighed and tears formed in her eyes, but she was too anxious and frightened to allow her thoughts to rest long upon the past.

"Oh, if Joe is not here!" she said to herself, with sinking heart.

Joe was not there, apparently. Annis went to the front door and tapped lightly. The shutters of the window were up and she could not see into the room. Then she passed round to the back door, and tried that; it was fast. The little low window of the kitchen behind had no shutters: she looked in, but could see nothing but blackness. As she touched the glass, leaning against it, in her attempt to see, the lower portion moved. Surprised at this, she put her fingers to the bar and without difficulty succeeded in throwing up the sash.

She pondered over this. How was it that the window was not hasped? It was impossible that it could have been forgotten when the house was locked up. She drew the sash down again, and ran her fingers along the junction between the movable lower sash and the upper one, which was stationary. Then she guessed how it was that the window was unhasped.

It was possible to thrust a knife-blade through the crevice, and with it to press back the hasp, and so allow the sash to be thrown up.

She at once guessed that Joe had been there. He had told her that he could enter the house without a key. As certain as that he had been there, was it that he was out at the present moment, for were he within he would most surely have fastened the window. Although it was possible for one on the outside to turn back the hasp, it was of course impossible to fasten it again.

But there was other evidence that Earnshaw had been there, for out of the gloom appeared a little white creature, which leaped on the window sill and plaintively mewed. It was the watchman's favourite cat.

Annis stood moving the window up and down, uncertain what to do. She could enter the cottage if she chose, but she hesitated to do this. The thought came upon her, that if within, Joe could come to her and there would be no possibility of escape; and though desirous of saving him from danger, she was fearful of him. She felt in her pocket for a pencil and a scrap of paper, intending to write a few words as well as she could in the dark, but though she had Martha's last note with her, with its blank leaf, she had no pencil. The bitter wind made her shiver.

"Oh! I wish I knew what to do," she said faintly.

"Annis."

She heard her name spoken in the soft musical note of a woman, and yet she knew that the speaker was a man.

"Joe," she whispered, whilst her whole frightened little body quivered. "Joe, is that you?"

He glided towards her: he was still in woman's apparel, as she could see indistinctly by the starlight.

"What have you come here for?" he asked in a low tone. "Have you come to see *Him*?" and his voice quivered with suppressed rage.

"No, no, Joe," she answered, putting up her hands appealingly. "I have come here to save you."

"To save me," he said, sweetly. "Me! So you still think of *Me*. Come to save *Me*."

"Indeed I have," feebly and yet vehemently, notwithstanding the weakness of the voice and faintness of the little spirit that urged her to speak. "Joe, the police have found out about my having been with the man–monkey before — before — you know what."

"Well."

"And I have to appear before a magistrate tomorrow, and be

309

put on my oath and make a statement of what I saw."

"Well."

"Oh! I cannot tell a lie. I must say that I saw you, and then you will have the police after you. I cannot tell a lie, if they ask me what took place."

"No," said the man, "you cannot. You would not be the little true Annie I have known and loved so — "

"Oh, stop, stop!" in terror.

"And what am I to do?"

"Joe, you must make your escape at once; the police will be after you tomorrow, not before."

"You will not have to go before a magistrate till Monday, you may be quite sure," said Earnshaw.

"Then you will have two whole days."

He gave a short harsh laugh. "They will be on my track tonight."

"No, they will not. They know nothing as yet."

"There is something else to make them hunt me down."

"What? The veil?"

"And something besides."

"Do not tell me what it is," she begged in her fear; "but fly at once, and in your present disguise."

"I have been seen. Before an hour is over, the police will know that I am in Sowden."

"You have been seen, Joe?" echoed the girl. "Who by?"

"By *Him*."

"What, by Hugh?"

"Yes. He saw me. Shall I tell you what I was doing, dear lassie? I was on the lookout to learn something of him for you — and for myself. God! I thought the fellow was dead!"

"Why, Joe?"

"Never mind, but I did. And I saw him, not half an hour ago. A fine faithful lover, Annis!" He burst forth into his loud booming tones, in his scorn.

"Oh, hush, hush!"

"Shall I tell you how I saw him?"

She clasped her hands over her bosom, on the little brooch of jet and Cornish diamonds, and looked up with a white imploring face. But it was too dark for that to be seen.

"I saw that true-love of yours speaking tender things to a lady, looking into her face, and she with her eyes lifted to his, and her hand clasped in his hands, just as I once saw him and you in this house. And I saw him bend over her and kiss her pretty fingers. Ha! a true lover that, a faithful lover that! I hate him more than ever for his forgetfulness of little Annis."

A faint quivering sigh, half sob, broke from her heaving bosom.

"And as he lifted up his face, he saw me," continued Earnshaw.

"Joe!" She spoke in a mournful voice. "Is it true?"

"Is what true?"

"What you told me of Hugh — of Mr Arkwright?"

"I swear by God it is perfectly true. Did I ever tell *you* a lie?"

Again she sighed heavily; and then after a moment of struggle with herself, in the same sad voice she asked, "Now what are you going to do?"

"I am as safe here as anywhere. I cannot hide amongst a crowd, as do other men. My face will not let me."

"Joe, has no one seem you here except Mr Hugh Arkwright?"

"No one."

"I will go and speak to him."

"That you shall not," said Earnshaw, fiercely, catching her by the arm.

"Let me go," she said calmly. "I will only ask him not to mention having seen you."

The man did not speak for nearly five minutes, but walked up and down the back of the house, never, however, taking his eye off Annis, who stood cowering against the wall, with her hands over her eyes and her heart beating wildly. In the bitterness of her suffering she forget Earnshaw and thought only of Hugh, unfaithful, and herself, deserted and miserable. Now she understood why Martha had not mentioned Hugh in her letters. Annis longed to throw herself into the arms of her cousin, and bury her head in a bosom which she knew was true, and there sob out her griefs.. Earnshaw stepped up to her, whilst she was thus thinking, and said, with his hands holding her wrists, and drawing her palms from her face, "Go, go and beg him to spare me. Plead with him for *Me*. Ah, ha! That will be charming. You will find him with his new love hanging on his arm, and you can tell him how you feel for *Me*."

"I will go," answered Annis, recovering her calmness and speaking in a constrained voice. "Yes, I will go. Where shall I find them — him, I mean?"

"In his uncle's house. You must be quick, if you would catch them together. And then, Annis, when you have heard what he says, and know what my fate is to be, and when you have seen him and his new deary together, then come to Me."

"Why?"

"Come and tell me whether I am to fly at once or not; come and tell me. Come and see me once more. Hark!"

Far away and faintly chimed Sowden church clock.

"That is nine o'clock. Before long they will be parting, — kissing and squeezing hands. Ha! you understand me. Go and see it all, and then speak to him. And at eleven o'clock come to me. Not here. No, it will be too late for you to come here. You will find me in Arkwright's mill-fold. You will find me at the mill door."

"It will be so late," said Annis.

"But do you not want to save Me."

"Yes, indeed I do."

"Then you will do that. Avoid the watchman, but he will most likely be at one of the other mills. At the stroke of eleven come to the door that you used to go in at day by day. If you cannot be there at that moment, I will be within; then tap thrice at the door."

"How can you get in, Joe?"

"I went off with the keys. Now, away with you!"

She turned and left him, with her heart as dark and sad within as the night without. She glided through the garden into the lane, then went to the bridge and there she stood still and leaning her hands on the rail, bent her head upon them and wept convulsively.

She remembered when that little bridge had been swept away, and when she had clung to the breast of one who had borne her through the swollen beck, and had felt his arms embrace her, and her own little heart glow with a strange rapture. Half a year had passed, and what events had taken place in those few

312

months! Her mother gone, the whole course of her life altered, her heart a prey to emotions she had not known before, her mind open to ideas she had not previously dreamt of.

When she had recovered herself, she hurried up the lane, wiping her eyes and steeling her heart for the approaching interview.

She felt her blood curdle as she passed the spot where the death of Richard Grover had taken place. She reached the branch in the lane, turned towards the Arkwrights' house, saw the light in the windows, and the illuminated conservatory, and stood still. How was she to manage to speak in private with Hugh? She did not like to go to the door and ask Sarah Anne to tell him that she was there, and wished to see him. She shrank from the smirk and knowing looks of the girl, and she knew that such a visit would become the subject of gossip all over the village directly, and its impropriety would be freely commented on. No, it would be better to trust to an accident.

She opened the garden gate and glided through; then, stepping off the gravel walk on to the turf, crept towards the conservatory. She looked at the brilliant flowers and the brilliant light with her dim forlorn eyes. There was no one within, but she could faintly catch the voices in the parlour, as the door communicating with the drawing-room had been left half open by Hugh when he and Laura returned to the company.

Annis stood and shivered outside, chilled without and weary and bruised in spirit. She heard music being played and a female voice singing, and she wondered whether that voice belonged to her who had supplanted her. She looked up at the stars with a longing to be with her mother beyond them.

"Leave it in God's hands," the vicar had said. But, oh, how terrible was the result!

She could not endure the cold much longer. She turned the handle of the greenhouse door, and found that it was not fastened. She opened it a very little way, and the warm air rushed out on her. What if she went in? She would rather see Mr and Mrs Arkwright than the servant, for they would not mention her visit, and would probably allow her to speak to Hugh for one minute. Still hesitating, she thrust the door further open and now the cold wind leapt in, swept through the conservatory and slammed the drawing-room door.

"Ach!" exclaimed Mrs Arkwright, looking up from her game of whist. "*Du lieber* Hugh. Will you have the goodness. That naughty greenhouse door is open, I am sure. Did you hear the shocking bang? Go shut it, dear fellow."

And so Hugh almost immediately went to Annis.

Without the least suspicion that she was there, he sprang from his chair, laid down his cards, opened the door into the conservatory and entering, saw standing on the garden steps, a little black-draped figure, with a face of deadly pallor, out of which two large dark eyes shone with a subdued light.

He recognised her in a moment, shut the door behind him hastily, and started forward. She came in now, leaving the step.

"I want to speak to you one moment, Mr Arkwright," she said in a calm unnatural tone.

"Annis, dear, dear, Annis!" He had her hands in his instantly. They were as cold as stone, and did not return his pressure; but he scarcely observed it.

"You dearest little girl," he said, devouring her with his beaming eyes. "How ill you look; have you been unwell?"

"I have been very well, thank you."

"I must have a kiss."

She repulsed him, turning her face aside, whilst a sudden twinge of pain contracted the muscles of her mouth.

"What is the matter, my own?"

"I am not yours, Mr Hugh."

"Annis!"

"I have come to speak about something else," she said constrainedly.

"You will drive me mad," he exclaimed. "What does this mean?"

"I want you to do me a great favour," she said, and then, with her voice softening, "in consideration of old times. You saw someone a little while ago — Joe Earnshaw."

"I did," with a puzzled look.

"Will you promise to tell no one you have seen him?"

"Annis, what do you mean?"

"For the sake of old days passed away for ever," she went on, in a mournful tone, "I want you to do this one thing. You have

314

ruined my happiness, make this amends. it is not much."

"I will promise you anything you like," answered Hugh. "But I cannot understand you, Annis. Why are you so cold with me? Have you ceased to love me?"

She looked up at him. Her great brown eyes began to fill, a tremor ran over her face and a flame kindled in her cheeks.

"Let me go, let me go!" she wailed, struggling from his grasp.

"Annis!"

She was gone. He stood motionless, bewildered, gazing at the night through the garden door. His heart stood still.

"She is no more mine — no more mine!" he repeated. "My God, my God! This is terrible. Anything but this!"

Then he heard his aunt calling him from the drawing-room. He shut and bolted the conservatory entrance and returned in a humbled condition of mind to the room he had so lately left, and reseated himself at the table.

"My dear fellow!" exclaimed Gretchen impatiently. "How shocking you play! *Frielich*! I had rather a dummy as you."

"He is preoccupied," said Mr Arkwright, with a wink at his wife, and then at Mrs Doldrums, and finally a sly glance out of the corner of his eyes at Laura.

"Excuse me, aunt; I am not fit to take a hand tonight. I have a good deal on my mind."

"And heart, too," said Mr Arkwright. "Ahem, we understand."

Hugh looked dreamily at him, and then tried to collect his thoughts sufficiently to go on with the game, but in vain.

"We will excuse you," said his uncle.

He threw down his cards and left the table.

Chapter Thirty–Four

"Mrs Doldrums' carriage is at the door," announced Sarah Jane.

"Oh dear!" Laura said. "I should have preferred walking."

"And then Hugh would have accompanied you home," put in Mr Arkwright slyly.

"I have no doubt that he would," replied Laura at once; "he is always ready to be civil and obliging."

"I will at all events see you to the gate," said the young man; and as he took Laura to the carriage, he whispered, "I have seen Annis."

"When?"

"This evening; but only for a moment. All is not quite right, I fear."

"Oh, stuff! Lovers are always full of fancies."

"I wish it may be only fancy," Hugh said despondently.

"I will seek her out tomorrow and insist on her coming to the Lodge," Laura said. "Good night, Hugh."

"Good night, and many thanks, Laura."

The carriage rolled away, leaving Mr Arkwright and his nephew at the garden gate. "Come and have a pipe and a glass of brandy and water in the greenhouse," said the former, turning towards the house.

"I will join you there presently," answered Hugh. "I want to run into the town first."

"It is rather late."

"I will be back directly."

"You will find me in the conservatory; don't be long."

Hugh passed into the lane. His uncle looked after him with a grim smile and said, when he was out of hearing, "We have you fast now, young fellow."

Hugh went at once to Kirkgate, and knocked at the door of the Rhodes's establishment. The shop was closed, but there was a light through the glass over the door, which showed that the family had not gone to bed. The poor fellow could not rest without an explanation from Annis. Her behaviour had maddened him. What had she meant by saying that she was no longer his, and by her intercession for Earnshaw? A temptation to connect these two facts together presented itself before him, but he turned from it in sickly horror. Annis and that awful watchman — the pure, simple maiden and that murderous maniac — what could be the connection between them? He knew the hateful creature's passion for the girl, and he was now made aware of her interest in him. And she could be no more Hugh's little Annis! Good God! Did she mean that she belonged to another? He recoiled from the thought. "I will not think of this," he said. The door opened to him, after he had been kept waiting some little while, by Susan, holding a candle.

"Lor, Mr Hugh! Whoever would ha' thought it were you?"

"Who's there?" called Mrs Rhodes, shrilly, from the back room.

"Susie," said Hugh, "tell me, please, is Annis with you?"

"Annis!" The girl stared at him and then laughed. "Nay, she's not here. Whatever put that in your head, sir?"

"Are you certain?"

"Ay, I'm as sure as I'm standing here."

"Where is Martha? I must see Martha immediately."

"Martha," called Susan, "there's a gentleman at t' door, seeking thee, lass."

"What's all this about?" cried Mrs Rhodes, without leaving what she was engaged upon.

"It's somebody wants me, Mother," said Martha, going into the shop. She was as much surprised as her sister to see Hugh at the door; she was distressed to observe his anxious expression. She went to him at once, without asking questions, and telling Susan not to fasten the bolt, as she would be back directly, she stepped out into the street with him.

"Thank you, Martha," he said. "Now tell me, where is Annis."

"I do not know."

"I have seen her tonight, and have spoken to her, so she is somewhere in Sowden."

"You have seen óur Annis!" echoed Martha, standing still in astonishment, and looking at him. "We thought it likely she would be sent for soon; that she might be coming, happen, tomorrow or maybe Monday, but not tonight."

"She is actually here."

317

"And you do not know where to find her?"

"No, I do not. I thought she would be with you."

"I could have made sure she'd ha' come first to me," said Martha, with a slight tone of disappointment in her voice; "but happen she thought otherwise."

"Where can she be?"

"I think it likely enough she is at the vicarage. If she didn't come first to me, it was because she wanted to see Mr Furness before others. And she may have felt a sort of reluctance to come here, after what's taken place. Yes, I reckon that is it," with some confidence. "She went to the vicarage, and is staying there. You may set your mind at rest. I feel sure that is what has happened. We shall see her, dear lass, tomorrow. I'll get back as soon as ever I can fro' my work."

"This is not all I have to say," pursued Hugh. "Annis is so changed."

"Ah! I thought she would be. She'll be a right lady now."

"That she always was," said the young man, with a sigh; "but she is altered in another way. She spoke to me so coldly and indifferently, as though I were a mere acquaintance."

"You wouldn't have her jump into your arms, now," said Martha in her blunt, offhand way.

"No. But she seemed not to care a bit to see me, not to be in the least glad to meet with me again."

"She was shy. Do you think she'd ha' come to see you, if she hadn't cared for you?"

"She came to ask a favour of me, quite concerned about a third person, and in a formal manner. I am afraid all is not going on smoothly. Martha, you must find out for me what is at the bottom of this."

"Psh!" said the girl; "I've no patience with you. Annis is all right. You should know her better than to mistrust her."

"She told me distinctly that she was no longer mine."

"Then she didn't mean it. She was silly. Maybe she is a bit jealous. Some folks love to make mischief and they may have been telling her spiteful tales."

"They must have been tales of pure invention," said Hugh, simply.

"Oh, there are a deal o' tales about, along of you and Laura

Doldrums."

Hugh stood still and laughed. "Is that all?" he exclaimed. "*You* never suspected anything, Martha, did you?"

"I trusted you," the girl replied.

"Now I must be going back. As you are so satisfied that Annis is at the vicarage, and that her manner towards me is the result of a misunderstanding, I shall rest more content. I was in a thorough fidget before I saw you. Poor little Annis! I cannot endure the thought of a cloud coming between us, if only for a few hours. Good night, Martha."

And he went, with lightened heart, towards home. Martha returned to find herself in a hornets' nest. Her mother, Rachel, and Susan were all prepared and waiting to attack her.

"Here's pretty goings–on!" exclaimed Mrs Rhodes, the instant the girl came in. "So much for your chu'ch ways. May we never have the like o' them i' our sect. And what is more, lass, I won't have my house treated like this. What does yond fellow mean by axing if we'd Annis here? What is he after, coming here this time o' neet? Look at t'clock, lass; it's nigh on eleven. I know what folks will be saying if they see young men come rapping at my doors at this time o' neet, and thy father safe and snoring i' bed half an hour agone."

"Eh! I wouldn't be a go–between," sneered Rachel. "It ain't I as would lower myself to that. I wouldn't strive all I could to make a leddy o' yond lass, and have her lookin' down on us, and shamed on us all as are her relations."

"Martha," threw in Susan, "so thou knows where Annis is a hiding. And thou'rt boune to bring her here for Hugh Arkwright to be sweethearting her."

"I'll have none o' that i' t' house," protested Mrs Rhodes. "If Annis is boune to come here, as I suppose she must, there being no other place for her to go into, I'll look sharp after her, and not have her trailing after all t' lads i' t' place."

"Mother," said Martha, with perfect composure, "I believe Annis would not think of coming here."

"No, I reckon not. We ain't grand enew for her fancy," sneered Rachel.

"There's many a slip 'twixt cup and lip," said Susan; "and if what folks say is true, Hugh Arkwright ain't a going to make a fool of hissen by marrying Annis, as thou'rt so chuff over."

"No," Mrs Rhodes exclaimed, in her harsh voice, with a toss of her head, "she won't demean hersen to come to her poor relations now. But when she's found out gentlefolks ain't going to make so much o' her as she thinks for, then she'll come sneaking here to be taken in, you'lt see!"

"Mother," said Martha, without showing the least symptoms of being put out of temper, "I think you have quite mistaken the dear lass."

"I mistake her! That's like enough, you saucy young minx. It's you is ever over right, and me is ever wrong."

"I beg your pardon, Mother. I did not mean that. I think you've mista'en Annis's motives in not coming here."

"Pray, what motives are they?" contemptuously asked Rachel, tossing away the piece of sewing she had been engaged upon.

"I think, Mother, she'd not like to come here after what you did to her."

"What *I* did!"

"I don't mean to offend you, Mother; but you know she mightn't feel over comfortable here, thinking how you'd deceived her, and sent her out to the man–monkey, pretending it were Hugh as wanted her." Martha spoke with great simplicity and quietness, but the words had their effect. Her mother darted at her a glance of fury, but was silenced.

"And what mucky hoile[1] dost think she's gone to now?" asked Susan.

"I think, lass, t' vicar has ta'en her in for t' neet."

"The vicar!" exclaimed Rachel.

"Well," laughed Susan, "happen t' vicar ain't much better nor us."

"Halloo there!" called a loud voice from the top of the stairs. "You womenfolk, ain't you going to stop them clappers? How can I go to sleep if you're fratching half t'neet through? Shut up, will you, or I'll leather–strap you all round."

It was the voice of John Rhodes from bed: it silenced the women.

[1]hole

320

Chapter Thirty-Five

As Hugh entered his uncle's house the clock of Sowden church steeple struck eleven.

He found his uncle in the conservatory, with his pipe in his mouth, lounging in his easy chair, beside a table on which stood spirits, and a small jug of cold, and another of hot water, reading his newspaper.

The lights in the drawing-room had been extinguished. The suspended lamp in the greenhouse was low, so that Mr Arkwright read with difficulty.

"Just in time," he said; "I can't make out this smudgy print any longer. There is no more spirit in the lamp, and it is going out."

"Shall I fetch you the moderator from the drawing-room?"

"Never mind. We can talk; we don't want light for that, I suppose, and obscurity will help to veil your blushes. The lamp won't go out altogether for another half hour, but give a sort of twilight glow, suitable for romance, eh!"

Hugh did not understand what his uncle meant, so he answered indifferently: "If you do not want light, I am sure I do not. My cigar-end yields sufficient for me." He drew his chair round, so that the back might be against the garden front. He remembered the horrible vision of the face glaring in upon him from the outer darkness, and, rather to avoid the reminiscence, than expecting a recurrence of the circumstance, he moved the seat so as to face the camellias.

"Dismal night," he said: "wind piercingly cold."

"But there is plenty of warmth within," with a nod of the head towards Hugh.

"It is a pity the gas is not brought along this lane, so that we might not have the trouble of lamps," Hugh observed.

"Oh!" said his uncle, "it is you who are changing the topic."

"We were on no particular subject, that I am aware of."

"No, but approaching one by slow degrees."

"What topic?"

"Well, I suppose I must dash at once *in medias res*. I

congratulate you heartily, my dear boy."

"You congratulate me!" exclaimed Hugh. "What on earth is the subject of congratulation?"

"Sly fellow. Do you think I do not know?"

"I am at a loss to comprehend your meaning."

"What a long *tête-à-tête* you had in this place, Hugh."

"Yes, I had something very particular to say to Miss Doldrums."

"And you kept us waiting for our game of whist in the most unconscionable manner; but we were not disposed to interrupt you. And she is quite agreeable, I suppose?"

"She is very agreeable," said Hugh, on whom his uncle's meaning dawned. He was provoked, but at the same time amused. He drew a long whiff of tobacco and blew it leisurely out, with his eyes on the crimson camellia.

"Uncle, I never saw a plant so full of flower as that. It is beautiful."

"Changing the topic again, Hugh! Sly dog."

"What is the native country of the camellia? Do you know, sir?"

"Timbuctoo. Hang your camellia! We are talking of Laura."

"I did not mention her."

"No, but you were thinking of her."

"She was far from my thoughts, which were then on the camellia."

"Laura, be that the subject of our conversation."

"Then, uncle, I shall go to bed."

"Fudge, boy. I know your heart is full. Talk to me."

"My dear sir, you are entirely mistaken if you think I take an extraordinary interest in Laura. I like her very much; indeed I am fond of her, as a sister, but no more."

"You don't mean to tell me," began Mr Arkwright incredulously, "that all those *tête-à-têtes* mean nothing. What were you chattering together in this snuggery for, this evening, unless you liked her more than a sister? Didn't you pop the question this evening? You had a glorious opportunity."

"Certainly not."

"Then you were a monstrous fool. You had the best possible chance. A bright, pretty winter garden. Flowers all round, air warm, hyacinths smelling, glass glittering — it was just the very time and scene for a romantic young fellow like you. Don't let it slip next time."

"I have no intention whatever of proposing to Miss Doldrums."

"Then why are you trifling with her affections? She is fond of you, is always talking of you, praising you, running after you. I should say she was madly in love with you. And you encourage her, and draw her on. You are bound in honour to make her an offer."

"Bound in honour I am to do no such thing," said Hugh, with temper.

"Gammon. I guess what you refer to. That is all over."

Hugh turned sharply on his uncle. Did he know anything which was concealed from him, anything which would sever Annis from him for ever?

"Why over?" he asked.

"Because — on my word," burst forth the manufacturer, starting up, "you are enough to make a man swear. I never do such a thing — I should be sorry to begin the practice. But I would give five shillings to be able to say, Damn you. I believe an oath is an escape provided by nature for the feelings when brought to high pressure. Upon my word!" he added, relapsing into his chair; "I think I never came across such a confounded fool in all my life."

"Uncle, I will not stand this."

"I am addressing the Turk's head on the bowl of my pipe."

Mr Arkwright and Hugh smoked on in silence, drawing hasty whiffs, and puffing the smoke out in little compact clouds.

"Shall we return to the consideration of the gas?" asked Hugh at last.

"No, decidedly not!" very angrily spoken in answer.

"Then I will finish this cigar and go to my room."

"Hugh! none of this nonsense. You must marry Laura."

"I shall certainly not. In the first place, she would not have me, and in the second I am otherwise engaged."

"Not have you! She'd jump at you."

"Then she is not the person who would suit me."

"No; none suit you but little sniggering — "

"Uncle, stop." He spoke firmly.

"Hugh. You do not mean to tell me that you persist in that absurd romance of last autumn! This is intolerable. I did not think such a jackass — I am alluding to the Turk's head, Hugh, don't go. Hugh, give up this folly, and be rational."

"I am quite in my senses."

"No you are not. Common sense points out Laura as the very girl who would best suit you. She is nicely educated, is full of spirit, fun, and good nature, is universally popular, has lovely hair and eyes, and a charming expression, and to crown it all, is immensely rich; and all to be had for the asking. Hugh, do you hear? — to be had for the mere asking. Here am I toiling and moiling to make a few hundreds, and there are thousands to be had for the mere asking — the mere asking! You have but to hold up your little finger and the money is yours. By George! I wish bigamy were legal, and I would try to get Laura for myself. It is tempting Providence to throw away such a chance. So much gold lying at your feet, and you will not stoop to pick it up. So many thousands extended to you, and you will not stretch out your hand to grasp them! You nincompoop! — Turk's head, I address you!"

"Would it not be as well, uncle, if you were to take a cigar and allow me to pitch that pipe away? It is likely to produce a quarrel."

Mr Arkwright paid no attention to this suggestion. "Boy," he said, taking the pipe out of his mouth and leaning his hand which held it on the table. "Listen to me."

"I am attention, sir, but please to address me in future, and not the Turk's head."

"I have reckoned on your proposing to Laura Doldrums, and my hopes and expectations have been built on the prospect of your marrying her and becoming possessed of her property. I must tell you that my affairs are by no means as prosperous as you might have supposed. I have had serious losses. The failure of the Leeds and Manchester bank clipped my wings a trifle. That rascal Armitage — you know — who bolted to America, lost me a couple of thousand pounds, not a penny of which am I likely to recover. Business has been slack, and I cannot dispose of the goods I have in stock. My yarns, made for the

German market, to German weights, will not sell in England, and they encumber the warehouse. The machinery wants renewing, and I have not the money in hand to order fresh. As long as this German war lasts — and there seems to be no prospect of it terminating in a hurry — I am in a losing condition. The flood did me damage to the tune of some hundreds; and I must have some prospect of money or I shall go to pieces. If you take Laura, you can sink money in the business, and we shall weather the storm and do well. What I want now is a few thousand pounds. With that I shall be able to hold on till the tightness is past, and afterwards the business may be extended, and I see my way to turning over a great deal of money. You must please to remember, Mr Hugh, that you have nothing whatever of your own, and that your future entirely depends on your turning your present opportunities to the best account. You are in a fair way to making a fortune now, if you will only realise the rare chances put in your way, and use them effectually. You are in a business which bids to be prosperous, you are beginning to understand it. There is a certainty of money sunk in it quadrupling itself in a few years, if we can only tide over the present crisis. A series of untoward events have affected the concern at present — the failure of banks, the fraud of Armitage, the Continental war, and the imperfection and wearing out of the machinery. You may ask, why I do not borrow. Because I never borrow if I can avoid it. I shall have to borrow at a heavy rate, and I care not to burden myself further. I have a loan already, which ought to have been paid off, encumbering me, and one I would have relieved myself of this year, but for this deuced German war. No. What I want is a partner who can sink money in the concern. You are the proper person to become my partner, and the opportunity of obtaining the requisite sum is open to you. For the asking, you may have enough to set me once more on my feet, and give the concern a push which will carry it on into success. If you are obstinate, pigheaded — I allude to the Turk's head — I shall pass you over, and take another into partnership. I have had an offer already, and I shall close with it unless you yield. Let me tell you, Mr Hugh, it is pleasanter to be partner than clerk. You wouldn't be particularly pleased to see young Jumbold put over

325

your head, and you to remain as salaried understrapper, eh? Of course I should personally prefer having my own nephew in the business with me, to a young man who is no relation; but the proposal has been made by his father, who is ready to pay handsomely for the partnership, and I shall close with the offer if you do not accede to my wishes, and become a wise man, and a rich one into the bargain."

"I am sorry to disappoint you," said Hugh calmly; "but I adhere to my determination. I am bound to do so as a man of honour. When I asked Annis to be mine, I encouraged her to form an attachment for me, and I should be wrong if I disregarded her happiness in the pursuit of my own selfish advantage. A girl's feelings are too sacred to be trifled with. I believe the poor little thing loves me. If I ignored her feelings and deceived her confidence, I might ruin her peace of mind, and cloud a beautiful spirit with distrust, and harden a green and tender heart to stone. I should outrage my own convictions. I am satisfied that Annis is the one woman best suited to me in the world. I love her, I trust her, I believe implicitly in her goodness, I am sure of her devotion to myself. I have borne much for her already, which has daily endeared her more to me, and she has suffered much for me. On my account she has been driven from her home, associates, and work, and has had to hide an aching heart and bear the desolation of her bereavement, among strangers. She has been worried and insulted, and made the subject of gossip and scandal, because of me. I have already lifted her into a position of observation, and I cannot fling her back into oblivion. How can I calculate on the effect on her of such treatment as you recommend? And how do you think I could bear the humiliation of loss of self-respect, and consciousness that by all honourable men I was regarded as an infamous, perjured scoundrel."

"Confound you!" exclaimed Mr Arkwright passionately; for now his blood was fairly up. "Do you mean to insinuate that I am not an honourable man?"

"Uncle," answered Hugh, who had worked himself into irritation by his long speech, "I am satisfied that what you recommend to me, in the case of another you would regard as dirty, dastardly conduct."

"No such thing," said the manufacturer, angrily. "No man with any sense in his head would do other than approve of what I advise. If a man puts his foot into a wrong box, he will get out of it at once, with a consciousness that he is in a false situation, that is, if he is wise. If he is an infernal idiot, he will put the other leg. in too, and proceed to lie down in his box. No reasonable man, I say, would think, that because you had been spoony once on a time on a little snivelling mill girl — "

Hugh bounded out of his chair, and in doing so knocked over the table.

"There you go with you damned precipitation! (You have made me swear, observe.) This is in keeping with all you do. You will plunge into a much worse mess than this with just a little thought. Gad! this water is hot enough that you have splashed over my knee, but that water you want to take a dip in yourself in a deuced deal hotter, let me tell you. Pick up the spirit bottle, Hugh. Look out for broken glass. You have smashed both tumblers. Confound the lamp! I wish it were not so near out. Turn it up, Hugh, and let us see where the fragments are: I don't want to get my feet cut with glass. You have boots on, but I only my slippers. What a jackass — I am addressing my Turk's head."

"Uncle!"

Hugh was standing where he had risen, his back was towards the garden front of the conservatory; facing him was the wall, trellised over with creepers, not now in bloom, before which, on a raised bed, were the camellias. As the lamp had failed, the rich carnation and white flowers had faded into the dusk. A single spot of flame remained, and by its light the white blossoms were faintly distinguishable, but the crimson flowers were not to be discerned from the leaves. But now, as Hugh stood, flushed and angry, with his eyes levelled at the gloomy bushes, the flowers gradually detached themselves from the darkness, and gathered distinctness, then colour. The white waxlike blossoms lost their pallor and flushed, the crimson ones grew scarlet. Hugh looking, and not immediately observing, his mind being preoccupied, saw his shadow flung back and distorted on the creeper-covered wall.

Then he started and turned, and turning, saw his uncle risen, and his face illumined with a coloured light, and his eyes dilated.

"Good God!" exclaimed Hugh. "The mill!"

Chapter Thirty-Six

The wind rushed along the vale, laden with sleet. Black vapours with ragged outline spread over the heavens, extinguishing star after star. The night seemed to be a great void of blackness, through which raced a blinding scud of frozen particles, that struck against every opposing surface, and on it built little walls and ridges of watery ice. A sickly nebulous haze clung about every gaslamp. Deserted causeways were crusted over with dissolving sleet; whitening roads were welted with black ruts; clogged bushes shivered and shook off the ice lodging on their twigs; windows were pattered on softly; leaves tingled, spouts gurgled, eaves dripped; Nature, oppressed with darkness and desolation, paled and blackened again, shuddering. An engine uttered far away a long protracted wail. A man slunk from the cold into a low public-house near the station, and shut the door behind him on the darkness and sleet.

A quaking girl ascended the steps of Arkwright's mill, her black dress patched with the outshakings of the cloud, that clung to her, and sucked the warmth from her, and feasted thereon, and dissolved into water drops. Then a hand, thrust out of the darkness, grasped her wrist, then hinges creaked, she was drawn within and the door was shut behind her, and black as it was without, she became aware that there was a blackness blacker still; and that if there was a horror of being without, there was a horror more horrible still of being locked within.

All this took place as the Sowden steeple clock struck eleven. The impervious darkness, the consciousness of being in it with one whom she dreaded, was unendurable to Annis. She bore it for a minute only. Her fears rose like a flood, and rushed over her. She would have fainted if she had not spoken. Her nervous system could not have endured the agony of terror longer by a moment without giving way.

"Joe, show a light or I shall die," she moaned.

"Go up to the spinning room," he answered gently, in his thrilling musical tones, full now of a strangely sad pathos. "Go to the old reel, poor little lass, and wait. You will find light there."

"I cannot see," she whispered. There was a tightening at her throat, as though she were strangling. "I cannot endure this darkness any longer."

"Feel your way. Shall I assist you?"

"No!" with a sharp cry. She started from the door. That stone stair she knew full well. Often had she tramped up and down it with light heart or with sad heart, with buoyant spirits or with wistful longings, but never before with the stunned sensation in her brain, or the contraction of heart that she felt now, as with her hand against the greasy wall she groped her way up the oil–steeped steps. The man followed behind. When she considered that he was drawing nearer, the thought goaded her on. The old familiar scent of the foul oil that impregnated everything met her once more; with woodwork she knew was saturated with it, the very stone distilled drops of it, the iron was polished with it, the wool clogged with it, the window glass blurred with it. And with the scent of rancid oil was also an all–pervading subtle odour of gas.

When she reached the door of the spinning room she thrust it open with her hand and went in. The light spoken of by Earnshaw was very faint; it was only that cast through the windows from without by the lamp above the gate into the millyard; this made a sort of yellow dusk within, especially towards the extremity of the long room.

"Go in there and wait for me," said Earnshaw.

"Joe, the gas is turned on, and is escaping," Annis said, as the hiss of the vapour and its nauseous scent met her on entering. "How is this? They generally turn it off at night."

"I suppose it is left on," he answered. "Wait here while I go down." He turned and left her.

Annis remained in the great machine–encumbered room. The mechanism was quiet now. The great straps did not rush along the roof, setting numberless wheels in motion. The floor did not quiver with the vibration of the countless movements in the delicately–constructed machines. But all was not quite still. Throughout the room sounded the *pfiff* of gas apparently escaping from every burner.

Annis heard the descending steps of Earnshaw, then his tread on the basement floor, slow, heavy, distinct.

She listened, anxious for his return, as she was in a hurry to be off. If detained much longer she would find a difficulty in getting shelter for the night. To the vicarage she had purposed going, according to Miss Furness's direction, and in her pocket was a note from that lady to her brother, asking him to give the girl a bed for a night or two, and promising to come to Sowden by an early train on Monday. Annis, waiting and wearying, crept down the room towards the end which was partially illumined by the lamp outside. As she went along, on all sides of her sounded the gas, and the air became more heavily charged with it. She could scarcely breathe. She put her hand to the taps and turned them. This occupied her, and diverted her mind from Earnshaw. Tap after tap was open. She went down one side, feeling her way and groping for the burners, then up the other side, doing the same. And as she passed the windows, she threw open some of the casements.

It was strange that the gas should have been left on. Usually each tap was shut off before the main was closed. This could not have been done on the present occasion when work was over. The gas must have been prematurely turned off at the main, and then let on again for some special purpose, and the unclosed cocks in the spinning room forgotten.

But this explanation was far from satisfactory.

Annis heard the tramp of the ex-watchman on the stair, then the sound of his feet entering the drying room. She was weary of waiting. She stood listlessly gazing out of one of the blurred windows into the darkness.

What seemed a fuming torch rushed by with a rumble, and a star changed hue over the railway bridge. In reality, she saw the illumined steam of the engine of a goods train, and the shifting signal-lamp. Presently a leaky joint of a pipe in the room began to fizz and splutter, and a whiff of white steam to blow out of it. Then a drum high up against the wall trundled slowly, playing with the loose flapping belt.

Annis was surprised, perplexed and alarmed. The steam had been turned on; wherefore, and by whom?

Then slowly up the steps from the drying room and across the landing to the door of the long spinning room, came Earnshaw.

331

"Where are you, Annis?" he asked, standing in the entrance.

"I am here, near the reel," replied the girl. "You have been very long, Joe. I want to get away."

"I can speak to you now."

"Well, Joe, I wish you had let me say my say first. I have little to tell you, except that Mr Hugh Arkwright has promised not to mention to anyone that he saw you. You are, in consequence, tolerably safe. Do make your escape at once; do, Joe!"

"Annis, it is impossible."

"I am sure it is not. You have two to three days clear for getting away."

"Annis, do you see me?"

"Yes, why have you taken off your disguise?"

He was in his waistcoat and shirt–sleeves. A broad–brimmed felt hat overshadowed his face. He was just distinguishable by the feeble glimmer through the window.

"I have thrown off disguise because it avails me no more. Escape is impossible."

"Not so; make the attempt."

"I will make no further attempts, Annis, you have seen my face."

She did not speak, but shrank away and putting her hand on the reel, turned it, looking fixedly out of the window.

"Can a man with a face such as mine disappear in a crowd? I tried the disguise of female attire, wearing a veil over my face continually. That disguise is known and avails me no more. The York police have discovered it."

"Oh, no," put in Annis earnestly. "You forget they have not discovered who the red–veiled woman was."

"Not yet, perhaps, but before Monday it will be known. Do you think the Sowden and York officers will not enter into communication with one another? If they do, all will be found out. Poor little girl, you do not know everything that has taken place."

"Do not tell me!" she pleaded.

"Yes, you shall know all. I killed Richard Grover."

"Oh, I know that. I made sure of that; but you did not intend it, Joe, it was an accident. You were protecting me."

"I killed him purposely."

"No, Joe, no!" she cried, thrilling with horror.

"I had been waiting my opportunity for years. I found it at last, and I killed him. Richard Grover was the man who mutilated my features. He it was who disfigured and mangled my face, and made me an object of loathing to my fellow–men. He it was who blighted my life, who poisoned my happiness, who ruined me, body and mind, physically and morally. He it was who drove me from my home, drove me into seclusion, drove me to the maddening misery of being cut off for ever from the joys of life. Worse, ten thousand times worse, Annis, he severed *us*."

Annis sobbed, shuddering, shrinking against the wall, cowering before him, as his voice rose and rolled through the deserted room in loud booming tones.

"Little girl, I have loved you, oh, madly! Madly is indeed the right word, for my love has been the love of despair, and it has driven me to do that which in olden days I would have hated myself for doing. But that I killed Richard, I rejoice, I thank heaven. I would not have caused his death, though, had he not insulted you. No. I would only have beaten and mashed his face with the slag on the roadside, till it was reduced to a state like mine. But I killed him — murdered him, if you prefer the word — because he dared to lay his cursed fingers on *You*."

"Let me go," pleaded, in mournful tones, the frightened girl.

"No, Annis, no! I have not done my history. You have not heard all. I hated Hugh Arkwright."

Her heart gave a great leap, and then stood still. She dropped her hands and her whole body went rigid.

"I hated Hugh Arkwright because he dared to love you; more than that, because he won your love. You still cling to him, do you not?"

She did not speak.

"I will have an answer. Do you love him, or do you not?"

"Oh, indeed, indeed I do! You asked me this once before, and I answered you then."

"Yes, I knew it. I hated him for having stolen your affections. I would have none love you but myself, and if you could not return my passion, I would prevent anyone else from assuming a right over you. I attacked Hugh, intending to kill him. I cut at him with my knife —"

A shrill cry of inexpressible anguish escaped from the girl; and she caught at the casement and held to it with both hands, fearing lest she should fall.

"I stabbed him, and plunged with him into the canal. I thought I had killed him, but his fortune has been better than mine. May be" — and he ground his teeth with rage — "those prayers of yours saved him. Ah! if you had prayed for me, as you did for him, I should have had more luck, and he would now be rotting at the canal bottom."

She relaxed her grasp of the window, and made a dart for the door. Earnshaw caught her, laughing wildly. "Little one, do not try to escape. You cannot leave this place. I have broken the key in the lock, and there is no more egress."

She staggered back to her window and grappled it again, in a stupor of despair.

"Annis, you have not heard my story out. When I emerged from the canal, I hastened to your old cottage; there I lurked till deep on into the night. At last I came forth, and I robbed the cottage of Widow Lupton. Not that I wanted money. No, I wanted a dress for disguise. Having obtained that, I sought you out. I had discovered your address. Tell me now, am I likely to escape? Is there the remotest possibility of a man, disfigured and conspicuous as I am, avoiding capture, when the police are on his track, thoroughly aroused, knowing him to be a murderer, a burglar and a would-be assassin? No, Annis, no, I cannot get away. Were I taken, I should be hung, or, worse still, thrown into a madhouse, to rage my life out away from you. Whether I die on the gallows, or whether I am locked into an asylum, I care not. In either case I should not be with you, and you would be at the mercy of Hugh Arkwright."

He burst into a demoniacal laugh, loud, gulping, hideous, continued in echoing peals, as the hyena may laugh in the desolate places and empty sepulchres of the east, over the bones of a benighted traveller, who has died of horror at the glare of the moonlike eyes looking down on him, lusting for his blood.

Then away he rushed towards the revolving drum, and about it he placed the leathern belt, and tightened it around a lesser cylinder; and running along the line of motionless machinery, he touched a lever here, turned a tap on, adjusted a strap there, and directly, the rush of the wheels, the whirr of the bobbins, the rumble of the cylinders began. The mechanism was set in motion throughout the room.

And Annis, clinging to the window bar, in a dream, looked out on the blank wall unrelieved by openings, belonging to the warehouse of the adjoining mill, and saw on the blank surface squares of lurid red, like illumined windows over which were drawn scarlet blinds; became slowly aware of an intense heat, and a smell of burning, and a thickening smoke — but these her senses perceived, without conveying their impressions to her brain.

Then suddenly Earnshaw came up to her, his eyes glittering with red reflections, the light cast back by the wall irradiating his horrible face, his black hair bristling, his white teeth flashing, his hands extended towards her, and laying them heavily on her feeble wrists, he said, "Annis, I have fired the mill. We shall die together."

She did not speak; she looked at him with unconsciousness in her dulled eyes, without repugnance, without appeal for mercy.

"Annis," he continued, speaking loud, to be heard above the rush and rattle of the machinery, but with a voice so full of volume that it would have been distinguishable in the midst of a thunder crash; "Annis, dear, dear Annis! I swore that no one should have you for his own. See how I keep my word. I will not be torn from you. We shall perish together."

The heat became more intense, the floors were slippery with the exuded oil that burst from every pore in little bubbling springs. A pungent white smoke arose from between the planks; a flickering blue flame, like a Jack o' lanthorn, ran along the floor, then stood still and changed hue to pale yellow, gathered size and luminous power, and shot up, a quivering tongue of light. Drops ran down the walls, or fell from the ceiling, as the heat dissolved the oil. It was as though the horror of death had fallen on the old factory and it sweated in its agony.

Now, without, appeared yellow walls and gleaming window glass. A bare elder tree in a corner became a tree of gold, the fold ground was brilliantly lighted with orange stripes, and in the light were seen black moving figures with illumined faces. Mill whistles shrieked, buzzers roared, bells jangled, and the gathering people shouted. Annis saw and heard, but neither spoke nor stirred. Earnshaw laughed over his handiwork.

The room was ghastly in the yellow light that smote in through the dingy windows. In the weird glare from the spout of flame near the further end, that stood up like a dancing cobra to the piping of a charmer, wavering and curling, rolling back and falling, and leaping up once more with lofty crest, the racing belts and rushing wheels were revealed, as they laboured at a profitless work. Phosphoric gleams flashed about, at a few inches above the floor, in an irregular, tentative manner, as though invisible hands were engaged in carrying flames from spot to spot. Then, all at once, the oleaginous vapour ignited with an explosion in several places, and began to gnaw at the heated boards.

A pipe burst with noise in the fire-consumed lower storey, and the steam rushed out in a volume, screaming. The flaming oil swam over the floor, igniting wood wherever it came in contact with it. There were timber supports to the beams of the roof, and the fire corroded their bases. The heat was that of a furnace. Annis stood still at the open casement, looking out in the stupor of her terror.

All at once a glimmer of life stole through her dim eyes; she stretched out her hands and tried to speak, her lips moved, but no sound issued from them. She had seen Hugh in the crowd below.

336

The scene from without was wildly magnificent. The first storey glowed like a furnace. The flame had not burst through the windows, but consumed the interior; the light began to appear, faint at first, gradually intensifying in the second storey, and cast a yellow glare through the windows of the long spinning room.

On the further side of the entrance–door and stairs communicating with the rooms, the flames had burst through the roof and spouted into the air, to be caught by the wind and borne away in flapping streamers of amber and scarlet. Here the fire raged with greatest fury, as it broke from the drying room, which was full of hot wool, that blazed at once, and, flying about in ignited masses, spread the conflagration. When the fire came in contact with copper, the flames turned green. Sparks and flaming particles rushed up at the over–hanging clouds, as though labouring to ignite them, and then fell away and went out.

The sleet had stopped; only a few stray spangling flakes rambled about in the glare of the burning mill. The boiling vapours which obscured the stars, reflected the light, becoming lurid, as clouds of floating, glowing copper.

The long window of the engine–house, reaching nearly the whole height of the factory, crossed within by landings of stone, was illuminated and the shadow of the huge engine in motion, leaping up, then sinking, starting up again, and again falling, was cast on the panes.

The great gates of the mill–fold were closed and fastened, to keep the crowd from the premises. All the women, and as many of the men as could be persuaded to go, were cleared out of the yard. The alarums of all the mills in the valley within sight pealed continuously, but no engine had as yet arrived. The fire was momentarily gaining strength.

"By Gad!" said one of the men in the yard, "there's two i't' miln. Dost tha see 'em, Wilfred?"

"Ay, lad; I sees 'em."

The shadow of Earnshaw, as he rushed about the spinning

room, crossed the lighted windows in succession. Annis remained at one little open casement.

"This is some confounded incendiary work," said Mr Arkwright. "What the deuce is the reason of it, I should like to know. Open the main door. Where is the watchman?"

"Here I am, sir."

"You have my keys. Get that door open."

"Uncle, the mill is on fire at three points. This is not the result of accident," said Hugh, coming up.

"Accident!" echoed the manufacturer, turning sharply around on him. "Look there!" He pointed to the second storey windows.

Hugh looked. A chill came over him as he observed the little figure standing at the casement. The face he could not discern, as the strong light in the background threw it into obscurity.

"Can't open the door," said John Rhodes, hurrying up. "The lock is hampered. So is most o' t' locks."

"Burst the door open," ordered Mr Arkwright. Hugh rushed off for a ladder.

"Come here, Fawcett," he called to one of the men who worked for his uncle. "Help me. We must rescue those people in the mill, whoever they may be."

"Eh! let 'em burn," answered Fawcett. "It suited 'em to set t' miln afire, and they mun take t' consequences."

However he accompanied the young man. "Tha'll find t' stee[1] ower short, I reckon," said the man, with stolid composure. "I say, master, did ya ever hear t' tale o' t' fire i' one o' them big hotels i' Leeds?"

"Oh, never mind the story now," said Hugh impatiently, as he laboured to unhook the ladder from the wall.

"Nay, it's a pity to do wi'out it; we shan't get this done a minute sooner. There was two men i' a room at top o' t' house," continued the imperturbable Yorkshireman, "and when there was a cry o' fire, they nip out o' bed, and grabble after their trousers. And tha sees, it were dark, and they were dazed like, and they got hold on t' same pair o' breeches. And t' one man claps his right leg into one leg o' t' trousers, and t'other man he got his

[1]ladder

338

right leg thrussen into t' other leg o't' same pair, and he war looking t' wrong road, so he'd t' seat right afore him."

"Have you got that unhooked?" asked Hugh.

"Bime by," answered Fawcett. "Well, so they started off downstairs, yoked together by t' pair of breeches, one pulling one way, and t'other pulling t'other; and in their fright and confusion away they go, tumble–jumble from top to t'bottom, and out into t'street fast by their legs. Now, master, this is loose."

"Up with that end of the ladder on your shoulder."

Fawcett obeyed, and proceeded to follow Hugh, who supported the further end.

"I say!" called the man, a minute after.

"Well, what?" asked Hugh, turning his head.

"Did ya ever hear t' tale o' t' robbers and t' apit[2]?"

"No, and I do not want it now."

"Because the way we're hugging t' stee reminds me of t' tale."

Fawcett proceeded to relate an anecdote, but it was lost on Hugh, whose attention was otherwise engaged. The man finished it, as Hugh planted the ladder.

At this moment a flame, which had been hurling itself against one of the windows of the lower storey, shivered the glass and shooting through, ran up the wall, licking it as a serpent lubricates the victim it is about to swallow. By this, Hugh saw the face that looked out from above, and two little hands held towards him supplicatingly. He set his teeth.

"Give me an axe," he called.

"Here, sir," shouted the engineer.

"I say, I've a better tale by half than that o' t' robbers and t' apit. It's a tale about an oud woman and her bairn and a beer[3]. But I won't detain thee now. I'll tell thee when tha comes down," said Fawcett; "and," he added, "if thee dosn't brussen thy sides wi' laughing, I shall be capped." Then to the engineer: "I say, Wilfred, dost tha know t' tale o' t' oud woman and t' beer?"

[2]beehive

[3]bear

339

"Ay, lad," answered the man he addressed, "tha'st toud it me mony a time. Now clap thy foit on t' stee bottom."

"I'm doing so, Wilfred. Gearge, dost thou know?"

"Know what, Bill?"

"Why, t' tale o' t' oud woman and t' beer."

"Nay, I cannot say I mind it."

"Weel, tak hold theere along wi' me, and I'll tell thee. Hast thee gotten fast?"

"Ay."

"Weel, there was a man and wife had gotten a baby, as war laid i' a rocking cradle. They were no but poor folks, tha sees, so they hadn't much o' a cottage. No but a house wi' a chamber ower. And they got up into t' chamber by a stee. One day there came a grizzly beer in at t' door. It had escaped from a menagerie, happen. That I cannot say for sure. Choose how he gotten loose, he gotten theere. He came right in at front door, standing on his hind legs and looking about him in a pined sort o' way. Weel, t' man, he were so flayed, he ran right up t' stee; and he'd heard beers was mighty climbing beasts, so he pulled t' stee up after him."

"And where were t' wife and bairn?" asked George.

"Nay, he never gave them a thowt; he were ower flayed for hissen."

Whilst this story was in progress, Hugh, axe in hand, was climbing the ladder. It was too short. It did not reach the windowsill. He kept his eyes raised, fixed on the little face that looked down on him from above, lit by the rushing fire blast from a side window of the lower storey.

By this time a beam had been brought to bear on the main door; it was rested on the stone platform at the head of the steps leading to it, and was driven with violence against the black, iron-studded valves.

"Gearge! thou arn't listening," said Fawcett, reproachfully.

"Eh, but I am!"

"Weel, then. In came t'beer and made straight at t' bairn i' t' cradle. T' woman hugged up t' poker and stood afore it. 'Gie him a crack ower t' ead, lass,' hollered t' man through t' hoile in t' floor above. 'Doan't thee lose heart. Mash his head for him, lass!' So t' wife gave t' beer a smart blow and down he fell.

'Won't thee come doun and help to finish him?' asked t' woman. 'Nay, lass, he might get up again. Gie him another crack. Bang him about t' ribs. Emtpy t' copper ower his head.' 'He's dead,' said t' wife. 'Art thee quite sure?' asked t' man, through t' hoile. 'Ay. He's dead for certain.' 'Cut off his tail, lass.' She took t' chopper and did so. 'He's safe enew,' said her husband. 'Now, lass, I'll come doun.'"

Hugh found the ladder far too short. The sill of the window overhung; and, standing on the topmost available rung, he could only touch it with his hands. Descending a step or two, he turned his head and called to the men below, "Lift the ladder. Put it on your shoulders."

"That reminds me —," began Fawcett.

"Never mind what it reminds you of," burst in his comrade. "Heave up t' stee, as t' lad bade thee."

"Don't tha see I'm about it?" retorted the story–teller. "Sithere, lad. I'll take t' eend o' t' stee on my shoulders, and tha mun steady it, Gearge."

"Ay, I'll do that."

"And while I'm houlding t' stee, I'll tell thee summut."

"If tha'st got wind to do 't; but I'm jealous tha 'asn't."

Between them they elevated the ladder. Hugh ran his hands along the wall, steadying it as it was raised.

"I say, Mr Hugh!" shouted Fawcett, "hast thou seen them monkeys in red coits and blew breeches on a stick, they sell at fairs? Happen thou'rt like situated now. Only don't thee go tummling over, like them monkeys."

"Gie ower wi' thy funning," expostulated George.

"I might as well let t' stee fall," retorted Fawcett.

Hugh's hands grasped the sill. The ladder was tall, and necessarily wavered as it was being elevated by the men, but he held it in balance. Now, close above him was the well–known, well–loved face, with its soft eyes beaming down on him, and the lips trembling with emotion.

"Annis, give me your hand."

She put forth her arm and Hugh grasped her fingers.

"Can you support me? Are you strong enough?" She put the other hand to his. He set the axe–haft between his teeth, clutched a stanchion, heaved himself up and stood in the window.

The opening was too small to admit him, but holding the stanchion, he used his axe to good effect, smiting at the window-frame, and breaking in the glass and leadwork. Those below shouted, but he cared nothing for their applause. Those working the beam for battering in the door rested for one moment, and then recommended their work.

When Hugh had made a sufficient opening he stepped through, sprang to the floor, and caught Annis in his arms.

"My darling, my own darling!" he exclaimed. She could not speak. Her heart was full to overflowing, but the deep earnest eyes told him how she loved him.

"My dearest," he said, "we have no time to lose. Come to the staircase. We cannot descend by the window; that is impracticable with such a short ladder."

He led her towards the entrance. *Crash* went the battering pole against the door, and the whole interior echoed at the stroke.

They came out on the landing. A fierce howl rang in their ears. Earnshaw was halfway down. The stone flight leading to the first storey ended in a platform of wood, movable, for convenience in hoisting bales of wool. Above this the second storey was wood also. Earnshaw, at the first sound of the ram against the main door, had descended the steps and fired the lower landing.

Looking down, they seemed to be gazing into a well of fire. Volumes of flame rushed out of the door of the drying room, bearing with them a blazing snow of ignited wool, which whirled up and around, and sank, as eddies of wind were formed by the draught that rushed in from all quarters.

The platform of wood below them was a waving lake of flame. At intervals the planks warped and burst, with little reports, from the nails that had retained them. Then the rafters cracked. The heated blast, driving against the gas-pipe that communicated with the upper rooms, exploded it. The timbers of the roof overhead were scorched and glowing in places. A spiral column of lambent blue flame, transparent as glass, rose, tremulous and graceful, in the air, detaching itself from the body of flame, and ascended to the roof, where it spread out into a cloud of translucid nebulous fire, and in a moment yellow spots, then puffs of flame, appeared in the midst of it, and it vanished, leaving the rafters in a blaze.

From below, with his hideous face rendered doubly awful in the scarlet glare, looking up, uttering howls of frenzied rage, came leaping through flame, over fallen burning wood, the man who had caused the conflagration.

"You here!" he yelled at Hugh, plunging up at him.

"Yes, I am here," answered the young man, pressing Annis behind him.

He had left his hatchet in the window. He drew back into the spinning room and shut the door.

Earnshaw cast himself with all his might against it, but Hugh kept it closed. There was a spinning jenny close to the door. He planted one foot against a projecting piece of the machinery, and laid his back against the door.

The madman raged behind him, beating at the panels with his fists, then thrusting his knife through between the interstices.

Hugh hoped every moment to hear the front door give way before the blows of the battering ram.

Earnshaw flung himself again with all his weight against the door. Hugh could barely hold his position. The iron against which his foot rested gave way. The he saw the floor sink, bending beneath the weight of the jenny — saw ragged red edges, like the bleeding lips of a great wound appear, and the machine sank through the consumed boards into the roaring gulf of fire beneath. It crashed down, tearing away posts, ripping beams out of their sockets, snapping polished rods of steel; and from where it had vanished came up a volume of black smoke, charged with a dust of kindled ash.

As the stay for his foot gave way, Hugh slipped and fell. The door burst open and in rushed Earnshaw, knife in hand, and nearly precipitated himself into the yawning chasm, whence rose the smoke mingled with fire. Hugh was on his feet again in a moment. Annis was at his side. The madman stood and glowered at him; a flame was gnawing into the planks between them, and breaking off portions, and throwing them half consumed into the furnace below.

"Young master's up yonder a long time," said Fawcett. "I think, Gearge, I'll happen go up mysen and see if I can do owt. Wilt 'a hawd up t' stee, lad?"

"Ay, I will. Come thee here, Wilfred, and steady t' stee."

So Fawcett ascended. "I say, lads," quoth he, looking down, "I hope ya feel mighty humbled in having me lifted over your heads."

"Nay," answered the engineer, with Yorkshire promptitude, "not so long as we've gotten the chance o' pitching thee down, i' our own hands."

"But you've hoisted me to a place whence ya' can't throw me," shouted the irrepressible joker, as he gained the sill.

"Mebbe, you'll find it a middling uncomfortably hot place yond," retorted Wilfred.

"Happen there's a warmer i' store for thee, lad," bawled Fawcett, before he swung himself into the room.

"Hugh Arkwright, where art thou?" Hugh shouted in reply, and in a moment Fawcett appeared through the smoke.

"Hold that fiend off, will you?" cried the young man.

"Why, Joe! it's never thou! They say bad pennies is sure to turn up. I think thee's gotten into t' mint again, to be melted up and made into a prettier picture. Eh, lad?"

Earnshaw looked at him, and stepping backward into the smoke, disappeared.

"What's he after?" inquired the lively Fawcett.

"He has gone raving mad," replied Hugh. *Crash.* The great entrance door had given way.

They felt it at once. A rush of wind poured in, blowing the fire into redoubled fury and carrying the flame to the further end of the room with a sudden sweep.

Hugh looked at the stair. The whole aspect of the place was changed. Instead of it serving as a chimney towards which the fire converged, and which drew into it currents of flame, its action was reversed. A blast of cold air poured in at the bottom, and gushed through the open doors on the different landings.

"We can descend, if only we can get the ladder to cross the fallen landing," said Hugh.

"All right!" exclaimed Fawcett. "It's yours in a wink."

He rushed away to the window, and after a little trouble, a

good deal of shouting to George and Wilfred, and a few playful sallies, he produced it at the door of the room.

"It's too long," said Fawcett. "Here's t' axe; shorten it."

It was impossible, without cutting, to make the ladder pass the door. Hugh chopped through the sides with the hatchet Fawcett had brought from where he had left it, and the two men descended the stone steps. The lower landing was not fallen; it was still on fire, and flaming in places; in others, it was glowing red. The planking had gone, but the rafters remained in a state of combustion, half charcoal, half fire.

Hugh knelt down and tried them with his axe. They were too brittle to support any weight, so he hacked them away, and they fell flaming and crackling to the bottom.

It was cool on the stairs and an intense relief after the oppressive, parching heat they had endured in the long room. But in safety they were not. The roof above them was blazing, and might fall at any moment. Sparks dropped past them momentarily.

"Down with the ladder," shouted Hugh, as the last rafter of the landing gave way. "Here, give it to me." He snatched it from Fawcett's hand, and cast it across the gap as a bridge, one end resting on the lowest step of the upper stair, the other on the topmost step of the other.

"Hold this side," said Fawcett. "Let me go over first. I'll keep it fast at the bottom for thee and t' lass." He walked cautiously along, placing his foot on the rungs, and balancing himself with his arms. The ladder was not quite level, the lower end being some seven inches below the other.

"It's not the pleasantest walk i' t' world," said Fawcett, on reaching a secure footing. "It's like t' Brig o' Dread, nae bigger than a thread, my owd mother used to tell me about. Now, sir, ower wi' t' lass and thee. Cheer up, sweet! don't be flayed."

Outside, Mr Arkwright waited anxiously. He knew nothing of what had happened to his nephew; he had been told that Hugh and Fawcett were in the mill — that they had entered by one of the windows. He hoped, by bursting in the door, to be able to reach the fire at once, but he was mistaken. The base of the stair and the floor of the hoist were so encumbered with fallen timber, still burning, that when the doors fell in, it seemed probable that they would be in a blaze before they could be dragged out.

But now was heard a heavy rumble, like that of a laden waggon with which the horse had run away. Then a distant cheer, running along from knot to knot of people clustered on the road and watching the blaze. Louder grew the rattle, noisier grew the shouts.

"Here's t' engine at last!" cried Rhodes, as the racing lights became visible, when the machine whirled over the railway bridge and came with horses galloping and foam-splashed, and then dashed through the millgates, flung open to receive it.

In two minutes, amidst a thundering cheer, a shoot of water rose up the side of the factory and burst over the roof, to the tramp of the firemen working the engine.

"In yonder," shouted Rhodes. "In at t' door."

"Ay, ay!"

"There are folks there," he cried. "Hand the hose here."

In another moment a volume of water was poured into the great door, and extinguished the fire on the basement.

"Where is Hugh?" asked Mr Arkwright. "He can't be in the mill now."

"He's not come our, sir," answered Rhodes. "Lend a hand here, lads; we'll clear them doors and rubbish away, and get t' stairs open."

To return once more to those within. "Now, sir!" called Fawcett, "I've got fast hold; lead t' poor little lass along."

Annis put one foot forward, shuddered and recoiled. "Oh, Hugh, I cannot."

It was a pass of no ordinary danger. Between the bars of the ladder, the eye looked down on smouldering logs, and still blazing fragments of plank, and on the shattered door, lying in the fire, with its splinters already kindled.

It required a steady head, and nerves under control, to cross without turning giddy.

"Annis, you must come," said Hugh. She looked again and became faint.

"I cannot, indeed. I should fall." Then timidly glancing into his eyes, she asked, "Oh Hugh, could you not carry me? I dare not cross that, indeed I dare not."

"Fawcett!" called Hugh. "Do you think this ladder would bear if I carried the girl over?"

"Happen it might, but I can't say."

"Do try, Annis, to go alone."

"Oh I would, I would indeed, but I know I should fall. If there were a plank, I might manage, but a ladder —"

He saw her lips whiten and a film come over her eyes.

"Then we must do our best. Annis, let me take you in my arms. As once I bore you through the flood in safety, so now, please God, I shall bear you through flame." He caught her up and stepped on the ladder.

"Do not stir," he said. "Pray to God and be motionless."

He put his feet on the long side poles of the ladder, he did not dare to trust the double weight on the rungs. Moreover, holding Annis, he could not look at his foothold. There was a red spot, a splash of paint, on the wall immediately opposite. He fixed his eyes intently on that as he slowly moved his feet along, sliding each forward, not venturing to raise them.

Then he saw a streak of light at his side, and heard a crash below, as an ignited piece of timber fell from the roof. Immediately after flaming laths flipped out of their places above and went spluttering down.

And next, and more horrible still, he heard a fiendlike yell behind him, and heard the leaping of a man down the stairs at his back. He felt the little girl in his arms tremble.

"Gad! Keep off there!" shouted Fawcett, as he saw Earnshaw bound to the head of the ladder, and kick at it, endeavouring to thrust it off the ledge.

Hugh dared not turn his head to look. Determinedly he kept his eye on the red stain. The ladder bent under the weight; he knew this by seeing the red spot apparently rise. Suddenly he felt a jar through every fibre of his body. Earnshaw had taken up the axe which Hugh had laid down, and had struck the end of the ladder posts with it. The jerk — as that on which he stood was shot forward a couple of inches — staggered him, and he felt uncertain of his balance. His head swam and his heart contracted. A blue mist formed before his eyes, and the red patch faded from his vision. An impulse to loosen his grip of Annis, throw out his arms to steady himself, came over him

347

with scarcely resistible force. It was the natural instinct of self-preservation.

Fawcett saw Earnshaw raise the axe again for a second stroke. He set his own foot against the end of the ladder near him, knowing, however, how impossible it would be for him to resist the jerk of a stroke from the hatchet. He saw the ferocious countenance of the madman blazing with rage and triumph. He saw that one other blow must infallibly shoot the ladder off the step, and send Hugh and his burden into the glowing depths.

Hugh, sickening and faint, pressed a kiss to the cheek of the girl he bore, and her arms tightened around him. Fortunately for him he did not see the uplifted axe, but he heard a rush as of a stream bursting from a sluice, and felt a sharp pang in his hand, and his feet slid along the poles with redoubled speed. The pain had restored him to full consciousness, the red blotch on the wall became distinct once more. A cry of keen anguish, loud and bewildering from its power of tone and intensity of feeling, pierced his ears. A moment more, and two rough hands clasped him, and he stood with Annis in temporary security.

Still he heard that rushing sound, and still the pealing of those awful cries.

"What is it, what is it?" he gasped.

"Look," answered Fawcett.

Then he saw that the lead cistern on the roof had melted, and was pouring in a glittering cataract upon the steps he had so lately deserted. And there was Earnshaw, writhing in the falling torrent, his face glaring in the flames from above, streaked with silver, his dress coated with glistening metal, with the molten streams rushing on him and leaping off him in shining spurts, uttering burst on burst of shrilling screams, then gathering himself up, and leaping forward, and plunging past them into an abyss of slivery metal and fire and smoke.

"Stand back!" shouted Fawcett.

He caught Hugh and Annis and drew them into the doorway of the willying room. He raised the latch and looked in. The fire seemed to have avoided it, and it was cool and dark. Scarce had they reached it before they heard the rush of water through the entrance door, and its explosion into steam.

"We should ha' been scalded yonder," said Fawcett. "Lucky

we got in here."

In another moment the steam, laden with particles of charcoal, and pungent with the odour of wood ash, was swept into the little room and pervaded it.

The splash and fizz of the water continued, and the room became hot, though the door was shut against the vapour.

"Did you ever hear t' tale," began Fawcett, but stopped; his audience was not disposed to listen. Annis had sunk upon a box in the corner, with her face in her hands, and Hugh was gazing out of the window. Then they heard a shout from below.

Fawcett started to the door. The engine had ceased to play through the entrance, and the stairway was clear of steam at the bottom, though it still hung in a cloud above.

"I think we may venture down," said Fawcett.

Hugh raised Annis gently, and they went out of the willying room. Now they saw anxious faces looking up through the doorway.

"Who are there?" asked Mr Arkwright, in a loud voice.

"It's me and Mr Hugh," replied Fawcett. "And I reckon thy nephew's gone a picked a bird out o' t' flames. Happen a phoenix."

"Come down, will you."

"Ay, we're coming," answered Fawcett. "Look out yonder, there's a dead chap somewhere yonder."

Yes, there he lay, encased in a leaden shroud that glittered like silver, with the steam from the engine water rising from off him.

"Put a board across to t' steps," said Fawcett. "We ain't a going to walk on hot ashes and scalding lead to please nobody."

"Good heavens!" exclaimed Mr Arkwright, as the three emerged. "Annis Greenwell!"

Chapter Thirty-Eight

Miss Doldrums kept her promise. On Saturday she took charge of Annis, moving her to the Lodge, and attending to her. Annis slept the greater part of that day, the anxieties, and the mental and nervous tension of Friday night, having completely exhausted her. Towards evening she recovered, and seemed fresh. Laura brought her to her own room for a talk. She had refrained from questioning Annis before, partly because she had been sound asleep and partly because Laura had felt the necessity of putting a certain amount of restraint on herself; but now she was determined to satisfy her curiosity, and seeing that Annis looked bright, with the colour in her cheeks, and a light in her eyes, she drew her into her own boudoir, shut the door, seated the girl in a comfortable stool by the fireside, and said, "Now then, tell me all about it."

"About what?" asked Annis, lifting her wistful eyes.

"About the fire, and Hugh, and the man–monkey and the watchman, and all that. I am dying to know."

But it was quite beyond the power of Annis to relate the circumstances in a compact and concise form, and she looked at Laura with a despairing expression, that made Miss Doldrums laugh.

"Well, well, begin at the fire," she said.

By degrees, the whole story leaked out. Annis could not relate the events of the past night without making allusions to other circumstances which needed explanation, and these in turn opened up other matters which had also to be made clear.

Laura was thus put in possession of the whole story — or very nearly all. Annis had mentioned Hugh as little as possible, and had not referred to their attachment.

"Now then," said Laura, "there is something more I want to know. Yesterday evening Mr Hugh Arkwright told me that all did not go smoothly between you. You saw him for a moment, I think, and he thought you cold and distant."

Annis hung her head and did not speak. Laura saw her bosom heave and her fingers nervously twitch. "Well, dear," said she, "tell me what was the cause of this, I am so eager to know. I take the profoundest interest in all that concerns you and Hugh."

The little girl shrank from disclosing this secret and still refrained from speaking.

Miss Doldrums went to her side, took her hands between her own, chafing them gently, and said again, "Please to tell me the cause of this. There is something, is there not?"

"Yes," in a low, tremulous whisper.

"Now tell me what that thing is. You have not fallen in love with anyone else, have you?"

"Oh, no, no!" looking up suddenly.

"Then what can it be?" Annis made no answer. "Has Hugh vexed you in any way?"

"I do not think he cares for me any more," she said in a low tone, with her head bowed down.

"Then I am sure you are out!" exclaimed Laura. "Why, he is always talking to me about you. Yesterday evening he asked me to look after you when you came to Sowden, and be kind to you. Now I am doing what I promised him to do."

"Were you at Mr Arkwright's house last night?" asked Annis, timidly, without raising her head.

"Yes, dear, I was."

"Oh, Miss Doldrums!" began Annis.

"Call me Laura," interrupted the other.

"Joe told me that he had seen Hugh — " she hesitated.

"Doing what?" to help her.

"With another lady." She stopped again.

"Of course, dear, he has to be with heaps of ladies. There is nothing in that."

"But he was kissing her hand, and — "

"Why the fellow, Hugh, did that to me last night. There is nothing in that." But Annis seemed to think otherwise. "No," said Laura sharply, feeling the hands struggling to escape from hers. "No, you misunderstand."

"Joe told me that he had seen Hugh speaking to a lady, looking into her face, full of affection, and she with her eyes raised to his, and her hand clasped in his hands; and then he bent his head—" there her voice failed her.

"That was me!" exclaimed Laura, with too great precipitation

351

to be careful about her grammar. "Do you know what it was all about? Look up, Puss."

Annis was unable to do this without revealing the fact that her eyes were full of tears. But one of the glittering drops fell on her knee, and Laura saw it.

"You must dry those silly eyes," said Miss Doldrums. "There is an old saying, Don't cry before you're hurt. That applies to you. You are not hurt in the least, so no crying, please."

"I cannot help it," pleaded Annis.

"Yes, you can. Now listen to me. Hugh was asking me to befriend you when that awful man saw him. I had just promised him that I would take you to stay with me, and he was so grateful, stupid fellow, that he behaved in a foolish way. I heard Hugh utter an exclamation and I saw him start. No doubt he caught a glimpse of the man looking in at him through the front of the conservatory. There! Are you satisfied?"

Annis lifted her face, bright and smiling, in reply. Every cloud was gone.

"You little know how Hugh has talked to me about you. I believe he has no one else in Sowden to whom he can speak about you, so I humour him, and he has told me so much about you that I seem to know you very well."

Annis pressed her hand.

"The great boy has been here today, to inquire after you. I have thought it best that you should not meet today, but he is coming here to tea on Sunday, and you can have a nice talk with him then. And your cousin Martha has been here; you were asleep at the time, so she is going to return somewhat later."

"I should so like to see Martha — dear Martha," said Annis.

"So you shall," answered Laura. "As soon as she comes, she shall be shown up here. I have given orders."

The young women did not continue their conversation for some while. Annis was thinking. When she looked up, she saw that Laura's eyes were fixed on her intently.

"You are so different from me," said Laura.

Annis coloured. "I suppose I am," she said with a sigh. "I feel it myself; and I doubt whether I shall ever be fit for Hugh."

"Fit!" echoed Laura. "Bless the girl! What does she mean?"

"I shall never be like you," said Annis, despondently. "I mean,

I shall not be a lady."

"Psh! you are twice as much a lady as I am," exclaimed Laura. "I see my faults clearly, now that I am set alongside of you. You are not harum-scarum, you know."

"Harum-scarum!"

"No, you are not. And it is the great blot in my character that I am so. I am frightfully so. The smoke-jack has got into my constitution and I twist and twirl all day long. I wish I was not so harum-scarum. If it had not been for the smoke-jack, I should have had to work for my living, and I know I should have been a noisy, pert, giddy girl, who would probably have come to no good. But money and education have been my saving. You — you are quite different. I see it, and I feel it. You would never be vulgar, rich or poor, with or without education. I with I were like you! Hark. There comes Martha."

Chapter Thirty-Nine

"Hugh," said Mr Arkwright on Monday morning, "where were you yesterday evening?"

"At church."

"Yes, but before church? We did not see you here at tea."

"I went to Doldrums Lodge. Laura was kind enough to invite me to meet Annis."

"Hold your tongue, sir!" burst forth the manufacturer. "I will not have you mention that girl."

"Then you are still as determined as ever to refuse me your permission to choose a wife for myself."

"No, I do not refuse, so long as that wife is chosen within certain limits."

"Pray mention them."

"An old woman on one side, and a poor one on the other. I do not think, however, that there is much risk of your throwing yourself away on one advanced in years; but young men are reckless about money. They think it will fall upon them out of the clouds, as it did upon — what's her name? Pasiphaë, was it? No, it doesn't matter."

"Danaë, sir."

"Yes, to be sure. Now that shower of gold in the story of Danaë, was, if I remember aright, a case of matrimony. And I wish young men would just take example from that lady, and look out for an opportunity to form lucrative marriages."

"We had enough of that subject the other evening, I think, uncle. Suppose we give it up as hopeless. Young men are blind, we will suppose, to their monied interest, and are infatuated on the subject of domestic felicity."

"Be hanged to your domestic felicity!" exclaimed Mr Arkwright. "What does domestic felicity matter to a businessman? He is in his office all day, and he will do well if he attends to his accounts out of business hours. Changing the topic — How the deuce came that girl into the mill?"

"That is a long story. I have not got to the end of it yet."

"I believe you carried her in there, for the sake of taking her out. I was never more provoked in my life than when I saw her ugly face —"

"It is not ugly."

"I am speaking of the Turk's head. I wish she had been roasted there. That would have been the easiest way of getting out of the difficulty. I suppose, now, you are more obstinate than ever."

"When a man has been through fire and water with a girl, he can hardly do otherwise than I have resolved on doing."

"Well?"

"I shall certainly make Annis my wife."

"You are a confounded fool. I address my Turk's head."

"It is not in the room."

"It is in my pocket."

"I don't believe it."

"Look, then."

Hugh snatched the pipe from his uncle, and broke the head on the bar of the grate. "We have had enough of this Turk's head. Please to drop all references to it for the future."

"Damn!" said Mr Arkwright. "Hugh, the guilt of my swearing is on your shoulders. You con—"

"The head is off. *De mortuis nil nisi bonum.*"

"Change the topic," grunted the manufacturer.

"To what, sir?"

"Hugh, I am not sorry about the fire. It has done me a world of good. The mill was heavily insured, and now I shall be able to get new machinery. The place, moreover, will be rebuilt, or repaired, and the work is brought to a standstill at a time when trade is at its worst, and when the running of the mill would have entailed loss. I did not like to dismiss my hands — now the fire has relieved me of my difficulty. That maniac could not have done me a better turn, and I am obliged to him. The books are safe. He had not the key of the office, and, as that was detached from the factory, it was unhurt. I'll do the best I can for the man, and bury him decently. He was not in a club, and has no relations, so that the parish would have to do the job."

"The fellow had money," said Hugh. "It turns out that he had a trifle in a Manchester bank, which brought him in a few pounds interest. His will has been found in his box at the cottage in the Sand Pit. You know he lodged there, and, when he disappeared, his traps remained. Rhodes did not like to disturb them; the cottage belongs to Annis Greenwell, and he did not think he had any right to interfere. But now that the man is undoubtedly dead, his things have been overhauled, and a will, dated a twelvemonth back, has been discovered, leaving all he has to Annis. This is not much — some five-and-twenty pounds a year perhaps — still, it is something."

"And you are going to marry on the strength of this — she being an heiress?" laughed Mr Arkwright.

Hugh took no notice of his uncle's rudeness. He continued, "The rest of his things are not worth much. They consist chiefly of books, for the unfortunate fellow was apparently a reading man."

"I could see, from his manner of speaking, that he had some education," said Mr Arkwright.

"Lately, he had been studying books on insanity and diseases of the brain; at least, so we conclude, for he had quite a library of late works on mental disorders. The poor fellow probably fretted over his disfigurement, and from allowing his mind to prey upon it, he became subject to morbid fancies, and then read himself into a conviction that he was insane. Certainly his acts have not been those of a man with a mind properly balanced; but whether he were actually mad, or only believed himself to be so, and behaved agreeably to this conviction, is more than I can say."

"Psh! Mad — of course he was mad."

"I remember once I told you that I thought he was not in his right mind, and you disputed my opinion."

"Because it was not grounded on facts. Here we have a fellow throwing himself with you into a canal, out of a railway carriage at full speed."

"The speed was being slackened."

"He thought it was at full speed. Here, again, we have a man setting fire to a mill, with no earthly object except of making a bonfire; and, like a fool, hampering the locks beforehand, so that when he tried to escape from the fire he had raised, he was unable to do so. These are facts and from them I draw the conclusion that the man was raving mad."

"I think your facts are not correctly stated," said Hugh. "My impression is that the poor creature had determined on self-destruction, and more than that, on making Annis Greenwell perish with him."

"Can you have a clearer evidence of insanity?" asked Mr Arkwright.

At this moment the door opened and Sarah Anne looking in, said, "Please, master, there's a lady wants to see you."

"Show her in," said Mr Arkwright.

Miss Furness was ushered into the room. Mr Arkwright had often met her at the vicarage, but Hugh had not seen her before. He was struck at once with her look and appearance. She was dressed in a silvery grey gown, which matched her whitening hair and contrasted with the pure colour of her transparent complexion. There was something cool and dovelike about her, which charmed him the moment he saw her. He observed the same features as those of the old vicar, but refined and more delicate. Both had the same sweetened expression, caused by much sorrow, and the same serenity of spirit beaming out of every lineament; but in the vicar there was the superadded force of the man, and the consequent deficiency of the tenderness of the woman.

Miss Furness had a pleasant word for Hugh. "I have often heard of you," she said, "though we have never met."

Then she expressed her sympathy with Mr Arkwright on account of his terrible loss by the fire, womanlike, supposing that the disaster was very great, and utterly ignorant of the matters beneath the surface, which make an apparent misfortune very often a great advantage. Mr Arkwright did not undeceive her, but hushed her regrets away with the remark, "In trade, you know, there are ups and downs, and we make our calculations accordingly." Then, suddenly remembering that he had not inquired after Mrs Furness, he repaired the breach of courtesy with characteristic promptitude.

"No news is good news, so I suppose Mrs Furness is pretty well?"

"Thank you, yes. She is much the same, day after day. She has her ups and downs, too, but not such startling rises nor such sudden depressions as in your case. I have got a kind friend to sit with her today, during my absence, who will do her best to amuse her until my return this evening."

"Are you going back so soon?"

"Yes, I must. I have no one who understands my mother to be with her at night. If little Miss Greenwell had been there, it would have been different."

"Has the girl been with you?" asked Mr Arkwright with surprise. "I always supposed she had gone to an orphanage, or a school, or something of that sort."

Hugh smiled. Miss Doldrums had told him the day before to whose care his little girl had been confided by the vicar.

"Yes," answered Miss Furness, "she has been with me and my mother is so fond of her, that I could safely have trusted the old lady to her; but of course Annis cannot return to York just yet. She is such a sweet child, Mr Arkwright — don't you think so?"

"Hugh," said the manufacturer, "will you be so good as to see John Rhodes, and tell him to tell me as soon as the insurance fellow comes."

"Yes, sir." Hugh knew that this was a mere excuse to get him out of the room; he, however, took the hint, and left. When he was gone, Mr Arkwright said, "My nephew is crazy over that milksop of a girl; so, when you began praising her, I sent him off."

"She is a very charming little thing," said Miss Furness. "I have seldom met with a better behaved, more simple-minded girl; she has all the delicacy of feeling that one is glad to find in a well-educated lady, but which is too often wanting."

"I don't care whether she is good or bad," said Mr Arkwright; "she is not the sort of person Hugh shall marry."

"I believe the poor child is very fond of him. I have carefully refrained from speaking to her on the subject, but I have seen her colour rise whenever a letter came from Sowden, and then fade, when she found in it no allusion to Hugh. I have observed her very attentively, and I am sure that her whole heart is wrapped up in him, and that her love is not a mere evanescent fancy, but a deep, strong passion."

"You forget, Miss Furness, that her origin is very humble."

"Yes, perhaps I do. But one has only to be with her to forget it at once. Whether it be a crime to be born in a low rank of life, I leave you to decide. I myself am exceedingly particular about all the proprieties of social life, and I strongly object, on principle, to a marriage out of the sphere in which one is placed by Providence. At the same time I do feel, perhaps I may have had cause to feel, that the mutual devotion of two hearts is too solemn and earnest a feeling to be rudely broken through. Is the humble origin of Annis the sole objection you raise against her?"

"For the matter of that," said Mr Arkwright, "I do not care so much about her origin as her means. In this manufacturing country, those who are at the bottom of the ladder one day are at the top on the morrow. If you went through Sowden, and picked out only those who could claim a position in the upper ranks of, say, two generations, I question whether you would find more than the vicar. Either the father or the grandfather of every one of our aristocracy here have risen from the ranks. No. I am not so particular on that point. But in this money–loving age, and country, and county, one must look for money, and I require Hugh to marry someone with a decent dower, or I shall not take him into partnership. I have already explained my views to him. He knows that he only retains a clerkship if he marries to please himself, but that if he can find a sufficient sum to sink in the business, I make him a partner."

"What do you call a sufficient sum?"

"Oh, I am not particular. A few thousands."

"If Annis Greenwell had, say eight thousand, would you reject her?"

"Certainly not."

"Then she shall have them."

"Miss Furness!"

"She shall have them," repeated Bessie with composure. "I do not give them to her, for they do not properly belong to me. But I have money in trust, and I shall be fulfilling that trust if I give them to her."

Mr Arkwright stared at her with a puzzled air. Miss Furness continued quietly, "A gentleman with whom I was intimately acquainted — he was an admiral in the Navy— "

"The Silver Poplar!" rudely interrupted Mr Arkwright, and then at once felt how ill–mannered he had been, and reddened with annoyance.

"The Silver Poplar," repeated Miss Furness, looking him straight in the face, with the softest possible heightening of tinge in her cheek. "Yes, the Silver Poplar left his money to me. He had been saving for many years, and the sum had mounted up. He died, and left all the savings to me — in trust. According to his will, I was his sole legatee; but there were private instructions as to what was to be done with the money, which I have not been able hitherto to carry out. You seem to know something of the history, so I may show you the paper; otherwise, I should only have told you of its contents."

"I beg your pardon, Miss Furness," stammered the bewildered man. "I meant no offence."

"I am satisfied of that."

"I had heard something, I own, of your engagement to Admiral Dalmaigne, and I knew, too, the nickname by which he was generally called; and when you mentioned —"

"Make no apology," said Miss Furness, "none is needed. To show you that, so far from being annoyed. I am relieved of an awkwardness by finding you acquainted with the circumstances, I show you, as a friend, this paper." She extended to him a small note. He took it with hesitation, and opened it, and read —

DEAR BESSIE,

I leave all my money to you; make use of it as long as you like; but when you want it no more, then employ it to make two young and deserving people happy, whose union is impeded by a barrier such as can be removed by money. It will console me to think that my poor savings, which did not avail us, have comforted others.

Yours ever
WILLIAM DALMAIGNE

Mr Arkwright folded up the letter again, and handed it back to Miss Furness, without saying a word.

"I think," continued she, "that you had better say nothing of this to Hugh, nor will I mention it to Annis. I will take the girl back with me to York, where she will be happy, and will be acquiring much that she would not learn among her relatives here. We must let the two write to one another, and we shall see what a year or two will bring forth. If they continue to be attached to one another, then, when suitable, they can marry, but for at least a twelvemonth Annis must remain with me; and I think I can promise you that she will do you no discredit, and that she will make your nephew a faithful and good wife. The money shall be hers as soon as she is married; till then she shall know nothing about it."

Mr Arkwright did not speak immediately; he was thinking. When he opened his mouth, he had determined to renounce the prospect of having Laura for his niece. "You see, Miss Furness, I had made up my mind that my nephew should marry a certain young lady who has got plenty of money, and I have been trying to force her upon him, with no success. One man may lead a horse to water, but twenty can't make him drink, and though I've brought my Hugh into that same party's society times out of mind, I doubt if all Sowden could make him propose. So I give it up, and I accept your terms. Done." He held out his hand.

Miss Furness smiled and extended her fingers. The manufacturer grasped them, and shook them heartily. "Now," said he, "we are more comfortable. The bargain is struck."

Chapter Forty

More than two years have slipped by. It is June. In May, Hugh and Annis were married. And now they come to Sowden, after a month among the lakes.

Hugh introduced his little bride to a sweet cottage, built in the sandpit. The old home of Annis is enlarged and ornamented and the garden in front stocked with roses in full bloom. The old house and garden have been so transformed, that it is difficult to recognise them again. The cabbage-beds in front have made way for parterres, the "house" window is now that of a little hall. At the side towards the river is a sitting-room with a bow window, and there is a cheerful bedroom over it. Joe's room has been altered into a passage. The cottage is small, but neat and comfortable. In the hall are the stuffed birds, and the white kittens gambol over the kitchen door, but General Garibaldi has disappeared.

The little wife looks round, with a flutter of delight.

"Oh, Hugh!" she says, putting her hands on his shoulders, and looking up into his face. "I want to ask one favour."

"Wait," he says. Then he draws forth a crimson kerchief, and puts it over her head, makes her pin it under her chin, and look up blushing at him.

"Now, Annis, what do you want?"

"Oh, Hugh! I wish you would let Martha come and live with us?"

"Martha!" shouted Hugh. The kitchen door opened and Martha came in. With a cry of delight, the bride flew from her husband to the arms of her cousin.

"There, that is sufficient," said Hugh. "I alone have come through Flood and Flame with you, so come back to me."

THE END

THE BARING-GOULD COLLECTION

The Reverend Sabine Baring-Gould lived from 1834–1924 and wrote over 130 books, covering a huge range of topics. Fiction, theology, folklore, social comment, travel, history, and more.

Red Spider.
First published 1887. A Gothic romance, set in a real Devon village in the early 1800s. A book overflowing with life and colour, and just as good a read now as it was in its time, when it was a very big success. £5.00 ISBN 0 9518729 1 5

Winefred
First published 1900. An exciting adventure story, set on the cliffs of Seaton in South Devon. It features a real-life character, smuggler Jack Rattenbury, and his romantic attachment to young Winefred. There was a dramatic landslip on these cliffs in the early 1800s and this fact is woven into the story. £6.50. ISBN 0 9518729 6 6

A Book of Folklore
First published 1913. A compendium of many of the most intriguing stories the author had gleaned throughout his long life. A wonderful book for dipping into, full of ghosts, doppelgangers, vampires and werewolves. £5.00. ISBN 0 9518729 4 X

The Mana of Lew by Cicely Briggs
The author was Baring-Gould's grand-daughter. This book charts the history of the great house which he restored throughout much of his life. There is also a complete family history and considerable detail of the surrounding neighbourhood. Many illustrations.
£5.00. ISBN 0 9518729 3 1